CONTENTS

For Betsy ♡ Hope you enjoy :)

THE
ESSENCE
of Fate

A SOULS REUNITED NOVEL

ALISON E. STEUART

Love you!

A Steuart

Somewhere deep inside you,
in the realm of past lives, intuition,
and your sixth sense,
is knowledge of which you are unaware.
You cannot control it,
but it can control you.
Do not be afraid of its power,
trust its wisdom.
For it knows your soul's desire,
the passion,
the pleasure,
the pain,
the craving for more.
It knows who I am
and senses when I am near.
It knows you are mine,
and I am yours.
That when we are together,
we are home.
Now
Then
again and again
For eternity.

~ Alasdair Stewart

ONE

CHARLOTTE

So much for getting out of my meeting in time to avoid the clusterfuck that is Miami rush-hour traffic. I missed it by twenty minutes, sealing my fate.

Case in point, it's been three minutes, I'm in the passing lane, and I've already got this guy going five miles *under* the speed limit in front of me, some chick texting and driving to my right, another person changing lanes randomly with no signal—I actually think he might be drunk—and I'm stuck in the middle of it all with no option of getting out. I don't do well in situations like this. My intolerance for people that mindlessly go about driving, not giving a damn that there are laws and basic rules that make this whole process run more smoothly, not to mention safely, is extreme. To put it mildly.

The minutes pass and things are not progressing the way I would like them to as I sit stranded, watching the rest of the traffic around us fly by. My hands grip tighter to the steering wheel. I'm teetering on the edge. The anger is building, though I'm trying hard to keep it in check. It's a fruitless effort, regardless of the breathing exercises I'm doing. I know what comes next... Sibel, my alter ego—or *Psycho*, as I like to call her —will make her appearance, and the road rage will ensue. It's kind of like what's-his-name that turns into the Hulk when the shit hits the fan. He has no choice in the matter, and it's the same for me with Sibel. Sometimes she comes in handy, but nine times out of ten, she causes issues I could do without.

I should blame the jerk in front of me who is now driving seven miles under the speed limit, and yes, he is *still* in the passing lane. Clearly, he doesn't know that the left lane is sacred territory meant for motivated people wanting to get from point A to point B in the quickest, safest way possible. *Not* to meander and create unnecessary traffic jams. I'm on his ass now, trying to get his attention so he will hopefully get out of the way. However, I'm not sure he can even see me in any of his mirrors because his seat is back so far, I can barely see his head. This has me somewhat confused since I see his elbow sticking out his window. That means his arm is resting on it, which doesn't seem physically possible, considering the position of his seat—let alone, comfortable.

Before I can ponder that pointless mystery any longer, Miss Text-n-Drive moves into the other lane, leaving an opening that I know Mr. Go-Getter in front of me isn't going to take, so I'm forced to pass him in the right lane. Glancing over as I go, suspicion confirmed—everything about this guy screams, "I have no life and I don't give a damn if you do!" Beyond the awkward seat-position and arm-out-the-window combination, his only contact with the steering wheel is the underside of wrist; that's terrifying! He also doesn't seem concerned about the cigarette dangling from his mouth that a simple gust of wind could knock into his lap. And don't get me started on the duct tape flapping in the wind near the passenger side mirror. There is no way that's doing anything constructive. Perhaps I should feel sorry for him. I don't know his story; it could be a sad one. But Sibel has taken over, and she's not interested in excuses.

I blare the horn as I pass, just because it makes her feel better to vent a little since she can't walk up to the guy and say, "What

2

the hell is your problem? There are signs all over the highway that say *Slower Traffic Keep Right*! It's not that complicated!"

Making my way back into the fast lane with Asshole getting smaller in my rearview mirror, I can relax; it's all clear. Finally, the road is mine. I turn up the volume and come back down to earth while I close the door on Sibel until she's awakened again.

As the music continues to calm my agitated nerves, my thoughts wander to this afternoon's meeting. Overall it went well, but I'm still frustrated with a few of the board members. The resort's common areas are looking tired and a bit dated. Now is the time to spruce things up before too many people get turned off by it. Savvy travelers don't like paying top-dollar to stay at a luxury resort that looks like it's been ridden hard by all the previous guests. Granted, it's not nearly that bad, but my standards are high. I want my guests to feel like they are the first to ever stay there. It makes a difference, a difference that is important to me. But our numbers are up from last year, so some of the misers in the group think we're good for a while longer, no need to spend the money until we absolutely need to. *Cringe.* Pointing out that this year's numbers are up for every resort and hotel on Miami Beach due to the hellacious winter they've seen up north didn't seem to matter, but the list of negative comments we've received, albeit a short one, gave them something to chew on until the next meeting.

My uncle James owns the resort along with several other five-star locations around the world. He's one of those people that just makes things successful. It doesn't matter what it is; if he acquires it, it will be successful.

When he bought The Clara Sea, I was fresh out of college and ready to take on the world. However, Uncle James is not a handout, start-at-the-top-because-you-are-family kind of guy. Therefore, I started at the front desk, working my way up to general manager in five short years. At first, I was a little insulted that my hard-earned business degree gained me a spot at the front desk of an oceanfront resort. But I trusted my uncle and knew I should follow his lead. Of course, he was right. I started at the bottom, learning everything I needed to know about successfully running a luxury resort and loved every minute of it.

Now, The Clara Sea is my baby, and I am proud of her success. So when board members with tight wallets and no foresight question my judgment and try to hold me back from continued success, I don't like it. I guess I'm somewhat of a control freak, but more so, I just think things should be done properly, with high standards. I can't imagine doing otherwise.

Several miles before my exit, I'm coming up quickly on another driver going slow in the left lane and not getting out of the way. *Dammit.* My body tenses with aggravation as Sibel wakes up, ready for a fight. Interestingly, this time it's not a car that would be better off in a junkyard; it's a *seriously* gorgeous black Lamborghini. I can't imagine the person driving that work of art is an unmotivated who-gives-a-shit jerk like the guy I passed earlier. But I can imagine that his or her ego and sense of entitlement will keep that car right where it is, and if I want to get around it, I'll have to pass in the right lane. Sibel does *not* like being forced to pass in the right lane.

Getting up on his tail, I wait for the right signal to flash, indicating the driver is finally paying attention and will move. That doesn't happen and Sibel has lost her patience, which was limited to begin with. I flash my lights to get his attention... Nothing. I move to the left a little, flash my lights again hoping he sees them in the side mirror... Nothing. Actually, I take that back. I think he may have slowed down. *Bastard!* I'm getting closer, moving left and right, flashing my lights, but Lambo stays in my lane, clearly challenging me.

Stupidly, I pick up the gauntlet.

Rarely do I resort to blaring the horn when I'm behind a car —I usually save that for the pass—but now I'm pissed and I'm on it, the nerve-shattering sound only making matters worse.

Regretfully, the horn blast doesn't work, and I'm about to

reach a new low because Sibel wants to start shoving her middle finger at the windshield yelling, "Fuck you, Asshole!" I yank her by the collar and throw her in the backseat before I become one of *those* people.

With my psychotic split personality temporarily diffused, reason takes over—which means if I want to go faster than Moneybags, I have to pass on the right. Ultimately, it's really not that big a deal; it's the principle, and it simply infuriates me.

As the signal ticks its steady rhythm and Sibel is fuming in the background, I pass Black Lambo with its equally black tinted windows and shiny perfection, not giving in to Sibel's insistence that I flip him off as I go by.

This is when I notice my exit is coming up on the left. *Dammit*, again! I must have lost track of where I was during my self-imposed duel with my highway nemesis. I should have just dealt with it, but I'm a Gemini and a stickler for following rules, even if they are my own. Geminis are also known for their split personalities, which explains Sibel. I'm actually a very kind, generous, hard-working person that values dignity, integrity, and honor. But my evil twin has major issues when others don't show the same regard. She has been known to react, or overreact, with free-flowing verbal assaults, a variety of hand gestures like the standard f-you bird, finger guns, hangman's noose, and some others involving private parts that I'm too embarrassed to acknowledge. I think her favorite is to show off her road-rage skills by flashing lights, tailgating, blaring the horn, and cutting in front of jerks that force her to pass on the right. Like she's getting ready to do right now. With a quick acceleration and a jerk of the wheel, I put my Mercedes right in front of the Batmobile.

Taking a moment to relish the satisfaction, I ease up my acceleration, forcing him to slow down. Not enough to be terribly dangerous, but definitely enough to piss him off. With a smile and a wave, I take my exit, feeling a little less defeated.

That mini euphoria lasts about five seconds, because I may

have underestimated my opponent. Bruce Wayne is *right* on my ass, and now I can see masculine hands on the steering wheel, confirming my assumption and giving me some relief that I don't have a potential cat fight on my hands.

Coming up to a red light, I get in the left turning lane knowing the lane next to me is open, providing the perfect opportunity for him to pull up, roll down his window, and let me have it. That would have been ideal. Because having that intimidatingly awesome car, jet black and shiny with what I suspect is an extremely pissed off man inside, pull up behind me is menacing. "Shit!" I asked for it... No, Sibel asked for it. Bloody nuisance!

Heart pounding, hands sweating, I curse my split personality and start to plan my getaway. As the green arrow finally lights up, I don't move. I continue sitting there until it turns yellow, waiting for the second when it turns red and take off. My hope is that Captain Menace doesn't want to chance a ticket or worse, wrecking his precious $250,000 car. *That* would have been ideal, as well. But once again, I am disappointed. He's hot on my tail and apparently has no intention of losing me until he's had the opportunity to personally rip me a new one.

"Let it go, jerk!" I yell as my anxiety spikes a little higher. At the next light, I realize there is no way I'm going to lose him in all this traffic, and there is definitely no way I'm going to let him follow me home. I have no choice but to suck it up, face the music, and diffuse the situation as quickly and reasonably as possible so I can get on with my evening, chill out, and possibly get drunk.

Up ahead I see Sommelier's convenience store. I love that place. It's an upscale, well-appointed quick stop where you can get excellent wine, gourmet cheeses, chocolates, and coffees; the most amazing pre-made dinners; and other random stuff you might need when you don't feel like dealing with the traffic and crowds at the main grocery store further in town. That seems like a safe enough place to have my inevitable confrontation with the Caped Crusader. Hopefully he's not unstable or prone to violence and simply wants to yell at me a bit for almost hurting his precious car...or potentially causing a major accident on the highway. *Thanks again, Sibel!* Maybe I could get hypnotized or something to shut her off permanently. It would save me a lot of grief.

Pulling into the parking lot, I pick a spot front and center, hoping for an audience. I put my car in park, take a fortifying breath, check for my big-girl panties, and kill the engine. "Here we go..."

I get out of the car and he's right next to me, but I can't see him since he has Secret Service tinting on his windows. Adding to the suspense, his engine purrs a little longer, and I do my best to remain calm, cool, and collected, leaning against my car, hiding my hands behind me so he won't see them shaking.

Staring at the opaque window, assuming he's only looking at me and not pointing a gun at my heart, I tip my head and raise one eyebrow as if to say, "Let's get on with this."

Finally, a minute later, the smooth hum of his engine dies and driver's door opens. Strangely, it seems like slow motion as his tall frame slides from the car and reaches its full height. I can only see the back of his head and a small portion of his profile and my heart almost stops. He's young, broad-shouldered with dark, shiny hair and what appears to be a stunningly gorgeous face. I silently pray that when he fully turns to look at me, he is cross-eyed or has a huge birthmark covering the rest of his face. Shallow, I know, but the way my chest just constricted, I need anything I can get to not have some god-like creature render me speechless, especially now.

Once again...no such luck. Making his way around the front of his car, he faces me fully. *Sweet Mary, Mother, and Bride! You have got to be kidding me!* I am literally looking at the most gorgeous specimen of a male human you can possibly imagine, no joke. Actually, maybe it is a joke because I am so overwhelmed by the humor in this whole situation, that when the stupidly hot God of Physical Perfection finally approaches me, I involuntarily throw my head back and laugh out loud.

It's not a total out of control, ugly-face, tears-pouring-out-of-your-eyes crack up. But it's a healthy enough laugh that releases the right amount of endorphins into my bloodstream to relax my strung-out nerves and clear my brain. At least somewhat.

Bringing my head down and my hand to my chest, I regain control as my laugh ebbs to a slight chuckle. With a slow, oh-the-things-I-get-myself-into head shake, I open my eyes and catch my breath on a small gasp. He's close—too close—and I swear I can feel heat coming off him as every nerve in my body has turned into a live wire. Although, it's probably my stupid hormones that were unexpectedly shoved into overdrive. *My God!* It doesn't help that his stunning eyes are staring at me with such intensity, I'm momentarily at a loss for words. Somewhere in the fog of my subconscious, I hear Sibel yelling, "Say something, you idiot!"

The stare-down continues for what seems like ten minutes but is probably less than one. The spell is broken when his eyes shift down to my breasts and a sexy-as-hell smirk lifts one side of his flawless mouth. That's when I finally notice the painful tightness of my nipples, which are no doubt casting shadows across my chest because this particular dress requires no bra. *Earth, swallow me whole!*

I can't do this. I need to get the hell out of here. He's obviously enjoying himself, and I'm starting to feel humiliated. Regaining my composure, I ignore my body's obnoxious response to his…his…I don't even know what. He has to be a vampire or something; real humans are simply not this flawless.

Finally, my brain cells snap out of it, and I say, "Surely, you're not going to just stand here, *in my space,* and stare me down until I turn to ash?" The smooth conviction in my voice boosts my confidence. Standing a little straighter, I square my shoulders.

With a voice as desirably masculine and beautiful as his physical being, he responds with, "Why would you turn to ash?"

Without missing a beat, I say, "Because you seem to have an unnatural heat radiating from your body...which happens to be inside my awkwardly too-close-for-strangers zone, and the intensity of your stare has me on edge, awaiting the laser beams that will finally do me in, effectively...turning me to ash." Honesty is the best policy, right?

Now it's his turn to laugh, though I wouldn't really call it a laugh—more like an annoyingly controlled and sexy chuckle. *Ugh!* I'm such an idiot. Time to cut my losses and retreat. "Okay, well...I'm sorry I cut you off on the highway. Since you so rudely wouldn't get out of my way and forced me to pass in the right lane, I almost missed my exit and was left no choice but to get in front of you." That came out faster than I would have liked.

The depth of his stare shifts, and his tone is commanding when he responds. "You had plenty of choices. The most important one being to have patience while control was taken from you. By doing so, you would have achieved what you wanted because I would have gotten out of your way."

God, he smells good, and I think his voice has hypnotized me because I just want him to keep talking.

"Instead, you lost control by using aggression to get what you wanted. I was watching you in my rearview mirror." The smirk returns. "Your beautiful eyes blazing. I read your lips, surprised that such language would come from such a lovely mouth." Now he's staring at my lips, and I swear on my life they swelled. *Ho-ly shit!* And dear God, I think my nipples are at it again! What the hell is wrong with me? This feels like freaking foreplay!

"Well, that is very charming...in a back-handed sort of way. And thank you for the excellent advice. Patience is a virtue, after all." I'm okay with that coming out a little snippy. He's got me so flustered, and I'm not really sure how. Either way, I don't like it. I am totally out of control with all these involuntary reactions my body has suddenly found an affinity for. Needing to regain some semblance of control, I continue. "Now that we've established you have an uncanny ability to read lips from the reflection in your rearview mirror while driving down the highway and you apparently have wisdom beyond your years, I think we're good. Plus, I'm sure you have places to be and more important things to do." *Like maybe some blood to suck and a coffin to get into.*

As he puts his hand on my car right next to my shoulder, a waft of his scent hits my olfactory nerve, instantly heating my entire body and numbing my brain. *What the hell?* Trying to shake it off, I hear his smooth voice ask, "What makes you so sure of that? Perhaps I have nowhere to be and am perfectly happy standing in this parking lot, sharing with you my wisdom on giving up control."

Wow, he's really good at this, and if I'm not mistaken, that was a very suggestive comment—one that my traitorous body thought had a nice ring to it. Did his nostrils just flare? *Dear Lord,* tell me he cannot smell me. The thought makes me heat up even more in all the places I shouldn't. Making matters worse, I swear when I look back at his eyes, they are dilated, which is evidently my body's signal that we need lubrication because my panties are now soaked with my wetness.

Oh. My. God. Is this even possible? I have no clue who this guy is, but my body is acting like the family dog when someone finally comes home after it's been alone all day.

Avoiding his suggestive comment and the sexual tension that is about to make me spontaneously combust, I retort, "Perhaps. But I *do* have somewhere to be, which would explain why I was in a hurry on the highway. Again, I apologize for my aggressive, out of control driving and promise to be a good girl and never do it again." Moving away from the door so I can open it and make an escape, I give him a quick, "Have a good evening."

But before I even get near the handle, he stops me. "Where do you have to be?"

His question surprises me, catching me off guard because I'm not sure how to answer. Clearly, I was lying, but it's none of his business either way.

For whatever reason, I decide to go with the old standby for getting rid of a guy and tell him, "I have a date...with my boyfriend." I'm really hoping that did not come out as awkwardly as it felt.

I'm guessing it didn't, because Mr. Impossibly Gorgeous And Cool In Every Possible Way suddenly shuts down, gives me a curt, "Very well, then," and heads back to his car. Once he's in, he starts the engine and puts it in reverse.

The finality of it lands heavy in my chest, like I've somehow made a terrible mistake. Is this guy some kind of sorcerer, taking control of my body and mind? What the hell? I should be happy he finally left—now I can get on with my life! To prove to myself that none of this matters, I turn to his retreating car and with all the confidence and attitude I can muster, I bring my hand up to my mouth and blow him a very sincere, very exaggerated kiss.

I realize my mistake when bright red lights flash on the back of his car and the engine revs as he shifts to reverse. I really need to check my horoscope for today. I'm starting to think I should have stayed home.

Racing backward to block my car, he screeches to a halt. As he throws open the door, I brace myself. For what, I'm not sure. All I know is that the look on his face scares the hell out of me, and the intensity in his turquoise eyes leaves me paralyzed. A freight train could be careening toward me, and I would stand here like a deer in the headlights, frozen, waiting for impact.

Hearing the firm cadence of his designer shoes tap across the pavement, a chill goes up my spine, and I take a deep breath, readying myself to beg for mercy. I don't get a chance because the next thing I know, he is fully up on me. Putting one hand under my hair to cradle the back of my head, he puts the other on my lower back as he masterfully brings me to him, dropping his mouth to mine, every move gracefully and impeccably timed.

My conscious mind takes a backseat, and I am suddenly his to do with as he pleases, and *God help me*, it feels amazing. The warmth of his strong body pressed against mine, his hands holding me in a way I can relax and fully enjoy this unexpected pleasure. His kiss is so delicious, I am lost. I don't even know what is happening around me; all I know is that—right or wrong —I don't want him to stop.

My body is hot and humming with a tingling vibration. His kiss is wet and warm and firm and soft all at once. The rhythm of our lips and tongues moving together is like a well-choreographed ballet. I can't help pulling him closer, my hands in his hair and around his broad shoulders. An unstoppable moan escapes as he deepens the kiss, lighting my body on fire.

In the back of my mind, I acknowledge what he's doing. Somehow, I managed to infuriate the beast, and now he's going to ruin me for all others. Because I can pretty much guarantee that no one will ever kiss me the way he is in this moment. All others will pale in comparison, and I will be left longing, never fully sated. It's okay, though, as long as he doesn't stop right now, I'll deal with the consequences later.

The kiss goes on and on, melting my core and leaving me hungry for more. As if sensing my need, he turns my body, pushing my back up against the car. I arch into him, desperate for more contact, more of his strength...more of his potential. Reaching up, he cradles my head with both his warm hands and long fingers. He moves his mouth around mine, kissing it slowly from every angle. He's savoring me as if he doesn't want to waste a taste or touch, like his body knows something neither of us is fully aware of. It's a heady combination; the experience in his touch, the comforting heat that surrounds him, the clean sweetness of his mouth, and his spicy scent are more powerful than anything I've experienced before. Add to that his obnoxious good looks and it's like every one of my senses is experiencing pure euphoria.

Holding me steady, he talks through his kiss, that deep voice penetrating my daze. "You taste so fucking good, I could devour your kiss for hours. But your submission tastes even better. Do you know that I can smell how much you want me right now? That I can feel the vibration of your desire radiating through your beautiful body?" He continues his slow perusal of my mouth, licking my lips, nipping the edge with his teeth. It's like I've been drugged, but he's not done yet. "Do you feel what that's doing to me?" He pushes against me so I can feel the hardness that causes a gush of wetness to completely soak through my panties.

As if reading my body, he asks, "If I were to reach underneath your skirt, would I find you soaking wet, ready for me?"

My breath hitches, and I'm suddenly aware that this is way out of hand. I pull away, breathing heavily, lightheaded and confused from being overly aroused...but I'm yearning for more, even though I know it's wrong. Terribly wrong.

I look up, his eyes penetrating mine and I swear they can see his soul and mine. *My God, who is this man?* Then his thumb slowly glides across my bottom lip, wet and swollen. His face is close, his voice deep and raspy with desire. "Somehow, I don't think your boyfriend would appreciate how your body reacts to mine. Perhaps he's not providing you with what you really need."

Thrown by his statement, I don't have time to react when he grabs my arm and brings it up over my head, stretching my breast, making it feel heavy and erotically exposed. My head falls back as he cradles that side of my body with his own.

His next move, though, will likely ruin my sanity and self-esteem forever, because when his hand glides up my ribcage and across to cup my swollen breast, he takes my erect nipple between his thumb and finger, giving it a masterful pinch, twist, and pull.

And I literally have an orgasm right on the spot.

My head falls to his shoulder; I'm trying hard not to make a sound, hoping to save some of my dignity. I squint my eyes, and my breathing becomes erratic as the pleasure pulsates through my core. I am somewhat grateful for the fact that he doesn't just leave me there, broken and humiliated. At least he held me through it, keeping me from collapsing onto the pavement. And when my body has completely come down from a high I couldn't fully enjoy, he politely opens my door and gently guides me to my seat, then he reaches over me, slowly pulling the seatbelt across and latching it with a loud click. Leaning in, he kisses my temple and whispers in my ear, "You are perfect, but don't ever lie to me again."

And then he was gone.

TWO

IAN

I may live to regret that. And not because of the throbbing erection that has become somewhat painful and is wondering why the hell I'm in my car, driving in the *opposite* direction of the most desirable female it's ever…almost…come in contact with. Truth be told, I'm wondering that myself. Unfortunately, my original plan—to locate her this weekend and ask her to join me for dinner—was completely disintegrated when she blew me that smartass kiss that screamed triumph after her blatant lie. That single move obliterated all reason, and my actions became instinctive, and my instincts said to punish her…in the most delicious way possible.

Her instincts were to submit and I can't deny, the ease at which she did so was both a confounding surprise and a mind-numbing turn on. Regardless, it was powerful and it stirred something in me I didn't recognize. As if it went beyond sexual desire, beyond physical attraction—it was more like possession, as if she belonged to me and we both knew it. Whatever *it* was, it was a potent aphrodisiac, like nothing I'd ever experienced before.

The more I analyze the singularity of our encounter the more it reeks of the essence of fate. The thought raises the hair on my neck. Something was there, something extraordinary, and I suspect she could feel it, too. Whatever that may be, I am suddenly grateful for the stars' alignment that crossed my path with hers. She is mesmerizing, and when she came up behind me on the highway, I could see her clearly in the rearview mirror —she was so close. That gorgeous hair, a natural mix of blonde waves over a darker base, as if she spends most of her time outside near the ocean, soaking up the sun. It artfully framed her delicate face with its tan creamy skin, clear light eyes, and sinfully full mouth. I just wanted to stare at her, frustrated I couldn't without the risk of crashing into something.

It was entertaining to watch her unleash her road rage on me, flashing her lights and moving from side to side, trying to get my attention. Little did she know, she already had my full attention, which meant I was going to drag out the game as long as possible. I would have eventually let her pass so I could get her tag number and have Jackson locate all her information. But she thwarted my plan when she decided to cut me off and quickly take the next exit, not giving me the time I needed to get the number and completely pissing me off with her reckless driving. So, I opted to follow her, waiting for the opportunity to see if she was worth the trouble. She is definitely worth the trouble and then some.

I knew my efforts would pay off when I pulled up next to her and she got out of her car, staring at my jet-black window without knowing who or what was behind it and waiting patiently for me to emerge. When that didn't happen, she cocked her gorgeous head and raised one eyebrow as if to say, "Okay, now what, asshole?" My fingers twitched at the thought of how much fun that sassy attitude could induce.

Yet her involuntary reaction to me was a thing of legend, from a time long forgotten. The raw carnality of it activating the traces of my caveman DNA that had me wanting to throw her over my shoulder, return to my cave, and mark her as mine. I saw her breath hitch, eyes dilate, nipples harden… God, that was beautiful. She even relaxed the tension in her muscles, subconsciously submitting, as if she'd been waiting an eternity for me to come and take her. There was something so primal, so visceral about her reaction that it tugged at some foreign place deep inside me. My grandmother is always commenting on my old soul and all the power therein. Perhaps today was a reuniting of sorts. It would certainly justify its intensity.

I smile remembering the sound of her laughter when she lost her composure. My breath caught in my chest as I momentarily stopped breathing as the sound wrapped around me and sent a tingling up my spine. But seeing her gorgeous head thrown back, exposing the creamy skin of her throat and neck, tested my willpower to its limit. I cannot believe how close I was to taking it in my mouth and marking her, as if it were my right to do so. The look on her face—when she opened her eyes and realized my proximity—was priceless. Remembering the sound of her gasp forces a laugh of my own, despite the fact that my cock is still throbbing and pissed off at me.

Without thinking, my hand comes up to run along the shadowing of my chin and jawline. Chills spread across my body. I still have her delicious scent on me, an exquisite combination of her arousal, nervousness, whatever spicy perfume she had on, and her own natural sweet scent doused with pheromones. I am suddenly tense and edgy with need and wondering why my sadistic ego just left her in that fucking parking lot.

A sudden burst of irrational anger ignites in my chest as I make a sharp turn and head back to the convenience store. What I intend to do when I get there, I don't really know. Perhaps I *will* throw her over my shoulder and take her back to my cave. All I know is that I want her with a force that suddenly feels violent.

A few long minutes later, I'm stopped at the red light barely a block down from the parking lot I had hoped she'd still be in, recovering from the unexpected orgasm I gave her. But she's gone.

"Fuck!" My hand hits the steering wheel right as my cell phone rings. It's Jackson, and I pray he has her information.

"What did you find?" I ask my right-hand man and best friend. Jackson and I grew up together, and the old cliché, *He's like a brother to me,* isn't a cliché with us. Our friendship was founded and solidified when he protected me from some of the local meat-headed bullies that decided the skinny kid was an easy target. I never backed down from them, but there was no way in hell I could have beat them physically. However, Jackson could. Even as a kid, he had the height and muscles of an oversized teenager, but it was his fierce stare that diffused any confrontation before it ever happened. As a black man with pale green eyes and sharp features, he was intimidating as hell and learned early on to use it to his advantage…and, thankfully, mine. Jackson has more honor and integrity than any other man I know and always has; it's his nature. So when he saw a bunch of punks picking on someone half their size, there was no question how that situation was going to end—with the little pack of dogs running away, whimpering, their tails between their legs.

"Charlotte LeFay," his deep voice sounds through the speakers. Some of the tension leaves my body as I hear her name. Charlotte LeFay…fucking beautiful. My imagination takes over with images of her naked and ethereal. "She's the general manager of The Clara Sea, a luxury resort and spa in South Miami Beach."

"I know the place," I respond, essentially cutting him off. "We need to book something there immediately. A conference, dinner party, cocktail party. Hell, a bloody masquerade ball, for all I care. Just make sense out of it and book it. We can go over the details tomorrow."

When I hear Jackson's baritone laugh, I notice how desperate I sound—which is totally out of character. I thrive on control; Jackson knows this and evidently thinks it's funny that I appear to have lost it, especially over a woman. "What's so funny, asshole?"

"Oh, nothing. Just can't wait to meet the girl that has your panties in a wad." He ends his sarcastic comment with a chuckle. Lucky for him, Jackson has no drama in his life. He doesn't create it, and he masterfully deflects it. He married his college sweetheart, has a two-year-old son, and a daughter on the way. It's like a storybook, all perfect and sweet.

"Yeah, I bet. Hopefully, that happens sooner rather than later." The flat tone in my voice indicates my mind is elsewhere. Like wondering where Charlotte is right now and how long it will take to have her, naked and screaming my name in ecstasy as I devour her next climax.

"All right, man. I'll be in touch with the specifics. Go home, have a drink, and call your grandmother. She's always good for a few laughs to snap you out of a bad mood. I talked to her last week and she asked me if Becca was having pregnancy wet dreams yet."

Our laughter mingles through the car, finally ebbing out with me asking, "What the fuck is a pregnancy wet dream?"

"Man, you have no idea what happens to a woman's body when she's got all that extra blood and hormones pumping through her. It's intense! Ask Nana, she'll tell you all about it."

On a half-laugh, I state, "I'm not sure I want to give Nana extra ammunition to talk trash. She does fine on her own." My grandmother is in her late eighties and no longer has a filter—not that she really ever had one. She's been known to make grown men blush, something Jackson and I find immensely entertaining. In her youth and even beyond, she was beautiful with dark hair and blue-gray eyes. She has a passion for joyful living, and something tells me that my grandfather was a very happy man during their long marriage. Although, I'm sure he was occasionally embarrassed by her sharp wit and inappropriate topics of conversation. "But I'll give her a call anyway. Thanks, man."

"You bet." And we hang up.

I'm almost home. Very much looking forward to the peace and tranquility of my sanctuary. That's what my penthouse is to me. It's my escape from everything and everyone. High above the city where no one can find me, no one can see me, no one can hear me. It's perfect.

Yet, this evening, as I walk through the foyer, it suddenly seems quiet and vast and empty. Putting my things down, I head over to the bar to fix a drink, the clink of ice cubes on glass echoing through the silence. Mindlessly pouring the scotch, I fill the glass a little too much. Not that I really care; I probably need it.

Standing at the window, I take a fortifying sip, relax my shoulders, and look out across the ocean, lit up and sparkling by the full moon hanging low in the early night sky. My mind is fully occupied by Charlotte, wondering where she is right now, what she's doing, what she's thinking. And there it is, that feeling deep in my core, the same one I felt when I was walking toward her for the first time. Like a magnet, being pulled by that invisible force of energy. If you let it go, they inevitably lock together with a snap, sometimes impossible to break apart.

I should tread lightly. My sudden obsession is new ground; this powerful attraction and bone-deep need for her is foreign. Initially, my easy confidence has no doubt she will be mine and soon. That's how it's always worked for me. But in the back of my mind, there is something telling me it's different this time. She's different. My grip tightens on my glass as I try to ignore the possessive longing that just came over me. This could get interesting.

I raise my glass to the moon, now blazing bright. "Here's to you, Charlotte LeFay, until we meet again."

THREE

CHARLOTTE

S taring out over the ocean, hypnotized by the full moon's sparkling reflection, I hear the door open as Erika comes back onto the balcony with our wine refills. "I don't care what you say, Charlotte. That is literally the hottest thing I have ever heard in my life! You don't even want to know what I was tempted to do just now when I went to the bathroom, I was so turned on. Why the hell doesn't awesome, sexy shit like that happen to me?"

Erika is my best friend, confidant, and soul sister all in one. She was the first person I called when the sadistic God of Orgasms and All Things Sexual left me neatly strapped into my car seat, humiliated and defeated. I'm still numb, questioning my sanity because there is no way that really happened to me.

"Yeah, the only problem is, it doesn't matter how sexy it was, how sexy he was, or how amazing the bastard made my body feel. It was fucking humiliating beyond words and I hate him for it!" Just saying it puts a lump in my throat. I've been crying off and on since I got home, which is frustrating as hell because I can't really pinpoint why. Strangely, it doesn't feel like it's because of the unbearable humiliation of being controlled and violated...*publicly*...by a stranger that looks like some superhero of hotness and sex appeal. No, that infuriates me beyond words, this is deeper than that, like it's connected to a part of me I've never known, pushing me off-center and well outside my comfort zone, which is something I guard and protect with my life.

Truthfully, I'm not a crier, I'm not a drama queen, and I have a really thick skin. But right now, I'm none of that. I'm insecure, exhausted, and kind of weepy, like PMS emotions times a thousand. The crazy thing is, I haven't even gone through an expected and completely justified fit of rage, smashing things that I picture as his face. Compounding my confusion and humiliation is the fact that my body doesn't seem to be as upset as my mind. Apparently it remembers, all too well, the effect my nameless nemesis had on it, because when I allow myself to remember his gorgeous face, those mesmerizing turquoise eyes with their intense stare, his mind-numbing scent, that mouth, that kiss—God, that kiss—and the feeling of letting go in his arms, it heats up and creates butterflies in my stomach that seem to have a direct line of communication with my clit. "Ugh...I hate that bastard!" bursts out of nowhere.

I put my head in my hands then rub my temples, making a mental declaration that I'm never talking to Sibel again for getting me into this mess. Crazy bitch.

"Drink your wine, honey. The third glass is the charm." Holding her glass up, Erika proposes a toast. "To healthy libidos and the ability to have spontaneous orgasms from intense nipple stimulation. May the universe pleeeeaaasse grant me this same ability so I can experience it too before I die!"

We bust out laughing, working up to hysterics as tears run down our cheeks. Coming up for air, Erika can't let it go. "I still cannot believe that happened to you. I swear, when you were all upset, telling me everything that happened, I was like, wow... this sounds pretty freaking amazing to me. Then you pop up with this sudden orgasm via nipple tweak and I almost tripped into oncoming traffic!"

I nearly choke on my wine trying to keep myself from spraying it across the table. "Oh my God! I didn't even think about telling you to sit down first, or better yet... Hold on to your hat, sister, you're not going to believe this one!" The latter I belt out in my best country accent and we've lost it again. The wine is clearly kicking in. I need this more than anything right now, and Erika knows it.

"Honestly, when I first answered and could tell you were crying I thought something terrible had happened, then you start going into this pornographic fantasy and I'm like, 'What the heck?' Is she messing with me? Is there a hidden camera on me somewhere?" She's turning her head side to side, mimicking herself looking for the camera. It is hilarious, and I have no doubt this is not an exaggeration.

"I'm so sorry! I was so out of it I wasn't even thinking about how ridiculous everything must have sounded or that you might faceplant out of shock!" I take a huge, reassuring breath. "You have no idea how much I needed to laugh about this. I feel more like myself, thank you. You always know how to keep me grounded."

"Yes, I do, and I expect the same from you when some alien from the planet Hot-as-Shit shows up and warps my mind, melts my bones, and makes my clit explode. Oh...and gives a bonus nipple orgasm!"

I smack her leg, cracking up. "You're losing it, Erika Fleming."

"You think I'm kidding? I'm going to be pissed if it doesn't happen to me. Dammit! Now I think you've ruined me for all others. How the hell is any guy I meet ever going to top your mind-blowing, roadside sexcapade?" Shaking her head, she mumbles, "Nipple orgasm. You gotta be kidding me."

"Cheer up, babe, it'll happen eventually," I encourage as if she's a child that just lost the All-star game.

"It's not fair. *I'm* the slut in this relationship. It should have happened to me." The petulant sarcasm in her tone sets us off again.

"Erika, you're drunk, and I'm getting you an Uber."

"No, don't bother. I'll sleep in your guest room so we can get up early, have coffee out here on the balcony, and talk more trash about Lambo man and his magic fingers."

Walking inside with my arm over her shoulder and our heads leaning into each other, I agree. "That sounds perfect."

Just before the sun rises, a long full-body stretch kick-starts my energy. I lie still for a few minutes, allowing myself to fully wake. As yesterday comes back to me, the first thing that drifts through my mind is how grateful I am that I slept through the night. If ever there was a time for me to toss and turn from mind-racing stress, it was last night. But I actually feel pretty good—physically, anyway. Mentally...I'll evaluate that once I've had some caffeine.

Making my way to the kitchen, I see the wine bottles and glasses from last night and smile. I should let Erika sleep a little longer. She's not an early riser. Although, once she gets a whiff of the coffee brewing, she'll drag herself out of bed and join me on the balcony.

The sun is beginning to peek over the horizon. I love starting my day out here in the fresh morning air straight off the ocean, the orange burst filling the sky as the sun works its way up over the edge, breaking that precise line with its glow. It's crazy, but on the days I sleep in and miss this event, I always feel a little off, with a little less pep in my step. It reminds me of one of my grandmother's favorite sayings: *The sunrise and coffee are to the start of your day what the sunset and wine are to the end.* Then she'd wink and say, "We must balance our vices."

Even though it's Saturday, I'm going to head to the office for a bit. After that last board meeting, I have some loose ends to tie

THE ESSENCE OF FATE

up. Plus, I'd like to stay busy so I don't sit around and obsess about being pleasured beyond reality and humiliated all at once by a total fucking stranger. The thought of it makes me get up and refill my mug that's only half empty. A pointless act meant to keep myself busy so yesterday's events don't rotate on replay in my head.

It's a futile effort because as soon as I'm comfortable again with the now blazing sun warming my skin, I can't help but remember my reaction to seeing him for the first time. Even if I get Alzheimer's when I'm old, I will still remember that moment. The flood of physical, mental, and emotional stimulation is something you only read about in books, never really believing it could be real.

It's not like I'm a virgin or something and have no idea what being attracted or even aroused feels like. No. Whatever the hell happened yesterday was not typical, not average, *not* normal.

Making matters worse, he had the upper hand. I'm admittedly a control freak; I have my reasons, but it's worked out pretty well for me so far. I've always worked hard, keeping to the high standards I set for myself. So having control taken from me and rubbed in my face is a hard pill to swallow. Actually, I'm not even sure I've swallowed it yet. It's just sitting in my mouth dissolving, acrid and burning.

I wish I had someone older and more experienced to turn to. Not to simply rehash the whole thing—Erika and I can and will do that for the rest of our lives—but someone to help me understand and justify the deep emotions that were awakened by a nameless man. Sadly, I don't have that someone, and I'm sure as heck not going to ask Uncle James. I laugh at the absurdity, knowing he would probably put a hit out on Joey Porn Star.

Oh my God! It's like that awful record scratch sound in my head. What if he is a porn star? No, he probably owns the freaking production company and website! Miami is huge for that. *Ugh.* And it would explain that over-the-top, I-have-money-to-burn car he was driving! Not to mention his unconventional familiarity with making a woman cum on command. "Oh. Dear. God!" I say, putting my head in my hands.

"What now?" Startling me, Erika appears on the balcony. "Don't tell me Magic Mike showed up in the middle of the night with more of his orgasmic sorcery."

"Thankfully, no. But it just hit me that he could be part of the porn industry and I'm completely skeeved out. Wouldn't that make sense? He's rich, flashy, hot, and clearly knows more about sex than your average person." My tone says that I've come to a conclusion on this and the sky is getting ready to fall.

"Ahhh… It kinda does make sense," she agrees, making a sort of cringe face. "He's probably an instructor that teaches all the newbies the tricks of the trade, like proper nipple stimulation techniques."

"Wow, that really helps a lot, Erika. You're supposed to disagree and give me all the reasons why it *doesn't* make sense and that he's actually a super clean guy that comes from a great background and simply had a momentary lapse in control because he was overwhelmed by our raw chemistry!"

Erika laughs. "Honestly, the porn guy scenario seems more believable than that fantasy. Don't worry, though. All you really did was kiss him. It's not like you guys had unprotected sex or anything. What's the worst that could happen, you get mono?" She seems so unfazed by the possibility that I may have had a seriously intense make-out session with a guy that's been with thousands of women and produces sex movies for all the world's creepers to masturbate to. I, on the other hand, am not okay with that notion.

"Please change the subject. My brain cannot properly process the potential of that scenario," I say, exasperated, rubbing my temples.

"You brought it up, I just agreed." Taking a sip of her coffee, Erika continues, waving her hand. "Okay, fine. What's on the agenda for today? Let's go get lunch and then go to your spa. It's been too long, and you could really use a good massage right now."

"Maybe, we'll see. I have to run in for a little while anyway and wrap up some things from yesterday. You know I can't stand getting behind." Right then, my phone pings a text notification. Glancing over, I see that it's Tracy from work.

Tracy: Good morning! I wasn't sure if you were coming in today or not, but there is a group that contacted us early this morning that wants to book the Garden Room. No big deal, I know, but they insist on working directly with you on the details. It's their "policy" to cut out the middleman.

Great...it's one of those deals. I know it all too well. I'm usually stuck with some snippy, wannabe intern with overdone makeup and wardrobe. Exactly what I don't feel like dealing with today. Doesn't matter, though; we'll accommodate, they'll pay.

Me: It's okay. I'll be there. But tell them I only have a twenty-minute window on such short notice and to be there at 11. Thank you!

"Great! My morning just got a slight interruption. I have to pacify some firm that's too important to deal with my employees and insists on dealing with me." It's happened before and it annoys me to no end. Do they really think I'm going to be intimidated or maybe impressed by this request? Only deal with the general manager so everyone looks and seems uber important, not only to their clients, but the employees working the event. Whenever a client is truly that important, they don't need to request my involvement.

Getting up and saying a silent goodbye to my spectacular view, wishing I had time for a walk on the beach, I take my last sip of coffee. "I'm going to jump in the shower. You stay out here and enjoy your morning." I get no disagreement from Erika as she winks and holds up her mug as if to say, "Cheers."

An hour later, I'm primped and ready, more done up than I had originally intended for a quiet morning of paperwork and no meetings. Erika is just coming in as I gather my keys, purse, and laptop. "I'll text you when my meeting's over. Let me know where you want to go for lunch, I've got a comfortable change of clothes with me so let's do kinda casual. I need to feel like it's at least a half day off. No heels, no layers, no synthetic materials." Dressing up for work every day in Miami can be exceedingly unpleasant. The heat and humidity can be uncomfortable when all you have on is a skimpy bikini, forget about work attire with its heavy materials that end up creating more heat. I keep telling myself I need to create a line of super stylish, professional clothing made of cotton and bamboo, specifically for women forced to dress up in a tropical climate.

"Okay, I'm heading home to get ready. As always, thanks for letting me crash here last night." Erika leans in and kisses my cheek.

"No, thank you for being here. You saved me from going completely insane. I'm not sure what I would have done without you." Sincere in my appreciation, I give her a tight hug. "I'll see you in a bit."

Arriving at work in what seems like only a few minutes, I'm in a surprisingly good mood. It must be the lack of traffic. It's so refreshing not having to deal with all that chaos and idiocy. During the week it takes me a minimum of thirty minutes to get here, and that's on a good day.

Checking in with Tracy, I get a quick briefing of the night before. No issues, problems, or cranky guests. Precisely how I expect it to be. She has the conference room set up for this morning's impromptu meeting and fills me in on the rest of the details there.

"It's a real estate development firm, McAlistair Architecture, Design & Development. They have a new client from Brazil arriving next week. According to the gentleman I talked to, there will be a total of twelve people, including those from the McAlistair firm. They requested the Garden Room and would like your recommendations for what to serve for lunch." Looking up from her iPad, she pushes her glasses back over the bridge of her nose, which she will do at least five more times during this conversation alone. It's a charming habit that suits her personality. "Since he had such an amazing voice and was being genuinely polite, I decided not to push the issue and explain that we have people that are paid very well to help them decide what to serve a group of Brazilians for lunch." Her monotone voice is betrayed by the smirk on her face.

"Hmmmm...an amazing voice, huh? Perhaps I'll have *you* escort them to the Garden Room while I 'finish my call' so you can put a face on that voice. You might be pleasantly surprised." I jokingly lift my eyebrows up and down. Tracy blushes and silently begs me with her eyes *not* to do that. She is extremely shy and reserved when it comes to the opposite sex, but something tells me that doesn't mean she has no desire. Quite the opposite I suspect. "Don't worry, I'm only teasing you. But you're welcome to accompany me, if for nothing more than to appease your curiosity."

She thinks about it for a minute, then opts out, as I knew she would. "I'm fine. Thank you, though." And she takes her leave.

I start organizing some of the notes from yesterday's board meeting so when I go over everything with Uncle James, it's quick and precise. He prefers to get business out of the way first when we chat so we can talk about more interesting topics like politics, world events, and any hospitality industry gossip either of us may have. I'm truly fortunate to have him. He's more like a father than an uncle, and he means the world to me.

The morning passes quickly, and before I know it, my phone buzzes with Tracy informing me that my eleven o'clock is here. At least they respect my time and have arrived promptly. Touching up my lipstick and making sure my appearance is in order, I make my way to the lobby.

I'm surprised to find only one gentleman waiting for me when I arrive. He's impeccably dressed and quite striking with his tall, well-built stature. As I get closer and his face is no longer shadowed, I notice his pale green eyes that almost glow against his dark skin. Wow! Talk about handsome. No doubt Tracy melted somewhere behind the front desk because I don't see her anywhere.

Holding out my hand, I greet him. "Hi! I'm Charlotte LeFay. Thank you for choosing The Clara Sea for your meeting. Tracy tells me your clients are coming in from Brazil." His handshake is properly firm without overdoing it in spite of the fact that my hand is about five times smaller than his.

"Good morning, Charlotte. Thaddeus Jackson, but please, call me Jackson." He really does have an amazing voice, deep and smooth, befitting his size and presence. He must be six and a half feet tall, at least. "Yes, they will arrive Tuesday, and the meeting is set for the day after. Thank you for accommodating us on such short notice."

"Absolutely. I think you will be very pleased with the Garden Room. It is our most popular for more intimate gatherings. Shall we go take a look?" I'm at ease with Jackson. He's got great energy and an old-fashioned charm. A pleasant surprise, considering what I was expecting.

"Yes, of course. But, could you ask someone at the front desk to direct Mr. McAlistair to us as soon as he is finished? He had to take an important call outside and will be a few minutes."

That was a totally reasonable request and nothing out of the ordinary. So why did I just get butterflies in my stomach?

On a slight pause, I acknowledge his request and ask Terrance to make sure Mr. McAlistair is directed to us since I can't find Tracy anywhere, poor thing.

Making our way toward the conference room, Jackson offers compliments on the decor and elegant features of the resort. He is so articulate I'm tempted to ask him to be the voiceover in our next round of ads. Listening to his deep, almost baritone voice say, "The casual elegance of your lobby is reminiscent of the West Indies style, yet you have masterfully incorporated a modern flare that makes The Clara Sea a singular resort," distracted me so much I almost forget where I'm going and miss the entrance to our destination.

Practically sliding to a stop, I rest my hand on his arm to keep us from colliding. "Here we are!" I announce with a laugh. "I'm sorry, but you honestly distracted me with your compliment. I hope you don't mind, but I may have to write that down and use it in my next ad campaign." Then with a wink and a double dose of charm, I add, "And I may be contacting you with an offer to moonlight as the new voice of The Clara Sea."

Entering the conference room, his deep laugh echoes as he turns and says, "I may take you up on that, Ms. LeFay."

He immediately walks over to the floor-to-ceiling windows overlooking one of our many well-established tropical gardens. It's what everyone does when they enter this room—head straight for the view. It's impossible not to, it's just that beautiful. "I must say, Charlotte, this is far better than I imagined. It's extraordinary and will be perfect for Wednesday's meeting."

"That makes me very happy, Jackson. I'm so pleased you like it." At that moment, I hear the steady tap of confident footsteps coming toward us from outside the door. It's familiar. Then something inside my gut is suddenly uneasy as chills creep up my spine. I don't have time to pinpoint why before the door swings open and my world falls apart.

Time is suddenly ticking by in slow motion. All I hear is the muffled sound of my pounding heartbeat inside my ears as my vision locks with the same turquoise eyes that belong to the man that almost ruined me not even twenty-four hours ago. He's here, in my resort, in my conference room, walking toward me like a predatory cat getting ready to pounce. Once again, I am powerless to move. My mind has shut down, but my body has come alive, heating up with the memory of what this man is capable of. I have to snap out of it. I will not be humiliated by him again. Ever. And he clearly has found an affinity for toying with me. I can see it on his face. He is very pleased with himself for having found me.

Before he can fully approach me and offer an introduction, I snap the hell out of it, square my shoulders, and offer him my back as I turn to make my way around the opposite end of the twenty-foot table and walk out the door. Once I'm outside, away from his godforsaken energy field that my body seems to be magnetically attracted to, I can breathe again.

"Son of a bitch!" I declare on a harsh whisper. How did I not see that coming? Impromptu, important meeting, can only deal with me specifically...the day after! How could I be so blind? Probably because I stupidly distracted myself with ridiculous notions of him being some porn mogul that I'd thankfully never see again.

Anger is now pumping a different kind of adrenaline through my veins. I hate how naive and out of control he makes me feel, and now I'm pissed. Yesterday I was confused, definitely angry, but also a little sad about what had happened. Now I'm fucking furious. The audacity of him to show up here, *where I work*, distracting me with his front man so he could sneak up on me. To do what? A repeat of yesterday, maybe lay me out on the goddamn conference room table? Not a chance, bastard.

Barely making it down the hall, I hear the door fly open and him jogging the short distance to get to me. "Charlotte, wait!" he says as he grabs onto my arm. The momentum of the sudden stop and him turning me toward him added nicely to the force of my hand slapping him across his gorgeous face. The sound echoes through the hallway, my hand stinging painfully.

"Don't. Fucking. Touch. Me." I yank my arm out of his grasp, turn on my heel, and continue down the hall.

"I came back," I hear him say, still standing where I left him. "Yesterday, I turned around and came back, but you were already gone."

That statement stops me in my tracks. My back is still to him as I digest what the arrogant bastard just said. Now he's done it. The floodgates are open, and I'm not feeling sorry for myself anymore. Sibel has busted out of the solitary confinement I left her in for what was supposed to be eternity, and she is out for blood. Slowly turning around, rage coursing through my body, I pause, trying to outdo the ferocity of his stare. God bless the heavens above, that man is physical fucking perfection and it makes me hate him even more. A burst of confidence has me marching right back to him. Even from a distance I can see the blazing red handprint on his cheek and it tightens my gut. "You came back, did you? For what?" My voice is venomous. "So you could gloat and humiliate me even more than you already had? What exactly did you think I would do upon your return, *Mr.* McAlistair? Drop to my fucking knees and beg for more?"

He doesn't answer my question, just calmly states, "It's Ian. My name is Ian."

For whatever reason, knowing his name, Ian McAlistair, seems intimate and so personal that it makes my chest hurt. I swear on my life, he is not human; he's from another time and place or bloody planet where it's normal for people to play sorcery on your body and totally mess with your head.

His voice is calm as he continues. "I wasn't sure what you would do. But I knew I had made a mistake, and I wanted to apologize." His voice wraps around me like a warm, freshly filled bubble bath, releasing the tension and dulling my anger. Sibel fends it off, holding on to my rage for dear life.

Crossing my arms in front of my chest, I respond, "And since you missed your opportunity for this heartfelt apology yesterday, you decided a sneak attack *here, where I work,* where I have a very important position and reputation to uphold, would be more appropriate than a phone call, email, or maybe even a handwritten fucking note?"

He raises an eyebrow at me, and, not to be outdone, I raise one back at him.

"You're right. I could have done any of those things, in spite of the fact each one is cowardly in its own way. By doing so, I would have left a clean opening for you to completely ignore me. And since my goal was to get your full attention, so I could look you in the eyes and tell you that I am sincerely sorry, I decided this was the quickest way to make that happen." Hands in his pockets, he is totally at ease in his own skin. He's so smooth and sure of himself, it flusters me to the point I want to childishly stomp my foot, growl out a deep-throated *Ugh* and disappear. I swear he knows it, too.

"Well, you said it. So you and your sidekick can be on your way." I'm not sure where Jackson is during this whole confrontation. He must still be in the conference room. "I have a day off to enjoy, and your twenty-minute window just closed." Turning to make my retreat, Ian follows close behind. I knew this wasn't going to be easy. I've now presented a challenge, and he's not going to let up until he gets what he wants.

When I hear him say my name, my first instinct is to stop and turn to him. But Sibel thumps me in the head saying, "Uh uh, sister." And I keep moving.

"Charlotte," he says again. "I had hoped we could finish discussing the details for Wednesday's lunch meeting. Even though I only saw the conference room briefly, it's perfect. I know my clients will be comfortable and beyond impressed. We just need to finalize the lunch menu." He has no problem keeping up with my fast pace, regardless I have no intention of stopping.

Once I arrive at my office door, I turn to him, one hand on the knob. "Understand this, *Mr.* McAlistair, you are more than welcome to entertain your clients in this resort. I will ensure that everything is perfect, as I always do. But I will no longer be your contact. I will not be helping you with the menu, flower arrangements, wine selection, or anything from this point forward. I would recommend Jackson deal directly with Tracy. They are already acquainted, and surely you have better things to do with your time than pick out a lunch menu." Turning the knob, I open the door only halfway, and once inside, I turn to him, blocking any entrance.

The look on his face is like a kick in the chest.

It doesn't matter, though. All I have to say to him is, "Goodbye."

FOUR

IAN

For several long minutes, I stand there, my hands braced on the doorframe, head hanging low. I'm trying very hard not to rip the fucking door off its hinges. It's a herculean effort because every instinct that I live by is telling me that she's mine and I need to go in and get her. Every knuckle is white, ready to explode from the force of my grip. I hold on a little longer as it helps release the energy that will otherwise have me doing something stupid.

On a deep breath, I slowly release the frame, stand up straight, roll my neck, and casually head back to the conference room where I left Jackson. No doubt he has a thing or two to say about what just happened.

Entering the room, I think about seeing Charlotte standing there. She had her hair pulled back in a ponytail, a few curls drifting around her face. She looked younger and more gorgeous than I remembered. My controlled steps couldn't get me to her fast enough. I wanted a proper introduction. I wanted her to know my name so I could hear her say it, watching her supple mouth form the words. Perhaps my ego overestimated the outcome of my surprise visit, because as soon as I was close enough to watch her fully register what was happening, the shock and anger was evident in her eyes, and I knew she was going to bolt.

I immediately went after her to the sound of Jackson's voice saying, "Wow, Ian. That went well. What the hell did you do to her?" He was more serious than sarcastic.

The urgency to get to her had my guard down, and when she turned all her fury on me with an unexpected slap to my face—that stung like a bitch—I knew my mistake was monumental. The fire in her beautiful blue eyes when she told me not to touch her, the venom in her voice, was like a punch to the gut. I deserve worse, I know I do, and I have a feeling she will make it so.

Three thoughts enter my mind as I make my way back over to Jackson, who is patiently waiting for me to return: 1. I have never had a woman reject me, 2. I have never had a woman slap me across the face, and 3. I have *never* wanted a woman as much as I want Charlotte LeFay.

The women I've been with don't question my intentions or resist my advances. Having mastered the art of physical pleasure, I know what they want, and they submit to it—every time. Today, however, my flawless record has been broken.

"I gotta say, Ian, I'm curious as hell to know what you did to deserve that kind of welcome. But truthfully, I'm afraid if I know, I might have to kick your ass because that has to be one of the most charming, sincere, and genuinely awesome young ladies I've ever come across. Other than Becca, of course." Jackson always tells me like it is, which is one of the many reasons why I trust him so much.

"Yes, Jackson, you probably would. Which is why I'm not telling you. And you're right, she's pretty damn awesome," I say, staring out the window overlooking a tropical paradise. "I'm going to have my work cut out for me this time, and I'm afraid I'm rather lacking in the art of the chase." I finish my thought on an exhale, rubbing the back of my neck, then the side of my face where she nailed me.

"Looks like I won't have to kick your ass. Apparently, she already took care of it. That's a hot little hand mark you've got there. Contrasts nicely with your eyes." He thinks it's funny, of course. Jackson and I are polar opposites when it comes to women. He's sweet and charming, old-fashioned and committed —his perfect marriage and lack of personal issues a testament to that. I, on the other hand, don't do commitment. My relationships lean more toward the *friends with benefits* kind where the benefits are the main focus. I can do dinner dates and attend functions together, but it never runs deep—no emotional attachments, no baggage. It's pretty cut and dry, and it has worked well for me. But now, a wrench has been thrown into my well-oiled, smoothly running machine, a wrench by the name of Charlotte LeFay. There is something different with her, and I won't let up until I know what it is.

Heading out the door, I'm firm in my declaration. "I'm glad you're enjoying this, asshole. But rest assured, I will have Charlotte. In every way possible."

Back in my office and back on my game, I focus on Wednesday's meeting with the Brazilian firm, Novas Alturas Development, which made it big during Brazil's economic boom, developing some of the area's most spectacular high rises. Their reputation is superior and their pockets deep. A move to Miami to expand their range and footprint makes sense since Brazil's boom came to a screeching halt. Unable to keep up with itself, it created an infrastructure nightmare that has yet to be resolved. This move to South Florida keeps up their momentum and stays in line with the Brazilians' love for all things Miami. I think they may have surpassed Cubans as the dominant subculture.

They contacted me a few months ago after acquiring a dilapidated warehouse building and two adjacent properties near the bay. It's an excellent location. However, if the city doesn't make it possible for them to implement the necessary changes to the existing traffic lanes and intersections, it may not be. In reality, that is unlikely. The city would be stupid to create any obstacles to the redevelopment of that area. It's long overdue and will dramatically increase the real estate values of the surrounding areas, not to mention the significant tax base increase, which means more money in the city's coffers. To ensure success, Novas Alturas needs a solid connection and partnership here in the States, preferably Miami. That's where I come in.

McAlistair Architecture, Design & Development is the company I created eight years ago after a two-year internship and working my way up the ladder at one of New York's biggest real estate investment and development firms. I had a knack for almost everything but especially enjoyed working with the architects and interior designers to come up with style signatures for each project. We always considered location, culture, history of the area—anything that helped tell the story of where the building was and why it was there.

It was a fascinating and inspiring process that made the less enjoyable aspects of real estate development much more satisfying and worthwhile. So when I moved to Miami, I included architecture and design departments as part of my development company, instead of contracting other companies when those services were needed. Doing so has created the opportunity for us to have a hand in more than just what we develop. Allowing the McAlistair brand to have a broader reach and my strict standards ensure our brand's reputation is solid.

A knock on the door announces Jackson's entry *and* the stupid smirk on his smug little face. "How's your afternoon going so far, boss-man?" Putting his hand up to his cheek and patting it gently, he continues. "That cheek finally cooling down? Hope it doesn't bruise, that'd be awkward." A laugh escapes, the sound bouncing across my office like a bass drum. I get why he thinks it's so funny, and because I'm not a complete asshole who can't ever find humor in himself, I laugh along with him.

"You're not going to let me live that down, are you?" I say, getting up and heading to the fridge to get a water.

"No, Ian. I'm not." His matter-of-fact tone contradicts the underlying chuckle. "You know I love you, man. But you've had it way too easy when it comes to the ladies. I don't even think you know what it's like to have to work for it, even a little. You never have, with your weird-ass good looks that melt panties everywhere you go. I swear I used to think you had some kind of mojo that warped a chick's mind into doing whatever the hell you wanted." He's a bit more serious as he concludes, "How can you fully appreciate the value of what you have if you need zero effort to get it? You can't. That's why nothing ever sticks with you." He raises an eyebrow and tips his head. "It's high time you start getting a taste of what you've been missing."

"Yeah, I know what I've been tasting, and it's pretty fucking sweet. And I'm not sure what you're getting at here. It's not like I'm going to walk into The Clara Sea, get down on one knee, and ask Charlotte to marry me." Simply making that idiotic comment sends heat down my spine. I chug the rest of my water, hoping to extinguish it. "She's a beautiful woman that has me intrigued. I've admittedly started out on the wrong foot with her, which is also…admittedly…a first for me." Walking over to him, I hold up my fist for a bump. "But I can guarantee you this, that wall that she's put up will come down, even if I have to break it down with my bare hands. So you're right, I may finally have to work at it, but I intend to enjoy it every step of the way."

Jackson returns the fist bump, and his face lights up. "Oh, I don't know about that, but I do know *I'll* enjoy it. This shit's been boring for the past eight years, at least. It's like watching the same damn movie over and over again."

"Good, since you're so damn bored, you can head back over to the resort and get with whomever your contact is…something with a T, I think"—I was too focused on Charlotte getting ready

to shut the door in my face to remember the name she said—
"and figure out the details for Wednesday. Regardless of
Charlotte's cold reception, I still intend to use that conference
room. It's fucking brilliant. I may even have to steal the idea." It
really was spectacular; the whole resort was spectacular. I'll have
to make a point of checking out the rest of it, give myself a
personal tour of what Charlotte spends most of her time
overseeing. The idea has me suddenly looking forward to it as I
have a vision of running into her in the hallway again. This time
with a more cordial exchange.

"You do realize it's Saturday, right?" Jackson says with a little
impatience in his voice.

"Yes, I do. But the Novas Alturas meeting is Wednesday, and
since I changed the venue at the last minute so I could stalk
Charlotte, the details need to be ironed out now so any snags can
be dealt with," I say, sitting at my desk and waking up my
laptop.

"And why exactly do you need to send me to work out these
details when you have two assistants that could do it for you?"
He's definitely getting annoyed now.

"Because I trust you more than I trust them." It's the truth. I
trust Jackson more than I trust anyone, and I know that he will
run into Charlotte again—and when he does, he will put in a
good word for me.

Right as he opens the door to leave, I hear him say, "It's a
good thing you pay me more than I'm worth."

FIVE
CHARLOTTE

I texted Erika right after I shut the door in Ian's face, my heart racing as my rage slowly faded to a steady anger that's still simmering, causing a slight headache. The audacity of this man has me completely shaken.

Me: OMG! Meet me at Laney's Cafe, like now!
Magic Mike just showed up as my impromptu 11:00
appointment!

Erika: WHAT THE FUCK??? Tell me what happened!!

Me: At Laney's. Hurry!

Erika: UGH!

Sneaking out the back door of my office so I don't get ambushed by Ian again, I don't even bother changing into my Saturday gear. I want to get out of here and go over everything with Erika so we can analyze what happened. I am totally on autopilot right now and am a little freaked out about slapping him in the face. Erika is going to flip!

Fifteen minutes later, we are walking toward each other in front of Laney's, our favorite go-to for something casual but healthy. Seeing me, she shuffles faster in a mini-run.

"Oh my God, Charlotte! I can't believe he showed up at the resort. Are you okay?"

"Yes, I think so. Let's get a table. I have to tell you everything. You are going to freak!" We opt for an inside table in the back corner for privacy and out of fear my mind-warping stalker nemesis will appear out of nowhere again. Sitting down, we both order our usual kale wrap. I contemplate adding some kind of alcoholic beverage to accompany it, but decide against it, saving that for tonight.

I go through everything, rambling it off to get it out of my head, telling her about my surprise at finding Jackson as my liaison instead of some pissy intern. How his charm and unique presence was disarming, in a good way. "That's probably why the bastard sent Jackson in first, the old distract-and-attack technique. Well, it worked. Because when he walked into the room, I was so caught off guard and hit with such a rush of adrenaline, I barely remember what I was thinking. It was like a fifty-car pile-up in my head!" My heart rate picks up again as I relive it.

Erika is so enthralled with every word, her eyes are dilated and she is leaning forward over the table. But, of course, she has to get to the important stuff. "Was he actually as hot as you thought he was yesterday?" She's dead serious, too.

Not wanting to disappoint her inner slut, I answer truthfully. "Hotter. And I'm not kidding. I swear to you, the sounds of his footsteps are even hot! How is that possible?" I exclaim, remembering the measured cadence of him walking toward the conference room and the butterflies that swarmed inside me. "But none of that mattered once my mind cleared and reality set in. I saw the look in his eyes and saw his intent, like he was coming to get me, and all I could think about was how humiliated I was yesterday when he arrogantly took over my body, my mind, all sense of dignity…then left me there, sitting in my car like a total idiot wondering what the hell just happened. All the while, picturing him laughing his ass off as he zooms away in his car that costs as much as a house."

The waitress interrupts my tirade, putting our plates down in front of us. Once she's out of earshot, I continue. "I don't know, Erika, something came over me. Maybe it was pride or just the anger I hadn't fully let out yet, but in that moment, I decided I wasn't letting him get the upper hand again. So I turned around and walked out, not giving him a chance to even speak a word to me." I laugh a little at her expression; she has no idea how good this gets. "Once I was out in the hallway and I wasn't overwhelmed by his presence, it hit me, hard, that I had been duped…*again*. I couldn't believe it. It made me *so angry*"—I pause, swallowing my emotions—"that when he ran up to me and grabbed onto my arm, asking me to wait, I turned around and slapped the hell out of him." With a sudden lump in my throat, I put my head down, trying to keep my emotions from bubbling over. Perhaps it's a letdown from the adrenaline rush, or maybe it's because I've never hit anyone before and it's honestly not as satisfying as it sounds, or maybe because I hit him and a part of me wishes I could apologize.

After Erika recovers, she asks, "In the face?" Her voice is high. "You actually slapped him in the face?" I knew she'd be shocked—hell, I'm shocked, and I'm the one who did it. "My God, that's pretty major. What did he do… What did *you* do?"

"He definitely took it like a man. I can't believe how hard I hit him. It stung my hand so badly, but he barely flinched. Then I told him not to fucking touch me, and the look on his face…*ugh*, it made me weak for a second. So I turned around, *again*, and walked away." In a frustrated voice I add, "I get so flustered and confused around him. I don't know who I am. I'm *not* myself! Look at what's happened with only two encounters. If this shit keeps up, I'm going to have to ask Uncle James if I can manage another resort, like the one in France!"

With a mouth full of kale wrap, she swallows. "If you do that, I'm coming with you. But in the meantime, we need to analyze what happened." Shallow Erika is gone, no longer interested in hotness and nipples. Now serious Erika is on the scene, ready to do forensics on this morning's sneak attack by Ian and his accomplice, Jackson. "First of all, did he ever mention why he was there?"

"According to him, he turned around and came back to Sommelier's yesterday, but I was already gone." Her jaw drops at that little tidbit. "He wanted the opportunity to *look me in the eyes and give me a sincere apology*. When I asked him why he couldn't just call or email instead of sneaking up on me and potentially embarrassing me at my place of employment, he said the other options were cowardly and left an opening for me to ignore him."

Erika chews on that for a minute. "Hmmm…I'm intrigued. This guy's got it for you…bad." Holding up her hand to fend off my argument, she continues. "Ah, ah, ah, not so fast, opposing counsel. Hear me out. You cannot deny that he had the hots for you yesterday. There was way too much fire between you two for it to be something that happens to the guy every other day. There's just no way. Then, you said his parting words were, 'You are perfect, but don't ever lie to me *again*.' That statement says it all, Charlotte. I don't know how we missed it last night!"

She's having a eureka moment, so I let her continue. "He had every intention of seeing you again, and he knew it before he even got out of his car and turned your brain into mashed potatoes. I bet he got your tag number when he was following you, then, once he tasted a sample of what you had to offer, the hook was set. His comment referenced the future, honey. You're right, he's smooth and he knew what the hell he was doing." It's like she just solved some decades-old mystery, like what the heck ever happened to Amelia Earhart? However, she does have a point. That statement did reference the future. How the hell did I miss that, too? It's like he's surrounded by an energy field that scrambles your memory so you can't remember any details that could incriminate him.

"Okay. I don't disagree. So what if he planned on seeing me again? That doesn't mean I wanted to see him! The arrogant jerk automatically assumes I'm good with that?" I pick up my uneaten wrap, turn it over, and put it back on the plate. More mindless bullshit brought on by Ian Von Kryptonite. "Oh! And did I tell you I know his name now?" I hear the slight hysteria in my voice. "Ian McAlistair. Not McAlister," I say, emphasizing the *er* sound. "Like it's supposed to be, all normal and every-day. No, it's McAli*stair*, all sexy and unique with that yummy little flare at the end." I roll my eyes and play with my wrap some more.

"Yummy is right," Erika says in a deep, sultry voice. "Ian, Son of Alistair, that is seriously fucking delicious. You're doomed, sister." It's like she's thrown in the towel on my fate. I'm not okay with that. Then to rub salt in the wound, she adds, "If he shows up in a kilt next time, I'm out. I simply will not be able to handle that level of hotness." She leans in to rest her head on one hand, giving me a slow, dreamy-eyed blink.

"Erika?" Her name comes out slowly as I wave my hands in front of her preoccupied stare. "Team Charlotte, here. I don't need you telling me I'm doomed then giving me ammunition to conjure up visions of this obnoxiously good-looking man in a kilt like some Scottish hero in a bloody romance novel! I need your advice on how to deflect any more of that shit!" The waitress approaches our table, but makes a quick turnabout at the tone of my voice and, more likely, our ridiculous conversation.

"Okay, okay, you're right. I'm sorry. I got distracted when you said his name." She laughs at herself. "Ian McAlistair… ooohhhh, this just keeps gettin' better." Looking up, she sees the impatience on my face, apologizes again, and reluctantly asks, "Is it safe to assume that he did not book the Garden Room for next week's pornography summit?"

I throw my head back and laugh. "You should see your face! It's like you're scared of my answer!"

"I *am* scared of your answer! *And* I'm scared of your reaction to my reaction to your answer!" She says it so dramatically, the last part flying off her tongue so fast we both have to stop and look at each other, replaying it in our heads to make sure what she said even made sense. As if realizing at the same time that it did, we both burst out laughing again.

A few minutes later, wiping tears from my eyes, I look up and say on a drawn-out sigh, "Oh, you're gonna love this one, too. He's the owner of McAlistair Architecture, Design & Development. Look them up, they're huge."

Her hand hits the table. "Are you kidding me? So not only is he wickedly good-looking, ridiculously rich, and capable of instigating spontaneous nipple orgasms, he's got brains, too? *There is no way.* He has to be a playboy that works for his father, Papa McAlistair, who owns the company and is probably terribly unattractive, but because he's stupid rich, he's married to a younger, drop-dead gorgeous woman who provided him with a son that isn't really his, but the spawn of her affair with the local fitness trainer." She's on a roll now, and I think we're starting to annoy the other patrons with our outbursts of laughter.

"That is some classic stereotyping there, Erika. And you're probably right. He can't be that successful. He only looks like he's in his mid-thirties, max." We look at each other as the same lightbulb beams over our heads, and we grab our phones to Google him.

"Holy...everything! Is this him?" She holds her phone up, and I nod in agreement. There he is. It makes my stomach hurt and my hands sweat to see him. I grab her phone and stare at him. Flipping to the next picture, my chest joins in the fun with a deep ache as I see him arm in arm with a gorgeous brunette, dressed to the nines for who-knows-what society function.

Quickly handing her phone back, I return to mine and

continue my perusal of his company's website. "No luck here. He's named as the Founder and CEO. Evidently, there is no unattractive Papa McAlistair to pin all the success and praise upon." Crestfallen, I set my phone down. "That was a bad idea. Can't say I feel much better."

Always the optimist, Erika looks on the bright side. "Why not, Charlotte? This has the potential to be fun! He wants you... big time. And from what you've told me and from what I see here"—she holds up her phone featuring his image— "that's a pretty major compliment. I hate to be shallow..." She tips her head and looks off into the distance, briefly questioning the sincerity of that statement before continuing. "But men that look like that, with money to burn and magic fingers, don't chase women. They don't have to. Ol' Ian McAlistair wants him some Charlotte LeFay. The question is, do you want him?" She matter-of-factly cuts to the chase.

Staring at my poor wrap that is probably going to end up in a to-go box, I sigh and answer, "Physically, I do. That's a given. My body has a mind of its own when he's around and it's game for anything, look what it allowed to happen yesterday! But he's nothing but trouble and I know it...all too well." The thought makes me sad, conjuring up memories I practice avoiding. "I have more sense than to set myself up for that kind of disaster. I've worked so hard to get where I am, and as you know, I've made it through some major hardships. It would be insulting to everything I stand for to let some arrogant jerk ruin my life. Guys that look like him, with that kind of money and experience, leave a trail of broken hearts everywhere they go. I refuse to be one of them." That last statement boosts my confidence as I sit a little straighter and lift my chin.

"You've got a pretty solid argument, girl. And I can't say I disagree, considering. But there is one thing you can take to the bank—Ian McAlistair is not going to give up easily. He wants more of what he had yesterday and he's not going to stop until he gets it. Men like him don't quit. They thrive on success, they thrive on control, and they relish the idea of a challenge." She reaches her hand over to cover mine. "You better put on a thick suit of armor, sister. You're going to need it."

SIX

IAN

"Good morning, Mr. McAlistair. I hope you had an enjoyable weekend. Your grandmother is on line one," Maria, one of my assistants, informs me as soon as I walk in the door Monday morning. Nana knows my schedule and my work habits. I'm always on time, 8 a.m. sharp, and I don't start booking calls or appointments until 10 a.m. She knows if she catches me first thing, the chances are good we can chat.

"Thank you, Maria. And yes, I did. I hope you did as well." I'm always polite and respectful to my assistants, but I never let it lean toward friendship. I keep it strictly professional. I made the mistake one time of being *somewhat* of a friend to an assistant, and she ended up falling in love with me. It was a disaster that I have no intention of ever repeating.

Sitting down, I pick up the phone, greeting my favorite person in the world. "Good morning, Nana. How has the world been treating you since our last chat?"

"Well enough. But you haven't called or stopped by, and you didn't answer my call yesterday. I thought maybe you were bound, gagged, and tied to a chair in some run-down warehouse nobody knows exists. I've been waiting for the ransom call for days." Hearing that ridiculous scenario told in her sweet voice is such a contradiction, it makes me laugh.

"Nana, have you been watching cable TV dramas again? You know that stuff never really happens, right?" She loves making up dramatic events based off the bullshit she sees on TV. She's addicted to crime mysteries and anything with raunchy sex scenes.

"If it wasn't that, I figured some husband found out you were tapping his wife, got jealous, and did you in." I can tell she's biting back a laugh. Nana loves trying to instigate trash-talk, and since she's made it to eighty-eight and is still going strong, I let her have her way.

"You know I don't *tap* married women. I have no interest in being done in by a jealous husband. Plus, there are plenty of single women to choose from."

"You're a smart man. Leopards don't change their spots. If she's cheatin' on him, she'll cheat on you. Dishonest women are dangerous, Ian. Always weed out the bad ones."

She's right about that.

"Not to worry, Nana. I can smell them from a mile away." Thankfully, I do have an uncanny ability to detect women that are lacking any moral standards. She can be physically beautiful, but if she's the shallow, back-stabbing, gold-digging type, she has an off-putting smell that I find totally unattractive. It's been easy to rely on that instinct, and it's never let me down.

"It's your old soul, dear. You've had enough past lives to ensure your instincts are sharp. You are fortunate to have it, so don't ever take it for granted," Nana tells me for the umpteenth time. She is very proud of our heritage and often insists that I am a reincarnated Scottish Highland Chief from somewhere way back in our history. She enjoys telling the stories, so once again, I let her have her way, redundant as it may be. "Never forget, our ancestry runs deep in Scotland, and the Scots have better instincts than *anyone*. We may be a superstitious lot, but it's for good reason. It's the Fey, Ian. That sixth sense has always been strong in you."

I've heard this story a hundred times as well, the legendary power of the Fey. In Scottish lore it's along the lines of clairvoyance. However, Fey, though spelled with an a, is also another word for faerie, and hearing it now conjures up that spectacular image of Charlotte and how fucking beautiful she is. Is it a coincidence that the first woman to fully occupy my typically preoccupied mind, who triggers unfamiliar instincts and awakens my inner caveman happens to have the surname LeFay? If I asked Nana, she'd be sure to say it was fate that brought her to me, then lecture me on the futile efforts of fighting it. Therefore, I will keep it to myself.

"Did I lose you there, Ian? I know you didn't hang up because I can hear you breathing. What's got you so distracted? Hopefully it's a woman. Tell me all about her... You know I like hearing about that more than tearing down buildings and putting up new ones." She's always trying to get me to tell her the private details of my relationships. Sometimes I give in and tell her the *very* vanilla version, only to be reprimanded by her, insisting she can get better from a daytime soap opera. She's relentless, and recently asked Jackson if Becca still gave good head because women tend to get over that after they've been married a while. Jackson almost fell out of his chair, and I laughed for days remembering the look on his face.

"You didn't lose me, and I'm not seeing anyone right now. But I was introduced to a very intriguing young lady this weekend, and if anything happens there, I'll be sure to fill you in." That seems appeasing enough, and it's basically the truth. Although it would probably make her entire year to hear the details of Charlotte coming undone in my arms, fully dressed, standing in a convenience store parking lot. Damn, that was absolute perfection. Imagining it heats my blood, making my cock begin to swell.

Nana's surprised tone snaps me out it. "What do you mean,

IF anything happens there? When the hell has anything NOT happened with a woman you're interested in?"

"Well, Nana, this time, I may have let my arrogance get in the way of a proper introduction and miscalculated how badly that would piss her off. She's a fiery one, and I'm going to have to change up my game a bit to cool her down." That's a bloody understatement, remembering the stinging slap she landed across my face.

Nana's voice perks up. "Ha! This is what I've been wanting to hear! You finally ran into a woman with a good head on her shoulders that can think for herself and doesn't melt just because you said 'Hi' to her. Hallelujah!"

Still, I laugh at Nana's enthusiasm. "Yes, well...she can definitely think for herself, and I'm glad that pleases you so profoundly. I will keep you posted on my pursuit. I'll get her eventually."

"Or perhaps she'll get you." Nana's ominous laugh gives me chills. "So glad I called you this morning. Goodbye, dear. I love you."

A few hours later, Jackson arrives to go over everything for Wednesday's meeting. Saturday went well, and he was able to get with his original contact, Tracy, at The Clara Sea to iron out all the details. I was pleased to hear the chef sat down with them, offering some creative suggestions for the menu with a fusion of our Miami cuisine and their Brazilian. Jackson is pleased with how everything has been handled—all the scheduling is in place, any minor details were taken care of, all recommendations were solid, and everyone has been accommodating and professional. The process has been seamless. Kudos to Charlotte. Since she's at the top of the food chain at The Clara Sea, it's a reflection of her leadership and standards. A little jolt of pride runs through me at the thought.

Regardless of my ulterior motive in moving the location of our meeting, I'm genuinely looking forward to sitting down with the lead partners from Novas Alturas. From the conversations we've had thus far, our rapport is spot on and they are completely onboard with our ideas. With McAlistair's experience and connections in the Miami area, they would be making a mistake by not partnering with us.

"That's all good news, Jackson. Thank you for handling it. I know it was a step down for you, and I'm sorry. I promise to make it up to you," I say as I finish jotting down the last of my notes.

"Don't worry about it, Ian. I know why you sent me. But so you know, I didn't see Charlotte when I went back." Jackson's tone is a little apologetic, and I'm momentarily speechless at his ability to read my mind. He offers a smile as if to acknowledge that, too.

"Yes...well, I appreciate you having my back, and when the opportunity does present itself, I look forward to hearing Charlotte's version of how you convinced her I am *not* the devil incarnate."

Laughing at the insinuation that Charlotte will engage in conversation and not slap me across the face again, Jackson replies, "You are smooth, Ian. I look forward to hearing how well I saved your ass. Now, onto more important things—did you talk to Jeremy down at zoning about our friends coming in from Brazil, and does he intend to clear the path for the project to get off the ground in less than a year?" He gets more annoyed than I do with the bullshit the city and county try to throw at us to create roadblocks. There is a lot that goes into developing a substantial building, be it residential or commercial, and many of the zoning requirements, permits, and other various hoops we need to jump through are necessary, but there is so much nonsense created to appease the jackasses that need to feel important by making the process more difficult.

"Yes, I had dinner with him last week. He said the zoning

board is quite enthusiastic about it. The city's been getting a lot of flack about that area being such an eyesore. They need this."

Jackson nods. "Good. That's what we need to hear." Shutting down his iPad, he finishes, "I'll head downstairs and make sure everything is lined up with the renderings and storyboard videos. They look good, man. Novas Alturas is going to be impressed."

If they aren't, it would be a first. Our rendering department is topnotch, and the three-dimensional replica of the finished project is outstanding. It's a twenty-story residential building featuring an exclusive retail area on the ground level. The building is wide, so we included a massive garden and pool area on the ground level, and lush sky gardens on the eighth floor, and the sixteenth floor, that will make the 175 luxury suites easy to sell. Each garden has a beach-entry pool with one attached hot tub and a second hot tub tucked into the garden for privacy. The state-of-the-art irrigation and planting bed design insure year-round lush vegetation.

"Yes, I saw everything earlier. It's spectacular. With all the land available to work with, this may be our best design yet. I'm tempted to buy the penthouse for myself."

"I have everything scheduled for setup tomorrow at The Clara Sea. I'll let you know when it's ready so you can come by and give your stamp of approval. Might I recommend arriving with a bouquet of flowers for Ms. LeFay? You know, as an olive branch, so she knows you're capable of being a gentleman and not always an overbearing prick." There's that annoying smirk again.

"An overbearing prick... Thanks, Jackson. I'll keep that in mind, although I cannot recall ever buying a bouquet of flowers for anyone. I'm not sure how I feel about it. Seems too cliché for me." I don't know why the idea of walking into The Clara Sea with a bouquet of flowers for Charlotte makes me feel like a fucking twat, but it does. There has to be something more original that makes a clear statement. I guess sending her an embroidered silk blindfold wouldn't go over too well. *Dammit!* Now I've got that delicious image in my head... Good thing I'm still sitting behind my desk. "Either way, I'll be there. Just let me know when."

Jackson finally leaves and I'm suddenly in a good mood, knowing tomorrow has presented me with an opportunity to see Charlotte again and maybe diffuse the flamethrower she's got aimed at me. If I can get her to stay still and converse with me, I'd feel like we had made some progress. Sitting back in my chair, hands steepled, I imagine her in front of me. Beautiful and relaxed, smiling at me as we discuss something mundane. That simple image brings on a sense of comfort and contentment that is so out of the ordinary it has me wondering if perhaps I *am* a twat.

On a heavy sigh, I get back to work. "I must be getting old."

SEVEN

CHARLOTTE

I'm grateful to be up in time to have coffee with the sunrise. It is especially beautiful this morning with extra pink and purple right before the full orange glow takes over the sky. It's simply breathtaking. I try to take pictures with my phone, but it never does it justice. If only I were an artist and could capture its beauty on canvas. I laugh to myself. I may have some talents, but painting isn't one of them.

I take a longer route to work so that I have time to pep myself up with some of my favorite music. It's my go-to therapy to set the vibe for the day. Today I needed a little extra bump in the right direction. Pulling into my parking spot, I sit for a few minutes while the song finishes. I'm thankful I wasn't greeted with any surprise visits from Ian yesterday, but something tells me he will be here today with Jackson to make sure everything is set up properly for their meeting tomorrow. The thought has me a little on edge. But after analyzing and rehashing everything with Erika over the weekend, I am more steady and more grounded since making the decision to *politely* deflect any more advances from the Ambassador of Carnality. Regardless of how much my body hates the decision, my mind knows who comes out the loser in the scenario he's expecting to come to fruition.

It was an easy decision, having watched my mother's beauty and light diminish to darkness after my father was killed in a car accident...*with* his mistress. It was the worst possible way to learn how destructive naivety can be. Therefore, I'm choosing the high road, where it's safe and uncomplicated, where my heart stays intact.

Tracy meets me in my office for our usual briefing. No major issues, just a guest that had to be moved to another room due to an annoying neighbor. Although our clientele tends to be more respectful of others and we don't typically have to deal with moving people around to find peace and quiet, we do occasionally get a group that acts like they are on spring break in Panama City. Unfortunately, I can't take Sibel's advice and throw them and their belongings out on the street. But I can make sure the staff is inattentive and mistakes are made that hopefully annoy them so much they don't ever return. Even if they leave a bad review, I don't care; it's outweighed by the number of five stars we get, and it usually makes them look bad, not us.

"So, are you excited to see Jackson again today?" Tracy blushes as I expected she would. I guess her meeting with him Saturday afternoon was almost too much to handle. As she put it, "He kept having to snap his fingers in my face to get me out of the trance his eyes put me under." Somehow, I don't think it was quite that bad, but she is definitely smitten.

"I guess. He's married with a son and a baby on the way. And it's not like he'd ever be interested in me, anyway. Guys that look like him don't typically go for girls that look like me."

I'm a little shocked at her declaration. "Tracy! Don't say that. First of all, you are a very good-looking woman, and secondly, don't just assume what a guy is attracted to based on your own insecurities. More often than not, it's the insecurity he finds unattractive." I give her a stern look, to which she pushes up her glasses and looks down at her iPad.

"I never really thought about it that way. I suppose you're right, though. I'll keep it in mind." I almost feel like she's saying it to appease me so I won't continue down this path. Out of respect, I leave it there.

"All right...it looks like you've got everything lined up for their setup today. They're scheduled to be here around eleven, correct?" I know what time they are scheduled, I just wanted a transition away from her self-deprecation.

"Yes, I am meeting Jackson in the lobby with a few extra staff members to help them unload and set up, should they need it." Perking up, she adds, "I'm really looking forward to seeing the rendering of their proposed project. From what he described, it sounds amazing." Tracy has a keen interest in design. She's my right (and sometimes left) hand when it comes to approving interior design features and other enhancements to the resort. She has excellent taste.

"That's great! I'm looking forward to it as well. I'll meet up with you later once they arrive." With that, I'm back to returning emails and phone calls, pleasantly distracted from a potential run-in with Ian at some point today.

As the morning wears on, I lose track of time. It's 11:30 when I finally glance at the clock. Instantly, butterflies are swarming around inside me. Ugh! I hate being nervous, and from the moisture that has formed on my hands, I'm definitely nervous.

Waiting a few more minutes while I deep-breathe and get my head in the game, I make my way toward the Garden Room. There, I am greeted with Jackson, several others from their office, and two of my employees. Jackson immediately walks over and offers sincerely, "Good morning, Ms. LeFay. It is a pleasure to see you again. I'd like to offer my highest compliments to you and your staff. Our experience here at The Clara Sea has been first-class."

Wow. Every time he says something about the resort, I just want to record it and play it on the radio. It's funny, I think he could say "The Clara Sea is mediocre, at best," and it would sound amazing in that voice.

A genuine smile spreads across my face. "There you go again,

Jackson. Popping out with radio ads and TV commercials with a simple 'Good morning.' I think you need an agent." We both laugh, then shake hands.

"I don't know about that. I've got enough on my plate as it is." Placing his hand on my shoulder, he asks, "Could I speak with you for a moment out in the hall?"

"Yes, of course." He's kind of serious now, and I wonder if I should be concerned.

Once we are in the hallway, I walk over to a sitting area overlooking the same garden as the conference room. There is an elaborate bird feeder beyond the windows that presents a fantastic show of the joyful flitting, swooping, and chirping that is the adorably charming display of various birds excitedly taking turns gathering seeds. I have several of these placed around the resort, and they are a huge hit. I've always loved the unencumbered beauty of nature and its creatures. Apparently, Jackson does, too. He's instantly drawn to the activity outside and smiles. "That's fantastic! I've never seen such a variety of birds in one place. You've really created something special here, Charlotte." I'm genuinely flattered by his compliments. Maybe because he is so sincere in offering them.

He continues with something I wasn't expecting but am relieved to hear, nonetheless. "I didn't get a chance to see you Saturday after Ian showed up. It's kind of weighed heavily on me since then, and I'd like you to know that whatever happened to cause your anger at seeing him again is between the two of you. I know nothing about it."

It's very kind of him to make it a point to set my mind at ease. I did picture Ian bragging to Jackson about our salacious encounter last Friday, but somehow I knew he didn't know. I don't know if it's just the vibe I got or what, but Jackson put me at ease from the first time we met.

"Thank you, Jackson. I appreciate you telling me that. It's a relief to know that you weren't a full accomplice to him sneaking up on me Saturday. I definitely didn't see that one coming." I laugh a little to ease any tension.

"Honestly, I can't say I wasn't an accomplice. He knows who you are and where you work because of me. But I didn't think you wouldn't want to see him when he did show up. It would be an understatement to say I was shocked at your reaction." He seems disappointed in himself for his part in Ian's games. I can't help but respect his honesty.

I laugh at the thought of it. "I bet you were. I was pretty shocked myself when he walked through that door. But that's over and done with, and hopefully we can move on. I said what I needed to say to Ian on Saturday. From here on out, I can be cordial and professional." I put my head down and play with the pen I'd forgotten was in my hand. Part of me would rather avoid him altogether than have to pretend he doesn't stir something inside me.

"For what it's worth, Ian is actually a good guy. Like I said, I don't know what he did to upset you, but clearly it wasn't good. I just don't want you to think he walks through life being a total jerk. He's been like a brother to me since elementary school." He smiles. "It was always known as the rich kids' school and I definitely wasn't zoned for it, but my father made sure I got transferred there, anyway. My neighborhood wasn't necessarily bad, but the school I was zoned for was, and he wasn't having any part of that kind of influence on me. Ian and I hit it off right away. He never thought twice about the color of my skin or my parents' bank account. He's generous and works harder than anyone I know for his success." He laughs, shaking his head. "Hell...his favorite person in the world is his grandmother! He can't be all that bad." I notice his smile spreads wider as his deep laugh fills the space around us, and I wonder if it has more to do with Ian's grandmother than Ian himself.

"That's a pretty good sales pitch, Jackson. Did Ian pay you for that?" We're both laughing now. "Listen, I've had a few days to cool down, and I'm feeling less like I want to strangle him.

However, that's not to say I'm interested in anything more, and I don't want him to expect it. Something tells me that Ian McAlistair gets what he wants when it comes to women. I'm just not one of them."

"No, you're not, and that's a good thing. But, should there ever come a time when you have the slightest inclination to wipe the slate clean and start over with him, do it. You might be pleasantly surprised." He's so sincere, and I don't know whether it's that or the idea of starting over with Ian that pulls at my heartstrings. Either way, it's more evidence that I should steer clear.

Standing up from our seats, I lean in and give him a hug. It felt like the right thing to do. "I'll think about it, Jackson. Thank you. You're a good man."

As soon as we end the embrace and are about to part ways, my spine tingles and my heart races at the sound of footsteps coming down the hall. Footsteps that I know belong to Ian. It's happening again. Somehow, my ears recognize, as if by instinct or some inexplicable memory, the sound of each step he takes. The worst part is, my body knows it too. Its chemistry has already shifted, quite noticeably. *Dear God, how am I going to do this?!*

I can't bring myself to turn around, even though I see Jackson smiling at him. A few seconds later, I hear Ian's voice deliver a curt, "Jackson," as his greeting. Now I have no choice but to turn and face him, pretending I'm totally unfazed by his presence.

Ooohhh...by all that is holy, why does he have to look like that? I plaster a pleasant smile on my face and hold out my hand to shake his as if he were an everyday client and not the man that made me orgasm in a parking lot five days ago, before I even knew his name. "Mr. McAlistair, welcome back to The Clara Sea. I think we are all set for your meeting tomorrow." I thought that sounded pretty good. But from the look on Ian's face, he did not.

Looking directly at *me* with a fierce expression, he says, "Jackson, could you please excuse us?" As I hear Jackson walk away, my anxiety level increases. I really don't want to be alone with him again. He does weird shit to my brain and I can't think straight. And he smells so freaking good I could cry. *Dammit!*

"It's Ian," he says, sounding slightly annoyed. "I'd like it very much if you would call me Ian and *not* Mr. McAlistair." He seems wound up like a tight rubber band today.

"Okay...Ian. I assume you're here to check on things before your meeting tomorrow. I think you will be pleased." Although, looking at him, I'm not so sure about that. The heated expression on his face is starting to make me sweat. I really wish one of my employees would walk up right now and say I'm needed elsewhere.

"No, I actually came to see you. I'm not concerned about the meeting tomorrow. It will go well."

Wow. Why the hell was that so damn sexy? Before I have a chance to respond, he continues. "It was recommended to me by a friend that I arrive here with a bouquet of flowers for you, as a peace offering, so that you know I am capable of being a gentleman and that I'm not always an overbearing prick. His words, not mine." He's smiling now. It's really quite charming, even though I know he's the devil in disguise.

He must be referring to Jackson, and on a laugh I say, "Well, looks like you didn't take his advice. I don't see any flowers."

Still smiling, he shakes his head, "No. You don't. For whatever reason, it didn't feel right. Perhaps it's because I don't do cliché very well." Yeah, I can't really picture that, either. "But I wasn't opposed to some sort of peace offering, considering how poorly my apology went on Saturday." His smirk is sinful as hell, and my body suddenly thinks he is going to offer me something along the lines of what he did last Friday and it's very excited about it. *Good grief!* If his nostrils flare, I'm walking away. I will *not* be able to deal with that again.

Reaching inside the leather-bound folder I didn't notice he was holding, he pulls out a piece of paper, but it's heavier, like cardstock or something. He's definitely piqued my curiosity because I have no idea what that could be. He holds it a bit longer, staring at whatever is facing him. He's hesitant and suddenly seems a little shy, which is completely throwing me off.

Looking up, he says, "Did you know the word *Fay* means faerie?" Of all the things I thought he might say, that was *not* one of them, not even close.

I stare at him for a minute, brows drawn together in confusion, and respond, "I may have heard that somewhere along the way. Why?"

"In Scotland, the word *Fay* has several meanings, but faerie is the most common. When Jackson first told me your name, Charlotte LeFay, I thought to myself...how perfect, how befitting. Charlotte the Faerie. I had this enchanting image of you in my head." He looks back at the paper he is holding, one finger following a line that is invisible to my eye. "Your gorgeous hair flowing in the wind; that beautiful face smiling mischievously, taunting me, tempting me; and a magnificent pair of wings protruding proudly from your naked body, so lithe and curved and deliciously feminine."

My heart is pounding in my chest, I am so caught off guard. The way he is describing me *as a faerie* has to be one of the most sensual things I've ever heard in my life. I'm literally speechless and heating up everywhere. It doesn't matter. Nothing matters, because once again, he's not done. The last time he ruined me with his arrogance, making me want to hate him for all eternity. Now he's going to ruin me with something so indescribable, my heart may never be the same.

He hands me the paper. A gasp escapes as I see what he was looking at. It is a pencil drawing, of me, *as a faerie*, and it is the most beautiful thing I have ever seen. I cannot stop the tears that well up in my eyes, it is that amazing. My fingers touch my lips to hold in the sound. There I am, from behind, walking down a path. I am naked, my hair flowing as if it's floating in a breeze. My wings are truly magnificent in their size and beauty; I cannot believe how perfect they are. My upper body is turned slightly to the left so that my face is in profile, a faint smile on my mouth. I am holding a single flower up to my nose as if to smell its sweet scent, the barest tip of my breast exposed just beyond my arm. The style, the technique and precision of this drawing are so beautiful I can't stop staring at it. But it's the one bit of color that is most poignant. The touch of pink that only brightens the flower I am holding.

For what seems like forever, I keep staring at this work of art he's given me, completely at a loss for words. Finally looking up, I whisper, "Did you draw this?"

His eyes are dark and glassy, lips held tightly together, he's tense with his hands held behind his back. His response is almost curt, "Yes. I did."

I don't even know what to say. This man that I wanted to hate or pretend didn't exist has just handed me something I can't even find words to describe—that *he* created—as a peace offering after he annihilated my pride and humility only five short days ago. Is the universe out to get me? Am I supposed to be left speechless and in pieces by this man at every turn? For good and for bad?

Running my fingers across the flowing lines, as he did before I knew what he was tracing, I smile. I love this rendering so much, I suddenly wish this were really me. Walking through nature, such graceful posture, shoulders so poised, so relaxed in my nudity, so feminine and sensual. This woman is powerful in a way that is raw and ethereal and maybe even a little dangerous. The expression on her face says she is pleased to have received the pink flower, but there is something else there she's not giving away, something mysterious.

The more I look at it, the more it reaches in and attaches itself to a place deep inside me, making my chest ache and my stomach feel like I'm falling off a ledge. Ian drew this...of me, for me, and there is so much meaning to be found here I'm suddenly overwhelmed.

In the faintest voice, not quite a whisper, I finally speak,

"Ian...I don't know what to say. It's so beautiful...so...I'm...at a loss." I huff out a breath I'd been holding, trying to breathe normally once again. What is the right thing to do and say in this moment? This man standing in front of me is more dangerous to my sanity and emotional wellbeing than I ever imagined. Prior to this, it was easy to see him for what he was—an arrogant jerk that has his way with women whenever and *wherever* he chooses. Now, he's showing me a side that is utterly enthralling in its uncommon depth and charm. The man he's exposing to me now is the kind a woman falls deeply in love with and is never the same again. I am more terrified of this Ian than the cocky bastard that was easy to despise.

His tone is calm if not somewhat hesitant when he asks, "So you like it, then?"

I can't help but laugh on another breath as it escapes my tight chest. "I don't think the word *like* comes even remotely close to how I feel about it. Ian, it's stunning... It's breathtaking!" I shake my head because those words don't justify it, either. "Do you draw a lot? I mean, do you sell your work? Surely this isn't just a hobby that no one ever gets to see but you?" He must be featured in galleries around Miami, at least. His talent is so far beyond novice it's ridiculous.

"No. I rarely draw. I don't have time." His matter-of-fact answer surprises me.

Holding the paper up, I question, "This is unpracticed? Ian, you must know how gifted you are. It's one thing to draw something well, but this is so far beyond that, it's like she's alive...like I can sense her energy." Looking up, I can see in his turquoise eyes that he is pleased I am impressed. My first instinct is to reach up and give him a hug, because I love this gift so much. But I know better than to tempt that kind of contact with him. "What made you decide to do this?" It seems so out of character from what I know of him it's almost shocking.

"I guess you could say I have a vivid imagination." A seductive smile forms on his lips. *Damn.* "I told you what I envisioned when I found out your name. The image was so magnificent, I was inspired. I wanted to see more of her, to play with her, like she called me to do. When I put what I saw on paper, I was mesmerized...enchanted." He pauses for a minute while his eyes roam around the features of my face. "Then I decided to give her a flower so she would be pleased with me." His voice got deeper, and another wave of heat came over my body. He's going to melt me again, right here in the hallway, this time with his words.

"But all she did over the past several days was taunt me and torment me. So I decided to give her to you, hoping maybe you would understand why I haven't been able to think straight or get you out of my head since you cut me off on the highway last Friday." He reaches up, placing his hand softly under my chin, slowly tracing the line of my lips with his thumb, his deep, almost menacing voice penetrating my soul. "You've cast a spell on me, Charlotte LeFay. Now, you have to deal with the consequences."

I'm going to pass out. I know I am... The blood is draining from my head and my vision is closing in. In an effort to prevent that embarrassing disaster, I quickly turn and sit in the closest chair, putting my head down as low as possible without fully putting it between my knees. I start to feel the blood leveling out and refilling my brain that has been overloaded by all five of my senses and maybe more that I am unaware of. Within seconds, I can *sort of* think again, and I realize he must know that I was getting ready to faint and I am mortified. He's suddenly there, kneeling down in front of me, one hand on my knee, the other cradling my face.

"Charlotte, are you all right? I thought maybe you were going to pass out. I think you should lie down. Please, let me carry you to a sofa nearby." He sounds panicked yet demanding at the same time. He doesn't know there is no way in hell I'm letting him pick me up and *carry me* anywhere. Right now, I wish I were that stunning faerie he drew, because she has wings and could fly away. That's all I want to do right now, disappear to some place safe and quiet where Ian's voice and touch and words and beautiful drawings of me are not causing an emotional traffic jam in my head, an ache in my heart, and major blood pressure issues. I need to be away from him, just long enough to regain my composure...and perhaps my sensibility.

"Ian...I'm fine. Could you please ask Jackson to come here?" He starts to speak, but I cut him off. "Ian, please. Just go get Jackson."

He hesitates, but gets up to do my bidding. A few minutes later, Jackson is there, kneeling down next to the chair where I am now sitting normally, the drawing face down in my lap.

"Charlotte, are you okay? What happened?"

"I'm fine, Jackson. But I need to speak with you privately for a minute." I can't bring myself to look at Ian. He's too much for me right now, and I know he can't be happy with me asking his best friend to help me. But, in this moment, I don't have a choice. For whatever reason, Jackson puts me at ease. He has since we first met, and after the conversation we had—before the Rembrandt of Sensual Faerie Portraits came along and took all my senses and emotions on a roller-coaster ride through space and time—I know in my gut I can trust him.

Jackson stands and turns to Ian. No words were exchanged, and thankfully, Ian walked away, heading toward the conference room. That godforsaken cadence ricocheting around my eardrums and making my stomach hurt. Once he was out of earshot, Jackson is seriously concerned, yet confused when he asks, "Charlotte, did he do something to you? He didn't hurt you, did he?"

A laugh escapes. "No...no, not physically, anyway. But I'm overwhelmed and terribly embarrassed and needed to be away from him. Could you please escort me to my office? I will explain once we have some privacy." I can tell my voice is strained; it's like Ian sucks the energy from my body, leaving me deflated.

Jackson walks me to my office, which is not far, and closes the door. Sitting at my desk with the bright sunlight shining through the windows, I take a deep breath and meet Jackson's concerned eyes. Smiling at him, I apologize. "I'm sorry if I upset you. I don't know what came over me... Well, actually, I do know. I'm kind of surprised and completely mortified that it happened." That's the understatement of the year. Erika is going to flip the hell out when she hears this.

"You don't have to apologize to me, Charlotte. I know Ian better than anyone. He's intense and driven, and sometimes his drive can push others over the edge." The low resonance of his voice and his paternal understanding are having a much-needed calming effect on me.

"Yes, and...did you also know that on top of his many other talents and otherworldly abilities, he's a gifted artist that should be famous for his unique skills?" There is a little sarcasm in my tone, regardless of the truth inside my question. Ian's drawing is now sitting in front of me on my desk, taunting me in a different way than it taunted him. I look up at Jackson and see him staring at the drawing with a surprised look on his handsome face.

He points to it, then asks, "Ian drew that for you? May I see it?"

I hand it to him, trying to read his reaction as he studies it. He slowly shakes his head, then smiles as he says, "This is good, Charlotte. I haven't seen Ian draw anything since high school, I think. And, yes, he is gifted and should have done something with it, but his father wanted him to be a businessman. He didn't think being an artist *suited* the family name. Sometimes I wonder if Ian's intensity comes from not being able to express himself through his art, like he truly wants to. His involvement with the architecture and design departments at McAlistair is certainly an outlet for him, but it's not enough, and whenever I tell him he should draw or paint, he shuts me down."

Wow, that's kind of sad. I can't imagine telling my child not to pursue a gift like Ian's.

"That is truly a shame. It explains why he seemed a bit shy when he gave it to me." With a smirk I tell him, "He told me that a 'friend' recommended he show up here today with a bouquet of flowers for me." I give him a knowing look. "Of course, Ian McAlistair couldn't do something as traditional as a bouquet of flowers. No, he has to melt my heart and rewire my brain with a portrait of me, as a faerie of all things, holding a flower he 'gave' me, that is so beautiful and meaningful, I almost fainted! Ugh...I literally almost *swooned* like some innocent little debutant." I drop my forehead to my palm in exaggerated shame.

Jackson laughs at my exacerbated rant. "I am sorry you almost *swooned*, but I will say I am relieved it was that and not something else that had you out of sorts. I didn't know what to think when Ian came in to get me. From the look on his face, I can tell you for a fact he wasn't happy about it." He's smiling ear to ear now. "It appears you may have gotten into his head. Ian doesn't act like this and now"—he holds up the drawing—"you've inspired him to start drawing again! He may have finally found his muse."

Smiling, regardless of my unease, I say, "I can see why that makes you happy, I really can. And believe it or not, I'm very flattered. But I've made up my mind about Ian. I am not getting involved with him...I can't. I know how the story ends. I have to protect myself from that." I can hear the desperation in that last sentence.

Jackson is still concerned, but I can tell he is also confused. "Forgive me if I am overstepping my bounds, but how does the story end?"

Exhaling heavily, my shoulders drop and I respond. "Tragically. That's how it ends."

"Oh?" he asks, somewhat surprised. "That certainly wasn't what I was expecting you to say. I can understand why Ian would overwhelm you and you've clearly got a reason not to trust him...but a tragedy?"

Letting out an insecure laugh as I exhale the pressure this

topic creates inside me, I shake my head and try to explain. "Listen, I'm not looking for pity when I tell you this, I just need you to know what I'm dealing with personally so you can know why Ian is not for me." Another deep breath. "You see...my father was a lot like him, very handsome, suave, charming and successful, every woman's ideal man. He and my mother had what I thought was a happy and loving marriage. They were wonderful parents and seemed to be each other's best friend. They held hands and kissed and laughed. It was...perfect. And my mother, she was beautiful and sweet and so kind." A lump forms in my throat as I recall my mother. I miss her so much. "But then, when I was seventeen, our world was shattered when my father was killed in a car accident in Utah." I stop for a minute, remembering the day that phone call came. I hate that day and the pain that came with it.

"Charlotte. I...I'm so sorry. I didn't mean to stir this up for you," Jackson says with heartwarming sincerity.

"Thank you, Jackson. It's okay. Sadly, the story only gets worse. You see...my father wasn't alone." Jackson raises a brow at that twist in the story but doesn't say anything. "There was another woman with him, obviously his girlfriend. She didn't survive the crash, either." My head is starting to hurt as I relive the most screwed-up thing I've ever had to deal with in my life. Losing my father that I loved so dearly and finding out a truth that tore apart everything I had ever believed him to be, all at the same time. It was unbearable, and I'm still not sure I've ever come to terms with it.

"Good Lord. I can't even imagine what that must have been like. I'm so sorry. Please...you don't have to go on. I'm sorry, Charlotte."

I get up and walk over to the window so I don't have to see that look on Jackson's face anymore, because it's about to make me bawl my eyes out, and finish the tragic tale that was my family. "As you probably can imagine, my mother was devastated in a way that words cannot describe. She never recovered. Two years later she finally succumbed to the addiction that she latched onto trying to dull the pain." I stay facing the window so I don't have to see the sympathy in his eyes. It will make me break and I've worked hard to *not* break anymore. Thankfully, he gives me the time that I need to regain my composure. When I turn back to him, I can't help but apologize for unloading so much on him. "I'm sorry, Jackson. That was a lot to take in."

Jackson stands and walks over to me. "Charlotte, stop. Do not apologize to me. You don't need to. I am honored to know that you trusted me enough to tell me what happened to your parents. I know that wasn't easy. But I'm glad you did. I understand now why Ian overwhelms you the way he does. It makes sense. Yet, I can't help but offer you some advice." His voice sounds so fatherly right now, the lump in my throat is starting to swell again.

"Uh-oh! Am I in trouble?" I ask with humor, trying once again to divert myself from crying.

His laugh echoes around the room. "No...no. You're not in trouble. However, you may not want to hear what I've got to say." He raises one brow and tips his head. "Ian isn't your father. Furthermore, it isn't wise to go through life making other people pay for someone else's mistakes. Not only is it unfair to them, but it is especially unfair to you." His features soften as he finishes, "You may think you are protecting yourself from a similar fate, but in reality, you are creating unnecessary obstacles that get in the way of living your life to its fullest potential. Your parents wouldn't want you to do that, Charlotte."

Smiling up at him as I wipe away the one tear I let escape, I tell him, "I think I might ask Ian if I can borrow you as my best friend for a while. Do you think he'd be okay with that?" We both laugh at my silliness. "Keep it a secret. My *other* best friend, Erika, would be devastated to hear me say that!"

"You don't need to borrow my friendship. It is yours from now on, no questions asked." He reaches over to give me a much-needed hug. "You are a very special young lady, Charlotte LeFay. I can see why Ian is so drawn to you." He lets go and pauses, those green eyes so caring and wise. "You may not want to hear this, either, and I completely understand, but believe me when I tell you...you and Ian McAlistair were made for each other."

EIGHT

IAN

Driving up I-95 at 110mph is a bad idea. And I don't give a fuck. I have to burn off this energy, this...anger, this...I don't fucking know what! "Dammit!" I hit the steering wheel on another outburst.

I wish someone could explain to me what the hell just happened back there. Even though Charlotte initially tried to act like I was some random person with that goddamn *Mr. McAlistair* bullshit, she seemed to be coming around after I gave her my peace offering. One I know she wasn't expecting and one that sure as hell had more meaning than a fucking bouquet of flowers.

I should have known it was going to blow up in my face as soon as I walked up and saw her gorgeous body tucked into that dress that was made for her, the curve of her ass so enticing, it made my hands clench. Or maybe it was because she was hugging my asshole best friend that she apparently has a crush on.

"Fuck!"

Seeing her in another man's arms, even a man I know and trust with my life, tightens my body from the inside out, making me want to destroy something. *That* may have been a better option than flying up the highway where I'm likely going to get arrested or killed.

Letting a trace of what's left of my sanity rectify the fried circuits of my brain, I take the next exit, only to realize I'm already past Fort Lauderdale, even though I swear I just got on the damn highway.

I'm fucking losing it! Driving like a maniac, wanting to destroy anything that gets in my way, I'm ready to beat the shit out of Jackson for the first time in thirty goddamn years. She *did* cast a spell on me, an evil one! She's a bloody witch, not a goddamn faerie.

That frustrating thought brings an image of Charlotte's portrait and the beautiful look on her face when I gave it to her. I didn't really want to part with it. I'd become somewhat attached to that image. But something in my gut told me I needed to give it to her, that she would know I wasn't the asshole she felt compelled to slap in the face last Saturday. That I thought of her as more than some roadside hookup I could command at will. It seemed like a good decision. She was obviously happy about it, emotional even. When her eyes welled up with tears, my first instinct was to take her in my arms and cover her mouth with mine, feel her relax, submit...just like she did the first time we met. Then she would know that her pleasure is my utmost priority... That in my arms, she is safe to let go, to give in to her carnal instincts, and know the true meaning of ecstasy. "Jesus Christ, I want her so badly!" I exclaim, hitting the steering wheel for the tenth time.

Regardless of how much she appreciated the gift, she shut me out, anyway. Completely. I don't know what happened, but I swear she was about to pass out. It scared the hell out of me and all I wanted to do was protect her, take her somewhere safe where I knew she would be okay. Instead, she wouldn't even look at me, wouldn't let me touch her...asked for Jackson to come in and save her...from me.

"Does she fucking hate me?" I yell again, confused by every

move she makes. I should never have let her goad me last Friday. I should have kept driving and never put the damn car in reverse. She weakened my resolve and I snapped, evidently making such a monumental fuck-up, I may never have a chance to make it up to her. I cannot let that happen.

If I could only get her to let down the walls she's built—to keep me the hell out—I could make up for the mistakes I've made, or anybody else has made, for that matter. I could take away any of life's pain and disappointment, and she could just… be. Unencumbered by obligations, expectations, or insecurities and bring forth her true self, her true power. Exactly how I imagined and put down on paper. Charlotte—raw, pure, and naturally magnificent.

A horn blasts from the car behind me, snapping me out of my daydream. God, this sucks. I can't fucking stand what's happening to me. She has me on edge, out of control, and it's so unfamiliar to me I'm at a loss as to what to do. I am *never* at a loss…ever.

Continuing through the intersection, I'm on A1A not far from the office, but far enough to give me time to cool down and get my head screwed back on straight. Maybe by the time I get there, Jackson will have finished his *private* meeting with Charlotte and he can tell me what the fuck is going on.

Finally back at my desk, I'm faced with a mountain of work that needs to be completed today. Apparently, I'll be working late, since I spent half the day with my head up my ass. I start prioritizing, creating a pile that I can delegate to my assistants, when Jackson knocks before entering. A familiar tension forms in my gut as I picture Charlotte in his arms. Even knowing he would never cheat on Becca and he would never screw me over, the agitation is still there.

He grabs a water then sits across from me, pretending to be at ease. I see through it; I can tell something is definitely bothering him. Either way, I have zero patience for beating around the bush. I need to know what the hell is going on, now. "Spit it out,

Jackson. I don't know how to read this bullshit, and I sure as fuck have no interest in playing games. Why did she need *you* to get rid of *me* so she could talk *privately* when, as far as I know, she barely fucking knows you?" Not wanting to speculate further, I let him answer.

"Yeah, I wasn't really sure about that myself when you came and got me. I know how much that had to bother you, and I'm sorry." He's sincere, but that was weak.

I can't even bring myself to laugh. I just look him dead in the eye and sternly respond with, "*Bothered* isn't even in the same universe as what I felt." I raise an eyebrow and tip my head communicating a clear, *don't fucking downplay this*.

"Yeah...I get it, man. I really do." Shaking his head, he rubs the back of his neck. "This is not going to be easy. You really stepped outside the box when you decided to pursue Charlotte. You're going to have to work at it, no doubt, but when that work finally pays off, I guarantee it will be worth it." He seems pretty satisfied with that encrypted code bullshit. I'm not.

"Jackson? What the hell is that supposed to mean? How am I supposed to interpret that vague nonsense? Tell me what the hell is going on, dammit!" It's a good thing I went for that drive to cool down. As pissed off as I am right now, I would have exploded an hour and a half ago if he fed me that simple bullshit.

He stands up and paces around my office, raising his voice when he says, "Cut me some slack here, Ian! I'm stuck between a rock and a goddamn hard place. I've got you on one side, and you know I've got your back, then I've got her on the other, and for whatever reason, she trusts me, so I can't betray that trust. It kinda sucks, man. I'm never involved in your life like this!"

"She trusts you because she's got good instincts. Which is one other thing I can pile onto the stack of reasons I find her so damn attractive." Sitting back in my chair, I rub my hands over my face. "Can you just give me enough information so I can at least work on a strategy that has a better chance at success than what

THE ESSENCE OF FATE

I've done so far? I can't do this fucking guessing game, and I'm about to kidnap her and take her to my place in the Bahamas where she doesn't have a goddamn choice but to be with me twenty-four seven." An idea that seriously has a tremendous amount of appeal.

Jackson laughs at my sarcasm, probably concerned I might actually do it. Coming back to my desk, he sits down and says, "Listen, Ian. She's a really smart, driven, and successful woman, as I'm sure you know. She's a good person, I know that for sure. But she's had to deal with some things that would cause any normal person to put up walls as protection. Charlotte has built a fortress, and it won't be easy to get through. If you think she's worth it, be prepared to put in the time and effort it's gonna take to prove to her you're worth it. You'll need to be patient with her, man."

At least that was something I can chew on; however, I'm concerned about this event that has caused her to be so insecure. I can't help but ask, "Has she been abused somehow?" The idea of someone physically hurting her makes me sick. If that's the case, when I find out who it is, it will be easy to make them pay.

"No, it's nothing like that, thankfully." The look in his eyes validates his next request— "Please don't try to get me to tell you, Ian. You know I would if I could, but it's not my place." He hates being in this position, and I have no choice but to respect him.

"All right, man. I won't, and I respect where you're coming from. Can you at least answer a few other questions that don't pertain to that? Like...is she attracted to me?" I feel like a fucking girl even asking that question. There has never been a time that females were not attracted to me, and considering Charlotte's reaction to my touch, I would be shocked to find out she is not.

"That's a first! You having to ask, I mean." Jackson laughs at my question—I guess that's a good sign. "I think you can rest easy on that front. Her finding you attractive is honestly part of the problem."

Ah, another clue. I'll tuck that piece away for later. "Did she like the drawing I did of her?" I nervously rub my hands together under my desk. Fucking twat that I am.

"She loved the drawing, very much. I think it was an excellent choice, since you opted not to go the traditional route. Very well done, Ian. Personally, I was happy to see you'd picked up your pencils again. I think you should continue. It's an outlet you've neglected to use for far too long. It's wasted talent, my friend."

Here he goes again. Guess I set myself up for that one.

"Yeah, we'll see." Brushing past that so he doesn't start badgering me, I continue. "I want to know what she said about it." The insecure artist in me comes out, but I don't care. I need to hear what she thought, what it meant to her.

He gives a knowing look at my deflection, but answers anyway, "Let's see, I think it was something like, 'On top of his many other talents and otherworldly abilities, he's a gifted artist that should be world famous for his unique skills.'"

God, that makes me happy, for several reasons. Now I want to draw more for her. Just to see her reaction, to make her see she doesn't need to be afraid of me, and perhaps to make her smile.

Jackson chimes in, "From the look on your face, it appears you've finally found your muse." I can tell he's pleased. He's been at me for years about getting back into my art. And here I am, ready to fill a gallery with images of Charlotte. What an unbelievable turn-on. Christ, this woman has taken over every part of me!

"My muse. Is that another word for obsession? Because I'm starting to think I'm fucking obsessed with her." Getting up from my desk, I walk over to the window, staring out over the city. I think about how to word the thoughts shuffling through my head without sounding like some love-struck teenage girl. "She's been in my head since last Friday. Shifting back and forth through different scenarios. Of course, a lot of them are mind-numbing visuals of what I plan to do to her sexually, but a lot of them aren't. A lot of them are your everyday, mundane shit like enjoying dinner together, hanging out on the boat, maybe fishing or diving, chilling on the balcony watching the sunrise." I look at Jackson, whose expression is like...*yeah, and?* "I'm sure that would sound totally normal to most people. But, it's not for me. No one has piqued my interests beyond something physical, *ever.*" Holding up my hand as if to stop Jackson from commenting even though he's just attentively listening to me babble, I say, "I know it's shallow, and I used to feel guilty about it. But eventually I came to terms with my reality. That's just how it was. I didn't choose for it to be that way, and it didn't seem right to try to force something to be there that naturally was not."

I walk back to my desk, take a swig of water, then chuckle, "I think it may have been easier that way. I can't say I'm particularly fond of the turn my life has taken in the last five days. I have only been in Charlotte's presence three times, none of which consisted of us being naked and sated. Although, the day I *unofficially* met her, I got a small taste of what that would be like."

I stand up straight. That's it! "Maybe that's my problem! It's unfinished business. Maybe I need to finish what I started, bring it to its natural conclusion, and I'll be good. No more obsession, no more distraction, no more of this gnawing need to have her." I'm kind of excited about this epiphany.

Jackson clearly is not. "Ian. Shut the hell up. That is the stupidest, most narcissistic bullshit I've ever heard come out of your mouth. And now that I personally know who you are talking about and consider her my friend, I suggest you watch what you say. I'm on your team because I'd actually like to see things work out between the two of you. But if you're going to take the low road and only be concerned with yourself, I'll make sure she wants nothing to do with you."

He's pissed and rightfully so. Charlotte didn't deserve that, and it's more proof that I am functioning outside my comfort zone.

I drop into my chair in defeat. "You're right. I'm acting like a little bitch. Feel free to kick my ass anytime. It sounded good in the moment, but it would never work out that way. Something tells me when I finally scale the walls of her fortress, it will be hard to find my way out...if I ever do."

Jackson stands up, looking me square in the eye. "Ian, my friend, the thing you need to understand is that when you finally get there, you won't ever *want* to leave."

It was a late night in the office making up for lost time. Now I'm home and it's a relief to be here, in quiet solitude. Just me, a scotch, and the moon sparkling over the ocean. Here, I am less edgy about my failures where Charlotte is concerned. It still bothers me, but right now I'm free to contemplate how I should go about overcoming the obstacles she keeps throwing in my path. Every time we are face to face, the situation deteriorates so quickly I lose my footing. Literally every time I am around her nothing goes the way it is supposed to and I am left feeling like someone put me in a fucking straightjacket, which inevitably pushes me to the point of throwing caution to the wind and just taking what I want...her.

Thankfully, my self-control is honed enough to prevent me from making that mistake, where I would be destined to the graveyard of overbearing, maniacal dickheads. I'm already standing at the bloody gate, I don't need to push it.

In the calm energy of my sanctuary, I can replay everything—from my interactions with Charlotte to the fatherly advice and reprimanding I've received from Jackson. Here, it is easy to see that my judgment was clouded by my overblown ego that has been molded and diligently refined by the women in my past.

Each of them spoon-feeding it with everything I asked for and expected of them, never questioning me, never denying me, never challenging me. At thirty-six, I have zero experience dealing with a woman that stirs a desire so deep within me that when I am near her, when I see her and smell her and sense her energy coursing through her body, the need to touch her is almost painful. Yet, she won't let me, and I'm forced into even more unfamiliar territory.

Whatever happened in her past was profound and upsetting enough she is determined to shut me out. She's attracted to me, though. She's affected by me, deeply, I suspect. But it doesn't matter; her need to protect herself is stronger.

Clearly, my selfish expectation to have her fall at my feet simply because I willed it to be so was the egotistical blunder of the decade. An even bigger blunder was putting my car in reverse after she challenged me, blowing me that damn kiss... Once again, the memory makes my spine tingle. But it may have been the smile afterward that did me in. God, she was so beautiful in that moment. If only I had maintained control and continued on, sticking to my original plan, I might have had a better chance. Instead, my ego took over and, in the process, handed her an army of reinforcements to stand guard outside the fortress she had already constructed. Fucking brilliant.

Now that I have some insight to go on, I need to rethink my strategy, backing it up with patience and precision. Slowly picking off each soldier, one by one, like a sniper hidden in the forest. When the last one falls, I will scale the walls surrounding her, then destroy every one of them from the inside out.

NINE
CHARLOTTE

I'm finally alone, curled up on my sofa in my favorite pajamas, a blanket over my legs and feet. I'm so drained after what happened with Ian today, I feel like I've been drugged. It was a struggle to even get through the rest of my day, but I had too much to do and ended up staying past five.

It didn't help that I can't seem to part with the portrait he drew for me. I find myself staring at it, like I'm doing now, while the rest of the world no longer exists. It draws me in, holding me there, ensnared by its beauty and potential meaning. Did he know it was going to have this effect on me? After all, he was masterfully aware of the effect he would have on me when he kissed me mindless then sent me over the edge with an unexpected nipple pinch. Was this portrait his second play at completely fucking with my head, making me aware that I am really *not* in control of myself... he is?

I'm probably overthinking it, and I really don't want to put any negative thoughts or energy toward my portrait. I love it too much. I feel happy when I look at her, and I wonder—is this really how Ian sees me, how he imagines me in his mind's eye? If so, no wonder he thinks I've cast a spell on him.

Dear God, when he told me that I almost died! The look in

his eyes, his touch on my lips, his voice all deep and sleepy sounding, his expensive woodsy scent swirling around me, putting me in a trance. I could hardly grasp what he was saying. All I knew was that 'dealing with the consequences' sounded so erotic coming out of his mouth, I nearly fainted. Laying my head back on the cushion, I stare at the ceiling, wondering how I will ever get past my embarrassment.

My phone rings, and I almost jump out of my skin, even though I was expecting the call. It's Erika downstairs with takeout. "Hey! I'll buzz you in."

A few minutes later, she's walking in with food that smells delicious. "Ohhh…this is what I need, stress food!" Leaning in for a hug, she squeezes out the rest of my words. "You're my savior. What are we having?"

"It's Thai, can't you smell it? I've been craving this all day, and after the little bit of information I got out of you earlier, I decided some sake was in order as well." She holds up several bottles of our favorite unfiltered, sweet goodness that not only goes perfectly with our meal, it goes perfectly to our heads.

"Yes! Let's open that first!" I do the honors of pouring us each an oversized glass. Screw it, I need a good buzz right now. Erika sets up our plates—apparently oversized food portions are in order, too. Fine by me.

As if on cue, Erika takes the opportunity to make a toast. "Here's to Mike the Magic Nipple Twister and whatever fun games he had up his sleeve—or maybe your skirt—today!" She winks as our glasses clink. I always tell her she missed her calling as a comedic writer, but she insists she's happy climbing her way up the ladder at one of Miami's biggest advertising agencies.

Taking a healthy sip, I laugh at her insinuation, shaking my head. "If only. That honestly would have been a more ideal situation considering what I was blindsided with."

Her eyes widen, knowing it had to be major for me to make that comment. Especially after we spent the weekend debating the pros and cons of pursuing anything with Ian McAlistair. Of course, Erika thinks I should just use him for sex. Which would be great, but that's not me. My heart tends to get involved too easily, and if anyone understands why I'm overly cautious about going there, it's Erika. "Oh, Erika...I think he may have topped Friday's sexcapade with today's little treat."

She looks shocked. "Are you kidding me? You had another spontaneous orgasm? What the hell did he do this time, suck it out of your big toe?" She's completely serious, and I can't help but throw my head back laughing. I absolutely love how crazy she is.

"Erika! You're such a freak! Where the hell did that come from? Suck it out of my big toe? Yeah...right there in the lobby!" I'm laughing at that ridiculous image, but the look on her face says, *What? I was serious.*

She continues with, "Hey! I'm not putting anything past Orgasm Man," then busts out laughing at her own joke. "Oh, God...I just had a visual of Superman, but in all black and red with a big O on his chest." Her tempo is going up as she laughs through her words.

Here we go...

"With sparkles swirling around his fingers, and a huge bulge in his pants!" We're both cracking up, wiping away tears. "Oh, this has endless possibilities... The Caped Crusader of Climaxes saves the day as a big smoke ring slowly rises over the city." I can see her brain working; she's not done yet and can barely talk she's laughing so hard. "And his little sidekick, Foreplay, is there: 'Holy cunnilingus, Orgasm Man, she was a squirter!'"

I'm done. I am laughing so hard, no noise is even coming out and my stomach muscles burn. This is a full-on ugly laugh, and we're both in deep.

A few minutes later, I'm finally coming out of my laughing fit. "Oh, my God, that was hilarious! Now the next time I see Ian I'm going to picture him in his skintight superhero uniform, a big O on his chest with his cape blowing in the wind as he stands there with his hands on his hips and his chest puffed out." Still laughing, I mimic the stance. Maybe that visual will protect me from whatever mindfuck he's got in store for me next time.

Wiping the tears from her eyes, she adds, "This could make the best porn series ever! Can you imagine?"

"Yes!" I agree with enthusiasm. "I would actually watch that! Although, I can't really picture his best friend, Jackson, as Foreplay. He's seriously way too cool to play that character."

"I'm writing this shit down," Erika declares as she starts typing into her phone. "Too bad Ian's not the porn producer we originally thought he was. That could have been our in!"

"Oh. Yeah. That would have been fantastic," I respond with zero enthusiasm, remembering how grossed out I was at the thought of Ian being in the porn business.

After riding out the high from our ugly laugh, we finally come back to reality. We finish up dinner and take our plates to the kitchen. Erika pours us each another glass of sake, and we make our way to the living room to get comfortable, each taking an end of the sofa where I finish telling her what happened.

"I was totally prepared, ready to be professional and act like it's no big deal, just another day, just another client. But no, it can't play out that way. *That* would be too easy. First of all, he looked good enough to eat and smelled good enough to scramble my brain right out the gate. Add to that the intensity of…him. It's so overwhelming! Then he tells me that Jackson recommended he bring me a bouquet of flowers as a *peace offering* and so I wouldn't think he was a total jerk. He said *that* was too cliché, and he *doesn't do cliché*…so what does he do instead? Goes about as far from cliché as possible and asks me if I knew the word *Fey* also means faerie."

She looks as confused as I felt when he asked me.

"Yeah…I know," I say, agreeing with her expression. "So then he explains that when he found out my last name is LeFay, he had a vision of me as a faerie."

Her mouth drops open and her head tips down, basically saying *what the fuck?*

"Oh, it gets better. He proceeds to describe this faerie vision of me, and it was the most sensual description of a faerie you can imagine. I was almost to the point you could knock me over with a feather, and then he hands me this." I grab the portrait sitting face down on the coffee table and hand it to her.

Her eyes widen as she puts down her wine, then covers her mouth with her hand. She looks up at me, mouth agape, and I think I see a little pity in her expression. I understand why. How do you not fall for a guy that gives you something so beautiful? "Charlotte...he drew this for you?"

I nod my confirmation.

"Oh my. I'm...stunned. This is magnificent."

"I know. I was so taken aback when I saw it, I got a huge lump in my throat and my eyes filled up with tears. I didn't even know what to say! Now you know what I mean by blindsided. If he wasn't wrong for me, I think I could have let myself fall in love with him in that moment." What a frightening thought.

"Yeah...I think *I* just fell in love with him." We both smile, not really able to laugh.

For me, this is serious, and she knows it. She knows that in my mind, Ian falls into the same category as my father. Over-the-top good looks, charm, success...everything a girl could dream of and more. But after the truth about my father was tragically revealed, destroying my mother's beautiful soul, my life was never the same. Once I mourned the loss of my parents and my storybook life, I swore I would never fall for a man like that—a man like Ian McAlistair. He may have every characteristic a woman could dream of, but there is no way a man his age and with his experience doesn't have a long list of women, probably spread all over the country, that are a simple phone call away, ready to do his bidding. The thought of it makes me sick, and I could never be secure or truly happy in a relationship that left me wondering if he was with someone else.

"I can't believe how much this looks like you. I mean...it *is* you. And the wings and that damn pink flower. My gosh, Charlotte...what did you say?"

"At first I could barely speak. I was caught off guard... Can you even imagine? Knowing that *he* actually drew it, and the reality of that alone was enough to knock the wind out of me. Adding to my torrent of emotions, the look on his face and this... almost...shyness about him was enough to twist my heart into a bloody knot. He literally asked me if I liked it!" My tone suggests that it was the dumbest question possible. "Of course, I let him know my feelings went well beyond liking it, and he was so pleased his smile seemed almost boyish."

"Wow, Charlotte. This guy throws it at you from all directions."

If she only knew what it was like to deal with him face to face with your mind saying one thing and your body saying another.

"Ha! He throws it at me from all directions, all right. As I'm standing there, still dumbfounded by everything that encompasses this drawing, he reaches up under my chin, nudging my head back so I'm forced to look at him. His thumb starts gliding across my lips when he says in a deep, sexy voice, 'You've cast a spell on me, Charlotte LeFay. Now, you have to deal with the consequences.'" I lamely try to imitate his voice.

Erika's hand goes directly to her forehead, her mouth dropping in disbelief. "You can't be serious. That is beyond panty melting! You cast a fucking spell on him, and he drew that...that masterpiece for you! Oooohhh, girl, good luck with this one. I told you he wasn't giving up easily." Here we go, Erika's thrown in the towel, again. Traitor!

"No...you don't understand how bad this gets. Erika... I was so overwhelmed with everything. Him, the intensity, everything he does to my senses, and then the freaking faerie portrait and the whole *'You've cast a spell on me'* declaration..." I put my head down in shame as I finish in a quiet voice, "I almost passed out. Literally, not figuratively. Thank God, I was aware enough to sit my ass in a nearby chair and get my head down enough so it didn't quite go that far, but it was close. Very close." I look up at her, seeing the concern and understanding in her eyes. "And I'm so embarrassed I could die."

She reaches over and grabs my hand. "Honey, you're only human. You'd have to be dead to not be affected by him and his twisted, magical fuckery. That guy is like a damn reincarnated wizard or something." She laughs, trying to lighten the vibe. "Boy, your road rage really got you in a pickle this time. Way to whack the hornet's nest, Charlotte!"

Yeah, it's more like Sibel got me into this pickle. I noticed she was in hiding during today's show-and-tell with Ian. Coward that she is.

"Uuugghh…I don't know what to do. I know he's going to be there tomorrow, and something tells me he will make it a point to cross my path again and again. Most women would think this is fun, but it's completely exhausting me. He's relentless on a level that scares me. I wish there was some way to just tell him why I can never be what he is looking for."

Continuing, I admit, "After my near-fainting episode, I had to get away from Ian, so I asked Jackson to take me to my office so I could clear my head. In an attempt to make him understand, I ended up telling him everything that happened when I was seventeen and how my life got turned upside down in the worst way possible." I take a long sip of my sake to wash down the emotion. "It seemed like the right thing to do, and he was so understanding… I'm actually glad I did, but it brought a lot to the surface that I work hard to keep buried," I finish with my hands fidgeting in my lap.

Erika puts down her glass and scoots over to me, pulling me into her arms. "Come here, babe. I know that was hard for you. Really hard. But it's good for you to talk about it, even if it's to someone you barely know. It worries me sometimes how you keep it balled up inside." She rubs my back as I relax and I'm pleased that only a few tears escaped. "You may not want to hear this, but do you really think it's fair to punish Ian for your father's mistakes?"

"That's funny, Jackson basically said the same thing. And the truth is, no, I don't. But right now, at this point in my life, I can't change the fact that Ian McAlistair makes me feel like I'm falling off a cliff and there isn't a safety net to catch me. Sadly, that is the same image I have of my mother right before her life ended."

That night I dreamt of Ian. He stood in front of me, staring at me with a look I couldn't decipher. I knew he wanted to tell me something, but there were no words. I tried to speak, but nothing would come out. It made me anxious, like something was getting ready to happen and it was vital that we speak. I started to panic, screaming at him to tell me something, but still there was no sound. My stomach started twisting and turning, like I was falling, making my panic worse.

Ian was calm, but his eyes were sparking with emotion. What does he want to tell me? *Ian! Talk to me!* But my voice was only in my head. Finally, he handed me a piece of paper. What I found there instantly stopped my panic, stopped the sensation of falling. It was a drawing and it was breathtakingly beautiful—of Ian standing there shirtless, muscles strained with me lying across his arms, staring up at him, as if he had caught me, saving me from my fall.

"Ian…" was all I whispered, but its meaning was so much more. Then I realized I could hear it, that I could finally speak. I looked up to thank him and ask him why he was there, but he was gone.

TEN

IAN

I may need to change my routine. I was out an hour early this morning to run the boardwalk through South Beach and got to enjoy the sun rising over the horizon. I see it from my balcony almost every morning, but this was different. To be outside, exerting myself, deeply breathing the fresh air off the ocean surrounded by the orange glow as it gradually took over the sky...it was awesome, like I was in it and not just observing it. I'm not sure why I haven't been doing it that way all along. I am more energized than usual, a welcome bonus considering how edgy I've been.

Last night I kept waking, tossing and turning, my mind busily trying to solve a problem. A problem that has nothing to do with today's meeting and everything to do with a certain blue-eyed enchantress with a penchant for messing with my head.

Mindlessly navigating my way to the office, I think about my next encounter with Charlotte and how to keep it from blowing up in my face, again. Maybe I should show up with a dozen—no, two dozen—roses and tell her I'd be honored if she would join me for dinner. Or I could just say *screw it* and go back to my kidnapping idea and hide behind a tree, nail her with a blow dart laced with a tranquilizer, throw her over my shoulder, and go enjoy a few weeks of getting to know each other in the Bahamian sunshine and salt air.

God, that sounds fucking amazing!

I don't have much time to contemplate that superb idea before my phone rings. "Good morning, Nana. How is my favorite person in the world?"

"Good morning, Ian. Your favorite person is getting old and feeble, but at least I've still got my looks going for me. You should have seen it yesterday when I was exercising at the Y, they couldn't keep their eyes off me!"

Ever since Nana turned seventy, she's been bragging about how good-looking she is. Though she's always been a beautiful woman, I think it's her way of doing a little reverse psychology...on herself. She's wise enough to know you can't fight the inevitable, but she's also witty enough to make the best of the ride.

"I bet they couldn't. I told you, you leave a trail of broken hearts everywhere you go. Poor fellas can only dream."

She's heard enough about herself and is more interested in getting the scoop. "Tell me about this girl making you work for your title and reputation. How many orgasms have you given her so far?"

I don't know why it still shocks me when she pops up with shit like that.

"Nana, please tell me you don't ask other people questions like that." I'm trying to stall because I'm not really sure what to say about Charlotte, and I'm definitely not telling her I've already given her one orgasm—and quite a spectacular one, at that.

"Of course I do! You gotta keep people on their toes, Ian. Besides, it's great entertainment for an old lady. They never expect it, and the look on their faces"—she pauses to laugh—"is priceless! I think I should have my own reality TV show or, at the very least, my own YouTube channel. I'd make a killing, I know I would."

She's right about that. They broke the mold when they made Nana.

"How do you know what a YouTube channel is, Nana?"

"I don't live under a rock, my dear grandson. Now quit trying to divert me from what I want to hear. Is she still wagging her tail in your face or are you getting some action?" I hear a noise in the background, and I'm certain she just lit a cigarette. I've confronted her about it before, but she swears up and down that she doesn't smoke.

"That's a great way of putting it, but honestly, I wouldn't even say she's wagging her tail in my face. If she were, at least then I'd know she wanted me to chase it." If she did that, I'd be back on familiar ground and know what the hell I was doing and how to plan my next move. "No, I think she is intentionally trying to avoid me, even though I know for a fact she's attracted to me, very much so. It apparently has to do with something that happened in her past. Yet, according to Jackson, it wasn't any kind of abuse."

"How the hell does Jackson know that?" she asks.

"Because she told him, but he says it's not his place to tell me. Which I respect, but it still annoys the hell out of me." She obviously trusts him way more than she trusts me. Yet another thing to make me nice and edgy.

"Hmmmm...the plot thickens. I like it. You must represent something that she is afraid of. I'll have to think on this one a bit and see what I come up with. If there's a will, there's a way. If you genuinely want to be with her, Ian, there is a way to make it happen. You just may have to struggle like hell to get there. You better make sure that's what you really want."

She always reverts back to wisdom and advice, and it's always spot on.

"You're right, Nana. And as of right now, she's all I can think about. I have this gnawing need to have her. So, I really don't have much choice but to find the *way*, because I sure as hell won't be giving up."

"That's what I like to hear, sweetheart. You are a McAlistair, after all. Well, I have to go now. Judy and I are going to breakfast this morning. I just wanted to catch you early and tell you I love you."

"I love you, too, Nana. Very much. Enjoy breakfast, and I will chat with you soon." With that, we hang up right as I pull up to the office.

Once inside, I'm faced with a list of messages, emails, and last-minute questions from staff members about today's meeting with Novas Alturas. Everything is set to go, and everyone is pumped.

This is what we thrive on—pitching the sale and closing the deal. My leaders are the best in the industry, and my staff is first-class. It's a smooth-sailing ship with excellent morale where everyone knows their comrades have their backs.

Back in the early days, we had a few backstabbers, whiners, and drama queens, but once those were weeded out, we were unstoppable. I'm very proud of my team and what we've created.

I've gotten an email from Jackson confirming that everyone arrived midday yesterday from Brazil and they are looking forward to this afternoon's meeting. Since they were traveling the day before, we decide to start the meeting at noon so we can mingle and enjoy lunch before we get down to business, ending with cocktails and dessert.

The owner, founder, and CEO of Novas Alturas, Lucas Azeveda, will be there, as will his son, Gabriel, who has recently taken a position next to his father as COO and is in the last stages of grooming before taking the helm when daddy retires. I've had numerous conversations with both gentlemen and feel good about the rapport that seemed to be there from the start. They are good men, and I respect the vision and hard work that has put them at the top. Novas Alturas is first-class, like us, making this union a splendid match.

Rounding out my morning with a call to my accountant, I'm ready to head over to The Clara Sea for one meeting I'm looking forward to and another that unfortunately has me a little nervous. We can definitely put that in the "first time ever" category, and it kind of pisses me off. I've never been so distracted by something in my life, and I can't help but wonder when the hell it's going to end. Surely this shit can't go on forever.

I'm suddenly hit with the idea that Charlotte may never come around, that she may never relax in my arms while I kiss away her thoughts and cares, that she may never look into my eyes while she comes apart and screams my name.

"Fuck!" I hit my desk and stand so quickly my chair flies backward. "Goddamn, I can't believe how badly she's in my head!"

She's bloody taking over everything, and I barely know the first thing about her. Maybe it's better if I somehow try to avoid her today. Get through this meeting, close the deal, and *then* go after her with everything I've got. Something tells me that won't happen unless she's laid up, sick in bed, and won't be there today. Otherwise, she will make an appearance because it's her job to do so.

"Get it together, McAlistair," I say to myself as I grab my things and head out the door.

On the way there, I get a text from Jackson saying that most everyone has arrived, mingling and chatting, and the vibe is good. I'm not late, more like exactly on time, with a few minutes to spare. I don't want to appear overly anxious, but I refuse to be disrespectful.

Pulling up to the front entrance, the valet directs me to a

reserved spot on the other side of the porte cochère, set aside for cars more valuable than they care to be responsible for. I tip him anyway as he shakes my hand and offers a personal greeting and assurance that he will keep an eye on things while I'm inside. Charlotte really does have a topnotch production here. Although, with her tenacity, I'd expect nothing less.

Walking through the main lobby, I am greeted by several more staff members and directed to the Garden Room. When I left my office there was a noticeable tension in my shoulders. Thoughts of Charlotte never truly being mine tend to have that effect on me. Now, I feel nothing but that familiar rush that only comes from closing a deal. My steps are light, my head is clear. This is going to be good. As I get closer to the conference room, I can hear the voices of people conversing in the hallway. A burst of excitement kicks up my pace. I'm looking forward to giving what I know will be a successful presentation.

Turning the corner, shortly before the entrance of the conference room, all my excitement is extinguished as my vision tunnels in on Charlotte standing in front of Gabriel Azeveda. She is looking up at him, a sincere smile on her lovely face as he takes her hand and slowly brings it to his lips, gently kissing the top of her fingers. A surge of explosive anger and jealousy courses through every cell in my body as I see how genuinely happy she appears with his charm and attention.

My first instinct is to walk up and tell the bastard to back the fuck off, but my rational side knows that at this point, it's not a viable option. There is too much at stake, and, as much as I hate to admit it, making any claims on Charlotte right now would potentially shut her down permanently.

As I approach, I can't help but notice that Gabriel is much taller than he appeared in the photos on their website and the few video conferences we had. It's also hard not to notice that he's decent looking. Maybe even what one might describe as handsome. Having never considered another man as competition, I'm surprised to find myself suddenly noticing every detail and nuance of Gabriel. Most notably, the intensity in his stare and that he hasn't let go of her goddamn hand yet. My spine tightens as my fists clench. *Motherfucker!*

Forcing myself to be calm and not break his bloody fingers when I shake his hand, I disrupt their little lovefest. "Good afternoon, Gabriel, and welcome to Miami. I see you've met our lovely hostess here at The Clara Sea." I release our handshake and turn to Charlotte. Her eyes are wide and so incredibly beautiful. As soon as she turns them to look at me, they dilate— significantly. That subtle reception feels like a triumph and my smile reflects it. "Good afternoon, Charlotte. It's always a pleasure to see you. I hope you're feeling better today." I can't help but throw out that little jab considering our last encounter when she almost fainted, then, quite soundly, sent me walking. I look forward to letting her know *that* will never happen again.

Her eyes soften a little as she responds, "Good afternoon, Ian." I noticed she didn't say Mr. McAlistair—progress, maybe? "I was just telling Gabriel today's lunch will feature a little Brazilian flair."

Okay...she didn't call him Mr. Azeveda, and now they are back to fucking smiling at each other and she just put her hand on his arm.

Gabriel is certainly pleased. I can practically taste how interested he is in her, and she sure as hell isn't deflecting him like she did me. She really does hate me. I quickly respond with the intention of getting Gabriel as far away from Charlotte as possible. "Yes, and if I'm not mistaken, it will be served shortly." Placing my hand on Gabriel's shoulder, I nudge him toward the conference room. "We should be getting inside." With a brief pause, I look Charlotte in the eyes, daring her to challenge me like that again. She is bringing out a side of me I didn't know existed. "Good day." And offer a curt nod.

However, Gabriel has clearly got his radar locked on my obsession and will not be swayed. He leans toward her, that deep accented voice grinding my nerves as he says, "It has been a pleasure to meet you, my dear Charlotte. I will look for you after our meeting. I would enjoy getting to know you, making a new friend here in Miami." He's about ready to make a lethal fucking mistake as he leans in and gives her one of those annoying cheek kisses that all foreigners do.

Evidently, Charlotte doesn't think it's annoying. "That sounds wonderful, Gabriel. Thank you." Her sugary reply has me turning on my heel to leave the scene before I make a very terrible mistake that I won't be able to undo.

"Dammit," I say to myself through gritted teeth as I force myself to continue toward the conference room. I have very clearly staked my claim. It's a first, and it's powerful, and my DNA is raging for me to fend off that intruder. *Un-bloody-believable.*

Entering the conference room, I briefly make eye contact with Jackson before heading straight to my main target, Lucas Azeveda. Regardless of the fact that I now have a major fucking issue with his son, I genuinely like Lucas and am looking forward to working with him on this exceptional project. "Lucas!" My enthusiasm is genuine as we greet one another with a firm and trustworthy handshake. "How are you, my friend?"

"Good. Good, Ian. How are you? I am so happy to see you." His thick accent and weathered appearance draw out a much-needed smile, defusing some of my agitation.

"I am happy to see you, as well." And I truly am. Lucas's smile widens, deepening his laugh lines and crow's feet. He is a distinguished man with slicked back white hair, tanned skin, gold-brown eyes, and a flawless set of fake teeth that are a few shades too bright for his warm appearance. "Have you seen the rendering?"

"Ian! It is magnificent! You have outdone yourself." He turns to face the replication of what will soon be the premier residence in Miami, gesturing with his hand. "Look at this. This, Ian. This is success." He reaches over, taking my hand in both of his. "*We are success.*"

In that moment, albeit fleeting, I am free of the whirlwind that took over my life only days ago. I am in my element. Back to center, where nothing can hold me back, where failure is never an option. "That we are, Lucas. Shall we get the meeting started? I think you are going to be very excited to see what my team and I have created for you."

Lucas nods as his face lights up, mirroring my enthusiasm. We are cut from the same cloth when it comes to truly loving what we do. I have tremendous respect for this man and I know he has the same for me.

Gabriel, on the other hand, has been relabeled. I now see him as an outsider sniffing around my female. Which is a rather significant problem, considering. I watched his every move throughout the meeting, sizing up my competition. I have to admit, the younger Azeveda has the potential to be a worthy opponent. He holds himself very well, and is excellent in his position of authority, regardless of his age, which I'm guessing is a few years younger than me. Adding to my ire, the more I look at the guy, the more I see why any woman would gladly drop at his feet...or *enjoy getting to know him better*.

The stars are significantly out of alignment for me, because not only has the girl I desperately want built a fortress around herself to keep me out, but some evil force has placed a Brazilian Casanova in her path—*and* she appears to be happy about it. This is definitely an obstacle I could do without.

One thing I could do *with* is having a drink, and thankfully, the resort staff just arrived with a full bar along with an impressive dessert table. I need to make a point of visiting the chef and complimenting today's meal and now this outstanding display. He is world class, and I'm curious as to where Charlotte found him.

Once the bartender hands me my drink, I make my way over to Jackson, who cuts directly to the chase. "That went well. You mind telling me what the hell happened before you entered the room? Please tell me it had nothing to do with Charlotte."

Now he's suddenly her protector. Maybe I should add him to my list of obstacles that keep pushing her further and further from my reach.

Taking a long swallow, I pause to enjoy the oaky citrus of this particular scotch, pleased with its elegantly smooth finish. I bring the glass up again to breathe in its aroma before answering in a low tone. "Gabriel has discovered Ms. LeFay. I almost had to wipe the drool off his mouth with my fist." That last part came out with a teeth-clenched hiss.

Jackson's expression changes from curious to an eyebrow-raised *Oh fuck!*, and it would actually be funny if I wasn't so pissed off about the situation. He adds the obvious, "Oh, man. That's complicated."

My head jerks up to look at him. "Yeah, complicated would be a good description, especially considering Charlotte doesn't seem opposed to his attention. I swear to God, Jackson, it's like I'm in a different universe when it comes to that woman. Either that, or this is some kind of penance for something my old, wicked soul has yet to answer for. Either way, I'm on the verge of doing something irrational."

Jackson shakes his head. "Something's up. You've got some bad mojo happening...compared to what you're used to, anyway." He tries holding in a laugh. "Although, this is the norm for your average mortals. You know...having to work for it a little." He seems to think that's cute because his laugh is now undisguised by the movement of his shoulders as he brings his drink to his lips. Which is just a lame attempt at hiding his smile.

Completely deadpan, I say, "I'm glad you're finding humor in this, asshole." I turn so my back is no longer facing the room. "The fun part is, Gabriel's not going anywhere any time soon. This project is going to take more than three years to complete."

"You do realize that competition is healthy, right? It brings out the best in everything and is the cause of all progression.

Evolution, survival of the fittest...that's all a competition, my friend. Modern technology? The result of one brainiac trying to outdo another. Hell, even losers improve due to competition." He seems very pleased with himself, playing the role of college professor.

"That's all well and good, Darwin. But I have no intention of being the loser."

ELEVEN

CHARLOTTE

Walking into work earlier, I was ready to take on the day, having already prepared myself for an inevitable run-in with Ian. I just hoped this time he wouldn't turn my world upside down. Wishful thinking, considering there has not been *one single* encounter with Ian McAlistair where he did not completely throw me off-balance.

Making matters worse, that damn dream I had is on repeat in my head. A part of me wishes I wasn't so scarred by what happened with my parents. Yet, there is another part that thinks life is hard and sometimes we learn hard lessons along the way, like not making the same mistakes as your parents. Isn't that what we are supposed to do? If so, why does the weight of it feel like such a heavy burden?

A knock at my office door jumps me out of my thoughts. It's Tracy, ready to go over her a.m. reports. It dawns on me, at that moment, it's time for me to take a break—a much-needed vacation to clear my head, reboot my drive, and calm my fried nerves. It's been a long time since I've felt this jumpy.

Once Tracy's list of problems are solved and questions are answered, I head down to see how things are going in the kitchen, where our head chef, Michael, and his staff are busily preparing for today's luncheon with McAlistair Architecture, Design & Development and Novas Alturas. Everything is on schedule, and I know they will be impressed with Michael's presentation. He's the best of the best, and beyond that, he's a great person. The Clara Sea wouldn't be the same without him.

On the way back to my office, I stop by the Garden Room for one last inspection, even though I know everything is set and ready to go. It's a habit; I want everything to exceed my client's expectations. But, in this particular case, I cannot deny that the notion of Ian being pleased about choosing The Clara Sea, regardless of his ulterior motives, gives me a noticeable sense of satisfaction. A smile touches my lips, as a part of me wishes I could be more at ease around him.

Staring out the window, I laugh at myself. *Be more at ease around him... Cut yourself some slack, Charlotte.* How can I be more at ease when we go from off-the-charts hot, flirtatious, and charming to sex master and arrogant jerk, then strategic ambush commander to manipulating bastard? And then to thoroughly confuse things, he showed up last time as a deeply intense, passionate artist that presents a stunning portrait in lieu of flowers and drops little poetic bombs like *you've cast a spell on me*!

Now that I think about it, Ian has more personalities than I do. I've only got Sibel; he's got freaking Don Juan, Napoleon, and Monet!

Just then, the door opens and Jackson walks in looking handsome, as always. A genuine smile stretches across his face, and I realize I'm very happy to see him. Walking toward him, I smile and reach up for a friendly hug. "Good morning, Jackson." Letting go, I finish with, "It's great to see you."

"And good morning to you, Charlotte. How are you feeling today? From the looks of you, like a million bucks." He gives me a charming wink that makes me laugh.

"I'm doing much better, thank you. Everything is set on our end. I've been down to see Chef Michael. The kitchen is in full swing." I give him a thumbs up as we turn and head toward the rendering of their proposed building.

"Wonderful! I have no doubt it's going to be outstanding. I was very impressed with Michael. You're lucky to have him."

I nod. "Don't think I don't know it. He's an artist, and I make sure he is a very happy one. It's the food that keeps 'em coming back, ya know." I give him a quick wink and a smirk.

He laughs. "Uhhh...I think we can both agree that there is a lot more to The Clara Sea Resort and Spa than just terrific food. You should take more credit than that, Charlotte LeFay." He gives me a stern look with a raised eyebrow. He's so fatherly, I truly adore him.

The noise of conversation and chatter stirs outside the Garden Room, so we head that way. I need to get back to my office to prepare for a few other scheduled appointments, and these guys have an awesome project to sell. Once outside, we mingle about with greetings and small talk, then Jackson and I depart with a quick *goodbye*.

Before I can make my way fully out of the crowd, I turn and almost run straight into a firm, broad chest that smells of expensive cologne. *Oh Lord, not again.* I look up to find an extremely attractive man smiling down at me. I assume from the dark skin, hair, and eyes that he is with the Brazilian Novas Alturas group. He confirms my assumption with his greeting.

"Pardon me, ma'am. I do apologize, I should watch where I am going." His voice is deep and accented, his smile beyond charming. "My name is Gabriel Azeveda, and I am with Novas Alturas. Are you here with the McAlistair group?"

Reaching to shake his hand, I respond, "No. I'm Charlotte LeFay, the general manager here at The Clara Sea. Welcome to Miami, Mr. Azeveda." His hand is warm, his grip politely firm, and I can't help but notice the spark of interest in his eyes. *Great. Just what I need.*

"It is very nice to meet you, Charlotte. Your resort is quite impressive. I've never seen gardens put to such use. It is true artistry." He turns toward the windows at the seating area overlooking the garden and bird habitat, hand raised in its direction. "They are so alive! It's absolutely spectacular."

"Thank you, Mr. Azeveda," I respond with pride.

"Please, Charlotte. Call me Gabriel. You see that old man over there?" He laughs, pointing to an equally striking man with white hair, clearly his father, but more weathered than old. "You may call him Mr. Azeveda."

We both laugh at his exaggeration. "Okay, Gabriel it is, then." He is easy to chat with, and I can tell he is being somewhat flirtatious; I don't feel like everything about him will swallow me whole like I do when I'm around Ian. To continue the conversation, I mention today's menu and its Brazilian inspiration, which I know he and his associates will thoroughly enjoy. I guess that was his cue to throw on the charm, because he reaches down and takes my hand in his, never taking his eyes off mine as he slowly brings it to his lips where I know he intends to place a kiss. None of this would have been a big deal, all things considered, but the familiar sound of Ian walking toward us suddenly made it seem like a very big deal, indeed.

How I know it's Ian—once again, simply from the cadence of his walk and the wave of heat and tingling nerves that come over me—is disconcerting and intriguing all at once. It's the same bloody sorcery I remember from the very first time I laid eyes on him. Yet, in this moment, it has me on the defensive. Literally like I need to defend myself, because the tension that is slowly approaching with every tap of his goddamn shoes on the granite floor is making me feel like I just got caught with my hands in the cookie jar, to put it mildly.

Making matters worse, Gabriel's lips are lingering awkwardly on my fingers, which may be standard protocol in Brazil, but that in combination with Ian's death vibes has me wanting to eject myself from the scene before I crash and burn, then peacefully drift to safety somewhere far away under my parachute.

Ian is closing in, and Gabriel has not let go of my hand. I'm trying to be normal and not appear as awkward as this is making me. Ian approaches with an outstretched hand and obviously forced pleasantries. The tension he's emitting is enough to fill the whole damn corridor, and it's suffocating me. When I finally bring myself to look at him—as he offers me a manufactured greeting—something inside me softens and I just want to stare at him, absorbing everything about him that I find so damn appealing. But he quickly douses that momentary lapse in judgement with an ice-cold bucket of water as he feigns concern with a reminder that I almost fainted because of him, then refused his courtesy. The look on his face says he wants to say more, as if it were even his place to do so.

His audacity and my insecurities were enough to bring Sibel out of hibernation, and she's feeling kind of bitchy. Little does Gabriel know, she's decided to use him as the needle in Ian's voodoo doll. Laying on the charm, Sibel calls him by his first name, then references their brief conversation as if it were part of some long-established relationship. That definitely had the effect she was looking for, because Ian just shut the whole thing down with a blatant attempt to get Gabriel away from me. Except it didn't work, and now Gabriel and I have paved the way for a *friendship* that may have a different meaning for him than it does for me. *Thanks, Sibel! Always there to lend a helping hand.*

Throughout the rest of my day, I picture Ian as he turned and walked away after I accepted Gabriel's clear advances. Everything happened so quickly, and now I'm a little off by my decision to have it play out in Ian's face. It really was a bitchy move, and knowing there is a side to Ian that isn't the devil incarnate, but quite the opposite, I feel kind of guilty....and maybe a little embarrassed to have been so tactless and immature. It can't be simple with Ian, can it?

Needing a distraction and to get it off my chest, I decide to text Erika.

Me: Hey! Flirted with one of the Brazilians...right in Ian's face today. May have even insinuated I'd go on a date with him. The Brazilian, that is...ugh!

Erika: Well that's one way of getting rid of him. Ian, that is...

Me: Yeah. Except now I feel like ignorant trash that thinks it's cute to play games.

Erika: It is a little out of character for you. But you are trying to get rid of him, right? If he judges you on the way out, it doesn't really matter if the mission was accomplished.

Me: Okay, Yoda. Do you have any other sage advice?

Erika: Yes. Go watch a hilarious cat video, laugh your ass off, and get back to work.

Erika: And you're not ignorant trash. Stop overthinking it. Love you!

Me: Love you...thanks babe!

Okay, I'm not sure if I'm much better off. But she does have a point. If my end game is to rid Ian and his sanity-twisting, emotional-knot-tying self from my life, then I guess I should relax. She's probably right. I overthink everything when it comes to Ian. It's one more thing to add to my long list of reasons why he's no good for me.

A knock at my door jolts my nerves...again. *Dammit!* "Come in!" I'm a little impatient, thinking it's Tracy for the fifth time today. The door opens as I start to tell her something— "I forgot to tell you..."

I stop cold as I look up and see Ian standing in my doorway, that godforsaken perfection making my stomach do flips. *What does he want?* I'm instantly nervous, and I hate it. "Oh...I'm sorry. I thought you were Tracy." Standing to give myself something to do, I ask, "How was your meeting? Should we be expecting that amazing vision of yours down by the Bay in the next few years?" That flowed well...I think.

"Three." That's all I get. That and blazing eyes accompanied by intense predatory vibes. *Ugh!* He's doing it again.

"Three?" I repeat with a silent...*and?*

"Three years. The project's scheduled completion." He clarifies with a one-sided smirk that creates a dimple I don't recall seeing before. *Really?*

"Oh! Yes, of course. Sorry, it's...it's been a long day," I say, trying not to sound as silly as I feel. "Congratulations, then! That's great news for you and your team. Everyone must be thrilled!"

"Thank you. I would say everyone involved is thrilled. It will be the premier location in this area and will likely sell out well before completion." No shortage of confidence where Ian McAlistair is concerned. I wish I found it irritating and not a total turn-on.

He takes a few steps closer as he continues. "I wanted you to know that lunch could not have been more outstanding. Chef Michael outdid himself, and I just stopped by the kitchen to tell him so. He is quite an asset, as I'm sure you know. The rest of your staff performed with the utmost respect and professionalism as well." His eyes soften a bit as he takes another step toward me, causing my heart rate to ratchet up several beats. "I'm very impressed with how you manage this resort, Charlotte. It's not an easy job. I've encountered seasoned GMs that couldn't hold a candle to you, and you're only what...?"

He wants to know how old I am. Why does that seem so personal with him?

I pause, "Twenty-eight." There's that dimple again. *Damn. Damn. Damn.*

"Twenty-eight," he repeats, and why in God's name it sounds delicious coming off his tongue is beyond me. My eyes zero in on his mouth with those magical lips, and I have visions of kissing him while he repeats...

Stop! I can't do this. I go to turn around and head back behind my desk for protection when he stops me.

"Charlotte, wait."

I stand there for a second too long with my back to him. On a deep breath, I turn back around.

"Before you sit down, I wanted to ask if you would please join me for lunch tomorrow?"

Even I have to admit that came out a little fast. There's no way in hell he's nervous. But the expectant look in his eyes tells me he might be, and after Sibel's games earlier, I'm suddenly feeling obligated to say yes. However, *yes* doesn't get me to an ending where Ian goes on his merry way and I'm no longer at a loss for which way is up.

An awkward amount of time passes without giving him an answer. He saves me from fumbling through my words by saying, "We started on the wrong foot, and it's entirely my fault. Perhaps someday I can give you an explanation for the stupid choice I made the first time we met. But if I tried to right now, you would probably still think I'm an asshole, and I'm trying very hard to get you to see that I'm actually not."

That was a little cryptic, but at least he acknowledges some of the truth. I can tell he's outside his comfort zone when he says, "I thought if we got to know each other better...at a pace you're comfortable with, then maybe we could open the lines of communication, be more at ease. I don't know...see where it takes us."

Why does that tighten my chest and make my stomach hurt?

"Ian...I'm not sure." I do turn and walk back to my chair this time, needing the safety of the desk between us. "I appreciate you making this effort, but I just..." I don't know what to say, and everything in me is telling me to run in the other direction.

"I guess you could say I have trust issues, and you really haven't given me a reason to trust you. I'm sorry, but that's not a good way to start off. Especially for someone like me." I hope that wasn't too much information.

He comes to stand in front of my desk with his hands behind his back. I know he's holding back, not wanting to say the wrong thing. There is something kind of endearing about that.

But when I look in his eyes, I can see how hard it is for him to say, "Charlotte, even if you decide to hate me for all eternity, I can accept it, if you just give me a chance—give us a chance—to get to know each other first. At least then we won't be left wondering, potentially regretting what was left on the table."

What do I say to that? He does have a point, and I really don't want to be a complete bitch, but at the same time I don't want to get hurt. I'm terrified of it. Putting my head down, closing my eyes, and mustering up some courage, I pop back up, open my eyes, and let out the breath I was holding. "Okay, Ian. Lunch. That's it." Holding up my finger to his triumphant smile, I add, "In a crowded restaurant, on land, no privacy and no ulterior motives."

His smile abruptly disappears, brows drawn in, and his head tips slightly. "Damn, Charlotte. You *really* don't trust me." With a subtle straightening of his spine, he quickly shakes off the disappointment and shifts back to being conciliatory. "But, I get it. So a crowded, land-based establishment it is, and I will leave all my *ulterior motives* at home." I can tell he wants to laugh, but he doesn't, and the expression it creates is seriously cute.

"You can laugh, Ian. Believe it or not, I actually do have a sense of humor," I say on a laugh of my own. This little exchange takes the edge off agreeing to have lunch with Sir Fucksalot and going against everything I've been committing myself to for the past week. So much for being a strong, modern woman.

He's smiling now, and it's such a stunning transformation of his face. *Wow.* It's like the universe dumped all its perfection on him and left nothing for the rest of us. Reaching into his pocket, he pulls out his phone and starts typing something. Without looking up he says, "What's your cell number so I can text you when I'm done investigating what restaurant in Miami will be the most crowded at noon tomorrow?"

Oh, he is smooth. Little trickster.

"Ian...I..." How do I say I don't think it's a good idea to give him my number? And why don't I think it's a good idea? It's feels like I'm giving him a key to my front door or something.

"Charlotte." He raises one eyebrow. "It's your cell number. That's how people communicate nowadays. If I lose all sense of dignity and become a nuisance, calling and texting all day, you can always block my number." His tone is slightly impatient, as if he's dealing with someone who isn't all there. Well...he *is* dealing with someone who isn't all there, at least whenever he's around. I think my brain cells are exploding as we speak.

Not wanting to appear silly or immature, I, once again, give in. "Okay. I'm sorry. That was unnecessary." Looking up at him, I use his same words. "Perhaps someday I can give you an explanation for my hesitance, but if I tried to right now, you would think I'm crazy." In an attempt to lighten the vibe, I purse my lips on a smirk and wink at him.

That was a bad idea. The effect it has is palpable as his eyes turn black, his nostrils flare, and his fist clenches. All of which, in turn, detonates an arousing sensation that rushes through my core, tightening my nipples, and forces my legs to squeeze together involuntarily to add pressure to the slight throbbing of my clit. I think I'm in shock as I stare at his eyes, unable to look away. My heart is pounding and I'm starting to get that falling sensation, which is exactly why I want to run as far away from him as I can, *not* give him my cell number or join him for lunch!

I snap out of it, and my tone is curt and impatient as I reach up and say, "Okay. Give me your phone, I'll put my number in." He slowly hands it to me, and I add it to his contact list. Handing it back to him, I don't meet his eyes as I say, "I will look for your text and see you tomorrow. Sorry to cut this short, but I still have some work to do." Taking another deep breath, I say, "Congratulations, again, on landing the deal, and I appreciate you choosing The Clara Sea as the venue for such an important meeting." With a stamped smile, I add, "We look forward to working with you and your team in the future."

He is not happy. Evident in the flexing of his jaw muscles, the slight squinting of his eyes, and the electrical charge that has taken over my whole office. The masochist in me wonders what would happen if he were unleashed. If I stood up and walked over to him, put my hand around the back of his neck, and pulled him into a passion-filled kiss. What kind of damage would he do? What kind of pain would he inflict? How much would I enjoy it? Thankfully, the sound of him walking away snaps me out of that random S&M fantasy.

I don't think I start to breathe again until he closes the door behind him. He left with a terse nod and "Good evening." Things between us are so hot and cold, it wipes me out. Physically, mentally, emotionally. This is why I don't want to start seeing him, even for an innocent lunch date. It's like we can't even have a basic conversation without it turning into some invisible sparring match that neither of us will ever win.

And where does my mind come up with the shit it comes up with whenever he is around? *How much would I enjoy the pain he could inflict...* Where the hell did that come from? I don't think I can even tell Erika that one.

I have to get these last few emails sent, and then I'm out of here. I really should go to the gym and work off some of this stress. Committing myself to doing just that, I hit send on the last reply, pack up my things, and head out. I am now looking forward to sweating, exhausting myself, and hopefully getting back to center.

As I'm walking toward the lobby to chat with Tracy before I leave, I'm surprised to see several people from the Novas Alturas group mingling there. I assumed they all left before Ian stopped by my office. Gabriel is there. He seems to be a head taller than everyone else and is looking my way, waving for me to come over. I really just want to leave right now, but I can't be rude. So I walk over with the intention of staying in my role as general manager and then moving on.

Gabriel enthusiastically brings everyone's attention to me with an introduction. "Everyone, this is the lovely Charlotte LeFay, the general manager of this fine resort. You have perfect timing, Charlotte. We were discussing today's fabulous meal and how impressed we are with your conference room and its wall of windows overlooking those spectacular gardens. I believe we have all come to an agreement that we are going to steal the idea." Deep male laughter mingles and echoes through the lobby. I can't help but be flattered, and I tell them so.

After a few more introductions and shared compliments, I bid them all farewell and head toward the exit. Gabriel excuses himself from the crowd, joining me as I leave. "Do you mind if I walk you to your car?" he says like a true gentleman.

"Of course not. Thank you." I'm not really sure what else to say. After my conversation with Ian, I'm not up for dealing with another man that is obviously interested in me. But at least with Gabriel, I can breathe when he's around. He doesn't feel like a threat.

As soon as we are outside, he says, "I would be honored if you would join me for dinner. I know tonight is late notice, but perhaps tomorrow?"

There is something so old-fashioned about Gabriel. It's charming and, in a way, kind of appealing. Which has me wondering why the hell Ian McAlistair turns me into a wet ball of goo every time he is near. Ian is *so not* old-fashioned.

For whatever reason, I guess to spite myself—and probably Ian—I turn to Gabriel and say, "That sounds wonderful! Tomorrow evening is open."

He looks so genuinely happy and his smile is so striking, I almost want to laugh. What the hell is up with me? I need to go home and really take a good look at myself in the mirror. I know

I am not a bad-looking woman, but between Ian and Gabriel, I've managed to attract two very successful, supermodel-looking men, all in a matter of a week. It's weird because I simply don't see myself as *that* good looking. It has to be something else.

"You have made my day even better, Charlotte. I will spend tomorrow looking forward to seeing you again." With that, we exchange phone numbers and a lingering goodbye. He opens my car door, then reaches down, once again taking my hand to his lips, his brown eyes soft with affection as he places a gentle kiss there. "Until then, my dear Charlotte." And he walks away.

Finally alone and safe from hot guys and wicked hormones, it dawns on me that tomorrow I am having lunch with Ian and dinner with Gabriel. I'm beginning to think I've lost my mind.

As soon as I walk through my front door, I grab my phone and sit down to call Erika. The drive home with loud music wasn't enough to help me sort through everything in my head.

She picks up after the first ring. "Hey, gorgeous! What kind of fun did you get yourself into today? I'm starting to look forward to these daily reports. It's like one of those cable series that sucks you in and won't let go."

"Haha...Erika. I wish that were the case. Then we could sit and watch it together and talk about everyone as if they were real. But in this case....it *is* real and I'm the main character! You're not going to believe what I did."

"That's probably true considering everything that's happened up to this point and the texts you sent me earlier. I'm guessing it has something to do with the Brazilian you mentioned."

"Yeah, I'm having dinner with Gabriel Azeveda tomorrow night."

"Damn. What's up with you and guys with sexy names? That's about as yummy as Ian McAlistair, just a different flavor."

"Yeah, that's not all that's yummy about Gabriel. He's gorgeous, like Brazilian hot-male-model gorgeous. And he's a gentleman!"

"Nice. This sounds like the distraction you need to get your mind off Ian. So what's the problem?"

"The problem is, Ian showed up at my office before I ran into Gabriel. I think he was trying to be normal and not some freakish sex god with an unexpected ability to draw portraits that steal your heart, because he politely asked if I would join him for lunch tomorrow. To which I said I didn't think that was a good idea, but then he put on the hard-sell with a sort of *apology, we got off on the wrong foot, let's just see where it takes us kind of thing*...and I said okay!"

"Whoa...that was a lot. Let me get this straight. Tomorrow, you're having lunch with Ian and dinner with Gabriel? This actually has ménage potential. You're such a bitch! What frigging hot-guy lottery did you win? I wanna play, this seriously isn't fair!"

"Erika! Stop thinking with your pussy!"

We both stop in a fit of laughter for at least a minute. "This isn't funny. Well, *that* was funny, but tomorrow isn't funny. I shouldn't have accepted Gabriel's invitation. I think I did it because I was mad at Ian and mad at myself, or maybe I was overwhelmed and wasn't thinking. I don't know!"

"Why were you mad at Ian and yourself? That doesn't really make sense."

"No, on the surface it doesn't. But there was an exchange between us that started off innocent, then the vibe changed to this intense sexual energy that I swear, Erika, it alters everything inside me. I can't explain it, but it scares the hell out of me. And the look on his face... God, it's enough to melt me right on the spot. When it happens, which is every damn time I'm around him, I shut down and mentally run for the hills. And that's exactly what I did, and I'm pretty sure he was livid about it because he left with barely a goodbye."

"Jeez, Charlotte. That's heavy. Especially for you, and I understand why it scares you, but he doesn't seem to be going anywhere so maybe you should just ride the wave. Quit fighting it so much. It's kind of like how we've always been taught about the run-outs at the beach—if you get caught in one, you go with it and slowly swim to the side until you reach calmer waters. If you swim against it, fighting its strength, you get exhausted and weak and that's how you drown."

"Wow...that was quite an analogy, Erika. You're getting wise in your old age."

"Careful, sister. Might I remind you I'm nine months *younger* than you."

Laughing, I reply, "Touché!"

"Listen, relax and stop beating yourself up about everything that involves Ian. Go have lunch with him, *be* yourself, and *enjoy* yourself. You're not obligated to him in any way, you're just having lunch. Then go out and enjoy your evening with Gabriel. You're not obligated to him, either. It's just a date. You don't even have to kiss either one of them, so it's not like you're double-dipping or something slutty like that."

I cringe at the thought. "Yeah, you're right. I'm not going to have either of them pick me up. I'll drive myself, that way I have an escape if I need it. And I'm definitely not kissing either of them. Bad things happen when I kiss Ian, and you're right, I'd feel kind of slutty if I kissed Gabriel." I don't tell her that the thought of kissing Gabriel tightens my stomach, but not in a good way. It's more like terrible guilt and betrayal. What the hell has Ian done to me?

"See? You've got it all figured out. Now stop stressing and go enjoy a glass of wine. Then you can fall asleep and have a wet dream about a threesome with Ian and Gabriel!"

She thinks that's hilarious.

"That's great, Erika. Exactly what I need. And now that you've put it out there, I'm probably going to have the freaking dream!"

"Okay, good! If you do, be sure to write it down as soon as you wake up so you don't forget any details. I'll want to know *all* about it."

"You're twisted, you know that, right?"

"Yes, and you love it. Good night, babe."

"Good night."

TWELVE

IAN

The steady echo of walking down the hall and through the lobby was my only focus after I left Charlotte's office earlier. Using the repetitive tap to discipline my brain and keep me moving forward. Otherwise, if I followed my instincts, I'd end up right where I always do...with her adding reinforcements to the fucking blockade she's got around herself, which is the complete *opposite* of what I'm trying to do.

If she didn't awaken such intense emotions inside me, I'd say *screw it* and leave her in the lonely goddamn tower she's so fond of. But that simply is not an option, especially now that Gabriel-fucking-Azeveda is sniffing around.

Sitting at the traffic light, I rev the engine, the vibration equivalent to the adrenaline pumping through my veins. I do it again and again, wanting it to move, to feel the power of the engine as I shift gears, controlling its speed, its tenor, its every move, eventually bringing it to its full potential. Like I want to do with Charlotte. She has no idea what I am capable of making her feel, that through that kind of pleasure she has the freedom to let go, to shed the baggage that weighs her down and become acquainted with her full potential. If she did, she wouldn't be avoiding me. She'd be fucking addicted, and she'd be mine.

But not yet. Charlotte's not going to let things be that easy. It blows my mind how every time I think I'm playing the right move, she blindsides me with a clean sweep of the whole goddamn table and I'm back to square one. I wish I knew what has her so afraid, what shuts her down at the blink of an eye. Like earlier when she briefly let down her walls and was being herself, playfully mocking me, pursing her lips, and winking. It was like she shot an arrow right through the center of my chest —the effect was immediate and intense. That's all she had to do, give me that brief glimpse and I was done. I wanted her so badly, it was painful. Making matters worse, I could, once again, see her reaction to me. Beautiful eyes shifting from light to dark, parted lips, her body softening from the heating of her blood. It was one poetic and primal and I didn't want it to end. Then she realized what was happening, and before I could catch my breath, she shut down and started treating me like I was some random client giving me a stamped out thank-you and 'we look forward to working with you again.' I think I actually saw red in that moment, so I left.

I'm starting to see a pattern here, and I can't say I like it very much. I must be a glutton for punishment, though, because I keep coming back for more. It will be interesting to see how lunch goes tomorrow.

Crowded, on land, no ulterior motives... I had to make an effort not to let my jaw drop when she laid out those ridiculous stipulations. Her fear controls her, and since Jackson won't divulge any details as to why, I'm left with a mystery, one on which I should not speculate.

Instead of going home where I know I will just be agitated and impatient, I decide to visit Nana, who always brightens my day. Pulling up to her waterfront townhouse with its perfectly manicured *everything*, I get out of my car only to be greeted by her neighbor Judy. *Dammit.* She's always trying to get me to date her granddaughter, and it's awkward because it's never going to happen.

"Ian! How good to see you, and looking so handsome as always." Her voice is a little too enthusiastic and irritating. I need to cut this short.

"Hello, Judy. Nice to see you, as well." I keep walking toward Nana's gate with my key in hand for a quick escape.

"My granddaughter will be here next week. I know she'd love to meet you. Maybe you could take her for a ride in your boat." I stop abruptly and find her practically running into me from behind. Turning, I have to grab her shoulders to insure she doesn't topple over.

"I'm afraid I can't do that, Judy. I'm seeing somebody. But thank you for thinking of me...again." It came out short and to the point, my intentions made clear.

"Oh. I see. Well, that's too bad. My Jennifer is quite a catch." She's a bit snippy now, as if I've somehow insulted *her* Jennifer, but I'm to the point where I don't care. She never lets up, even when I tell her no. She mumbles something else as she walks away, probably something about me being an asshole, and once again, I don't care.

Nana greets me in the foyer, as sweet and adorable as ever. "Hello, dear. You look weary. Did your meeting not go as well as you expected?" Reaching up as I bend down, she grabs my cheeks and kisses my forehead.

"No, the meeting went as planned. We partnered. You're likely seeing the annoyance of having to deal with Judy trying to set me up with her granddaughter again. I don't know how you put up with her. Doesn't she get on your nerves?"

Nana laughs. "Yes, she can be annoying. We all can when we get old, so we tend to overlook it in our peers. But she's always willing to go do anything. She's not a stick in the mud like everyone else, and she actually has a pretty great sense of humor. We have fun together." She has a big smile on her face, but it has a sort of cat-ate-the-mouse look to it. When she sits down and finishes her statement, I know why. "You would never guess, but Judy is obsessed with erotic romance novels. Not warm and fuzzy romance novels. I'm talking about the heavy stuff, and the more detailed the better."

I'm definitely surprised, and it must show on my face because Nana is laughing even harder. "Wow. What a strange obsession for a woman her age." I sit in the chair opposite her.

"She got a Kindle for Christmas a few years ago from her son. Little does he know, he gave her Pandora's box instead." Her tittering laugh shakes her body as the mischievous sparkle in her eyes brightens. "Once she figured out how the thing worked, she ran across a book with a raunchy cover and was curious. She's been hooked ever since." Her tone is matter-of-fact as her hand smacks down on her lap with the finality of a judge's gavel.

"Don't look so scandalized, Ian. It's endless hours of fun for us old ladies. She tells me all about each book and we laugh until we cry. I bet we're both going to live longer because of it! Do you have any idea how funny it is to hear an eighty-seven-year-old woman talk about butt pl...—"

I hold up my hand and give her a firm look. "That's enough, Nana. I really don't need to hear that. You can save your trash-talk laughing fits for Judy." I can't wait to tell Jackson this one. He will laugh for a week straight. I hold in a laugh of my own so I don't encourage her to keep going. She's like a child that way. You give an inch, she'll take a mile, so to speak.

"What? It's not like you've got virgin ears or something. You've probably done everything she reads about. Hell, I've done at least half of it."

Here we go; she's trying to take the mile.

"I'm sure you have, and I'm very happy for you...and Grandfather." I give her a wink, and she loves it. "However, that is not a conversation I'm comfortable having. You really should save it for Judy." I tip my head and raise an eyebrow.

"Well, you're no fun. What's the matter, are you not getting any lately? Charlotte still holding out?"

That catches me off guard. "Nana...how did you know her

name is Charlotte? I don't recall ever giving you that information." I sound like I'm talking to a child that is attempting to lie about an obvious truth.

She looks out the window and down to the floor, avoiding my eyes, her exaggerated guilt like the performance of a soap opera actor. Finally she says, "I called Jackson and asked him... well, begged him to give me her name. But don't be mad! It was all for a good cause. After our last conversation, I thought about what you said...about her avoiding you, that she's afraid of you. So, I wanted to do some research."

Oh boy. I can't believe Jackson fell for this. Well maybe, I can...but still.

I'm not mad at her, but I am definitely surprised. I think I would have rather she just ask me for her name, not be sneaky about it. "Nana, isn't that prying? Have you ever *done some research* on anyone else I've been seeing?"

"No! Never had a reason to. You barely talked about them. This one is different. And if you'd stop acting like you're my father, I'll tell you what I found out. It may be helpful." Now she's serious, a stern expression accentuating her tone.

She's piqued my curiosity. "Okay, let's hear it."

Taking a deep breath, she begins. "I figured something major happened if she was so adamantly resisting you the way you've insinuated. Let's face it, Ian. You're prime real estate, and any woman that doesn't fall for you is either a lesbian—and even then she could still fall—or she's had some sort of emotional trauma. Now, you said Jackson insists she hasn't been abused, thank goodness, so it has to be something else that hits close to home." Her eyes soften, and I'm suddenly struck with a need to protect Charlotte...and I don't even know what the hell happened.

"What are you getting at, Nana?" I'm impatient because the look in her eyes says she found something and that it's not good.

"I did some private investigative work on Google, and I found an obituary for Michael LeFay, Charlotte's father. It mentioned that he was *tragically taken,* so I searched for any information on what this tragedy might have been. It took a while, but I found what I was looking for, and I believe it is the key to why she is so afraid of you and her feelings."

My brows draw together, concerned as to where this is going.

Nana continues. "Eleven years ago, her father was killed in a car accident in Utah. According to the local news report, he wasn't alone. There was a woman with him who died a few days later in the hospital. The woman wasn't his wife, Charlotte's mother."

"Are you saying this woman was his mistress or something? Not just a passenger in the car?" It doesn't seem right to speculate, but it's also a legitimate question.

"I didn't find anything specifically saying *that,* but wisdom tells me it is the case. You see, her mother passed away two years later." The sadness in Nana's eyes is no match for what's going on inside me. Charlotte was so young—only seventeen—when her father died, and nineteen or twenty when she had to say goodbye to her mother.

"Was there any information on how her mother passed away? My God, that's so much for a young person to deal with." I wish I could talk to her about this.

"No, but I found another article about Charlotte and her success at the resort she manages. She's quite beautiful, by the way. It mentioned that her charity of choice is drug rehab and awareness, and she *always* donates in her mother's memory." Nana pauses to give me a look that says, *Do the math, Ian.*

That's when it all sinks in. I look back at Nana, and she nods her head in agreement to my unspoken conclusion.

"I see you've put the pieces of the sad puzzle together. That, young man, is what they call a tragedy."

I rub my hands over my face as a way of trying to clear my head. "A tragedy, indeed. And you are suggesting that I'm some kind of reminder of her father's infidelity that was ultimately the cause of her mother's death."

"I believe so, Ian. You said yourself that she is clearly affected by you, deeply at that. Her feelings for you probably terrify her. Can you imagine the effect of all this on a teenager, the impression left in her mind and the pain left in her heart? My God, it's a wonder she functions as well as she does." Nana shakes her head, and I can tell she is genuinely sad for Charlotte. I wish I could bring her here. Something tells me Nana would be a good friend to her, one she could probably use after all these years.

"That is quite some investigative work you've done here, Nana." I get up and walk over to the bar to fix us each a scotch. "I went to see Charlotte after the meeting. I asked her if she would have lunch with me tomorrow."

Nana smiles at that; I do not. I've just had a major dose of reality handed to me, and for the first time in my life, I am extremely pissed off at myself. "She was very reluctant to accept. She told me that she has trust issues and that I haven't given her any reason to trust me." I can hear the misery in my own voice. "Seems I'm off to a *very bad* start considering everything you've just told me. My arrogance may have destroyed any chance of ever being with her. I may never be able to break through; she may never look at me as worthy. The thought of it fucking kills me, Nana."

"Ian, dear, whatever you did to make her not trust you probably has more to do with her not trusting herself, and now you can understand why. Don't expect it to be easy. It shouldn't be, otherwise it would be like everything else, and where is the value in that? Fate has a way of making sure you don't take true love for granted."

Surprised, I look up from the glass in my hand and laugh. "Are you telling me I'm in love with Charlotte?"

With a sweet smile and knowing eyes, she responds, "No. *You* just told me that you are."

THIRTEEN
CHARLOTTE

After tossing and turning all night, *not* due to erotic threesome dreams, I decided to sleep in and take the morning off for the first time in a long time. Apparently, two dates in one day, each with a different guy, was too much for my conscience to deal with, even though I keep telling myself that neither is really a *date*. It doesn't matter what I call it, though. I was extremely nervous about having lunch with Ian, and I couldn't shake the guilt of leaving there and joining Gabriel for my next meal. It rotated in my head for hours until finally, Sibel chimed in with a sleepy, *Just change your date with the hot Brazilian guy to another night and go back to sleep, dammit.* That seemed to do the trick, and I fell back asleep around 3 a.m. Now I hope it works that well in reality.

Me: Good morning, Gabriel. I apologize, but would it be all right if we move dinner to tomorrow or Saturday? Something has come up for this evening.

That seems generic and polite enough. Now I can focus on the fact that I'm having lunch with the man that twists me inside out and backwards with just the look on his face and the smell of his skin. This would be the same man that I've *repeatedly* committed myself to avoiding, yet manages to be standing right in the middle of my path at every turn. I knew that once his meeting was history, he would find new excuses to see me. I just didn't expect it to be the *next* day with me sitting across a table from him sharing conversation and *getting to know each other*.

Walking over to the console table under my TV, I pick up Ian's drawing. I look at it every day, several times a day. I can't help myself, even though I get a strange swirling in my gut when I think about the fact that he actually created it and was able to draw emotion into it—the confidence her posture exudes that, in turn, makes her sensual beyond her feminine naked form. She knows she is powerful, she isn't afraid of it, she embraces it and encourages you to embrace it, as well. I love it. More than I care to admit.

He said this was his vision of me, but I don't see myself as I see her. Yet I do have a deep connection with her...and then I think I've lost it because she is a drawing. Setting it back down, I huff out a laugh. I shouldn't be surprised at this point. Everything that involves Ian McAlistair is blanketed with mystery and confusion.

Right then, my phone pings.

Gabriel: Good morning, my dear Charlotte. I am disappointed this evening will not work for you, but I understand. Friday will not work for me, so I will look forward to seeing you again Saturday evening. I will be in touch with details. I want to pick a place you are sure to love.

Wow, he's so polite it's almost awkward. I wonder if he is like that all the time or if maybe he's trying harder because of the whole culture, language barrier. It's charming, no doubt, but a little bit goes a long way nowadays. Too much and it starts to seem phony. It doesn't really matter. Gabriel is a distraction—a sweet and kind one that will hopefully keep me from becoming obsessed with Ian and the adrenaline rush that courses through my body whenever he's around.

Me: Okay great! See you Saturday. Thank you!

Once again, generic and polite.

Finishing my second cup of coffee, I'm ready for a quick workout before I get ready. I'm hoping that will get more energy flowing since I missed my morning sunrise. Plus, it should help get rid of the butterflies I get every time I think about sitting down with Ian, face to face.

What am I supposed to talk about with him? He's so distracting it's hard to keep a clear head, yet I'm supposed to come up with random conversation and act like he didn't pleasure me in the most intimate way possible...standing in a parking lot...before I even knew his name. I think I'd rather take Gabriel's overly sweet, borderline annoying charm over whatever the hell it is that happens when Ian is around. I'm starting to think I should have told him *no*.

Right as I'm getting ready to jump on my treadmill, my phone pings again. When I see Ian's name, my heart drops and my stomach does a flip. *Why, why, why does that happen? I can't stand it!*

Ian: Good morning, Charlotte. I hope you slept well last night. Admittedly, I did not. Although, I wouldn't say it's a bad thing because I spent the entire night thinking about you. The only downside was that it made the time tick by slowly, which was like torture considering how much I am looking forward to seeing you today. I chose the Four Seasons' main restaurant, EDGE, as our crowded venue. I suspect you will recommend meeting me there, but I ask that you reconsider and allow me to pick you up and properly escort you myself. It seems terribly impersonal to do otherwise.

Staring at my phone, I drop into the nearest chair and put my forehead on my hand. What. The. Hell? Even his goddamn texts make my heart pound and bring on that all-too-familiar sensation of the floor disappearing from under my feet. I read it again, then one more time...slowly. It's charming, but in a sexy, commanding, Ian McAlistair kind of way.

He stayed up all night thinking about me? And unapologetically told me about it! What am I supposed to say to that? *I actually did, too. But it was due to guilt because I stupidly accepted a dinner invitation from your new business partner?* I need to write back and cancel. I should have stuck to my original plan because my heart is not going to end up intact when Ian is done. Jesus! That text alone is enough to make me fall for him! And what is his end game? It's not going to be happily ever after, that's for sure!

I want to call Erika, but she can't be my crutch for everything. I'm twenty-eight years old, for Christ's sake! Pacing around the room, arms waving, I talk to myself for a few more minutes before I respond.

Me: Hi Ian, I'm sorry. I have to cancel. Something came up. I'll be in touch.

Delete

Me: Hi Ian. You overwhelm me and I don't think I can handle being alone with you, even in a crowded restaurant. I have to cancel.

Delete

Me: Hi Ian. In an effort to save myself from tragic heartbreak, I need to avoid you for all eternity. So I have to cancel.

Delete

Dammit, dammit, dammit.

Me: Good morning, Ian. That's seems like a long night, indeed. You must be exhausted. We can reschedule for another day if you need to rest.

That's a nice setup for an out. But something tells me the outcome I'm hoping for won't come to fruition.

Ian: Nice try, beautiful. Not happening, though. I'll pick you up at The Clara Sea or the front door of your building at noon. Just let me know which one.

Ugh! Arrogant...as I expected.

Me: Okay, then. I guess I don't need to tell you my home address since you've already stalked that information. Or should I say, you had Jackson stalk that information.

Ian: All that matters is that I know where to find you. See you at noon.

"Well!! Just take over my world, Ian...no big deal! I don't know what *your* address is, jerk! Shouldn't I be disturbed about that? A little worried that you're a weirdo or something?"

Yelling at the phone only makes me feel moderately in control. Cancelling lunch would make me feel fully in control, but something tells me he'll show up at my *actual* front door, to which he probably has a fucking key, and waltz right in, throw me over his shoulder, and take me to lunch. *Bloody hell!*

Nixing the exercise that was supposed to rejuvenate me, I head to my closet to find something to wear. I'll fix him... I'm going to look and smell so good, he won't be able to think straight for the next three days. Two can play this game! The sad part is, he's not playing a game. I'm starting to learn this is *how* he is and ohhh, how I wish it repulsed me.

I take my time getting ready since the morning is dragging on and making me more edgy. I decide to wear a long sleeve, off-the-shoulder fitted dress. It's solid slate gray, which is one of my best colors. It's casual but nice, and I pair it with neutral strappy heels that are high but not slutty. My only jewelry is a turquoise bracelet and earrings set Uncle James gave me for my twenty-fifth birthday. It's handmade by a Navajo artist and is my absolute favorite, and since turquoise is said to hold the power of protection, it seems befitting that I wear it today.

Standing in front of the mirror, I assess the finished product. My hair is down with a loose wave, my makeup is neutral except for my lips which I decided to accentuate with a dark mauve tone that pops against the gray of my dress. I think I've done pretty well. Hopefully Ian thinks so, too, and has difficulty concentrating and feels like he's the one falling off a cliff...a thought that makes me laugh.

I send a quick pic to Erika just for fun and to get some ego-boost reinforcement. My pose is overexaggerated, lips pursed for a kiss, and I'm holding up two fingers for the peace sign.

Erika: Damn girl! I thought you were trying to get rid of him?? You won't accomplish it looking like that...he's never going to leave you alone after today!

Me: Haha! This is my revenge for the text he sent me this morning.

Erika: Yeah? What was it...him standing in the mirror naked with a semi?

Me: Lmao! How do you always manage to take us back to the gutter?

Erika: Hey, don't knock the gutter. There is a lot of fun to be had there! Made you laugh didn't it?

I throw my head back, laughing out loud. No matter how low she goes, she always manages to make it funny. To me, at least.

Me: It did. But it also left a spectacular vision in my head that I DON'T need right now! Thanks!

Erika: That reminds me, I never got a report on the juicy threesome dream with you in a hot man sandwich. Don't be holdin' out on me!

Me: Wtf?? Don't make me laugh! It's going to mess up my makeup! A hot man sandwich?? That is so lame it's hilarious!

Erika: It gets the point across. Give me some deets!

Me: The only deets I have on that front is that I cancelled tonight with Gabriel and rescheduled for Saturday. I couldn't follow through with two dates in one day. Don't give me shit about it...I feel so much better now. Way too much pressure.

Erika: I get it. No shit giving here. You don't need any added stress for lunch with Magic Mike. You'll be busy enough dodging his magic fingers and spontaneous orgasms.

Me: Stop! Lol! I have to go, MM is going to be here soon. I'll call you later.

Erika: Pins and needles!!

Putting my phone in my purse, I go to the mirror to check my mascara and make sure the tears didn't smudge it. All good. I take a deep breath, shake off some of the nerves, and head to the elevator. It's a long ride down from the fourteenth floor as I continue my steady breathing and try not to make a big deal out of seeing Ian any second.

None of that really mattered, because once I made it halfway through the lobby I could see him outside, right in front of the two glass doors at the main entrance, casually leaning against his car. He looks amazing in a pair of dark jeans that couldn't possibly fit more perfectly and an untucked fitted white dress shirt with some kind of detail along the outside edge next to the buttonholes. As I get closer I can see his shoes are over-the-top sexy in a brown that is a little darker than the detail in his shirt. And those sunglasses... *Damn.* He looks like he stepped right out of a magazine ad. I wish I could take a picture without him knowing and send it to Erika. She would die! That silly thought makes me laugh at myself and in turn, relaxes me enough to walk out the door confidently and greet Ian with a smile.

"Hi!" I say and look to either side where I see people looking in our direction, most likely wondering who the hell he is, looking like that and driving that car. "You're drawing a lot of attention out here."

He doesn't bother looking around to confirm my assessment. *His* attention is fully on me, and its potency has piqued a self-awareness that wasn't there before. Like the wind across my shoulders, my hair tickling my skin as it glides across. The tightness of my dress and how it moves with my body, soft and stretching. The heaviness of my bracelet, the slight discomfort of the straps on my heels. When he takes his glasses off and I see the desire in his eyes, it takes every ounce of composure I have to stand in front of him and not turn back to the safety of my condo, because in that moment *my* awareness is fully focused on the weight of my breasts and my traitorous nipples that have become painfully hard.

I have an urge to put my head down in shame, feeling wanton and undignified. This is why I can't stand being around him. I have no clue who I am when he is near, and it totally wrecks my self-confidence. Thankfully Sibel, who has confidence in spades, jumps up, gracefully rebounds into a swan dive down my spine, and straightens it with a fortifying burst of strength.

Her timing couldn't have been better, because right then, Ian reaches up with his right hand placing it gently on the side of my neck. His palm is just under my ear, his thumb following the line of my jaw up to my cheekbone. His fingers reach around the back of my neck into my hairline, warm and strong. He moves forward, and I'm afraid he's going to kiss me on the lips. Instead, he brings his mouth to my left ear, our cheeks softly touching, and says on a deep whisper, "Don't be afraid, Charlotte." Then he kisses me below my temple.

It's like my body is floating and my mind's gone hazy. I'm surrounded by his scent, the heat of his body, the slight touch of his hand, and it's not enough. I want more. And it does scare me, beyond words. But how does he know?

Leaning back enough to see his eyes, I try to sound confident. "Why do you think I'm afraid?" Looking at him this close, his expression, the depth in his stare, I suddenly have the urge to touch him. To lean into him and press my lips to his.

"Because I see it in your eyes and I can sense when you try to shut down your response to me. It's a pattern I've come to recognize." Moving his hand from my neck, he softly glides his thumb across my cheek, eyes roaming over the details of my face, a slow smile forming on his lips. "But I'd rather not talk about that right now, my bewitching faerie, or you might turn around and leave me here, desperate and wanting to peel off my own skin...like you always do." He accentuates that last comment with a raised brow that's almost like a reprimand. Regardless, it's still unbelievably sexy, and I'm still unbelievably high on the scent of him.

Trying to play it cool, I reply with, "Peeling off your own skin seems a bit extreme, don't you think?" I smile, hoping he will become a little less serious.

He steps back, giving me some breathing room. Yet he's more serious when he responds. "No. Actually, I don't. You have a very powerful effect on me, Charlotte LeFay." With that, he turns to open my door. A perfect gentleman in every way.

Except I know what lies beneath. I know what he wants, and I know the havoc he is capable of wreaking on my heart. I have to keep my wits about me, don't let him break through the armor that protects it, and get through lunch.

FOURTEEN

IAN

I close the door for Charlotte once she is comfortably seated and make my way around the front of the car, trying not to run so I can quickly get in and lock the door before she decides to disappear on me again. The woman has me paranoid with her propensity to turn on a dime and bolt from the scene, be it physically or mentally.

When she walked out the door looking more beautiful than I have ever seen her, in a dress that shows off every incredible detail of her body and a smile that was enough to bring me to my knees, a flood of desire came over me that was so powerful it drowned out everything but her. No wind, no birds, no pedestrians, no cars passing…just her. It was a singular moment, one that will be etched in my mind forever. I am now fully convinced that she has placed some kind of spell on me. I just wish she would open her mind, let down her walls, and explore the possibilities therein.

She responded to my explosive reaction immediately. It's the same response she had the very first time we laid eyes on each other, and it has to be the most spectacular thing I have ever witnessed. To watch her body become aware of me, of my need to touch her and pleasure her. She doesn't realize it—her submission. It's like she's programmed to do so the instant she senses my presence. It triggers a reaction in me that is so powerful, keeping it under control almost hurts. To stand there, doing nothing while I watch her desire blossom and spread throughout her body, ending with her nipples stiffening and screaming for me to abuse them the way I know brings her the ultimate release, is a form of torture that has me on the verge of begging for mercy. I am not accustomed to this kind of restraint.

Predictably, when her conscious mind catches on to what is happening, her fear takes over and she shuts down. Leaving me in worse condition than the description I gave her just moments ago. But she's here now, and I'm going to make a concerted effort to keep her from fleeing. Now that I know why she runs, why she is afraid of me, why she's built such solid reinforcements around herself, my approach is more compassionate. Adding to my list of challenges, I now have an overwhelming need to protect her and repair the damage caused by her father's indiscretions.

Getting in the driver's seat, I close the door only to be bombarded by her scent and the energy surrounding her. It feels like it's attached to a fucking homing device inside my body. I turn and look at her as I start the engine. "Just out of curiosity, do you have any idea how stunning you are?"

She's nervous, I can tell, but my compliment makes her smile. Making her smile has become my latest addiction. I intend to do it often.

"Stunning? I don't know if I'd go that far," she says with slight sarcasm, and it's fucking adorable. "Although, I did put a little extra effort into my appearance today." She gives me a sideways glance accompanied by a pursed smirk, and I can tell she's being playful. I love it.

"Did you, now? If you were trying to impress me, it worked," I say, attempting to keep it light and not tell her she looks good enough to eat...right here in the goddamn car.

"Actually, I wasn't trying to impress you. It was more along the lines of revenge."

Hmmm…that was a compliment if I'm not mistaken.

"Revenge, is it? So it was your vindictive intent to blow my mind when you walked out the door. Hoping to keep me distracted and unable to think straight through lunch…eh? How clever of you." Little vixen.

"Yes…but my intention was to blow your mind, keep you distracted and unable to think straight for the *next three days,* not simply through lunch." With that straightforward declaration, she gives me a playful wink that has me ready to pull the car over, drag her into my lap, and kiss her until neither of us can breathe.

"Well, you'll be happy to know that you've exceeded your expectations… I will *never* be able to erase the image of how beautiful you are today, Charlotte." I want to tell her that my eyes see her as a beauty that cannot be perfected, for it has already surpassed perfection, but she might misinterpret my honesty as poetic flattery. She doesn't understand how she affects me or even why, and the innocence of her power is disarming.

"Then perhaps we're even," I hear her say under her breath as she turns her head and looks out her window.

Her mood is shifting. She doesn't like it when I compliment her that way. The truth is, she probably loves it when I compliment her that way, she just doesn't trust the way it makes her feel or my intentions in saying it.

Ever since my conversation with Nana last night, I am able to read her more accurately. Her reactions make sense now, no matter how misplaced they may be.

Changing the subject so I don't lose her completely, I ask, "Have you been to EDGE at the Four Seasons before?"

"Yes, I love it. That was a great choice. They have a ceviche that's to die for." She's back to smiling; neutral conversation will have to do for now.

"Excellent! We're almost there. Are you hungry?" I say as I

downshift into a turn.

"Yes, especially now that we're talking about award-winning ceviche."

I have a sudden urge to take her to every five-star restaurant in the world to get ceviche. I think Jackson's right—when I finally scale the walls of her fortress, I will never want to leave.

Pulling into the portico, I put the car in park as the valet approaches to open her door. I would have preferred to be the one holding her hand to help her out of the car, but it would have seemed strange to request it. I don't get the chance to hold the door for her, either, as the doorman does his job, but I gesture for her to enter first so she, as Jackson put it, *knows I'm capable of being a gentleman.*

Walking to the entrance of the restaurant, I can't help but put my hand on the small of her back. It may be going too far, but right now I don't care because I've already spotted five different men staring her down like a predator to prey, and something tells me she's oblivious.

After a personal—albeit nervous—greeting from the hostess, we are seated at a table that isn't what I'd consider private, but it's not in the middle of the damn restaurant, either. Before we sit down, I give Charlotte a sarcastic look and hold out my hand as if to say, *Does this meet your criteria?*

She laughs. Then, rolling with the punches, she says with a shrug, "It'll do."

The waiter brings us water, and I take the liberty of ordering us a bottle of white wine. I can tell Charlotte is skeptical as her eyes shift from the waiter to the table then back again. Yet she doesn't refuse. After he's returned and filled our glasses, I order us both a ceviche. Winking at her, I jokingly say, "I was going to get one to share but reconsidered, thinking it may have done in any chance I had at impressing you."

She laughs out loud. "Smart man. Unlike most women, I am not afraid to eat. I intend to take full advantage of your invitation."

God, she's amazing.

"And just for the record, you've already impressed me, so you don't need to keep trying."

"Oh? You're surprisingly full of compliments today. We're five minutes into our lunch date, and you're already impressed to the point I no longer need to try. You're not setting me up for disaster, are you?" I give her a look filled with skepticism.

She laughs again, and the pleasure of hearing it makes the hair on my neck stand. Reaching for her wine, she holds it up, proposing a toast. "To reverse psychology."

Bringing my glass up to hers, I still play like I'm skeptical of her motives, even if I know she's only teasing. "To reverse psychology."

We each take a sip and set down our glasses, but she continues holding the stem of hers, swirling the wine around in the glass. She stares at it a few more seconds as a smile appears on her beautiful mouth. This one, however, is not mischievous; it's tender and endearing. When she looks back up at me, her eyes are soft with deep emotion.

"I'm referring to my portrait. Being impressed...I mean." She looks down again, almost shyly. "I love it...very much. It just..." She looks up at me and laughs. "See! I'm still speechless over it!"

My heart is pounding. I wasn't expecting her to say that, and the smile on her face has me wanting to fill a room with portraits of her. She really does love it—I can see it in her eyes, and all I can think is that I want her to think of me that way. I want to reach across the table and touch her. I want to kiss her, to hold her in my arms and beg her to trust me.

"It makes me very happy that you feel that way. I was actually nervous about giving it to you. I haven't drawn anything in quite a while, and even though I thought it was beautiful, I wasn't sure if you would think so." I can hear the shyness in my own voice. Normally that would bother me, but sitting here with Charlotte, knowing the raw truth in her words, makes it okay.

"I can't imagine anyone *not* thinking it's amazing. And I'm beyond flattered at your impression of me. Of course, some people might think it's inappropriate... She is naked, after all." Her cheeks flush pink, complementing the shy look on her face. "I think she's very beautiful, Ian, and it's deeper than just physical. It's as if you gave her emotions and strength...a soul." She pauses, shaking her head. "I hope you don't think I'm crazy for saying that."

All I can do is stare at her. She sees the meaning in the drawing, but not herself. "You are everything you see in that drawing and more, Charlotte." I can't help reaching over and curling my fingers around hers, rubbing them gently with my thumb. I probably shouldn't have done that, because she's looking at our hands and her expression has suddenly shifted to that of fear, and it isn't superficial. She does fine with harmless banter back and forth, but when it runs deeper, she shuts the door.

I'm saved by the waiter as he brings our ceviche and places them in front of us. I let go of her hand without a word, hoping the thick tension surrounding us is short-lived.

We thank the waiter, pick up our forks, and dive in. It's delicious with the perfect balance of salt and lime, not too much onion or pepper, and plenty of fresh fish. The look of pleasure on Charlotte's face as she tastes her first bite sends a jolt of arousal down my spine and straight to my cock. I quickly look down at the bowl in front of me so she can't see any evidence of what came over me, and I pray she can't sense it, either. I have a vision of her excusing herself from the table and not returning. Shifting the conversation to something generic, I compliment the dish and she wholeheartedly agrees. From there, we move on to safer ground.

After placing our orders for the main course and finishing our first glass of wine, we easily keep the conversation flowing with questions about each other's career. I am impressed with her background. She worked to get where she is as the general manager of a five-star resort, regardless of who owns it. She clearly earned her position. I take a sip of wine, not taking my eyes off her as she animatedly talks about her excellent employees, potential renovations, board members with no foresight, and ideas for the future that will keep The Clara Sea's five-star ranking for a long time running. I am enjoying this more than I anticipated. She is fascinating. *My God! Look at her!* Her slender hands helping her tell her story, moving here and there, fingers acting out little details. She smiles a lot when she's talking and every now and again she pulls her hair over her shoulder, only to brush it back over minutes later.

"Tell me about your business. Surely that's enough about me."

Ah...no. Should I tell her I could sit and listen to her talk about herself for days? Probably not. "What would you like to know?"

"Hmmm...lets go with the obvious...how did you create such a successful development firm?" And so I told her and found that she is genuinely interested in my business and what I've dedicated so much of myself to. She continues asking smart questions, comes up with accurate conclusions, and is inquisitive about things she doesn't know or understand. I'm finding her to be an enchanting conversationalist and am thoroughly enjoying myself. It appears Charlotte is, too, as her demeanor is relaxed while she is smiling and laughing with ease.

She takes the liberty of pouring us each another glass of wine, which finishes off the bottle, then surprises me with, "So a little birdie told me that your favorite person in the world is your grandmother. Is that true?" She looks proud at having that card up her sleeve.

I wonder why Jackson told her that? Probably an attempt at boosting my character after my monumental fuckup of an introduction.

I chuckle, "Jackson told you that, did he? Did he also tell you she's one of *his* favorite people in the world, too? Nana is quite special to me, yes. I'm closer to her than I am to my parents, whom I love and respect. We just don't have the same connection that Nana and I have. She's my grandmother, but she's also my friend. I think you would like her very much." I have every intention of introducing them, preferably soon.

"That's very sweet, Ian. How lucky you are to have her in your life." I can tell she's happy for me, but I also see the sadness behind her words.

"My uncle James is like a father to me, but he travels a lot and has a home in France, so I don't get to see him that much. He has four other resorts in various countries around the world. But we talk all the time." She pauses. I know she's thinking about her parents and how they have obviously been left out of the conversation.

She probably assumes I'll ask about them, so instead of waiting for that awkward moment, she tries to brush past it. "My father passed away when I was seventeen. James is his brother. He's been like a father to me ever since. My mother passed away a week after I turned twenty. It was a rough few years, and I don't know how I would have made it through without him. He's very special to me."

It doesn't go unnoticed that she made that statement more about her uncle than her parents. Out of respect, my response is short but sincere.

"That's terrible, Charlotte. I'm so sorry." I reach over and squeeze her hand, as a show of sympathy more than anything else. "I can tell by the look on your face that you don't want to talk about it, so I won't ask. Should you ever want to, though, I'd be happy to listen."

She gives me a look that says she appreciates me not prying further.

"Thank you for that, Ian. I'd rather talk about Nana, anyway. I assume she lives nearby?"

"Yes. I surprised her three years ago with a townhouse on the water. I like to spoil her because she makes such a big deal out of it and acts like she's mad at me for doing too much, but the happy gleam in her eyes always gives her away." Thinking of Nana's antics brings on an uncontrollable smile. "She's a character, though. Hopefully when you meet her she doesn't pop out with some inappropriate question that pertains to sex or something else extremely personal."

The look on Charlotte's face is one of disbelief.

"I'm not joking. She's a tiny eighty-eight-year-old woman with the sweetest voice and biggest heart, but she loves to talk trash." Both of us laugh at the absurdity of it, transitioning us away from the sad subject of her parents.

"There is something adorable about that. She should meet my best friend, Erika. She's the queen of trash talk. They'd probably keep each other in stitches for hours." She reaches into her purse to look at her phone, then her eyes widen. "Ian! It's almost 3:30! Oh, my gosh, I can't believe how much time has passed. I really need to stop by my office for at least a few hours today. I'm sorry, but I really have to go."

She's antsy, and I can't tell if it's because her story's true or that she's shocked she just spent three and half hours with me and that's well past her limit.

"Of course. Would you like me to take you directly to the resort? I can send a driver to escort you home later." *Or maybe show up there myself, drive you to the airport, put you on my plane, and hold you captive in the Bahamas for two weeks.*

"No. That's not necessary. Really. But thank you." She starts to gather her things and stands. "I don't want to burden anyone, and plus, I'm a bit of a control freak and prefer to have my own car available when I need it."

She doesn't realize that one innocent statement has set my blood on fire with need. She also has no idea how liberating it will be when she hands over that control and lets me take her mind, body, and soul to places she doesn't know exist. I am hoping today was a step in that direction.

FIFTEEN

CHARLOTTE

Leaving the restaurant, I can tell something has shifted in Ian. He seems wound up all of a sudden, agitated, and I assume it's because I've abruptly cut our lunch short.

Truthfully, there was nothing short about it. I don't know how three and half hours passed by so fast, and since I had my ringer off, I missed several calls and probably a dozen texts. A quick glance showed none were emergencies, thank God.

As we approach the car, Ian hurries to my door and opens it for me. It almost appeared he was trying to get there before the valet. The thought of it makes me want to laugh, it's so cute. I don't though, offering a sincere "thank you" instead.

On the way back to my condo, I'm at ease enough to enjoy the ride more so than earlier when my nerves were fried. His car is beyond amazing. The leather seats are soft, creamy beige with dark stitching that complement the black and brushed metal surrounding us. The dash is completely uncluttered, although the console between us appears extremely high tech and very important. *Like James Bond important*, I joke to myself. It's masterfully created, and I'd say he definitely got his money's worth.

Watching him drive it is a whole other experience. I'm

tempted to shoot a quick video of him and send it to the head of Lamborghini and tell them I found the guy for their next ad. He is, hands down, the sexiest man I've ever seen, and how I managed to pique his interest is something I still can't wrap my head around.

To make matters worse, I truly enjoyed lunch, minus a few tense moments where things got a little deep. But I've come to expect that with Ian.

The drive to my place is short and the small talk neutral, but I can sense something is different. I'm not going to push it, because it ultimately doesn't matter. I'm still not going to allow myself to start seeing him, especially after today. He keeps adding more reasons to easily fall for him, and it makes me wonder how long the trail of hearts is he's left behind. Probably miles.

As he pulls up to the front doors, I go to let myself out, but he puts his hand on my arm and says, "Please, allow me." A few seconds later, he opens my door, holding out his hand to assist me. It's warm and sends a tickling sensation up my arm and into my chest. As soon as I can let go, I do. Now we are at the awkward "Goodbye" moment, and I hope he doesn't try to kiss me. I'd probably melt into a puddle right here on the pavement.

"Thank you, Ian. That was an excellent lunch. I enjoyed it very much." I'm suddenly nervous because there is so much more to say, but I can't. Plus, I can sense the tension in him, and it makes me wonder what's going through his mind.

"You're welcome, Charlotte. Thank you for joining me. I had a wonderful time. Though I may not be able to concentrate for the rest of the day as I sit in a daze replaying our conversations over and over." He finishes with a smile that is almost sad, making my lungs tight with emotion. He's so open with his compliments, yet I can tell it's not everything he wants to say. I can't help but wonder what the hell he would say if he felt he could speak openly.

"Surely you'll be too busy to sit in a daze. You did just land a major project that needs to get started." I try to be light and steer this goodbye away from his intensity. No luck there—he's always foiling my attempts to keep things from getting too heavy.

"You truly have no idea how spectacular you are or the effect you have on me, do you? I find it both endearing and maddening all at once." He takes a step closer and my heart rate increases. He takes my hand, holding it gently and stares at me.

This is where I start to panic because the ground has been yanked out from under me.

He continues. "Would you do me the honor of joining me for dinner tomorrow night?"

I knew this was going to happen, and that's why I didn't want to go down this path. Now I've opened the door for him to pursue me as his latest conquest. I should have played dumb at lunch or been shallow and talked about his money the whole time. Something I would never lower myself to doing, but these are special circumstances.

I don't want to tell him no while we're face to face because he'll undoubtedly convince me to go anyway just like he did in my office yesterday. I keep the ball in my court by saying, "That sounds nice, Ian. Let me check my schedule and see what's going on. I'll text you and let you know." I try to look in his eyes but have to look away because I can tell he's on to me, and he is *not* happy about it. I need to make my exit. "Thank you, again. I really have to run, but I'll be in touch." I don't know whether to shake his hand or give him a hug. Neither seems like the right thing, so I opt for a touch on the arm. He doesn't say anything, just gives me a quick nod and turns back to his car.

As I open the door to my building, I hear his car roar down the driveway. Once inside, I turn to see him take off onto A1A, tires screeching. I stand there for a minute longer, feeling guilty, sad, and a little angry with myself. Why the hell can't I be more carefree about this whole thing with Ian? I know my body would surely love the opportunity to jump in bed with him and have mind-blowing sex for days. But my stupid brain has been programmed to not allow a man like him anywhere close...just in case my heart gets involved. Since Ian practically gives me a daily dose of reasons to fall head over heels for him, I'm forced to keep myself at a safe distance. Where I'm protected.

Back inside my condo, I call Erika, as promised. I think she actually answered before it rang.

"I want every detail and don't hold back. But first, give me a sneak peek...any surprise orgasms?" I can tell she's got people nearby because she's talking under her breath.

"Give me some credit, Erika. You know I wasn't about to let that happen *again*. We had a really nice time and an excellent lunch. He picked me up, of course, and took me to EDGE at the Four Seasons. As you know, it's one of my favorite restaurants—score one for Ian."

"What's this *really nice time* crap? That's not what I've been waiting around all day for! You've got to have something better than that."

"Oh, lighten up, smut queen. The unfortunate truth is that I thoroughly enjoyed myself, and there are more reasons than I care to acknowledge that classify him as the perfect guy. Except for the most important one."

"Which is?"

"Guys that look like him, act like him...ugh! That *smell* like him and are stupidly successful have way too many temptations offered up on silver platters. I could never hold a candle to the stunning women I've seen him photographed with. I'm too vulnerable with Ian, and I know it. I can't be blatantly stupid, ya know? I know better than anyone the dangers of falling for a guy like him."

"Charlotte, I get what you're saying. But I can't help thinking you're making a mistake. You can't make Ian pay for your dad's indiscretions. And, honey, you can't avoid potential happiness because of your mother's weakness. That's simply not living a full life. Surely that's not what you want."

Ugh...she's about ready to make me cry. "I understand what you're saying, but for right now, I don't know any other way to be. I'm not ready to step outside my safety zone. Okay?"

"Okay...I'm sorry. I wasn't trying to push. I just wanted to give you some food for thought because I love you."

"I love you, too. And I'll think about what you said. In the meantime, I've got to go to work for a while. I haven't been there at all today, and I really need to check in on things."

"Yeah, I've got to get back to correcting problems created by other people's stupidity. Remember that chick that works here I told you about? The one that thinks she's God's gift to humanity and has the worst taste in wardrobe? Well, we've got a huge presentation tomorrow and she's got it so jacked up, I may be here all night fixing it. I'm definitely getting her ass fired over this one."

"Wow...that stinks. If I can do anything to help, let me know. Even if it's to bring you dinner or something."

"Thanks, babe. I'll let you know. *Muah!*"

Hanging up, I gather a few things before heading out the door. I'm so preoccupied I'm afraid I'm forgetting something. Thinking about Ian and the conversation I had with Erika is causing a train wreck in my head. I know she's right, and there is a big part of me that wants to text Ian right now and tell him, yes...I'd love to go to dinner, every night for the next month. But then I think about my mother and how her vibrancy and will to live simply disintegrated from a broken heart. The sudden pain in my stomach is almost unbearable. Ian has forced me to visit the ghosts of my past, on a daily basis, bringing to the surface a vulnerability I thought I had finally worked through.

Back at the resort, I find Tracy practically wearing out the carpet with her pacing. "Good afternoon, Tracy. What's got you so wound up? I didn't get any emergency calls so it can't be that bad."

"Oh, hey...there you are! No emergencies. Just busy and didn't think you'd be gone so long. Not that you can't take a day off, of course. I'm better at dealing with order and not chaos. I've barely had a chance to come up for air all day. I've always respected you, but when I have to wear your shoes, I respect you even more. I've never even seen you break a sweat!" She's so flustered it's almost funny. Tracy is great at keeping things in order, but for some reason she doesn't accept she's very good at dealing with chaos, too. I think it's when the dust settles and she analyzes everything that happened she gets wound up. Luckily, I know this about her, and I know how to get her feet back on solid ground.

Once we're in my office, I sit at my desk as Tracy takes her usual spot in front of me. "Okay. So give me the rundown of today's chaos. Should I pop some popcorn? Is it that good?"

When she looks up, a little confused, she sees me laughing. She laughs too, pushes up her glasses, and starts going through the day's events. This is where she is comfortable. Giving me a detailed blow-by-blow of everything from employee issues, maintenance updates, guest complaints, compliments and suggestions, and so on. It seems she handled things perfectly, and I tell her so. After I give her solutions to a few problems she wasn't comfortable handling herself, she leaves, and I get to my email that is unsurprisingly full.

The next few hours are spent returning phone calls, texts, and emails, going through mail, and other monotonous routines that would typically be spread throughout the day. Sitting back in my chair, I rub my neck and shoulders, trying to release the tension that isn't entirely from sitting at my computer too long. One more day and I'll have a weekend to regroup and clear my head.

Except I have to go out to dinner with Gabriel. *Damn.* Part of me wants to cancel, but that would be rude on a level I'm not comfortable with. Plus, it will be good to have Novas Alturas as a friend. That kind of networking is excellent for The Clara Sea. I'll go and enjoy myself, but will avoid doing so again, should he ask. I really need time to absorb everything that's happening with Ian and what my feelings truly are for him. I keep trying to deny it, but something is there, something deep that is both intriguing and completely terrifying.

Tracy knocks at the door and pops her head in. "Hey. Something just arrived for you."

Looking up, I see her mischievous smile, and it awakens the butterflies in my stomach. I have a suspicion it has something to do with Ian. As she walks toward me holding a beautiful box that is small and rectangular with an elegant finish that looks like antique linen, my heart starts beating faster.

She hands me the box, so light it seems empty. I set it down and stare at it, waiting for Tracy to leave. Her voice sounds like a mumble as she's walking away. I have no idea what she said.

I wait a few seconds longer, hoping whatever's inside doesn't make my heart explode and my body beg to be near him. Wishful thinking, as Ian McAlistair has made it his mission to slowly break me down, piece by piece, until I finally surrender to his will. Inside this simple box, lying on a bed of soft white silk, is a single pink rose, identical to the one I'm holding in his drawing. Its classic, elegant perfume infuses the air around me and permeates another layer of armor protecting my heart.

SIXTEEN

IAN

It's Friday, almost noon. Twenty-four hours ago I was on the proverbial *cloud nine* as I pulled up to Charlotte's condo for what would turn out to be an amazing lunch date, filled with interesting conversation, charming humor, and a blossoming hope that maybe we'd crossed a threshold and could move forward, albeit slowly.

Apparently I was wrong, because she dug her heels in the sand when I asked her to dinner tonight with her bullshit, *let me check my schedule and get back with you,* that actually pissed me off so badly I had to walk away to keep from calling her out. Now I'm stuck here, completely on edge, waiting for her to text me her answer, knowing it's going to be no, yet hoping, almost desperately, that it will be yes.

When I got back to the office yesterday, after I'd calmed down a bit, I did sit in a daze replaying our conversations again and again, as I told her I would. I kept picturing her face in all its expressions…happy, curious, serious, sad, thoughtful—each one beautiful in its own way.

I had never taken the time to observe the nuances of a woman's facial expressions before, other than what I expected to see during sex. Strangely, the effect it had was that it's made me miss her, badly. I wasn't even thinking about all the things I want to do with her physically; all I wanted was to sit and converse with her, watching her emotions shift and change from a breathtaking smile to a shy blush, an eye-opening surprise to sad longing and everything in between. It's like listening to an orchestral film score as it follows along with the story, making it more interesting, exciting, and emotionally provoking.

When I replayed the conversation about the portrait, a happiness swelled inside me. I thought about the deep affection she has for it, like I do, and how it's like a connection between us.

That's when it hit me, the flower…that delicate pink rose that made her smile in my vision. I decided to give her one for real, hoping it would make her smile again.

I wanted to personally choose the flower. It had to be perfect, so calling the florist and placing the order wasn't an option. Luckily, my first stop had what I was looking for. The rose was exactly like the one I drew and was so flawless it almost looked fake. When the woman took it out of the case for me to look at, its scent filled the space around us.

I'm not a big flower person. I know quite little about them and never really bothered to consider how magnificent it could be. Yet that one literally smelled so good it was sensual. I imagined Charlotte's reaction. How it would make her happy, knowing it will make her smile. I pictured her eyes slowly closing as its fragrance surrounded her, having the same *bewitching* effect it had on me.

"This is the one," I told the lady behind the counter.

She smiled and placed it in a beautiful box lined with silk. "You have excellent taste. Bewitched is one of the most popular tea roses out there. Revered for its classic beauty and scent."

I was a little confused. "You said *Bewitched*. Are you saying that's the name of this particular rose? I thought a rose was just a rose. Maybe distinguished by color or something." What the hell do I know?

She laughed. "Roses are big business, Mr. McAlistair. There are actually rose breeders that create hybrids, all of which are given specific names. They can go on to win awards at various shows around the world. It's quite a big deal. This one happens to be named Bewitched. An appropriate name, wouldn't you say?"

I had to laugh and told her, "Yes, and you have no idea how fitting that is for the woman who's about to receive that lovely rose." What are the chances the rose I drew for her, that I found *in the flesh*, per se, is known as Bewitched? I'm looking forward to telling Charlotte that story.

I paid the woman extra to make sure it was delivered right away, and she guaranteed that it would be. Yet I'm beginning to wonder if it had the desired effect, since I still haven't heard from her. I'm tempted to just text her and tell her I'll pick her up at seven. Patience and consideration be damned.

Jackson gives a quick knock and opens the door, and I'm happy for the distraction. "Jackson. How's your Friday going so far?" I say, trying to act normal.

"From the looks of it, better than yours. What's got you so lost in thought? A certain faerie named Charlotte?" He's still thoroughly entertained by my predicament with her. I know why—dear friend that he is, Jackson sees it as a payback of sorts. I look past it, because I'm now seeing that I've had it way too easy for way too long.

"As a matter of fact, yes. I thought yesterday went exceptionally well and was hoping to have a repeat tonight. But she wouldn't commit while we were together. Said she would *let me know*. She hasn't, and it's making me fucking nuts." I'm tapping my finger annoyingly on my desk.

"I told you, you've got your work cut out for you with her. She's more complex than what you're used to. Be patient, man. She'll come around."

At least he seems hopeful.

"After Wednesday's meeting, I stopped by to visit Nana."

I give him an inquisitive look with a raised eyebrow. He looks down in guilt, exactly like his cohort did when I questioned her knowledge of Charlotte's name.

"Mmm hmm...little do you know, she took it upon herself to do some private investigative work on Charlotte. Not because she was being nosy or looking for dirt. It was because she wanted to see if she could connect the dots on why Charlotte is so afraid of her attraction to me."

Jackson's brows pull together. "You must have been having some pretty in-depth conversations with Nana on that topic. Should I be regretting giving up her name?" He doesn't like the idea of potentially betraying Charlotte, but in reality, he didn't. My tenacious grandmother has a way of getting what she wants.

"You know Nana. Nobody reads between the lines like she does. She knew something was up and believes she figured it out."

Jackson's concern is visibly noticeable as his entire face melted, leaving his mouth slightly open. I can practically hear the, *Oh Shit*, that just echoed through his head.

"She found an obituary for Charlotte's father, Michael, which led her to an article about the accident that took his life. He wasn't alone. She made an assumption that the woman with him was his mistress."

Now Jackson's face has transformed to more of a *holy shit* expression. Nana must have been on the right path. "Adding to that tragedy, two years later her mother passes away, but there's no information as to why. Yet Charlotte consistently donates to charities that revolve around drug addiction and rehabilitation...*in* her mother's name."

Gobsmacked would be a good description of him now. "From the look on your face, Nana hit the nail on the head."

"Damn. It never dawned on me that's what Nana was up to, let alone that the information would be out there. I'm impressed, but I also feel guilty because Charlotte trusted me not to say anything."

"You didn't say anything. So don't beat yourself up. If I had any insight and stopped long enough to see past the hard-on I had, I could've easily found the same information. Nana knew what she was doing. All she needed was a name, and Charlotte didn't ask you not to tell anyone that." I give him a look that says, *you know I'm right, so chill.*

"I guess it's better this way. At least now you know what you're dealing with. It's heavy, man. I think she keeps it bottled up inside because when she told me what happened, I could tell she was trying hard not to cry. It was even getting *me* choked up."

It felt like someone kicked me in the stomach. The idea of her hurting like that messes with my head. Who does she turn to? Does she even have anyone to turn to? I would help her if she would simply let me.

"That bothers me more than I care to admit." I can see the sympathy in Jackson's eyes, not only for Charlotte, but for me, as well. That's my cue to change the subject. "Have you reviewed all the contracts with Novas Alturas? I've been through them twice, and it looks good to me."

"Yep. Looks good. T's and i's all properly crossed and dotted. Now comes the fun part," Jackson states sarcastically. He hates dealing with the city, county, and state and all the hoops they make us jump through more than I do. It's a long process before we can get to the actual fun part of putting up an amazing building, then adding the finishing touches.

On a chuckle I say, "Let the schmoozing begin."

To that, I get a deadpan stare that clearly means, *don't remind me.* Neither Jackson nor I are very good at kissing ass. Thankfully, having to do so is a rare occasion, since everyone we deal with has a boss that is a close friend of ours. Regardless, the process is still tedious, and it will likely be a year, if not more, until we can even break ground.

My phone pings. Not wanting to appear overly anxious, I let it sit a minute before checking the message.

*Charlotte: Hi Ian. I won't be able to join you for dinner tonight.
I forgot I made plans with a friend of mine. Thank you for the
invite and thank you, again, for lunch yesterday. Enjoy your
weekend*

The tension that text has triggered throughout my body is
causing a slight headache. It's complete bullshit and generic on a
level that's insulting. Enjoy my weekend? How the hell am I
supposed to do that when I'm not spending it with her? *Dammit!*

Jackson knows what the text says without seeing it. "A no-go
for tonight, eh?"

"Jackson, I kid you not, I am about to get in my car, drive
over to her goddamn office, and kidnap her!" I raise my voice in
frustration. "I know she wants to be with me. I can see it…I can
fucking feel it! God, if she would just give it a chance, she would
know it was meant to be." I slam my phone down, probably
cracking the screen. Rubbing my hand across my face, I blow out
a breath to relieve some of the tension and see Jackson staring at
me, somewhat in shock. "What? Go on…spit it out. I know you
think it's funny."

"No. It's not that I think it's funny. I'm just surprised you're
in this deep. Hell, you've only known of her existence for a week
and you've had pretty limited contact with her, yesterday being
your most extensive. The crazy thing is, I honestly don't think
it's because she's not letting you have what you want. You've got
feelings for her, man. And if you want to get anywhere with her,
you better start being honest…with her *and* yourself."

He's completely serious and probably right. But that kind of
reality is so foreign to me, I don't even know where to begin.

"Unfortunately, I feel like a lumberjack performing brain
surgery and my patient is about to bleed out." I stare at her text
again, wondering what the hell I'm going to say back to her.
Maybe something along the lines of, *I'll be there in ten minutes, be
naked and ready,* would be good.

"I don't know, Jackson. I don't do clumsy very well. I'm used to being steady on my feet with everything I do. This is the first time in my life I've had to tiptoe around, watching everything I say and do. I respect why I have to do it, I'm just not good at it and I'm paranoid as hell that I'm going to make *another* mistake."

Afraid like I'm starting to whine, I cut the conversation short. "I'll figure it out, Jackson. Thanks for listening." With that, I start going through papers on my desk.

"It's all good, man. And don't worry, like I said, she'll come around. Whatever it is that's going on between the two of you is pretty fucking heavy. Seems inevitable to me. Be patient, my friend." He gets up and heads to the door, stopping before he exits. "If you don't end up convincing her to go out with you tonight, come on by my place. Becca and Braden would love to see you."

"Thanks, Jackson. That sounds great. I'll let you know," I answer in a low tone and give a small nod as he walks out the door.

Once I'm alone, I can think about my response. *I told you not to lie to me*, is the first one that comes to mind. *I'll let you off the hook tonight, but tomorrow you're mine*, has a nice ring to it. Or I could ignore her altogether and say, *I'll pick you up at 7*. In the end, I go with my gut.

Me: I would tell you to enjoy your evening and tell your friend I said hello, but I know you are lying to me, again. That's okay, for now.

Do me a favor though. When you're alone tonight, I want you to lie comfortably on your bed, naked, relaxed, eyes closed. Focus on your body, the surface of your skin chilled and exposed. Be with that sensation for a moment. Feel the cool air tighten your nipples and raise the hair on your skin. Then I want you to think about what you feel when we're together, what sensations go through your body when I touch you. The heat that starts low and spreads throughout every cell until it reaches all the way to the tips of your fingers and toes. The vibration that starts at the point of contact, the electricity that lights up inside you, stealing your breath and making your heart beat faster. Be with it, let it expand.

Then I want you to think about what it is you want most in that moment. Be honest with yourself, Charlotte.

I'll be honest with you. What I wanted most in that moment was to have the warmth of your naked body surrounding me, your soft skin like a blanket smothering the chill that has clung to me for what feels like an eternity. Your scent drugging my mind so that all it knows is you, your touch, the kiss of your exquisite mouth, the wetness between your legs guiding me to where I belong. Then, after I make you scream my name as your body writhes and pulsates around me, I do it again and again and again until you have reached the point of pure ecstasy. And when you have enough energy to open your eyes, the first thing you see is me and you finally understand that you are mine.

SEVENTEEN
CHARLOTTE

W hen I get in bed after what seems like an extremely long day, I continue to repeat Ian's text in my head. I must have read the damn thing fifty times, so I've got it memorized.

I should have known it wouldn't be a normal *it's okay, I understand*. No, he has to melt the skin off my body with his sensual meditation exercise that was enough to have me rushing home to do exactly what he said, then break out some toys and thoroughly enjoy myself while imagining what *he* wanted most.

When I read it to Erika, she told me if I didn't put my parent issues aside and *"just fucking go get me some of that,"* she would personally take matters into her own hands by drugging me, tying me up, then calling Ian and telling him to come get me and keep me for a week. Oh…and to fuck some sense into me. Which made me laugh, until I realized she was serious.

The truth is, I didn't even need to go through with his exercise to know the answer. It's right there, clear as day, and it's been there since the moment I laid eyes on him. I want him, badly. I just don't know if I can trust him, which is a deal-breaker for me. Maybe if he hadn't left me humiliated in the parking lot the day we met, after making me feel more alive than I had in over a

THE ESSENCE OF FATE

decade, I would have felt more at ease about his intentions. He said he'll explain it to me someday, but I don't really see how that would make a difference. I was beyond humiliated, I was hurt by what he did, and I'm not sure I can get past it.

To his credit, he has surprised me with his efforts to change my mind. The portrait he drew of me is so special, so meaningful that I probably would have forgiven him if I didn't have *parent issues*. Then yesterday's lunch date was enough to make me at least want to try—until I started to get that falling sensation and I panicked.

Lying between my soft sheets, I adjust to the darkness that turns blue as it mixes with the moonlight. I pull off the sheet that's protecting me from the chill Ian wants me to feel. I don't want to be cold, exposed, vulnerable. But I can't ignore his request. He is an enigma. Everything about him is everything I swore I'd never want, but I cannot deny that something else is there. Something that intrigues not only my curiosity, but very deep emotions I'm not prepared to acknowledge. He stirs something to life inside me that scares me and leaves me yearning, all at once. I need to go through the motions of his exercise to see where it takes me.

My nipples harden and the hair stands on my skin, exactly as he said it would. I don't like the cold, but I stay with it, regardless. I'm surprised to feel movement in the air I thought was still, subtle shifts and waves gliding across my body. I hesitate before letting my mind go to him, still insecure about opening that door. It doesn't matter—he's relentless, even in my mind.

There he is, the masculine beauty of his face stopping my heart, those eyes drawing me in, hypnotizing me, evaporating my armor as a slow smile softens his bold features. Almost instantly, a wave of heat runs through me. It starts in the center of my body and spreads to the extremities. My fingertips are hot, and the back of my neck feels like it would be wet if I touched it.

I don't, though; I keep still, amazed at what is happening to me, simply imagining Ian.

I stay with it, like he said to. I'm not afraid. There is no sensation of falling. I don't want to run. I feel alive as my blood pumps through my heart and rushes out to every limb. It's exhilarating, and in it there is joy, like an explosion through my chest. As I imagine him touching me, his hand on the side of my face, that familiar tickle of electricity flashes through my body, expanding in my core. When his hand glides down my neck, then my chest, and firmly takes hold of my breast...thumb swirling against my hard nipple, my back arches in wanton invitation.

On a startled inhale, my eyes pop open. *My God! What happened to me?* I lie there staring at the ceiling, my breathing heavy, body suddenly cooling in the shifting air. He did it again. He grabbed hold of my mind, my body, my soul, and this time he wasn't even near me. He was able to drive his point home through written words he sent to my phone, words he knew I would obey and he knew what the outcome would be.

Because right now, in this moment, the thing that I want most —so much it almost hurts—is him. I want him touching me, kissing me, bringing me pleasure I know only he can provide. I want to hear his voice vibrating through my chest. I want to smell him, not from a distance, but up close while my mouth is on his skin. I want to wrap my legs tightly around him and hold him close, deep inside me while I release around him.

I wish I was confident enough to call him and tell him that I did his exercise, that I want him as much as he wants me. If I did, I know he would come over. He would be here with me, tonight. The reality of that thought flips the switch from an exciting joy and desire, to the frightening sensation of falling with no chance of survival. Inevitably, that brings to mind a picture of my mother, the last time I saw her, a shell of her former self. The next day she was gone, suffering no more.

I get up and put on my robe, no longer able to handle the

cold air on my skin. I go to the kitchen to fix some tea to help me relax and hopefully fall asleep. Halfway through the cup, I'm calmed down enough to let my thoughts go back to Ian. Nothing as drastic as potentially calling him and enticing him to come over—clearly I wasn't ready for that—but maybe I could slowly get to know him, establish a kind of friendship and see where it takes us. That seems safe and responsible, where I'll have more control. Where I'm not diving in head first. Satisfied with my decision, I get up and put my empty mug in the sink and head back to bed. No more sensual meditation exercises to mess with my mind.

I turn off the light and snuggle into my blankets. Tomorrow I will hit the refresh button with Ian. I won't purposefully avoid him, and I'll approach him with a friendlier attitude. I still have to get through my dinner date with Gabriel tomorrow night, but I'll keep it neutral and not give him any signals there might be a chance for more.

I really wish I had never accepted his invitation. I was overwhelmed and not thinking clearly. Gabriel is a very nice and extremely attractive man, but I feel nothing when I'm around him. Unlike the avalanche of emotions I feel whenever Ian is around. Nothing compares to that.

After finally dozing off and sleeping soundly through the night, I'm awakened by an incoming text. I'm surprised how late it is and disappointed that I missed the sunrise, again. I must have needed the rest. Grabbing my phone, I'm even more surprised to see the text is from Ian. It's barely 7:00 in the morning. What the hell?

Ian: Good morning, Charlotte. Did you do what I told you to do?

If I were close enough to the edge of the bed, I think I would have fallen onto the floor. I cannot believe he just texted me that…direct…demanding…

"Ugh!"

I sit up, flip my hair out of my face, and stare at my phone. "Well, good morning to you, too. Jerk!" I am *not* responding to that. Here I was, all happy about trying to start over with a new attitude, giving him a chance, and he throws ice water on it with his controlling bullshit that makes me crazy. I knew I shouldn't have given him my number.

Getting out of bed, I head to the kitchen for coffee. I don't even want to deal with him until I've had at least one cup. Getting the brew started, I'm back in the bathroom to brush my teeth and wash my face. I think I may have stomped from the kitchen to the bathroom and back, I'm so annoyed. Once I'm on the balcony, I sit down, breathe in that rich aroma, and take a fortifying sip. It's as if it flows directly through my veins and up to my brain where it starts connecting neurons, giving me some clarity.

"Did I do what you told me to do? Really? As a matter of fact, yes. I did! But you won't be hearing about that any time soon. I'll be keeping that whole event to myself and you can sit there wondering," I say out loud.

I pretend to occupy myself with my phone, going through news feeds and emails. I honestly have no idea what I looked at, because I'm too busy thinking about Ian and the fact that I *did* do what he told me to do and very easily confirmed what I want is him.

Making matters worse, I have an intense need to tell him so. Maybe I'm misreading his text. Maybe the tone is more sweet and pleasant, not the demanding, control-freak tone I'm imagining. What if he's just excited about the idea that I did it and wants to know what happened?

Another bucket of cold water gets dumped on my optimism with his next text.

Ian: Charlotte? Stop avoiding my question.

Oh my God! "You've got to be kidding me!" I slam my phone down on the table. Is he watching me or something? I stand and look around, but there's no way he could be. I'm up too high, and nothing close enough is facing me. Presumptuous egomaniac.

Of course, it pisses me off that he's right. He's probably always right, and if I start seeing him, he'll destroy my self-esteem with his need to prove it. On that note, Sibel opens one sleepy eye, thinks about it for a second, and crawls out from under the covers. She's not too keen on the idea of anyone messing with my self-esteem. She's also not too keen about sitting here saying nothing in a volcano of frustration...that hasn't erupted yet. So she kicks the top off and lets the lava flow.

Me: I'm not avoiding you. I was attempting to enjoy a cup of coffee on my balcony. You're interrupting me.

Ian: Then we're even. You're always interrupting me and you don't even know it. Tell me about the exercise.

Me: What exercise?

Ian: Charlotte. I know where you live.

Me: So you're just going to show up here? Then what? You can't get in.

Ian: Really? Care to see me try?

What the hell? Would he really be able to get in my condo? Sibel definitely wants him to try, just out of curiosity. I, on the other hand, have instant anxiety thinking about it.

Me: No

Ian: Why not? We could enjoy a beautiful Saturday morning, leisurely discussing the outcome of your meditation.

Me: Not happening. Besides, if you show up, I won't be here. Have a lot going on today.

Ian: Liar. I'm looking forward to the day you no longer feel the need to bullshit me.

Me: You assume too much.

Ian: Really? Then join me for dinner tonight. We can discuss it.

Sibel thinks he deserves to have ice water thrown on him for a change. At least I won't be lying this time.

Me: I have plans.

Ian: You're lying again.

Me: I'm not lying.

Ian: What are you doing then?

My heart is pounding and I'm getting a slight headache. I don't want to tell him. It's like I'm betraying him somehow, but that doesn't make any sense because I'm not seeing him, and I'm not interested in Gabriel. I'm just being polite because we already made plans. Sibel doesn't give a shit, though. She doesn't like being questioned or bossed around.

Me: I'm going out to dinner.

Ian: With?

I don't want to do it. I need to lie to him. But, before I can make a rational decision, my vindictive alter ego hits send.

Me: Gabriel

I wait for a response. The whole time he's been rapid-fire responding to everything I said. Now, there's nothing. The longer I sit and wait for him to reply, the worse I feel. That was a mistake. I know it in my gut.

"Dammit!" I get up, too antsy to stay on the balcony. I go inside to make another cup of coffee, but my appetite for it is gone. I can't stay inside. I'll go insane staring at my phone and second-guessing myself for hours. I send Erika a text and pray she's up.

Me: Hey! Please tell me you're up for meeting me at the beach for some one on one volleyball. I'm super stressed, cannot stay inside, and need to burn some energy.

Erika: I'm on it sister. Meet me there in 15?

Me: Yes! Thank you!

Erika: Plan on sweating. I'm feeling aggressive

Me: Good! I need my ass kicked.

Erika: Looking forward to hearing the details.

Fifteen minutes later, we are at our favorite spot. It's close to South Beach, but not over-crowded or sketchy. I'm happy there is a breeze coming off the ocean so it won't be too hot and we can play longer.

Erika walks up spinning the ball between her fingers. She gets right to the dirt. "So, what's wrong? Did you finally have a threesome dream with Ian and Gabriel? Too much deliciousness to handle and you need to sweat it out, or did you actually do that little exercise routine Magic Mike recommended?" She has one eyebrow raised.

"The dream might have been a better option. I did the exercise, and it wasn't really hard to determine what I want." I've got my head down because I'm afraid I may have screwed it up as soon as I admitted to myself that I actually want to be with him. "I made up my mind last night that I was going to give Ian a chance. Maybe try to be friends first and see where it goes. Nothing hasty that overwhelms me and makes me run."

"Okay. So what's the problem?" she asks, tossing the ball from hand to hand, giving me the, *what am I missing here?*, look.

Grabbing the ball from her because it's distracting the hell out of me, I reply, "He pissed me off this morning by waking me up with a demanding text that said, *'Did you do what I told you to do?'* I tried to ignore him, but he kept at it with that bloody ego of his, then Sibel took over and told him I was going out to dinner with Gabriel tonight."

Erika makes a grimace, then a kind of whistle sound. "Ooooo, yeah. That's not good. You really need to have some kind of exorcism done to get rid of her. She's nothing but trouble."

Her honesty doesn't make things better, but she's right. "I know. I feel like shit now. I tried justifying it because I'm not seeing him, and I have no intention of being anything but friends with Gabriel. Plus, Novas Alturas is a great contact. I want them to turn to The Clara Sea for everything from room accommodations and spa visits, to dinners and private meetings. They're going to need it over the next few years. But I know that's not how Ian is looking at it, and I'm a total bitch for shoving it in his face."

"You may be forced to make the next move, and I doubt he'd ignore you. He's too into you to be that stupid. Don't beat yourself up, honey." She pats me on the shoulder and grabs the ball. "Come on. Let's burn this pesky guy bullshit off. I'm going extra hard on you today!" Laughing as she runs to take her position.

She wasn't joking, either. Twenty minutes into it and I'm soaked, sweat running down my neck and chest, heart pounding. I definitely needed this, but wow. I think she's trying to kill me! "Easy, girl! Are you out for revenge? I didn't piss *you* off, did I?" I ask between heavy breaths.

"Nope. No revenge here. Just too much coffee, I think. Plus, I'm a good friend and I know when you need a good ass-kicking."

We both laugh and walk over to get a sip of water. After taking several big gulps, I pour a little down my chest to help cool me off. When I look back at Erika, her face is frozen and somewhat pale; she looks like she's seen a ghost. "What's up? Are you okay?"

"Ummm...you may not want to know this, but there is a seriously hot guy standing over there staring at you, and I'm pretty sure it's Ian."

I jerk my head around, and there he is—more glorious than ever. My heart jolts as I see his naked torso for the first time. Dear Lord, I should've known. It is simply unfair for the rest of mankind to be at such a disadvantage. It's honestly intimidating. Making matters worse, he's covered in sweat, so the light is reflecting off every curve of every muscle, accentuating the sculpted sinew of his body.

He sees my blatant inspection, but he doesn't smile that cocky smile that acknowledges his own superiority. No, he simply stares at me. Intense, angry, and clearly disappointed. He briefly looks at my body, equally sweaty and exposed in a sport bikini, then runs his hand through his wet hair, turns around, and jogs away.

I'm not sure what to do, because the ground got yanked out from under me...again. I stand there and watch his retreating figure get smaller and smaller until it's out of sight. My chest finally exhales as Erika says in a soft voice, "Are you okay? That was pretty intense."

"No. I don't think I am, but I'm not exactly sure why. I mean, I'm pissed at myself for being scared and weak when it comes to him, but I'm also pissed at my parents for freaking me out emotionally. I'm pissed at my stupidity for telling him about tonight. I'm pissed at him for being unnaturally perfect and obnoxiously overbearing. Ugh! I'm even pissed at Gabriel for asking me out to dinner!" I plop down on the bench. "I'm not cut out for all this. It's too much. I swear, I'm going to end up being an old spinster."

Erika busts out laughing.

Glaring at her, I raise an eyebrow in question.

"I'm sorry. That's too funny. I get that you're overwhelmed by the Thor-looking creature who was just standing here burning holes in you with his unbelievable eyes, but women who look like you don't end up as spinsters. You bitches get to pick whoever you want."

"Really, Erika? I've seen seriously hot men wreck their bikes and walk into light poles because they were too busy checking you out. So don't act like you don't get to pick whoever you want." I roll my eyes.

"Yeah, you're right. I've honestly never had a guy I was interested in turn me down."

We look at each other and laugh. Erika is gorgeous with her dark, shiny hair and whiskey colored eyes, and she loves men, she just doesn't like commitment. She says it's because there are too many options and too much strange, and strange is fun.

"I'm definitely right, plus you don't have debilitating insecurities holding you back," I say in a serious tone.

"Your insecurities aren't debilitating. Give me a break," she retorts.

"Really? Well, my insecurities prevented me from getting some of the hotness that just took off in the other direction without a hello or goodbye. I think that qualifies as debilitating." I challenge.

"Well said. That's actually a valid argument. Because now that I've had an up-close look at what's been begging for your attention, I'm pretty well convinced there's something wrong with you." She sets the ball on the bench and grabs her towel to dry her face.

"There is. Don't remind me. Coming down here was supposed to make me feel better. Now I'm ten times worse *and* I'm afraid he's going to jog by again. I have no idea if he was coming or going. Can we head out, maybe go get some lunch somewhere?"

I really am upset. I hate the way he was looking at me, almost like he was hurt. It's making my stomach feel weird, and I can't stand here waiting for more.

"Sure, babe. Let's meet at Laney's in thirty minutes." After a pause she says, "Come here." Reaching up, she puts her hand on my shoulder and looks me in the eyes. "It's going to be fine. Everything is going to work out. You'll see. Okay?" Then she gives me that loving, best friend smile.

"Okay." And we head back to our cars.

It's 6:15 and I'm waiting for the Uber driver to pick me up and take me to The Capital Grille where I'm meeting Gabriel at 7:00. I'm hoping to get there a little early so I can have a drink at the bar by myself. But with traffic, that may not happen.

I keep telling myself that it's nothing more than a business meeting to help establish a good rapport that will be beneficial to the resort. I know Gabriel doesn't see it that way; I'm not going to fret about it anymore. I've been in knots all day, and I'm over it. I just want to get through the night and maybe plan a few days off to regroup and screw my head on straight.

Thankfully, I do make it in time to have a quick drink and ease the tension in my nerves. Right at seven, Gabriel walks through the front doors looking stunningly handsome. I head over to greet him and, as expected, he's dripping with charm as he takes my hand for a kiss. "Good evening, Charlotte. Is it possible that you are more lovely than the last time I saw you? You have no idea how much I have been looking forward to tonight."

My stomach tightens with guilt. *Dammit!* I put on my best smile. "Thank you, Gabriel. It's so nice to see you, too. You picked a fabulous restaurant. Have you been here before?" I'm trying to steer away from his over-complimenting.

"No, I have not. But Jackson recommended it to me. He said it is one of the best in Miami." His smile shows that he is pleased with his choice; however, my heart just stopped because Jackson knows we're here. Which means there is a good chance Ian knows we're here. This has been the day from hell!

The hostess seats us and I notice that it is busier than usual, even for a Saturday night. The noise is making me edgy for some reason and I'm thankful Gabriel ordered us a bottle of Cabernet before the waiter had a chance to ramble on about specials and what he recommends. As we look at the menu, he asks for suggestions. Not wanting to be rude and say, *"Everything is good, just pick one,"* I recommend two of my favorites—the filet and the sea scallops. Keeping it simple and not wasting time staring at the menu, he chooses the filet.

The waiter returns quickly with the wine, thank goodness. I am more edgy now that I know this was Jackson's recommendation. Right as I go to take a sip, Gabriel picks up his glass and holds it up for a toast. "To a long-lasting friendship and endless possibilities."

His deep, accented voice echoes in my ears. *Endless possibilities?* Yikes! Where is he going with that? I don't make a comment because I don't even know what to say. I simply smile and take an unladylike sip and hope the kitchen isn't slow tonight.

Shifting the conversation to something neutral, I ask him about the new project he's doing with McAlistair. That was a good move because it keeps him talking about business for the next fifteen minutes and not whatever *possibilities* he was toasting to earlier. He's obviously very excited about working with Ian and his team and is extremely impressed with the design of the building. He said his father holds Ian in high regard with how he conducts business, the professionalism of his team, and the outstanding product they create. He's right—Ian's standards are very high; he's driven, and I don't think second-best is an option for him.

I reach for my wine glass and mindlessly swirl the last sip around as Gabriel continues on about the details of the project. Bringing it to my lips, I breathe in its strong aroma and glance across the rim to the other side of the restaurant.

The whole room turns quiet.

Everything around me becomes blurry, and all I can hear is the sound of my blood swooshing in my ears to the pounding of my heart. Ian is here, staring at me with a look so fierce, so menacing, it scares me.

I'm suddenly lightheaded, and my brain is scrambling to figure out what to do. I look back at Gabriel who is still talking and smiling at me, having no clue this evening could potentially take a very bad turn. My God, what if Ian comes over here and says something to Gabriel? He could ruin his reputation, not to mention an extremely lucrative partnership. Adrenaline is coursing through my veins, trying to help my brain function, but it's no use. I don't even know what Gabriel is saying right now.

I can't do this. I cannot sit here with Ian giving me a death stare all goddamn night, and I won't allow him to screw up his partner's impeccable image of him. I finish off the last sip, pour another for both of us, drink one more gulp, and excuse myself to the ladies' room.

I'm nervous and unsteady as I make my way over to where Ian is seated. His long frame is stretched out almost awkwardly in the chair, one foot over the opposite knee. He looks a little disheveled compared to what I'm used to seeing, and I'm starting to wonder if he's had a lot more to drink than just the one in his hand.

"Ian. What are you doing here? Is there something wrong with you? You can't let Gabriel see you like this, he's your business partner!" It comes out like a hiss because I'm trying to whisper but can't. I'm too wound up.

He doesn't answer or even look up at me right away, still staring at the table where I was seated with Gabriel. His elbow is resting on the table. He's barely holding his drink, as if it were dangling from his fingertips. Slowly, he brings it to his lips and finishes it off in one swallow.

The glass hits the table with a loud thud, and he gradually pulls himself up out of the chair, his full height blocking the light over the table, casting me in his shadow. He stares at my face, sad eyes roaming over every detail as if to memorize them. In this close proximity, I feel that familiar heat flow from my core out to my hands and feet. I close my eyes and take a deep breath because I am suddenly dizzy, more from him than the wine.

His deep voice penetrates my haze, and I notice it has a scratchy edge to it that makes him sound tired. I look up, directly into his eyes when he says, "Yes, I believe there is something wrong with me, Charlotte. I believe you have accomplished the impossible with that wicked spell you cast on me." His words come out deliberately and a little slurred.

"Ian, what are you talking about? No wicked spell has been cast on you," I say, still trying to whisper and suddenly feeling a little uncomfortable with his demeanor. I quickly look over my shoulder to make sure Gabriel hasn't noticed us talking.

"You're wrong, Charlotte. You have no idea what you've done to me. As I sit here watching you have dinner with another man, the pain it's causing in my chest is so excruciating I want to destroy this whole restaurant with my bare hands and curl up in a ball and weep like a child...all at the same time." He huffs out a weak laugh. "Pathetic, isn't it?" He moves closer, and I let him because I can't move. I'm paralyzed. He reaches up and cradles my neck and head with his warm hand, bringing his thumb around to sweep it across my cheek, and I suddenly have the urge to cry.

"I've come to realize that I'm in love with you, Charlotte LeFay. Rather deeply, I'm afraid. And I hate myself for making you not trust me. I'm sorry for that, more than you'll ever know." The sadness in his eyes is like a knife in my heart. "But I get it now. I understand why you can't be with me...and I promise, from now on...I will leave you alone." He slowly bends his head and gives me the most tender kiss on my lips. Afterward, he holds me there, resting his forehead against mine and taking a few slow breaths, his eyes closed.

Straightening, he lets go and walks away.

EIGHTEEN

IAN

Staring out over the ocean, I don't register anything but darkness. My mind is numb, although I can no longer blame it on the alcohol. It must be the aftereffect of coming down off an intense adrenaline rush.

This morning, when Charlotte told me she was going to dinner with Gabriel, I snapped. For whatever reason, I knew she wasn't lying. And the thought of her with another man, of him looking at her beautiful face across the table, imagining he might touch her hand during dinner, put his own on the small of her back as they walk side by side, that he might get to kiss her good night or potentially more, was enough to make me lose my mind.

Needing to escape my condo, I went for a run, hard and fast, attempting to burn off my fury. Of course, that only brought me face to face with the source of my madness. I was so caught off guard when I saw her, I almost face-planted on the boardwalk. Once I'd regained my balance, I walked over to get a closer look, hoping she wouldn't see me right away so I could play voyeur a little longer.

Watching her in such an unrehearsed, natural state may have been when the lock clicked shut around my heart. She was so beautiful, laughing with her head thrown back one minute, then fiercely concentrating on her next move a moment later. She didn't have on any makeup, her hair was in a ponytail with sweat-drenched flyaways around her face, and I had never seen her look more stunning than she did in that moment.

My eyes finally broke away from her smile to focus on her sculpted, athletic body, so healthy and feminine and unbelievably enticing. The urge to run my hands across her wet skin while holding her close to me was so powerful it made me angry. I see her as mine, but she doesn't, and it's killing me.

When she finally discovered I was there, I could see the shock on her face and wondered if there was a part of her that was happy to see me. I wanted to say something, to tell her she's the most beautiful thing I've ever seen and that I'm sorry for making her not trust me. I wanted to beg her not to go with Gabriel, not to let him touch her. But then her eyes strayed to my body, her lips parted, and I had to leave. I felt like I was being ripped apart by fierce desire and vicious rage.

For the first time in my life, my soul is screaming to be with a woman—one woman in particular—and it's not my physical body looking for sexual release. I want to protect her, provide for her, make sure she knows there is no one on earth that is more important than her, make her laugh and smile, and yes...show her the true meaning of ecstasy. But I managed to fuck up everything by making her scared to trust me.

When I got back home, I showered and tried to eat breakfast, hoping the effort to burn off my anger paid off. It did, but in its place was a deep sorrow like I've never felt before. I was so steeped in misery my body felt heavy and weak, tired in a way no amount of sleep could cure. The only thing that could take the darkness away was Charlotte. That's when I knew Nana was right, as always. I'm in love, passionately, deeply...painfully in love with the captivating faerie that cast her spell on me only eight short days ago.

Admitting the truth to myself must have been somewhat of a

shock, because all I could do was lay on my couch and stare at the ceiling for hours. Half that time was spent thinking about myself, my feelings, and how much I want her. When I was done feeling sorry for myself, like the selfish little prick that I am, I thought about her. I imagined her at seventeen when everything she thought was true turned out to be a lie. How profound that must have been for someone so young. Then watching how that deceit slowly deteriorated her mother to dust. I think my heart broke for her in that moment, and in the next, I felt hatred... toward myself for giving her a reason to believe I would do the same to her. It made me sick to my stomach for being such an arrogant, self-centered son of bitch to a woman so deserving of respect and compassion and tenderness and love. That's when I made up my mind to stop pursuing her, to stop pushing myself on her as if I had some bloody right to.

It wasn't a decision that was easy to swallow, so I washed it down with scotch. A lot of it. Which is how I ended up at the restaurant like a goddamn stalker on the verge of ruining my reputation as well as a valuable partnership. Thankfully, Charlotte came to me first and I was able to tell her what needed to be said without causing a scene. I wasn't lying when I told her I wanted to destroy the restaurant with my bare hands. I have never felt that kind of passion, the kind that is born out of fury. It was like being shackled in chains with no chance of escape while someone took Charlotte away from me. I had to leave, but at least I was able to tell her that she was free of me and my relentless pursuit before I walked out.

Now it's just me, the night sky, and the faintest horizon, barely visible in the distance. The alcohol has worn off, adding to the fatigue that is heavy on my body, but I know I won't rest any time soon. Maybe I should have another drink. Perhaps it will make me fall asleep so I don't have to sit here and pay attention to how fucking miserable I am.

I hear my phone vibrating on the table next to me. It's facing down so I don't see who it is. Likely Jackson or Nana, and I don't feel like talking to anyone right now. Then the thought that Nana might not be well and needs my help snaps me out of it. Leaning over, my body heavy like it weighs a thousand pounds, I grab the phone and see that it's not Nana; it's Charlotte. I stare at it for a second, not fully registering what I'm seeing since she's never called me or initiated any other form of communication. Before I stupidly miss the call altogether, I answer, "Hello." My voice doesn't sound like my own.

"Ian...I..." She sounds like she's crying. It jolts me out of my misery-induced fog and I sit straight up.

"Charlotte, are you all right? What's wrong? Did he hurt you?"

"Yes...I'm fine. It's just...when you left...I..." Her voice is barely above a whisper.

"Charlotte, listen to me...I'm coming to see you. I will call you in fifteen minutes from outside your condo." I hang up, not giving her a chance to tell me no. Running inside to grab my keys, I fly out the door, leaving the hopeless bastard I was, thirty seconds prior, on the balcony.

I'm at her building in ten minutes, calling her from the outside security phone. She answers after one ring, but I cut her off. "Let me in and leave your front door unlocked."

In the lobby, I run to the elevator. The goddamn thing crawls to the fourteenth floor. I pace back and forth like a caged lion. Finally the bell signals and the doors open.

Her condo is down the hall, and the door is unlocked. I walk in, and she is the first thing I see, standing by the window in her living room, facing me. She wants me—needs me—I can see it in her eyes. Moving quickly, I toss my keys on the counter as I pass the kitchen, my long strides taking me directly to her without a word. My eyes are laser-focused. She's so fucking beautiful, even through the evidence of her tears.

As soon as I'm close enough, my hand reaches up to cradle the back of her neck, pulling her to me as my mouth urgently claims hers. My other hand wraps around her lower back, bringing the rest of her body flush with mine. *Finally. Finally, Charlotte is in my arms.*

The kiss is ravenous, and I'm afraid I might be hurting her though I am powerless to pull back. But then she moans into my mouth and devours me as much as I'm devouring her. She's not fighting me. Our need for each other is exhilarating in a way that is impossible to express. It's savage in its demand to be unleashed. The electricity sparking through us, between us, is like nothing I have ever known. Yet hidden somewhere deep inside are the undertones of familiarity that have me tightening my hold and digging my fingers into her flesh in a possessiveness that borders on anger.

She calms my aggression with her warm hands as they move slowly across my shoulders, then reignites it when her fingers glide up into my hair, pulling just enough to take my explosive arousal a few degrees higher. When she presses herself into my hardness, a violent surge erupts through my body, and I can no longer tolerate the clothing separating our skin.

"Forgive me, Charlotte. I need to touch you." Bringing my hand to the zipper on the back of her dress, I pull it down. "If this is too much, too fast, you need to speak up now." Her dress loosens, then falls off her shoulders without protest.

My breath hitches as my hand finds her exposed nipple, hard and tight under my thumb. I involuntarily pull away as my eyes insist upon seeing what they've only imagined. Looking down, I find the perfect, simple sculpture that is the naked female breast. But hers...with its dark pink areola, erect and unyielding against the pale skin covering its weighted volume, is a masterpiece created by the gods.

Pausing to circle my thumb across one hard nub, I look her in the eyes. "You went out to dinner with that bastard without a fucking bra on?"

She's breathing heavily, lips shiny and dark and swollen. Her eyes widen, but she doesn't answer, so I continue. "When I take this dress off completely, if I find you're not wearing panties, your pretty little ass cheeks are going to be bright pink for the next two hours." The thought makes my hard cock jump inside my pants. But the way her eyes dilate and her mouth opens in invitation makes my balls tighten almost uncomfortably.

Stepping back enough to pull the dress all the way down her body, I follow it until I'm on my knees in front of her. I let the dress fall the rest of the way to the floor, and I'm met with a lovely pair of slightly modest pale blue panties. Looking up from my position, I smile, and her expression says she's happy I'm pleased, making my heart expand with an indescribable joy.

My hands glide up the back of her thighs, then form against her splendidly round ass and pull her to me. Heat is coming off her as I finally breathe in the scent I knew would be like a drug. She smells so damn good, I run my nose across the front of her panties and down.

Growling, I tell her, "You were made for me, Charlotte." I finish by giving her unexposed pussy an open-mouth kiss, right over top of the thin material that's hiding her from me. Licking, biting, sucking, then letting my tongue slip around the lace edge, allowing for enough direct contact to make her scream out. She's wet and my mouth waters from the pure taste of her.

I can't play much longer. My cock is about to rip through my fucking jeans.

I slowly pull her panties off to fully expose her to me. Leaning forward, I kiss along her tan line on one side, then the other while my hands move inward from her ass to the uppermost part of her inner thighs, just below her delicately soft lips. With a gentle squeeze, I pull apart, opening her enough to allow my tongue to sweep under to her wetness then across her clit in one slow, precise lick that has her calling my name as her legs start to give out.

Holding her waist, I stand and pull her to me, clutching her tight and kissing her mouth like I did her sweet pussy. She's shaking, her breathing erratic as she reaches up to unbutton my shirt. I only have patience for her to open one as I pull away, reach behind my head, and remove it in one swift motion.

The cold air surrounds my heated body as I stand there with Charlotte fully naked in front of me. My voice is strained when I tell her, "You are so beautiful, Charlotte." Bringing my hand up to cradle her face, my thumb traces her full lips, and I notice the slight tremble of my fingers. My eyes drift up to hers, shining and exquisite.

I stay there, drowning in their depths. "I swear, I want you so badly it's painful. To be here, holding you, looking in your eyes...knowing this is real. You know how I feel about you, Charlotte. What I said tonight was not a lie." I lean down and kiss her mouth, softly, unable to resist taking the fullness of her bottom lip between my teeth. "I will try very hard not to be rough, but I don't know if I can." There is tension in every muscle of my body, each one screaming for release. It's more powerful than anything I have ever experienced. "I'm afraid I might hurt you."

She takes a step toward me and reaches up to gently touch my chest, then her fingertips touch my nipple, sending chills up my spine. "Ian..." she says in a whisper that makes my heart pound, as she leans down to kiss my chest. Breathing deeply, she closes her eyes in pleasure as a delicate smile curves her lips before moving them up to my neck, where she kisses and sucks the tender part of my skin, driving me completely mad.

"...I *want* you to hurt me. I need to feel how much you want me." She puts her hands up to hold my head while she looks me in the eyes, then takes hold of a part of me I didn't know existed. "When you said goodbye to me tonight, it felt like a light inside me went black." Bringing her hand around to the side of my face, she tips her head to the side, eyes bright with emotion. "That was more painful than anything you will do to me now."

My arms grab onto her, strong and possessive. I fill her mouth with another passion-filled kiss as an indescribable sensation flashes through my body. Like a lifetime of need, of waiting, of wanting has finally been released from confinement. I swoop her up into my arms and carry her toward the bedroom I assume is hers.

I set her down in front of the bed, and we both start to undo my pants. When my rigid cock springs free, she takes it in her hand, slowly moving up from the base then back again. My body is vibrating with desire, and when she squats down to take the head into her mouth, I pull away—fast. "No. I'm sorry. I can't do that right now or I'll fucking explode. Forgive me, but I have to be inside you." Lifting her chin, I bend over to give her a gentle kiss and I say against her lips, "I promise to make it up to you…tonight."

I take a step backward, removing my shoes and socks then step completely out of my jeans. "Move back. Lie in the middle of the bed."

She does my bidding as I walk over to turn on the light. "I need to see you," I say with a smile as the glow of the light illuminates her exquisite body, hair fanned out across the pale duvet. *Un-fucking-believable.* Standing at the foot of the bed, I can't believe I'm looking at her like this. Not even an hour ago I was sitting on my balcony, depressed at the thought of living without her and hating myself for making it so. Of never touching her, tasting her, loving her. Now she's here, telling me without words that she loves me as much as I love her, and it's the most beautiful thing my eyes have ever seen.

"Spread your legs for me, Charlotte." She only hesitates for a few seconds. She's wet and her body senses my desire, evident in the way her back arches as her hand glides over her torso, across her bare mons and down toward her wet core. I come undone as her fingers slide across her lips, spreading them for only a second before her hand moves up her thigh and she whispers, "Ian."

My mouth is suddenly between her legs, drinking in the taste and smell of her, devouring her, pushing her hard to climax for teasing me, yet holding off just enough to keep it at bay. The thrust of her hips combined with the sound of her pleasure are more than my will can withstand. Enjoying one last lick across her swollen clit, I move to position myself on top of her. My hands are on either side of her head, my hips between her thighs, and as I bring my lips to hers, I confess just before they touch, "I cannot wait another second." Then I enter her in one powerful thrust as my mouth takes hers in a brutal kiss.

My mind goes numb as the pleasure of being inside the woman I've craved explodes around me. As I slide out to enter again, the sensation is so intense, I fall to my elbows and cradle her head in my hands. "Charlotte..." I kiss her through my thrusts as they become harder and harder. "I'm sorry..." I've barely given her a chance to catch up as my body involuntarily takes what it needs.

"Don't, Ian. Don't say that...please...don't hold back." She's staring into my eyes, and I swear I shatter into a million pieces. "I need this as much as you do, please..." When she pauses to take a breath, I bring my lips back to her mouth, my tongue sweeping across as my body pounds into hers. She stays with me, though, and I feel her tighten around my cock as her hips begin to thrust, matching my rhythm and increasing the pressure. She's panting hard, my name escaping on a strained breath, forcing me to drive harder and harder. When she reaches down and digs her fingernails into my ass cheeks, my mouth and teeth latch on to her neck as we both erupt into an all-consuming climax that is raw and bone-deep, marking us as each other's, exactly the way nature intended.

Riding it out as long as possible, we stay connected, breathing through the exertion and lingering pleasure. I can still feel her throbbing around me as she ebbs out of her orgasm. It was beyond anything I could have anticipated, and I will never be the same.

I'm too weak to hold myself up, so I roll onto my back, holding on to her as she rolls with me. We are still connected, though I am softening, as the pulsing of lingering pleasure prevents us from letting go. Resting her head in the valley of my neck and shoulder, she hums a sound that mimics how I feel as she swirls her fingers around my chest.

I did not know it was possible to be this sated...to be this content. It's like I'm home, I'm complete, like I finally found what I've been looking for after searching several lifetimes.

Wrapping my arms around her, holding her firmly, I can't help the words that escape me. "I love you, Charlotte. Don't be afraid of me. I will protect you...I always protect what's mine."

NINETEEN
CHARLOTTE

I've been awake for thirty minutes, replaying the last twenty-four hours in my mind. I really need to go pee, but my muscles are like jelly after the orgasm marathon Ian took me on last night.

I truly did not know it was possible for sex to be that good, to feel that powerful. Maybe it's because he's a master at it or because I've finally accepted that I have feelings for him. Perhaps it's something else. What I do know is that I have to stay strong and continue moving past my fears, because now that I've walked through this door, I'm never turning back.

Rolling onto my side to stare at him while he sleeps, I smile. He's so much less intimidating this way. Still abnormally good-looking, but he isn't radiating that magnetic energy that makes it hard for me to catch my breath, or staring at me with those turquoise eyes that put me in a trance. Like they did last night when I saw him sitting across the restaurant.

It's hard to believe that was a little over twelve hours ago— when I stood in front of him after getting past the heart attack he gave me, and he told me that he had fallen in love with me. I felt like my entire life changed in that moment and I was someone else. For that brief time, I felt so happy, like something clicked into place and I was finally my true self. Then it all came crashing down when he told me goodbye, for good. I was so distraught, I don't even remember going back to the table. Gabriel was concerned because I didn't seem well. I do recall that—it's how I was able to cut dinner short. There was no way I could maintain my composure for very long.

Once I got home, it took me an hour to drum up the courage to call Ian. I'm not sure what I was expecting to happen when I did, but him barreling through my door ten minutes later and changing the meaning of my existence wasn't something I fully anticipated. Though a part of me was terrified, not so much of him but of what could happen by letting down the walls that protected me, I'm actually glad he did. Knowing his feelings for me combined with the intensity of all that was sparking between us, before we even touched, I may have fallen in love with him, *again*, in that split second before he held me in his possessive embrace.

There was a raw power radiating from him when he walked through my front door, slamming it behind him as his momentum never faltered. His wild eyes focused on nothing but me, he took me in his arms without a word or need to ask, and kissed me with such desperate hunger I was on the verge of weeping. I will likely relive last night in my mind until I take my last breath…and maybe beyond that.

No longer able to hold it, I quietly get out of bed and head to the bathroom. Once I've relieved myself, the soreness in my body makes itself known and is screaming for a hot shower. Turning on the water, I wait for it to heat up as I stare at myself in the mirror. Naked and flushed…and young, healthy, beautiful, like Ian imagined in his drawing of me.

I want to be more like her, strong and confident, not controlled by fear brought on by the mistakes of others. Erika's words of wisdom echo in my head, and she's right—I can't live my life according to my mother's weakness, and I can't hold my father's infidelity against anyone but him. Last night was a major step in that direction, finally moving past the anxiety that controlled me for so long.

I step into the shower and let the hot water run through my hair, down my face and body. The heat feels amazing as it warms my skin and soothes my muscles. Taking a few deep breaths, I shut out everything but the darkness that held on to me for so long. I envision the fear and anxiety, black like ink, rinsing off my body, mixing and fading in the water at my feet before it washes down the drain. I stay there, my lungs expanding further through my exercise, letting the shower continue to wash away the lingering negative emotions until the murky water runs clean. I open my eyes and take a deep, invigorating breath, letting it flow through my veins, giving me a natural high I haven't felt since I was a child.

I stay there for a minute or so, wondering if I'm imagining what just came over me. It's as if I'm lighter, freer. There's a rush of energy swirling through my core, I swear it's as if I can genuinely *feel* more than I could. Like the tickle of water running across my skin, the heat penetrating my muscles, the ache between my legs, the butterflies in my stomach as I think of Ian sleeping in my bed. I turn around and step out of the water flow to open my eyes and take another deep breath. The heat feels too good to completely step away, so I stay under enough to let it flow down the front of me.

"Stay…just like that."

Ian's deep voice startles me, and I shift to turn to him. "No. Don't turn around." I stop, surprised by the command. He's in the shower with me; I can feel him though he's not touching me. "Close your eyes, Charlotte." He's closer now. His voice right there behind my ear. My heart is suddenly pounding as a surge of warmth gathers between my legs. *Dear God, he hasn't even touched me yet.*

He continues. "Do you know what this is doing to me right now? You, naked, water running down your perfect body, over your mouthwatering ass. I don't think I'll ever get enough of you."

I suck in a breath as he places a warm kiss on my shoulder, tongue gliding over my skin, teeth scraping, giving me chills as his stiff erection presses against me.

"I want to look at you," I say as I start to turn toward him again.

"No. Just stay like this. All I want you to do is *feel*. When your eyes are closed it heightens your senses. When your eyes are open, you know what's coming and anticipate how it will feel before you actually feel it. You'd be amazed at how much that can dull down your pleasure." He steps back, then says, "Put your arms down by your side and move your feet apart."

My arms fall, exposing me, and the sensation of the water spraying down on my breasts and nipples is suddenly erotic. My head falls back a little. But when I spread my feet, it opens me just enough to allow a stream of water to run down my slit and across my sensitive nub. There is barely any pressure, but I know Ian is watching me. His energy vibrating behind me, magnifying the subtle pleasure's intensity. I involuntarily arch my back, lifting my ass up at the same time my hands reach back to glide up my cheeks, pulling slightly, spreading me as an invitation for him to touch where the water is tickling me.

Ian startles me with an abrupt, "Don't do that, Charlotte."

I let go, upset that I did something wrong. Opening my eyes, I say, "I'm sorry. I didn't know…"

"You don't need to apologize, I do." He comes close behind me again and kisses my ear. "Close your eyes, beautiful. My mission here was to bring you intense pleasure. Not to have you make me explode before I've even had a chance to touch you and make you cum at least three times." He laughs and kisses down my neck. "Your spell on me is too powerful. I need to learn to adjust." Hearing his words rekindles my arousal. Stepping back again, he says, "We are about to be out of hot water, so no more misbehaving." He gives my wet ass cheek a loud smack, sending a jolt of pleasure directly between my legs where I feel another wave of heat.

"Put your hands out in front of you, lean forward, and rest them on the wall."

I do as he says, and the new position ratchets up my excitement. The water is now spraying down my lower back, my breasts are hanging and vulnerable, tingling in the cool air. Leaning forward with my legs spread has the water running across me from the other direction, and it's just as enticing.

He leaves me like this, allowing me to focus on the new sensation for a minute, then surprises me by gently reaching around to play with my nipple. My head falls forward and my breath catches. Just that slight touch, *dear God*. He lets go; I barely have a chance to recover and he's onto the other breast. This time, my abdomen tightens, making my hands almost slip down the wall.

Through the fog that's taken over my brain, I hear his deep voice say, "Jesus, woman, the sounds you make are enough to drive me insane." I didn't even know I made a sound; all I'm focused on is the sensation of the water running across my ass all the way to my clit, him teasing my nipple and the sound of his sensual voice. It's literally enough to trigger an orgasm. But I hold back, hoping he will touch between my legs.

"Stay like you are and turn off the water," he says.

I do it. Then he releases me and steps away. The suddenness of the air moving around my wet body, the leftover sensations of his hand on my nipple and water running across my sex has me biting my lip so I don't beg him to fuck me. Before I'm fully adjusted to the change, he touches the inside of my ankle and I whimper, as the walls of my entrance squeeze together, throbbing as they relax, then tightening again.

He slowly meanders up the invisible erogenous line of my leg to the back of my knee. My hands slip a little as my head falls forward—the pleasure has become so intense. The wet heat between my legs is pumping, readying itself for him. As he passes my knee and spreads his fully open hand on the inside of my thigh, my breathing becomes heavy and my whole body is hit with a hot flash of intense arousal.

The hunger and anticipation to have him touch my wet core is almost unbearable. Yet, when he gets there, right as the side of his hand touches my outer lips, he lets go. I cry out, pushing my ass toward him, begging for him to finish. A second later, he drags his fingers through the slick secretion from my clit all the way to my ass—slowly, precisely, gently massaging, bringing my climax to surface, but not allowing it to escape. Seconds prior to finally releasing, he grabs onto both sides of my ass, spreading me apart, and drives his rigid cock into my wetness, detonating an orgasm that is so intense I almost collapse.

Thankfully, he leans forward to put one hand next to mine on the wall and the other around my stomach so his strong arm is holding me up, because there is no way I would be able to hold myself up through his relentless pounding and the strength of the orgasm spasming through me. I give up all control, handing it over to him as my body floats through the euphoria as my contractions start to diminish around him.

He is nowhere near completion and I am so turned on by his primal need, the sound of our wet skin slapping together and his growling exertion, I feel another orgasm building before the first has fully subsided.

"I feel you tightening on my cock. Cum for me again." He reaches down and rubs my clit, sending me over the edge. I scream out his name as my hips thrust back toward him forcing him to go deeper. He makes an agonizing sound as his orgasm takes hold and finally ignites. It's so powerful I can feel it releasing inside me.

Wrapping both arms around me, he straightens, lifting me up so my back is to his chest. He quickly turns and leans against the shower wall. His body is angled so I can relax against him; my toes are barely touching the floor as he pumps through the last waves of his release.

My body goes limp in his strong arms, my head falling back to his shoulder. His breathing is heavy as he asks, "Are you okay?"

All I can do is nod. I can't move or open my eyes, not while I'm still throbbing around him.

We stay like that for several minutes longer. "Let me dry you off and lay you in bed. You need to rest after that."

I don't disagree, although I'm concerned I may not wake up. Is it possible to die from too much pleasure?

Turning me around as our bodies detach, he puts his hand on my face and I open my eyes. His expression stops my already struggling heartbeat. "That was unreal, Charlotte. How have I lived this long without you?"

I look in his eyes a second longer, smile a weak smile, and lay my head on his chest. I don't have the strength to respond. All I want to do is hold him.

Picking me up and setting me on the rug outside the shower, he dries off my body then grabs another towel for my hair. He takes me back into the bedroom and gently guides me to lie down so I don't collapse. I'm so relaxed as I watch him dry off his sculpted body, completely sated by the post-orgasm hormones tingling in my veins. I'm floating on a cloud and I have the sudden urge to confess my love to him. But I don't.

Finishing, he looks back at me and smiles, tossing the towel on the floor, then crawling back in bed beside me. Bringing the sheets up to cover us, he leans down to gently kiss my lips, "If you keep looking at me like that, I'm going to start writing sonnets and other poetry about your beauty and how you've enchanted me."

I can only summon a weak smile. "I would like that." My eyes close, the weight of my eyelids wining the battle over what little strength I have left.

A few hours later, I'm awakened by the smell of coffee. It is well past sunrise, and I'm a little off as I muster the energy to get out of bed. After splashing cold water on my face and brushing my teeth, I wrap my naked body in my favorite robe. Looking at myself in the mirror, I whisper on an exhale, "What have you gotten yourself into?" and laugh as I open the door to go find Ian.

When I enter the living room, my heart stops. He's sitting on the balcony sipping coffee and reading the paper, wrapped only in a towel at his waist, the late morning sun shining on him. The scene is so domestically comfortable I'm struck with an overwhelming sense of joy, and strangely, nostalgia. I stand there for a minute longer, taking it in as a tickling vibration swirls around inside my chest.

No longer able to *not* be near him, I walk out onto the balcony, take the paper out of his hand, and set it on the table as he puts his coffee down next to it. He looks up at me with those gorgeous eyes as I step over to straddle his lap and sit down. Smiling, I bring my hands up behind his head and lean in to give him a slow and sensual kiss, ending with my teeth dragging across his bottom lip in a tender bite. "Good morning, Mr. McAlistair."

"It is a good morning, indeed. But I need to warn you. If you kiss me like that again, I'm going to open this towel, set you down on my stiff cock, and fuck another orgasm out of you right here on the balcony. I still owe you one from the shower." His voice is deep and delicious, and it sends my body into complete, hot arousal.

He chuckles and adds, "From the look on your face and the size of your pupils, I won't have to wait until you kiss me again. Tell me, Charlotte, if I reach into your robe and touch your sweet pussy, will I find you soaking wet for me?" His eyes are now dilated, and my whole body flushes with another wave of heat.

"Yes, as a matter of fact, you will. You seem to have magic powers over not only my pussy, but my entire body. I'm now convinced you could make me cum with just the sound of your voice," I say, sitting up straighter and arching my back enough to put pressure on his fully erect shaft.

"I'm this close, Charlotte," he says in a strained voice, holding up his finger and thumb, barely a half inch apart. "I wasn't joking when I said I'll never get enough of you."

"Okay, I'm sorry. That last move was somewhat... involuntary." I lean down and give him a peck on the lips. "*I wasn't joking when I said you have magic powers over me.*" Getting up, I go inside to fix a much-needed cup of coffee. Back on the balcony, I notice his erection has not subsided—at all— and the look on his face has me nervous and excited at the same time.

"Can you take some time off work? I want to be alone with you, with no obligations or potential interruptions. I have a place in the Bahamas that I think you will love. We can fly out this evening." He's dead serious, and my brain is still sleepy enough to have a hard time registering his question and everything it implies.

"Umm...I...don't know. Can I finish this cup of coffee? That's a lot to think about after coming out of a coma." I take a sip from my mug, both because I need it and also to buy me some time. Fly to the Bahamas and stay with him? For how long? Is that too much too soon? I feel myself starting to panic.

Apparently reading my body language, Ian interjects my over-firing mind with, "Don't overthink it, Charlotte. My intention may be to have you all to myself, but it is also to show you what it's like to fully let go and relax. It's paradise, and there's something about that particular breeze off the crystal blue water that takes away all the pretension and expectation of everyday life. You're going to love it."

He's a good salesman. I'm ready to go pack my bags right now. But I do have responsibilities at work that I can't just walk away from without proper planning.

I look at him. There's something there, and I'm wondering what he really wants to say. Regardless, it makes my heart do flips and butterflies flutter through my stomach. Now that I'm getting used to the feeling, the one I call *the Ian Effect*, it doesn't scare me as much, but that doesn't mean it doesn't scare me at *all*…

A little uncomfortable, I respond with, "You have me ready to pack a bag, Ian. That sounds amazing and I'd love to go, but I have to see what's going on at work. I can't simply up and leave without giving my staff notice and setting up a transfer of power, so to speak. I can go in today to get a better idea of when I could make it work."

He doesn't know that I've already been setting up for some time off after all the stress he put me through last week. I could probably leave this evening, but I would still have to go in today to confirm everything and tie up loose ends.

"Would you think it strange if I told you I don't want you to go into work today because I don't want to be away from you?" Once again, he's dead serious.

"No. I'd think it's charming. But how else am I going to prepare for a trip to paradise?" I wink at him, hoping to take the edge off his humorless vibe.

"I guess that means you've had enough coffee to determine your answer is yes…you'll go with me." He's smiling now, showing off those sexy dimples that melt my heart.

I can't help but say, "Getting your way looks adorable on you, ya know."

He lifts one brow and responds with, "Does it? A sun-kissed tan is going to look adorable on you. How long do you need to be at the office to determine when we can leave?"

Okay…guess we are back to business.

"A couple of hours, I suppose. I don't even know what time it is."

"It's almost 11:30. Why don't we get dressed, go grab some lunch, I'll drop you off at the resort and pick you up when you're finished." He's giving me a look that says, *don't argue,* and at this point, I don't because it's one less thing for me to think about. Although, I can tell Sibel is getting antsy about Ian controlling everything. I shut her down before she says something that gets me in trouble.

Leaning forward, I whisper, "Come here." He does, and I give him another slow kiss that has me wanting to stay here and start another marathon. "Thank you for coming over last night. I haven't had a chance to say that yet." I give him a few more soft kisses. "After you left the restaurant, I was a bit…distraught, I guess you could say. There is a lot that needs to be said." I laugh over my awkwardness. "We've shared some intense physical passion in the past twelve hours, but not a lot of words." I put my head down, suddenly shy.

Putting his finger under my chin, he says, "Eyes up here, gorgeous."

I do as he says, feeling both nervous and excited.

He continues. "I'm not sure anything needs to be said after what we shared, Charlotte. I think our souls have made it pretty clear. They want to be together and they will, whether we try to fight it or not. Besides, we'll have plenty of time on the island to *talk*." He stands, taking my hand so that I stand with him. Reaching around my waist, he pulls me to him tightly and playfully kisses and bites at my neck. "Come on, my little faerie princess. Let's go get some lunch before I change my mind and tie you to the bed for the next two hours."

Chills race across my body, and once again, the promise in his words leaves me breathless.

TWENTY

IAN

Me: It's been two hours. I'm getting impatient.

Charlotte: Getting impatient? That would imply that you were previously patient. I don't know if that's a word I would use to describe you.

S he's getting cheeky, and I love it. It reminds me of the first time we met and she drove me mad with her sassy attitude.

Me: If I weren't patient, we would be entering our second week in the Bahamas.

Charlotte: Really? How so?

Me: Because I contemplated kidnapping you and taking you there. But my patience allowed me to maintain control and not take such drastic measures.

Charlotte: That's actually kind of hot.

Me: I'm on my way. Be ready.

Grabbing my keys, I'm out the door in less than a minute. The past two hours have crawled by, and I wasn't joking about my lack of patience. Not having her was a form of torture, dulled down through copious alcohol consumption, but painful, nonetheless. Now that I've had a taste of what I was missing, there is nothing that will dull my need for her.

The tires screech as I pull out of my parking garage and into traffic. The sun is as bright as my excitement to see her again, so I put on my sunglasses to cut the glare. As the traffic slows, I think about last night and the passionate way we made love. It was a first for me. Having never been in love, the intensity of our pleasure was indescribable. I know a lot about sex, but that was so far beyond anything I've ever experienced.

With Charlotte, it's beyond physical, beyond emotional. It's somewhere in the realm of spiritual, but not simply for me. There was a connection between us, and I know she felt it as much as I did, although she may not be ready to admit it. Being alone with her on the island and exploring that connection is going to be life-changing, I can feel it in my bones. The thought sends a wave of excitement through me, and I pick up my speed.

Pulling up to The Clara Sea, I see she is at the front doors talking to Tracy, her smile radiant as she gives a little wave. Getting out to open the car door for her, I pull her to me as she walks up, making her laugh with a kiss just under her ear. "Tell me we are leaving tonight. I want to wake up in paradise with you in my arms."

She leans back, giving me a sexy smile. "I'm tempted to tell you no, I've decided not to go, so you'll follow through with your kidnapping plan." Her face turns serious with arousal as she runs her thumb across my lips, pushing it in just enough to wet the tip. "I've been thinking about it ever since that text." She leans in, licking my lips before fully engaging in one of her sensual kisses that blows my mind.

I am so turned on. The urge to spread her legs and slam into her while she's bent over the hood of my car is so powerful, my muscles lock in restraint.

Turning her toward the car, I say through clenched teeth, "Get in the car, Charlotte." I make my way back to the driver's side, hoping no one notices what she's done to me. I get in and lean toward her. "Give me your hand." She does, and I place it on my now-throbbing erection. "When you do this to me in a place I'm not able to follow through by making you cum all over me, there will be retribution...with you begging me to let you cum after brightening your ass cheeks to a lovely shade of pink."

Her lips part as she sucks in a breath, eyes wide with longing. Her blatant arousal makes my heart pound in my chest. Then she wraps another tendril around my soul when she finally speaks.

"Ian...when you talk to me like that...I..." Her head drops in shyness. "Are you being serious when you say those things? Is that really what you want to do to me?" Her voice is so thick with desire, yet so innocent in its questioning, I'm momentarily incoherent.

"You're going to be the death of me, Charlotte LeFay," I say, moving back to sit straight in my seat so I can get us the hell out of here and somewhere I can show her how serious I truly am.

Once we are back out on Collins Avenue, I turn to her, the look on her face now mischievous. Smiling, I continue. "I am very serious when I say those things to you, and your response to it is further proof that we are perfect for each other. This morning, in the shower, was a small sample of how I want to pleasure you." Downshifting as we approach a red light, I can sense her staring at me. Glancing over, I see her beautiful eyes filled with desire and curiosity. I finish by asking, "That was fucking amazing, wouldn't you agree?" and laugh at her expression. It's something along the lines of, *Really...you have to ask?* and, *Hell yes, can we do it again?*

Answering, she says, "Ahh...I'm not sure *amazing* can suffice as a description. At one point I was seriously concerned I might blackout, the pleasure was so intense." Her smile is lighting up her face, and it takes my breath away. She laughs, adding, "I'm not kidding."

Reaching over to take her hand, squeezing it gently, I hold it for a minute. "Your pleasure is my pleasure, Charlotte. It's as simple as that." I bring her hand up to my lips, holding it there to breathe in the smell of her skin. Spicy, feminine with undertones that could be described as floral and sweet. To me, it's intoxicating.

Closing my eyes, I travel to the inside of her wrist where her scent intensifies. On instinct, my mouth opens, biting and licking her tender skin as I hear her whisper my name. My eyes open to see she is as affected as I am, making my voice sound muffled in my ears as I tell her, "I will never cause you any pain that does not bring you pleasure. I will never hurt you, Charlotte. I promise."

She doesn't respond as she looks away. I understand why—she's still afraid, and it will take some time to fully get past it. This trip to the Bahamas will help.

A few minutes later, she looks at me and says, "Thank you." I nod and give her hand a gentle squeeze. We continue to her place in comfortable silence, both of us riding out the euphoric buzz brought on by our exchange at the last traffic light.

Pulling into a parking spot, I go around to help her out of the car. When she's standing in front of me, I kiss her softly and say, "You're welcome," as she smiles up at me. "Always remember, trust is the most important thing we have between us." Nodding in agreement, she leans up and kisses me gently with her soft lips.

On the elevator, I finally ask, "How much time were you able to get off?" She gives me a fake frown and holds up one finger. Raising a brow, I confirm, "That better stand for one week." I grab onto the finger, biting it playfully.

Throwing her head back laughing, she wraps her other arm around my neck, pulling us closer together, giving me a quick kiss on the cheek. "Yes. One week. I hope you don't get tired of me, though. You don't even know all of my idiosyncrasies. You might be begging to come home after three days." She lets go and winks at me as the elevator doors open on her floor. At her front door, she fumbles, almost nervously, with her keys then pushes it open, but I stop her before she walks in, startling her as she drops her keys back into her purse.

"I'm sure any idiosyncrasies you may have will soon become endearing little quirks that make me love you more than I already do." Putting the side of my finger under her chin to lift her shy eyes to mine, I say, "Look at me. I'm not afraid of my feelings for you, Charlotte. I have always been driven, focused on success. And if I wanted something I went after it, never considering that I might not get it. I have never been in love and never looked for love. Until you."

I move my hand from under her chin, gliding my thumb across her jawline, admiring her skin with its little imperfections here and there, making her more perfect in my eyes. "When I realized I was in love with you it was at the same time I realized I had potentially ruined any chance that we might be together." I lean down to gently kiss her beautiful lips. "For a man as passionate and controlling as me, a man that cannot accept the notion of failure, a man that wanted you more than he wanted to take his next breath…walking away was the hardest thing I've ever done. But I did it anyway, for you…because I love you…all of you."

I remember how awful it felt knowing she would never be mine and hating myself for making her not trust me.

"Then you called me and there was that sliver of hope that brought me back to life." Kissing her mouth harder, I talk between the wet contact. "Then I tasted you…held you in my arms…and when we finally came together it was like nothing I even knew was possible…" I'm still all over her mouth, biting and licking, making her body become more and more aroused with every word and every kiss. "…And now that I have you…nothing…" I'm holding her now, tight, as my mouth moves along her jaw to the sensitive place below her ear, biting her as I finish. "...nothing will keep me from you again." I suck hard on her neck, not only to take her arousal to the next level, but to mark her beautiful, smooth skin.

Her breathing becomes heavy, her erotic moans driving me to madness, testing my control. Releasing her neck, I bring my mouth up to her ear as I push her against the doorjamb. "Do you know how tempted I am to make you cum right now, right here in this doorway without even touching your wet pussy? Your reaction to me is enough to make me lose my mind."

She puts her hands on my shoulders to stop me and hold herself up. "No. No, Ian...please, take me inside. I need to feel you...all of you, please." Her eyes are black with desire and I can't help but do what she wants, pushing the door open and backing her into the foyer. The latch clicks behind us, her purse drops to the floor as I push her hard against the wall, continuing the onslaught of kissing, licking, biting. Pulling away, I lift her shirt over her head and almost rip her bra away from her body, her breasts falling free. They are perfectly sized to her athletic form with just enough weight to make them hang naturally. Her dark nipples, so beautifully feminine, are tight and begging for attention. My mouth latches on, swirling my tongue around the hardness, sucking it as her hips begin to thrust toward me. Ten more seconds and I could make her cum, but I won't. I want this orgasm in my mouth so I can taste her response to my affection.

Releasing her nipple, I kneel down and yank her shorts off as she kicks out of her shoes. Her panties are next, and I pause, removing them slowly, taking in her scent that is now potent with lust. *Goddamn, my cock is going to fucking explode.* On instinct, my lips are on her thigh, kissing and biting as her hips thrust toward me again. Reaching behind her knee, I lift up, commanding, "Over my shoulder."

She does and is now open to me, allowing me to see how wet she is. "You didn't already cum, did you?"

She shakes her head quickly as she breathes out my name, her hand moving around the front of her hip to her lips, spread open and waiting for attention. I allow her to touch herself briefly, only because it's so fucking hot, but not enough to make herself release.

"That's enough." My voice is harsh as I pull her hand away and finally take what I want.

She tastes so good, I moan into her, the vibration making her cry out. Her leg starts to shake from exertion, so I reach under the one on my shoulder and support her with my hand, allowing my thumb access to her tightest entrance. My mouth continues to devour her as I glide my thumb around her ass, slippery and wet, driving her wild. She rides the pleasure for a few seconds longer before I apply enough pressure to send her over the edge. She screams out my name as I take her throbbing climax on my tongue.

After holding her through the last waves of her orgasm, I gently bring her leg down. She knows I'm not finished; the anticipation in her eyes is driving my desire to painful heights. Holding her head steady, I drop my mouth to hers in a savage kiss, forcing her to taste herself as I steal her breath.

No longer able to wait, I guide her to the bedroom where she immediately turns to me, impatiently removing my shirt then grabbing onto the button of my jeans, the backs of her fingers touching my skin and tightening my spine.

The sight of her standing naked in front of me, desperately trying to unclothe me as the scent of her heated arousal surrounds me, activates a primeval DNA that sends a surge of testosterone through my blood that is dizzying in its potency. As soon as she frees my engorged cock, I grab her, turning her so that her back is against me, wrapping my arms around her for maximum contact. With one hand on her breast, tormenting her nipple, and the other reaching down to spread her wet lips, I tease her, enticing the moans, whimpers, and cries that flood my body with need. "I want you on the bed, ass in the air with your knees spread apart."

She does what I ask, without hesitation, then pops up on her elbows to look back at me. Once my jeans are completely off, I stare at the sight before me, trying to inhale. "I'm going to draw you like this. You are absolutely exquisite."

Her eyes drop to my erection, the skin taut and shining. I reach down and take it in my hand, slowly stroking it, more for her pleasure than mine. "You like that, don't you?"

She nods and whispers, "Yes," as she arches her back and thrusts her ass toward me. Absolutely amazing.

"Put your head down on the bed, eyes closed." Coming forward to gently stroke her ass cheek, I tease her skin with light touches, letting my fingertips gently roam around her ass and thighs and back. When I sense she's ready, I draw my hand back and smack her firm cheek several times, softly rubbing the sting between each strike.

She moans as her pale skin reddens, her body relaxes, and her slick pussy pulsates with need.

Her physical reactions are a request for more, so I do exactly that. Give her more. More of the sensual, rhythmic cadence that awakens a desire she didn't know she had. Her body loves it, her mind will become addicted to it and her soul will crave this intimate connection that only we can share.

She's fully relaxed now, submitting to the pleasure-filled pain that has her ass glowing an enticing shade of red. Her entrance is begging for me as her labia swell with arousal... The female erection, it's fucking fantastic. One last smack, then I spread her apart to rub the slick head of my cock between her wet lips, pushing in slightly so only the swollen tip enters her.

She whimpers, wanting more. She needs it deeper as her legs fall open trying to force me to enter fully. But I don't let her have what she wants...yet. Instead, I pull out and rub the head around her puckered hole that tightens from the contact. She sucks in a breath, both from pleasure and fear. Holding it there, I push gently. "Are you a virgin here?" My voice is gravelly with desire.

Her whisper comes immediately. "Yes." And she instinctively tightens the strong band of muscle again.

"Good. I will teach you to enjoy that kind of play. But not today." I give her ass another smack. "You'll be surprised how hard it will make you cum." Rubbing the red mark on her cheek, I slide my cock down to where she wants it and is begging to be filled. I continue to torment her, gliding past her warm opening to circle her clit with my hard tip as she moans and pushes herself against me. Not wanting her to release too soon, I move back so I can return to the violent contact she's been craving.

Admiring her firm, round cheeks, bright from the attention they've received, I begin again, running my hand softly across her smooth skin, teasing her nerves before lighting them up with a stinging smack. I can see her sex throbbing with each contact of my hand, a succession that has no pattern. It's unpredictable and driving her pleasure higher.

I reach down to tease her, smiling as her legs spread instinctively to allow it. She wants to beg me to fuck her. I can tell as she repeats my name over panted breaths. Taking her slick secretion on my hand, I spread it over her red cheek, cooling and soothing her swollen flesh then starting again. The slick moisture increases the sensation of my next round of spanking. It's wet and loud and driving her as close to the edge as it is me.

It's on the verge of too much. This is a first for her and although she is fully enjoying every second, I don't want to over do it, distracting her from the pleasure that will make her next orgasm mind-numbing. So I lean down to lick and kiss over her hot skin, then spread her apart and insert two fingers into her softness, sliding them in and out in a slow twisting motion that has her growling as she pushes against me.

I kiss my way up her back, biting and sucking. I'm trying hard not to hurt her. It's never been like this; no other woman's pleasure has affected me so intensely, and I'm crazy with a need to mark her. Permanently. I don't, of course. I won't ever hurt her that way, but I *will* make sure she never desires anything but my touch for the rest of eternity.

Just before her climax hits, I pull out my fingers and drive my throbbing cock into her, pulling her cheeks apart to increase the contact as I pound into her. I watch myself sliding in and out, her muscles tightening as she moans out my name. Wanting to push her just a bit more, I lean over in search of her tight nipple and tease it with my wet fingers, then I squeeze.

We both fall into a pleasure that has no words. It's blinding and euphoric and deadly, and I will crave it like a wicked drug from now through the end of time.

As soon as my mind clears enough to register thought, all I can think is...how will I ever express how much she means to me? Telling her I love her isn't enough, though it comes out anyway.

"Charlotte..." I say in a raspy whisper through heavy breaths as our rhythm ebbs to slow and easy. I kiss her shoulder softly as she continues to catch her breath. "I love you." Moving gently, we disconnect so I can roll her sated body over to look her in the eyes, glazed and drugged from our lovemaking. Pulling her farther up on the bed, I spread her legs so I can lie between them, our bodies touching, wet and hot. I cradle her head in my hands, lean down, and give her a small kiss on the lips, then take my thumb and wipe away a tear that has escaped her eye. "Did you hear me, Charlotte? Those words are not enough for you to understand what you are to me, what you mean to me." I kiss away more tears, salty and warm. "I didn't know I was dead, my little enchantress, until you brought me back to life."

Her eyes look through me, reaching in to touch my soul. Then she pulls me down to her mouth and kisses me with such emotion, I have no need to hear the words. She tells me what I want to know in a way words could never communicate.

TWENTY-ONE
CHARLOTTE

After taking a recovery nap from round three of Ian's pleasure tour, I'm packed and ready to go on our trip to *paradise*. I'm not thinking about being nervous. I'm trying to focus on what to bring. He told me it's about as casual as it gets. That bikinis, cover-ups, sundresses, and flip-flops will suffice. With the lack of bulky items, I've managed to get a week's worth of clothes and necessities into one medium-sized duffle bag, which kind of has me concerned that I forgot something important.

Giving up on trying to figure out what that might be, I walk into the living room to find Ian staring at my portrait he drew, now framed and proudly showcased on my console. He reaches down and picks up the pink rose he also gave me, sitting next to the portrait in full bloom and breathtakingly beautiful. Bringing it up to his nose, he closes his eyes as the aroma penetrates his senses.

"That rose is amazing, Ian. I don't think I ever properly thanked you." Moving to him, I put my hand on his back and lean in. "Not only is it stunningly beautiful, the scent is so wonderful it's almost hypnotic."

He brings it back toward me so that I can smell it, as well. It's divine and I wish I could bottle it, then spray it all over me and everything I own.

"You have a knack for disarming me with your unexpected chivalry." I move behind him and wrap my arms around his firm waist, resting my head on his back. Noticing he hasn't said anything or responded in any way, I let go and ask, "Is something wrong?"

He puts the rose down and turns to me. "Your phone is on the counter. You've had several texts come in...from Gabriel." The look on his face makes my chest hurt. Does he think I want more than a friendship with Gabriel? Surely he knows better than that at this point.

I turn to retrieve my phone, nervous about what I might find. My stomach drops when I see several texts in a row, the first few words visible: *Hello beautiful... I've been thinking about you... Are you feeling better... Please join me for dinner.*

I feel awful. I hate the thought of him thinking I might want Gabriel's attention this way. I stare at my phone too long, wondering what to say. Ian and I have spent the past twenty-four hours together in a way that I haven't even spent six months with someone. Our connection is deep and uncommon, to say the least, but we still don't really know each other.

Looking up at him, I start talking. "Ian...I'm not interested in Gabriel that way... I shouldn't have accepted his dinner invitation. I was only thinking—"

"Stop." The sternness in his voice startles me. He's standing in front of me, but not close, with his hands in his pockets and tension radiating in all directions. "Just the idea of another man coming on to you makes me goddamn insane. But knowing that one has access to you, that he can text you...refer to you as beautiful and tell you he's been thinking about you... Charlotte, I've never been a jealous man, but then again, I've never cared enough to be jealous." He stares at me in the heavy silence. "Now I do. I care so much it fucking hurts."

My first instinct is to grab onto him. Wrapping my arms around him, pulling him to me as I rest my head on his chest, holding back tears. The thought of him hurting because of me is making me sick, so I squeeze him tighter. Finally, he takes his hands out of his pockets and softly wraps them around my back. He's hesitant, though, so I try to reassure him.

"Ian...I am not attracted to him and have no interest in being with anyone but you. I had already cancelled one dinner with him and didn't want to be rude, because a connection with a large Brazilian group like Novas Alturas would be great for business. I was hoping he would realize that I wasn't interested that way...but I think things are different in Brazil. He's very persistent." I pull back so I can look in his eyes. "All I want is you, Ian. I know this is all new, but whatever this is between us is...different. I don't know how to explain it. It's so deep, surely you can't question that."

His hands glide up my back and neck, stopping to cradle my head. Holding me there, staring into my eyes in wonderment, he says, "You feel it, too. Don't you?"

"Yes," I whisper.

"When we are near each other..."

"Yes."

"When we touch..."

"Yes."

"When we kiss..." His lips gently touch mine.

"Yes."

"When I'm inside you..."

Butterflies swirl in my stomach. "Yes." My eyes close.

"Say it, Charlotte. I know you feel it. Let me hear you say it." His voice is gravelly and his grip tightens, my heart beats faster, harder. I feel like I'm falling again, losing my breath. What am I so afraid of? Why won't the words come out?

He kisses me again, slowly, pouring his love into me. It anchors me, filling me with a happiness so pure I swear it brightens a light inside me that is tangible, literally visible behind my closed eyes. It's invigorating to all my senses as it races through me, shifting and swirling, tickling me from the inside out. He continues, deepening his passion as the light brightens to a blinding white.

Then suddenly, as if someone flipped a switch, I am no longer standing in my condo. I am someplace else, in a beautiful scene, vivid and serene. It's a meadow on the edge of a grand forest so green it seems impossible. The sun is shining brightly through a crystal blue sky and across the mountains in the distance, sparkling water runs through a rocky stream nearby and the distinct smell of brine is thick on the wind. There are purple flowers and green grass so thick and starkly colored it looks fake. This place is stunning in its beauty, and even though my conscious mind knows I have never been here before, it's familiar to me nonetheless, and I'm overcome with a sense of nostalgia that is both joyful and saddening all at once.

Ian's arms are still around me, warm and strong. I can smell him, taste him, feel his lips moving across mine, making my skin shiver with excitement. My mind is shifting back and forth, trying to decipher what is reality and what is a dream. There is no way I can physically be in this magical place, but somehow, I am—and Ian is here with me. Holding me and loving me as a sense of freedom comes over me, and I can finally tell him how I feel. When I release the kiss to look up at him and say the words that have been on the tip of my tongue, I see that his eyes are the same intense, vibrant turquoise that makes my knees weak, but he is different otherwise. It confuses my already clouded mind, and before I can fully register the subtle contradictions beyond his long hair and rugged features, I snap out of it on a startled gasp.

Ian grabs onto me as my knees give out, calling to me through the haze of whatever just occurred. "Charlotte! Are you all right?" Not waiting for an answer, he scoops me up in one swoop and takes me to my bed.

The strange thing is, I really didn't feel like I was going to faint. I was so relaxed I couldn't stand, and there was a part of me that wanted to go back to wherever I'd been, even for a moment longer.

"I'm fine, Ian. It's okay," I say from my now prostrate position on the bed. He's sitting next to me, draped over me with one elbow on the bed and his other hand touching me everywhere, as if to make sure I'm really there and that I'm really okay. His face has a look of such concern, I feel guilty for worrying him. Reaching up to put my hand on the side of his face, I say, "Ian, I promise it's okay. I'm sorry... I don't know what happened." I'm smiling as I remember the overwhelming joy that came over me minutes ago. I'm still a little freaked out about being catapulted into a dream that clearly had significant meaning, but more than anything, I need to tell Ian the truth.

Pulling myself up to a sitting position, I scoot closer to him and lean in to touch my lips to his in a chaste, playful kiss. "I can't handle another kiss like the one you just gave me." I kiss his cheeks and lips in quick succession. "At least not right now. It does strange things to my head and"—I hesitate as leftover nervousness flutters through my insides—"I have something important to tell you." I kiss his lips one more time, then look into his eyes, eager with anticipation. I pause to take him in and everything that has happened between us in such a short period of time. The explosive energy of our connection, the fear I've overcome that has allowed pure happiness into my heart, the lingering emotions from the dream I just had and every subtlety in between, make it easy for the words to flow from my soul.

"I love you, Ian McAlistair, in the purest way possible, with all that I am...body, heart, and soul." I finish on a whisper as a warm tear escapes. My eyes close as Ian leans in, taking it between his lips, the sensual touch sending chills across my body. He pulls back, mesmerizing me with his intent focus as he studies my face, stopping at my eyes, a slow smile forming on his beautiful mouth.

"Say it again, Charlotte." The deep tone is hypnotic as he

leans forward, gently pushing me to lie back on the bed as he lifts my sundress up to kiss me below my navel.

"I love you, Ian." My breath hitches as he removes my panties.

"Again." His voice is deeper now, his expression severe as the energy shifts and he is suddenly naked above me. My legs spread automatically, allowing him to press against my entrance with his hard, thick shaft.

"I love you," I say, barely audible through the emotion, right as he thrusts himself directly into my core, where a fireball of sensation shoots through me, making me scream out his name.

"Again," he says on a growl through gritted teeth as he drives another hard thrust, reaching the farthest point inside me and holding it there, igniting an electric shock of pleasure-pain that causes my fingers and toes to tingle before going numb.

"I love you, Ian." I'm trying to fill my lungs, but he claims that, too, as his mouth crashes onto mine and he breathes into me, forcing me to take the air from his lungs. I'm already lightheaded, and he pushes me further as he takes my exhale through his devouring kiss.

Desperate for oxygen, I turn my head, giving him access to my neck, where he sucks hard through the steady rhythm of his taking. And he is taking me, claiming me as his own in a way that is primal, beautifully articulated through an instinct that is as old as time.

I let him mark me. I want to be his in the deepest way possible, and as my body adjusts to the force of his rhythm, the pain turns to an intense pleasure that has my mind floating in some surreal place outside my consciousness. I feel the involuntary tightening of my orgasm begin as Ian's movements become stiff and labored.

"A-gain." He barely gets it out as his own orgasm takes hold, triggering mine to erupt, the contractions milking him as his face contorts and his muscles bulge and strain to maintain control.

"I love you," I say, louder, through the force of my climax. I reach up, pulling him down so I can have his mouth again. Kissing him until he relaxes, I push him over to his back so I can ride him through the last pulsing of my release. *Oh God.* My back arches as I moan out in pleasure. This new position has put pressure in all the right places, reigniting the flame I thought was burning out. "Ian." My fingernails dig into his chest as I start to move, my pelvis rocking back and forth. I lean forward enough so his hard abdomen puts more pressure where I am most sensitive.

"Christ, woman...you're making me hard again."

I open my eyes to see his glorious body under me, so masculine and powerful. His eyes are black, his lips red, his skin wet from exertion.

"The way you look at me, Charlotte..." He grabs onto my hips, pulling them down and forward as he thrusts up into me again, making me scream. "...it triggers something inside me, and I lose control." He's pushing and pulling and thrusting, harder and harder. I can barely breathe. "Just like the first time you looked at me." His fingers are bruising my hips, and I don't care. "That's when you did it... That's when you cast your spell on me."

I can't hold myself up anymore. I fall forward, and he wraps his arms around me, holding me firmly in position so he can drive himself into me. "You're mine. You've always been mine," he says through the strain of his effort. Grabbing onto my sweat-soaked hair, he holds it tight at the back of my head, sending a shock of pleasure down my spine to where our bodies are connected, pulling my head back so I can see him. "And you will always be mine." His mouth connects with mine as his other hand reaches down, slipping through our wet secretions to tease me on my tight, virginal hole, pushing us both into an intense release that has me seeing stars.

Time passes slowly as we come down from our lovemaking. I

am altered, permanently, by what we shared. This is different and well beyond anything physical. I am still on top of him, my legs straddling his waist. His breathing is slow and even, as if he is asleep, so I lie there, listening to his heartbeat.

A few minutes later, as I start to doze off, his voice echoes in his chest—"Again."

Smiling, I rub my hand across his chest, the skin tight over sinuous muscle, the hair coarse, his nipple erect. Lifting my head, I find his eyes closed, face content in its deep relaxation.

Moving farther up his body, I put my lips on his and say, "I love you, Ian McAlistair." Then I kiss him once...twice. "Body, heart, and soul."

He smiles against my mouth. "Hmmmm...I expect to hear that often." His lips pucker in a playful kiss. "Although it does crazy things to me." He nips at me in a tender bite. "Turns me into a caveman." His fingers move through my hair, pushing it over my shoulder. "I didn't hurt you, did I?"

"Yes. But in a good way." I run my finger across his lip. "In a *very* good way. I've never known such pleasure, Ian. Such emotion. It scares me as much as it makes me happy...but happy doesn't describe how you make me feel." I pull his bottom lip down, letting it pop back up as we both laugh. "Don't you think it's strange that we've fallen in love when we don't really know each other? I mean...we've shared a lot and declared a lot, yet you don't know much about me as a person." The thought that he may not like something about me or my history makes my stomach uneasy and a dull ache settles in my chest.

The sadness must show on my face because he taps my nose and says, "Look at me, Charlotte. Stop it. We settled this earlier. I'm in love with you, and it's not something I take lightly. And, for the record, the only thing that scares *me* is the thought of *not* being with you." The look in his eyes makes my heart swell. "You just told me that you love me, six times...I counted." He winks as his face lights up with a smile. "But I already knew it when I walked through the door last night and saw you standing there. I could see it in your eyes, feel it in your kiss. And when our bodies finally came together, there are no words to describe it..." His voice goes low as he runs the back of his fingers across my cheek. "There are no words for the reuniting of two souls. There is only what we feel, and it is ours. Only you and I know what is between us, Charlotte. It would be impossible to explain, even if we tried. Wouldn't you agree?"

"Yes." I suddenly have a lump in my throat.

"Then how could anything else matter? Do you have any idea how much I'm looking forward to getting to know every single thing there is to know about you?" He sits up then, so that I can straddle his lap, my arms around his neck.

"Yes. I feel the same way. But..." I pause, uncomfortable bringing up my past. "...I have some insecurities when it comes to something that seems too good to be true."

"Our story is our own, Charlotte. It doesn't belong to anyone else. Look at me," he says, pausing until I comply. "I know what happened with your parents, and not because Jackson told me. I can explain how I know later, but knowing that part of your history, the pain that you endured at such a young age and the fact that you persevered, blossoming into the magnificent woman that you are, was one of the reasons I fell in love with you." He leans forward and kisses one cheek, wet with tears... then my mouth, then the other cheek. "I will protect you, my love. I told you, you're mine, and that means you're safe. I will never hurt you and I will catch you if you fall."

Grabbing onto him in a tight hug with my arms and legs, I remember the dream I had, where he handed me a drawing of him holding me, catching me from a fall. A surge of emotion runs through me, and for the first time since tragedy struck my life, the thought of my parents' story and how it ended doesn't make me want to hide inside my fortress, locking away my ability to trust and love. "Ian. Thank you. Thank you for finding me, thank you for loving me." I pull back to look at him. I can't help the smile that takes hold. It's big and easily spreads across my face, like it did when I was a child. I haven't smiled like this in a very long time.

"My God, Charlotte. I could sit here and stare at you like this. Promise you'll smile at me like that always."

"Always." I give him a quick kiss and say, "Will you please take me to paradise now?"

Laughing as he stands, with me still holding on, he gives my ass a hot little smack, saying, "Get dressed, LeFay. The plane is ready."

We landed in the Bahamas around 6:00 p.m. and it is indeed paradise. Between our pitstop at his penthouse, the flight over on his private jet, and now this magnificent island getaway, I'm a bit overwhelmed.

My father was a successful businessman and my uncle is a *very* successful businessman, so I'm accustomed to the luxury houses, cars, and designer everything that come along with that kind of financial freedom. But for some reason, seeing what Ian's apparent success has earned him is a little intimidating. I keep telling myself it's his age, because he is very young to have achieved so much. But I know it's also the fact that he's every girl's dream, and it goes well beyond the superficial *looks and money*. He's a phenomenal artist who is shy about his talent, he's sharp and intellectual, wise beyond his years, and his passion knows no bounds. He's dominant in a way that is grounding and sexy at the same time. He has a lifelong best friend who's one of the most honorable men on the planet, he adores his grandmother...I mean, he's literally perfect, and I can't help but wonder how many other women have felt the same way I do. There is no way any sane female could keep her heart intact after being with him, and as always, thinking of how long the list of broken hearts is makes me a little queasy.

Needing some reassurance, I excuse myself to call Erika. She's ready to kill me anyway for not calling her earlier. As usual, she answers on the first ring.

"Where the hell have you been and why have you not called me? You've barely even texted!"

"I know...I'm sorry. My life has just taken a rather drastic turn, Erika. I'm in the Bahamas right now...with Ian."

"WHAT? The Bahamas? With Magic Mike? What the fuck, Charlotte? We left off with you upset about going to dinner with Gabriel. What the hell happened?"

I laugh, not only at her reaction, but at my reality, as well. "It started with Ian showing up at the restaurant last night, giving me a heart attack. I excused myself so I could go beg him to leave so he didn't ruin things with his new business partner, only to have him melt my heart by telling me that he'd fallen in love with me and then immediately breaking it by telling me he won't bother me...ever again!"

After a long pause, she finally responds, "Are you kidding me? He told you he loved you? That is so romantic!" Her voice is all high-pitched and sweet as if someone just handed her a kitten.

"I know. I couldn't deal with Gabriel after that, so I cut dinner short. When I got home, I called Ian."

"Wow...that's major."

"Yeah. You have no idea how major it's been since he walked through my door and took over my body and soul. I'm not kidding when I say that, either, Erika. I have had more sexual pleasure in the past twenty-four hours than most people have in an entire lifetime. And even then, it still probably wasn't as good as what that man is capable of doing."

"Are you serious? God. I'm so jealous!"

"Actually, you should be. It's bloody amazing."

"Well give me details, dammit! I need to replenish my spank bank."

I crack up laughing. "You are so twisted! You would actually spank to a visual of me having sex?"

"Ah...yeah. Why the hell not? You're hot, he's hot. What more do I need?"

"I should be disturbed by that confession."

"But you're not because you love me unconditionally. Now give me some details!"

"I'll give you details when I get home. I don't have enough time right now." I can hear her huffing through the phone. "I'm sorry, I know that's what you live for, but something really major happened earlier today." My stomach does somersaults thinking about it.

"Okay...and? You found out he has an identical twin that I get to play with?"

"No, silly...I told him that I love him, too. And I do, Erika. So much it makes me hallucinate."

"Wow...and wow...I've never even heard of such a thing. Are you sure he didn't drug you?"

Laughing, I respond, "Yeah. He drugged me, all right. With his overwhelming passion and need to take over my body. This may sound completely weird, but I swear there is something more to our connection than simply raw carnality and physical attraction. It's...I don't know...so deep and intense. Like we are desperate for each other, but in a way that's...kind of familiar, I guess."

"Obviously he's your soulmate, dumbass. I could see that from a mile away."

I'm so caught off guard by the frankness of her easy explanation, I sit there letting the truth of it sink in. "My soulmate. Oh my God...that would totally make sense. Why didn't I think of that?"

"Because you were too busy making excuses for why you couldn't be with him. It was a losing battle, though. When I saw the way you two looked at each other at the beach, I knew it was just a matter of time. This isn't the first go-round for you two little lovebirds, and it won't be the last."

"That's very romantic, especially coming from someone who doesn't believe in commitment and has mastered the art of *playing the field*."

"True. But my soul's always been a little slut, so I'm comfortable with it."

We both laugh as her sarcasm takes the edge off my worry. "You are hilarious! The eternal slut... This has the makings for a great cable series."

"Oh my God! It does! And I totally have to be the star."

"That may be your calling, Erika. And to think, all that promiscuity was character building for your future Oscar-winning performance."

"Wow...funny how there's a proper word for slutting around...and you just used it!" She changes her voice to an exaggerated British accent. "Erika Fleming stars in the new hit series, *Promiscuity—Don't Knock It Till You've Tried It.*"

I have to sit down, I'm laughing so hard. "Ooooohh...that is too much. You're going to have to be one of the writers, too, or it won't be as good."

Right then, Ian walks out looking delicious in nothing but a pair of blue-gray board shorts and a smirk that has my stomach doing flips. Walking straight to me, he takes my hand and pulls me up to stand in front of him and kisses me. Erika is saying something, but I can't decipher the words. Finishing, he says, "Let's go swimming." A smile spreads across my face. There is something so adorable about him coming out here to get my attention.

"Erika. I'm sorry, I need to run. I'll try to call you tomorrow or the next day. I just wanted to let you know where I am." I wink at Ian.

"Jesus, he's got a great voice. I am so jealous. Take notes so you don't forget any details. I love you...and Charlotte, I'm happy for you. Don't overthink it! Things may have happened kind of fast, but that doesn't make it wrong. Love doesn't need an explanation or justification. Got it?"

"Yes. It's just funny to hear it coming from you. I love you, too. Thank you."

I end the call and turn to Ian. He has a look on his face I haven't seen before, so I ask, "What?" a little shyly, wondering if I did something embarrassing.

"I've never seen you laugh so hard. It was beautiful and it made me happy." He reaches out and wraps me in his strong arms. His skin is warm and smells so good my eyes involuntarily close as my nose meanders across his chest and up his neck, settling under his ear. "But then I wanted you to get off the phone because I needed you...all to myself. I'm sorry, I know it was selfish."

I lean back so I can see his face. With a peck on his lips, I agree, "It was. But that's okay. It's also adorable, and I'd rather go swimming with you than talk on the phone. Even if it is to my best friend, Erika, who happens to be the funniest person I know." I set my phone down as he guides me to the pool.

It's absolutely beautiful, tucked into coconut palms and other tropical foliage, overlooking the Sea of Abaco on one side and the Atlantic Ocean on the other. I've barely seen anything on the island except what we passed on the way in and a quick look around his house, all of which is amazing, but this pool area alone could be considered paradise. It's breathtaking.

Once we're in the water—it's temperature perfect—he pulls me to him so that my legs wrap around his waist. "So, Erika is the friend you mentioned at lunch? The one that would get along well with my outspoken grandmother?" His eyes light up just mentioning her, and I fall in love with him a little bit more.

"Yes. I hope you get to meet her soon. You'll love her. That is, once you get used to her sense of humor. It's pretty raw. I expect it, and she still manages to shock me." I laugh, thinking about some of the craziness that is Erika Fleming.

"She sounds exactly like Nana, so I'm pretty well-versed on that kind of humor and shock factor. We will have to be cautious about putting the two of them together," he says with a raised eyebrow.

"True. Although, I can't wait to meet Nana. She sounds like fun."

"Oh, she is that. But beyond her unexpected trash mouth"—he pauses to laugh—"she's an amazing person with an amazing soul. I look forward to introducing you." He's slowly moving us through the water, and it's heavenly, almost soft in the way it washes across my skin.

After a few minutes, I break the comfortable silence. "It's totally off-subject, but can I ask you a question?"

"Of course, anything."

My head automatically drops in shyness. It's kind of an awkward question, but it needs to be asked. "Why don't you use condoms when we're together? We really don't know much about each other, and what if I'm not on any birth control? Was that ever a concern for you?"

His eyes shift, the color changing to a deep blue, and I'm momentarily lost in them. Then a sexy-as-hell smirk lifts one side of his mouth, sending a tingling rush through my body. He studies me, then confirms, "There will *never* be anything covering my cock when it's inside you. The thought of not connecting with you completely, naturally, the way it was meant to be, makes me crazy…and *not* in a good way. As for your other concerns, I have always, always used a condom in the past, and if there was any chance I wasn't…clean, I would have never been inside you." He pauses, holding me tighter. "I was already deeply in love with you when I walked through your door and took you into my arms, Charlotte. My instincts are to protect you, that's why I was willing to walk away. If making love to you would potentially harm you, I wouldn't have done it."

My heart almost explodes with love, then his serious expression becomes mischievous as he finishes with, "And if you aren't on any birth control, then…sooner rather than later…I get to fall more in love with you as I watch your body transform, becoming beautifully round as our baby grows inside you."

I catch my breath, suddenly emotional. "Sooner rather than later?" Where did that come from?

"Yes. You *will* be the mother of my children. Though, admittedly, I'd like to wait a while so that I can have you all to myself." He kisses me slowly, then continues. "We have a lot of catching up to do. There are no words to describe how much I'm looking forward to getting to know everything about you. So, selfishly, I'd like to wait, but if you told me tomorrow that you're pregnant, I would be the happiest the man in the world." He pecks my lips one more time.

"Do I get any say-so in this?" I ask, leaning back and giving him a raised eyebrow.

He laughs at me, the deep rumble in his chest making me giddy. "Don't even try it, princess. You have more than say-so. It's entirely in your control."

"Oh? How so?"

"I don't see you as the irresponsible type, Charlotte. If there were a chance you could have gotten pregnant, you would have brought up the topic of a condom well before now, so I wasn't really concerned. But, more importantly, I'm completely under your spell. All you have to do is say what you want, and I will make it happen. Therefore, if you want to have a baby now or five years from now, it's ultimately up to you. I will do what makes you happy." He is so unabashed in his affection. Knowing this powerful, talented, uncommonly handsome man has such strong feelings for me is overwhelming, but in a way that makes my love for him expand, taking on a life of its own. The experience of such deep emotion is so joyful, so exhilarating, I won't let my fear even show its ugly head. I still can't believe fate has brought Ian McAlistair to me.

"How is it that you can make me fall more in love with you

with just a few sentences? You're the one casting spells," I say sincerely.

Without hesitation, he responds. "We've only just begun. I intend to make you fall more in love with me in every way possible...and the possibilities are endless." His voice deepens, and his expression becomes playfully devious. "Like when I take off your bikini and set you up on the edge of the pool, then devour you until my mouth is filled with your cum."

And so he does...again and again.

TWENTY-TWO

IAN

I didn't think I could enjoy my island retreat any more than I already had. It has always been the place I go to reboot—not only my brain, but my soul. My life is fast-paced, overflowing with money and success and all the trimmings. It's what I do, all I know, and I have no intention of changing.

But unbeknownst to anyone but me, it wears me down. Recognizing it for what it is, I don't make excuses. I simply take a break, here in the peaceful solitude of this small island. The breeze off the water—that is therapeutic on its own—combined with the sounds of small, rhythmic waves gently breaking on the shore and the rustle of coconut palms in the wind, the fronds long and flowing, are hypnotic and rejuvenating to everything that I am: internally, externally, spiritually, and beyond.

But having Charlotte here with me has been like nothing I ever knew was possible or ever cared to contemplate. I laugh at myself because I truly believed I was happy, that my life was perfect. Yet looking back, I see that it was empty, and the depth of that emptiness is terrifying to me now. I won't even allow myself to imagine a life without her, and as grateful as I am that I found her, I can't help but wish it had happened sooner.

The scratch of pencil lead on paper continues as I finish the sketch I've been working on for the past forty-five minutes. She was so beautiful in the brightening light of the Bahamian sunrise, I had to draw her. She's asleep next to me, hair fanned out across her pillow, head turned toward me, her extraordinary mouth relaxed, showing off its fullness and splendid design. The white sheets are gathered around her and over her in beautiful disarray that speak of the love we made in the night. One breast is exposed, its dark nipple a focal point against her fair skin and the bright white of the room, lit up by the rising sun. This unstaged presentation is complemented by one exposed leg, bent in relaxation. She's a work of art and her raw beauty tightens my stomach with desire.

Continuing the sketch, I am suddenly thankful for this God-given talent instead of being frustrated by its persistent nagging in the back of my mind, looking for an outlet—or more likely, a muse. It's been a source of intense frustration for many years, yet now I feel fortunate to capture moments like these through the patience and skill of my hand, letting them become a part of me, and not through the mindless push of a button. I will likely have enough to fill a small library by the time I die of old age.

As I put the finishing touches on the sketch, I find myself reciting words in my head. It seems my muse has inspired the poetry I warned her about. My pent-up creativity must be overflowing now that it has tapped into emotions I didn't know existed.

In the whitespace on the bottom left corner of the paper, I let the words flow…

I see eternity in your eyes
I've been lost there
I've been home
Breathed my last breath
Been born again
In your eyes I can travel through time
I know there is pain but I am not afraid

Because there is a constant
Truly never ending
Shining bright and pure
Guiding me
Filling me with an indescribable joy
Driving my passion
Comforting my soul
Bringing me to life
Again and again...

I pause to savor the truth in my good fortune, having found this incredible woman. It's easy for me to imagine spending this life and ten others with her. Never getting bored, never falling into complacency. Each day building onto the next, creating a life of privilege, abundance, and wealth that has nothing to do with money and material things.

She rolls over, distracting me from my poetic daze, the sunlight finally bright enough to wake her. I laugh to myself, because I've never seen white sheets look so lovely. Her spell has turned me into a sentimental artist that sees beauty in everything from the magnificent to the mundane. I have to force myself to adjust, otherwise I'll be controlled by the distraction of my heightened senses.

She laughs a little, her back to me, saying in a sleepy voice, "How long have you been staring at me? I can feel it, you know." She quickly rolls to her back, smiling up at me. "I hope I wasn't snoring or making some silly face you'll never let me live down."

God, she's adorable.

"No. You were not snoring or making a silly face. Though, I would have found either endearing." I pause to stare at the drawing I made of her, reading over the words she inspired. "You were so enchanting, I decided to sketch you. I hope you don't mind."

She quickly sits up, her expression both excited and

concerned as she reaches for the paper. She stares at my work and her hand automatically goes to her mouth, fingers gently touching her lips. I can tell she's reading the poem, and I'm suddenly nervous.

"Ian," she whispers, then looks at me with glazed eyes. "It's so beautiful. The drawing...the poem. I didn't know you could write like this."

"I didn't, either. It just came to me as I finished the sketch. Apparently, the artist in me is very happy you are here," I joke, trying to hide my shyness. Confidence has never been an issue for me, except when it comes to my drawings, and now, evidently, my newly found ability to write poetry.

She stares at me for a minute, her freshly awakened appearance so alluring my hands twitch with wanting to touch her. Finally, she speaks. "You are perfect on a level that is intimidating, Ian McAlistair. Are you aware of that?"

"I hope that was an exaggeration. I don't ever want you to be intimidated by me. Excited out of your mind with anticipation, maybe. But not intimidated." I reach over and pull her to me, laying her across my lap. "Of course, if I'm being honest, I can say there is a part of me that understands. Sometimes I'm a little intimidated by how much I love you." I smile at her sweet expression, then laugh at myself. "Look what you've done to me, Charlotte. I barely recognize myself."

"Oh? And who was the pre-lovestruck Ian?" she says playfully.

"Hmm...let's see, pre-lovestruck Ian was the arrogant, presumptuous bastard that made the mistake of insulting you in the parking lot the day we met."

I know she can see the look of regret on my face, and with a show of compassion, she says, "I remember that guy. That's a pretty accurate description of him. He was seriously hot though." Then she teases my nipple with a light pinch.

"Careful, girl. It doesn't take much. My cock is always at attention when you're near." We both laugh because there's a lot of truth in that statement. We had to take a few days off because she was getting too sore; my appetite for her is insatiable.

"I'd like to apologize for that and try to explain myself." Her expression says I don't have to, but it still weighs heavily on me. Pausing to gather my thoughts, I get straight to the point. "I thrive on control. I always have. And as we discussed, controlling your pleasure sexually is where I derive pleasure."

She gives me a slightly impatient look, apparently wanting to hear something she doesn't already know. Smiling, she interjects with, "You're a Dominant. I get it."

I chuckle, wondering what her definition is. "Actually...I'm dominant, not *a* Dominant. Yes...I prefer to be in control when it comes to sex, and I'm not opposed to using toys every now and again, and I'm definitely not opposed to administering various forms of sensual punishment, but I'm not into controlling *everything* you do or putting you in situations that push your limits when it comes to pain. And I am really not into the kinky shit some people get into. To each his own, but I find a lot of that to be creepy, and it takes away from the beauty of what can be shared during physical passion."

She traces her finger around my chest. "Soooo...I don't have to worry about you showing up holding a whip, wearing painted-on black leather pants with chains crisscrossing your chest while you strap me to a wall and put a ball-gag in my mouth?" She's trying not to laugh.

My tone is serious as I respond, "Ah...no. However, there will be retribution for putting that freakish image in my head. It will be in the form of you replacing it with something real and mind-blowing...on the boat, perhaps," I clarify, giving her a suggestive look.

"That sounds fun," she says playfully then she kisses me.

"You can count on it," I respond with a little nip. "Now, back to what I was saying," smiling at her humor. "I am dominant in the bedroom, which means you will never be unsatisfied, but I also expect honesty between us. It's *very* important to me. *Trust is everything.* I don't see how you can have a healthy relationship without it, especially when I'm controlling your pleasure. The day we met and you lied to me about having a boyfriend, I was pissed off and left, yet I had every intention of finding you. But, then you blew me that triumphant, smartass kiss and I was done. In that split second, I just reacted. But, I reacted as if you were already mine." I pull the sheets down to expose her nipple, giving it a gentle pull, watching it tighten to a hard point as I remember her intense reaction that fateful day. "I had no right to do that. But I swear, when I look back...and I do often...the connection I felt with you was the same as it is right now... That we belong to one another. It doesn't excuse it, but it's the truth."

My eyes are suddenly transfixed on hers and the look of understanding, and maybe a little sorrow, I find there. It's like a kick in the gut that reminds me of how I almost lost her. "I'm sorry, Charlotte," I say in a low voice, looking down to where our hands have come together before reaching up to touch her face, gently following the lines and curves, drowning in the depth of her beautiful eyes. Through the tightness in my chest, I finish. "Thank you for forgiving me." I stare at her a minute longer.

The tenderness in her eyes is pure compassion that makes my heart expand. "Ian, it's okay. I appreciate your apology, and you know I accept it. But we've moved so far past all that it's like ancient history. Also, now that I know you, I get it." She reaches down to play with my fingers. "I understand, and...now that I'm no longer afraid of you, but actually have you wrapped around my little finger"—she's looking down at our hands now held together, laughing at her own cheekiness—"it's pretty hot."

As her eyes look up at mine, a coy innocence accentuating her playfulness, I grab her and pin her down on the bed as her laughing escalates to hysterical. Through it she squeals, "No... no...I'm sorry, I was just being silly!"

I cut her off with a kiss that lasts several minutes. "I'm not disagreeing with the fact that I'm completely wrapped. You accomplished that on day one. It's the *pretty hot* I'm not on board with. That was well beyond *pretty hot*... It was off-the-fucking-charts, immeasurably *hot* and completely messed with my head."

Her eyes soften as a smile lifts the corner of her mouth. I can't help but lean down and kiss her there. "Let's get some breakfast and go out on the boat. I've got an idea for your retribution. Don't think I forgot." With a quick nip on her neck, I jump off the bed then take a moment to stare at her lying there naked, her tan lines sexy as hell on her browned skin.

"Can I have that for breakfast?" she says, pointing at my erection, jutting proudly toward her. The look of desire in her eyes makes it increasingly harder, almost painful.

"You can have that for brunch." Grabbing onto her feet, I pull her across the bed to the edge where I quickly spread her legs, lean down and kiss the inside of her thigh, moving toward where she wants it most. She's moaning out my name, heating my blood and testing my willpower. I give her wet pussy an open-mouth kiss, my tongue diving in to drink up her arousal, leaving her on the edge of climax...exactly where I want her. And then I stand.

"Ian, no...please...I can't wait," she says as I walk away to prepare her coffee. At the door, I turn to see her hands moving down to finish the job herself.

"Ah-ahh. No touching. That orgasm is mine. Now get your sexy little ass out here so I can feed you breakfast." I have to force myself to follow through; the temptation she presents is all-consuming, and I mentally pat myself on the back for showing such discipline.

Unsurprisingly, breakfast goes by quickly, both of us anxious to get out on the water. It's a beautiful day with a cloudless sky, slight cooling breeze, and calm seas. Thankfully, it's the time of year that we practically have the whole place to ourselves with only a random boat passing here and there, most likely locals going about their daily routines. It's perfect—I need privacy for what I have planned today.

The water is like glass as we carve through its flawless surface. I love the feel of it, the full power of the engines enhanced by the boat's design, totally unencumbered by waves, chop, or wind. Charlotte is sitting next to me, staring off at the view of various islands as we pass. Each cay has its own story and personality, every one charming in its own way.

I often think about the people that settled these islands in the late 1700s and the tremendous challenges they overcame. For all its beauty and resources, it was still very isolated. Many of the smaller cays have only recently, in the past few generations, become somewhat modernized. But that's part of the charm and appeal that stays with you even after you've returned home, leaving you with a longing to walk through the narrow streets lined with tropical foliage and brightly colored cottages, to breathe the salt air and swim in the crystal-clear water over white sand. I've always had a strange connection to this place. From the first time I visited with a friend, many years ago, there was something about it that seemed familiar, like I was supposed to be here. It was on that trip that I bought my house on the quiet end of one of the smaller cays. It was one of the best decisions I've ever made.

Up ahead I see our destination, a sandbank so massive it would take more than twenty minutes to drift from one side to the other and probably extends a mile from the shore. The huge expanse of white sand covered by turquoise water makes it glow in contrast to the surrounding depths and grassy shoals, like a beacon leading the way. The nearby island is uninhabited, and there isn't a soul in sight.

Charlotte notices the brightness of the sandbank up ahead and asks, "What is that? It's so pretty." She stands up in excitement to get a better look, confirming my suspicion that she will love this place. She's been combing the beaches for treasures and snorkeling just off shore to see what's waiting to be washed in. But here, on the sandbank, you have to dive ten to fifteen feet to get anything you may want to take home.

"It's called Tilloo Bank. It's basically a giant sandbar covered with water. We can dive for sand dollars, the occasional conch or helmet, and tons of other shells." I lean over to kiss her smile, "I figured you would like it here."

"Like it? I love it! I just can't believe no one else is here. It's huge, and we have it all to ourselves," she says, looking around the bank's expanse as we slow down to find a spot to anchor. My stomach tightens in anticipation as I think about her naked body swimming through the crystal-clear water. The vision has already inspired another drawing.

Setting the boat to idle, I head to the bow to drop the front anchor. The current is not too strong today, otherwise we would have to drift with the boat, and that can be exhausting. The anchor sets easily in the sandy bottom, so I tie off the line and go to cut the engine only to find Charlotte already preparing to get in with her mask and snorkel in hand. "I've created a monster, haven't I?" I ask.

"I don't know, maybe I was a mermaid in another life," she says with a glorious smile. "I just love being in the water, and I feel like a child at Christmas. I'm so excited about what I might find."

Her laugh echoes under the canopy of the boat as her enthusiasm wraps around me, motivating me to grab my gear and join her, putting my plans aside for now. The water is perfect, slightly cooler than the air, like a swimming pool heated to the ideal temperature. We spend more than a half an hour in this spot, diving down for what seems like every shell within a hundred-foot radius. My little faerie may actually be more of a mermaid. Every single thing she finds is treated like a treasure made of gold.

She is different here, more relaxed, undistracted, and carefree. But mostly she seems so genuinely happy and it's contagious. I've always loved the Abacos, for obvious reasons, but having her here has taken the whole experience to a different level. We've been here for five days, and I'm ready to stay another month, maybe two.

Finally ready to dry off, we get out of the water and lie on the bow, letting the sun warm us as the boat gently rocks to the rhythmic sound of tiny waves dancing along the hull. It's so relaxing we both doze off, but not long after, I wake up and start feeling impatient. Not willing to wait any longer, I sit up, letting the blood get back to my head then move to the bench across from us that's positioned under the canopy, facing the bow...and Charlotte. After a few minutes of simply taking in her natural beauty, I speak. "Take your bikini off, Charlotte."

Popping up on her elbows, eyes blinking, she says, "What?"

"You heard me. Take it off." I give her a slight nudge of my head as I look at the parts of her body I want uncovered. She smiles nervously and looks around, instinctively worried someone might see her. But no one will, I wouldn't let that happen.

"Ooookay. Is this where my retribution begins?"

"Yes," I respond matter-of-factly.

"Should I be nervous?"

"No. But I'm sure you will be, anyway." I raise a brow. "Off."

And she obeys. Lying there, naked and glorious, her damp hair naturally messy around her face that is free of any enhancement, her dark nipples hardened from the sudden exposure to the slight breeze, her perfectly smooth pussy so pale against her tanned stomach and legs...it's a magnificent scene. There isn't one thing I would change about her. Her body is muscular and athletic but soft and curved at the same time.

"You have no idea how amazing you look right now, do you?"

She puckers her lips, playing along with what is suddenly turning into self-torture as my unexposed cock jumps with a quick rush of blood. It will be a bloody miracle if I make it through this to completion. "How often do you masturbate, Charlotte? That is...before you met me," I ask, giving her a knowing smirk.

Surprised, she fumbles for the right words. "Umm...I don't... know." She ends with a shy—if not embarrassed—laugh.

"Do you know how to make yourself cum?" I ask, "I can walk you through if you don't," I reassure her with a devilish smile.

The challenge I presented appears to have worked. She knows what I want, and it turns her on. I can see it on her face and the way her body relaxed, one leg shifting outward...just slightly. "Yes...I know how to make myself cum. Is that what you want me to do, Ian?" Bringing her fingers up to her mouth, she wets them, her tongue coming out to tease me, then slowly she brings them down to slide between her bare lips. Those gorgeous legs are now spread, exposing her fully. *Goddamn, she is stunning!* Her finger rubs gentle circles around her clit as her head falls back and her eyes close, the sun shining directly above her. Hard shadows contrast against the light's reflection, following the curves and lines and details of her form, creating something that is both fantastically real and abstract all at once. I let the image burn itself into my mind so I can retrieve it...

frequently. A sound escapes her as she lies back completely onto the bow, her other hand reaching up to tease a tender nipple.

I stay quiet and continue to watch her, knowing the pleasure is heightened by my role as voyeur. The proof is there, wet and glistening, making my mouth water. "You're already wet, Charlotte. Reach down. I want to watch you spread it around that gorgeous pussy."

Without hesitation she does my bidding, sliding her fingers down, coating them with her essence. A moan escapes as her back arches, legs spreading farther apart. She wasn't lying when she said she knows how to make herself cum, and imagining her by herself, doing what she's doing right now, has pushed my erection to its maximum. No longer able to keep it contained, I remove my board shorts, take my rock-hard cock in hand, and rub my thumb across the tip where it's slippery and anxious for what it craves. I'm ready to explode and could walk over to her right now, and with a few strokes, mark her flat stomach with the intense orgasm that's waiting to be released. But I won't. I want to cum inside her because there is nothing that compares to *that* particular ecstasy.

"Now put your fingers in your mouth. Act like it's my cock... like you want to make me cum."

"Ian, I want *you*. Please...come here." She's thrusting against her hand now, and I'm ready to give in.

"Fingers in your mouth, Charlotte... Now you can watch me while you do it."

She turns her head, eyes glazed with wanting, and slowly brings her wet fingers up to her mouth, licking from the base then taking two of them deep, sucking hard. She's watching my hand intently as it moves up and down my shaft, shiny and bulging as it begs for her. She squeezes her legs together, trying to create pressure where she needs it most. "Do you like that... watching me pleasure myself? Imagining it's your mouth taking me deep, tasting my cum as it spills across your tongue." I'm thrusting into my hand now, tightly cupping my balls with the other. She whimpers as she nods, bringing her fingers out to run her tongue along the tip. *Goddammit!* "Spread your legs and put your fingers in your pussy." I can hear the edge in my voice; I need to cum.

"Ian. My God, I have to have you inside me. Please..." Her breathing is heavy as she starts to fuck herself, the wet sound of her fingers moving in and out in rhythm with my own hard strokes. She has to cum soon or I will never last.

"Bring your other hand down and put pressure on your clit."

She does, and by the hitch in her breathing and the familiar moans escaping her, I can tell she's close. I walk over to her, out from underneath the canopy and into the sunlight. "Look at my cock. Look at how hard I am for you. Look what you do to me." I'm stroking harder now, the head wet, making her lips part with wanting. "Harder, Charlotte." Three seconds later she's writhing through her orgasm, legs twitching then squeezing together as she looks for more. This isn't enough. She's already programmed to only find full satisfaction through me...and it's completely blowing my mind.

Giving her less than ten seconds more to ride through her pleasure, I demand through gritted teeth, "Roll over and put your ass in the air."

Her movements are weak as her orgasm hasn't fully subsided. I help her get in position. Standing back to admire her, spread open, beautifully exposed, enticingly wet. On instinct, I reach down to coat my own fingers, spreading it across her ass cheek. "What do you want me to do, Charlotte? Tell me what you need."

"Please...Ian. Do it."

"Say it. Tell me what you want."

"Ian." She's begging without words. But I want to hear it.

"Say it."

"Hard...now! Dammit...spank me hard...Ian." Her back arches and she turns to look at me. Suddenly confident in her demands. "Mark me...I need you to mark me..." My hand lands in a stinging smack that echoes down my spine. *Fuck!* This is better than I anticipated. Pushing her to be comfortable with herself, with her own wants and desires. All of it heightened by the freedom of being out here on the water, the full exposure of being outdoors enhancing every touch, every sound...every sensation.

Another smack echoes, and I see her pussy tighten with the contact. I do it again...and again...and again, harder and harder. She's pushing herself toward me, ass cheeks bright red, her perfect lips pulsating and begging. Barely holding herself up, she looks over her shoulder, hair in wild disarray across her body, her face lethal with desire. It triggers a madness inside me like I have never known. My adrenaline spikes, making my heart pound as her pleasure becomes more intense...as her brain is injected with endorphins. It's like a drug, and she's already addicted.

One last smack and I spread her apart, then bury my face in her wet cunt. I drink her in before taking my throbbing cock to her entrance, sliding it between her swollen lips all the way to the base and holding it there, hands firm on her hips. I pump hard against her core as I yank her toward me, buried as deep as I can go before slowly pulling it out again, admiring how she is perfectly stretched around me. Just before the head comes out completely, I drive it back in, slow and measured, pushing her limits. When her slight contractions begin to squeeze my shaft, I pick up my pace and start pounding into her, my grip still tight on her hips, pulling her to me, our wet skin slapping together.

Growling out, I hear myself say, "Mine. You're mine." My voice sounds otherworldly as it becomes saturated with emotion and pleasure. She screams out my name as I continue fucking her through orgasms so intense and so drawn-out I'm afraid we both might black out.

As the intensity finally wanes, I fall forward, unable to stand any longer. She collapses underneath me. "Charlotte?" I ask weakly. "Are you okay?" I get a small nod in response. Still inside her, the feeling is indescribable as she slowly milks me dry, the gentle, involuntary contractions like an exquisite dessert after an unforgettable entrée. Every now and again my cock jumps, making my breath hitch from the flow of lingering pleasure.

My back is starting to burn, and our sweat has mingled together all over her back and my chest. Getting up so we can sit in the shade, I pull her with me and cradle her in my lap.

Once we are comfortable, her head falls to my chest, and I know she's still there—in that strange place between consciousness and unconsciousness. That place that is like being awake in a dream you don't want to end. It's beyond peaceful. It's pure and healing and powerful...and she will crave being there as much as I crave putting her there.

Time passes as I hold her, staring at her and thinking of all the ways I want to spoil her and make all her dreams come true. When she eventually comes around, she doesn't open her eyes, but she smiles and says, "I think I just died from intense pleasure exposure...literally. IPE...I've wondered if it was possible more than once over the past week, but now I know it is." She opens her eyes and asks in the most serious tone, "How did you bring me back to life?"

Laughing, I respond, "That's cute, LeFay. Plan on being permanently afflicted with IPE, a condition that is *not* deadly but quite rejuvenating. Although it may not seem that way when an acute attack occurs; the benefits tend to build with each experience." She's giving me a look that says, *Oh really?*, so I continue. "It actually makes you stronger. Before long, you'll have superpowers." I smile down at her and my heart skips a beat from the happiness shining in her eyes. She is very much in love with me. I can see it...I can feel it.

We seem content to simply look at each other. Studying each other's eyes and all the features we find so appealing about one another. With a straight face, she breaks the silence. "Erika said something to me the other day, when we first got here. I needed to talk to her because I was confused about my feelings for you, how intense they are." She laughs a little. "And that I told you I love you after being with you for...what? Two days, maybe? And that I meant it, with all my heart." She looks away— evidence of her lingering insecurities.

"Charlotte, you do realize this is all a good thing, right? You don't need to be afraid of it."

"Yes. I know. It's not that...really. It's that it's so different, like nothing I've ever even *heard* of. But Erika told me I needed to chill out because it was quite obvious you and I are soulmates. I believe her words were...*this isn't the first go-round for you two lovebirds, and it won't be your last.*" Her expression is serious again as she continues. "Do you believe that, Ian? I know you've made reference to it before, but do you think that could be true?"

"Yes," I say succinctly. "There is something uncommonly powerful between us. But I don't question it. I think I see it for what it is, whether we give it a title or not." I hold her a little tighter.

"For me, it may be easier to accept the idea of having a *soulmate,* if that's what you want to call it. You see, my family is from Scotland, and Nana is quite proud of our Scottish heritage and all the superstitions therein. She's been telling me since I was a boy that I have an old soul because of my 'wisdom, sharp instincts, and turquoise eyes,'" I boast as we both laugh. "She says the McAlistair line runs deep within me, and I agree with her... There is something there, but it's not something I can pinpoint or really describe. It's just there. I think that's why she and I are so close—she has an old soul, as well, and a sixth sense that is never wrong," I explain, but Charlotte only half smiles, as though her thoughts are elsewhere. "What is it? Did I lose you with all that boring stuff about Scotland and old souls?"

Sitting up to straddle my lap, she looks at me and almost seems bashful. Finally, she says, "Ian, I hope you don't think I'm crazy when I tell you this...because it *is* kind of crazy, but it's true and I don't know what to make of it." She's looking down to where her fingers are tracing paths around my stomach and chest.

"I love your kind of crazy, now out with it." I'm growing impatient with curiosity.

"The other day at my condo when...Gabriel texted me..." That last part came out uncomfortably. About as uncomfortable as it makes the inside of my chest feel. Good thing she let the nuisance know before we left to back off, she's taken. "You kissed me." She looks up with a smile that lights up my world. "And it was amazing, as always, but different somehow."

"Yeah...you fainted and gave me a fucking heart attack," I sternly add.

"Yes, well, no. I didn't faint. It was...something else entirely. I don't know, maybe because of the tension of the moment or the fact that you were pushing me to come clean with my true feelings for you..." She's serious, yet her eyes are distant. "But something happened during that kiss." Looking away, she takes a deep breath, then continues. "It was really strange, but there was this sudden bright light, then out of nowhere we were standing in a meadow that was the most beautiful place I've ever seen. We were still kissing, but I was seeing this strange place at the same time, almost like I was watching myself. The sky was the purest blue, there were mountains in the distance, purple flowers everywhere, a stream running nearby... I could hear the sounds of it and smell the clean air and feel the coolness on my skin. Ian...it was *so* real, but I knew at the same time that it wasn't. Regardless, I felt so happy I didn't want it to be a dream. I wanted it to be real. I wanted to stay there...with you. But then, what made my legs give out was... Oooh, this is the part that really freaks me out, and I know you're going to think it's weird." She's running her hands through her hair, then to her neck, as if to rub away the tension.

"Honestly, I'm totally intrigued by everything you're telling me. So please, don't stop now."

"Okay"—she takes another deep breath—"when we stopped

kissing, I noticed a stone building not far in the distance. It was old, had to be more than three stories high. It was huge! But then I shifted my eyes back to you...and the only thing that was *you* were your eyes. Exactly as they are right now, that amazing turquoise with jet-black lashes... Oh, and your smell, that was the same," she says, giving me a coy look. "But your features were different. Your nose, your mouth. You had long hair that was pulled back in a low ponytail! And now that I think about it, you had on a navy-blue jacket with gold trim and a high collar. I mean...it was so strange, like I suddenly woke up in some historical movie or something!" I can tell she's relieved to get this off her chest, but more so, there is something about this image that makes her happy.

"That's when my legs gave out!" she enthusiastically clarifies. "I didn't know what the hell was happening, but Ian?" She pauses to look at me, taking my hands in hers. "When I finally caught my breath and cleared my head, I had this overwhelming need to tell you how much I love you. It was like, I could finally say it. Like I was given a chance that had been taken away and it was so wonderful, I don't even think words can justify the feeling." I can see tears forming in her eyes, but she smiles through them, stealing my heart for the tenth time today.

"Wow, Charlotte. I have to say, that is a pretty powerful story. I think you must have had some kind of memory from a past life, as strange as it may seem. I'm not sure how else to make sense of it. Extraordinary things happen with no explanation, and this is one of them." Reaching up to touch her suntanned face, I still see the skepticism in her expression. "Relax, you. Just let it be what it is. Look at it as a gift. Your soul is letting you know that this is okay, that we are meant to be together. The idea that we have loved before, in some other place and time, is beyond spectacular." I pull her closer, wanting her warmth and scent that has become comforting and grounding. "I'd be disappointed if that weren't the case, Charlotte." Holding her face, I kiss her softly. "Stop overthinking it. We are together now, and that's all that matters. Got it?"

She nods and gives me a knowing smile. We stand and I guide her to the back of the boat, then with a quick smack on her bare cheek, I say, "Now get your sexy ass in the water to cool off. I want to watch you swim naked. You're a masterpiece and I could look at you all day."

And so she does, swimming around as if it were some kind of choreographed dance, so graceful and effortless. I stand there completely ensnared by all that she is and the significance of everything we just discussed. A sudden flush raises the hairs across my body as I thank God and the universe along with every ancient god and goddess known to mankind for making her mine...in this life and any other that has been or will be.

TWENTY-THREE
CHARLOTTE

S itting at Laney's, I'm lost in thought as I wait for Erika to join me. It's been four and a half months since Ian and I returned from the Abacos, but time has not faded the memories or the longing to go back. There was something ethereal about our time there, about how we came together in a way that was so much more than physical. Although, the physical part could actually be considered spiritual since, on more than one occasion, I ended up in a dreamlike realm that is so peaceful— where nothing of this physical world even exists to cloud what really matters. I can't help but think that is what heaven would be like, and then I wonder to myself, is that blasphemy?

Ian was right, though—it is rejuvenating, and I am stronger, like I've tapped into a power and confidence I didn't know existed within me. Now, when I look at the drawing Ian did of me, portrayed as a faerie that is so comfortable in her own skin, with her natural beauty, strength, and power, I recognize more of myself in her. It's as if Ian knew who I was before I did, which is fitting considering everything that has happened between us.

"Bet I can guess what's going on in your head right now," Erika says, startling me out of my daydream. "It starts with Ian and ends with orgasm. And don't try to deny it... It's written all over your face."

Laughing out loud, I respond, "That's only partially correct. I was thinking about our trip to the Abacos."

"Really? Still? What the heck did he do to you over there?" she asks, getting comfortable in the seat across from me.

"Good question. I'm not sure there is even a name for it. But it goes way beyond good sex."

"Well, from what you've already told me, I would say that's a pretty accurate statement!" Erika says enthusiastically. "The only sucky part of this whole thing is that, now, my sex life pales in comparison. Which actually doesn't make any sense, because I'm the one totally focused on super-hot sex where I get spanked and tied to the bed and penetrated...everywhere...by a super-hot guy that makes my toes explode with intense, rapid-fire orgasms. The Law of Attraction is supposed to make this *my* reality. You haven't been focused on this kind of juicy love, so how the heck did it come your way?" she finishes, genuinely confused.

"Huh...maybe your subconscious mind felt sorry for me because I wasn't getting any love, juicy or otherwise, and it redirected the focus toward me." I pause for a second to smile at her and the catty expression forming on her face. "Erika, how sweet of you!" I reach over and put my hand on hers, trying not to laugh. "You are a true, and very generous, friend."

Her face goes expressionless. "You want to know what's so screwed up? That seriously has merit! While I've been out slutting around, trying to figure out who is the best lay in Miami, I've been feeling kind of guilty because you weren't getting any at all. I literally would tell myself...*I wish Charlotte would get some good booty, she deserves it more than anyone.* That is no lie! I seriously bet my Law of Attraction did rub off on you!" She stops to look at me in mild shock. "Uhhh...you freakin' owe me. Big time!!"

I bust out laughing from the look on her face and the fact that she's starting to believe I reaped the benefits of her begging the universe for more hot sex than she was already having. "Oh, Erika! This is hilarious!"

"Yeah, I bet it is. Except I feel like you stole my winning lottery ticket. Bitch."

Wiping the tears from my eyes, I say, "Stop! You're making my stomach hurt!" Holding it, I continue, "Blame Sibel. It was her psycho road rage that caused everything."

"Yeah…Sibel. Your aggro alter-ego swiped my mojo. I'm having a hard time accepting *that* injustice!"

"Okay, okay! I'm sorry we swiped your mojo… I promise to make it up to you," I concede in a sugary tone.

She looks at me with one raised brow and an undeniable smirk. "Really? How so?"

I can only imagine what naughty thoughts are going through her head right now. "I will commit myself to a daily meditation where I ask the universe to bring Erika Fleming her very own Magic Mike to play with, that spanks her, ties her up, and gives her toe-popping orgasms every day."

She thinks about it then adds, "You forgot spontaneous nipple orgasms. I want those, too."

"Of course, you do. How silly of me to forget," I say, rolling my eyes while Erika's smile beams back at me. "What now? You've done a complete one-eighty on me and I'm not sure what to make of it."

"I'm just happy for you. Seriously…all selfishness and joking aside. I see a dramatic difference in you. Like you've come out of a shell I didn't even know you were in. If that makes any sense."

Thinking about her observation, I agree, "Yeah, it actually does, and that's a pretty accurate description. Whatever it is that you see, I feel and it's powerful. Here I was, all this time, thinking I had it together and, considering the hellish nightmare I was faced with by the age of twenty, I thought my confidence was well intact. But I swear, Erika, I would have never in a million years thought that submitting to Ian, that trusting him to control my pleasure, would have such a profound effect." I pause as a sense of excitement flashes through me, like it always does when I think about what he does to me. "Apparently, relinquishing control, at least for a little while, reboots the control that makes me successful at my career, that makes me confident...sharp...happy...everything! It probably sounds unreal, but I swear it's true."

"No, that makes a lot of sense. It's like how meditation rejuvenates your mind. You wouldn't think that when you stop thinking and only focus on your breathing, your brain gets smarter, but it does. It must be the same thing with submission," she states, totally on board with my logic. But as the seconds pass, I can see her mind has traveled at warp speed to reach a conclusion that will likely have her signing up as a member at the nearest BDSM club right after lunch.

Right as her eyes widen, I try to stop her. "Erika. I can literally read your mind. Stop it!"

"I am suddenly overwhelmed with the potential of all this fabulous information! Think of the possibilities! I can freely do all that kinky shit I've been too afraid to even consider. I'll just relinquish myself over to some Dom that will whip me into perfection!" Her eyes are actually black with misplaced desire and now I fear for her safety.

"Erika. Stop being ridiculous! You are not relinquishing yourself over to *some Dom*. How did you left turn this conversation into Kinktown? I'm not talking about whips and chains. I'm talking about a mutual trust between two people that are in love. There is a big difference." I'm trying not to be too reprimanding.

Letting out a huff, she retorts, "I know...chill out. It was fun to think about it for a minute. But it's a completely unrealistic idea. I couldn't be with a Dom that's already Dommed someone else. He'd have to buy all new equipment and sanitize the entire house...and himself! And the hotness level I'd require him to meet sends the whole idea right off a cliff." And, as usual, she's dead serious.

"Oh my God. That was the weirdest, kink version of 'Squirrel!' I've ever heard. Now stop highjacking my love story!" I say, trying not to laugh at the silly look on her face.

"You're right. I totally highjacked your story. I'm sorry."

"You're forgiven. And back to your earlier point, yes…it's very much like the benefits of meditation. Honestly, there are times he pushes the pleasure so far, I end up in a meditative state. But it isn't only my mind. It's my whole body, maybe even my soul. It's deep, and according to Ian, that's where most of the healing takes place," I explain, hoping it doesn't sound strange. Though, it did seem strange to me, at first, there is no denying the sense of freedom within myself.

I can see that Erika is loving this conversation as she adds, "I know some people…well, a lot of people…would think that's weird or total BS that excuses what they would consider disgraceful, it's really not. It's beautiful! I mean, it wipes away all pretention, cuts through that thick layer of expectation that society bogs us down with, and exposes the real you. And!…the only way you get there is through trust and love and the most fantastic gift we, as humans, received…*carnal pleasure*. This is truly poetic!" She announces that boatload of information loudly, causing me to look around the restaurant, worried someone might be listening.

Laughing, I shake my head and say, "Yes, it is. That's why humans have been writing about it for thousands of years. But I'm curious… How many cups of coffee have you had today?" I ask, laughing a little harder as I see her counting them in her head.

"Haha! Funny. I can't help it if you and Ian inspire me to think about sex more three-dimensionally, so to speak. I mean, it's always fun and feels amazing, even beyond amazing if he's especially good at it, but you guys add this extra layer. It must be the soulmate factor. It makes it so deep…almost primal," she says, lifting her arm up toward me. "Look! It gives me chills!"

Laughing at her reaction to my sex life, I go to respond, but my phone pings an interruption. "Speak of the devil."

Ian: You need to bring the rest of your things over to my place. It's time for you to officially move in.

"Ugh!" I groan without thinking.

"What's wrong? Surely the devil had something yummy to say."

"He wants me to officially move in," I reply, hearing the doubt in my own voice and wondering why the hell I'm making this so complicated.

"Yeah. And?" Erika questions. "Sounds like heaven to me. Last time we all got together at his penthouse, I told Jackson and Becca that Ian must have the best view in all of Miami. It's awesome! Living there, you'd have your sunrise, the sunset, and everything in between. What else could you ask for? And it's free!"

Before answering, I text Ian back.

Me: I pretty much live there now, Ian.

"I know. I'm there all the time and I love it so much and…I mean…I know I'm going to move in eventually, it's just…" I pause because I know my justification no longer has any merit, yet it stands firm in the back of my mind like the Queen's Guard at Buckingham Palace, not budging from position, no matter what. "…I like having my condo, available and paid for by me. I know it has everything to do with my mother's dependence on my father and it is clear evidence of the deep scars left in their wake. You'd think acknowledging it would make it go away, but it doesn't," I finish just as Ian replies.

Ian: It's not the same. I want you to consider my home your home. I thought that's what you wanted. You seem happy there. I don't understand why you fight me on this every time I bring it up.

Damn, he's getting upset with me, and I hate that. So I send a reply that could probably be considered a white lie since the truth would likely not go over well. For him or me.

Me: Please don't be upset with me. It's more me putting off the hassle of packing all the stuff I hardly use. Everything I need is already at your place

I've barely turned my attention back to Erika and he's already texted again and hasn't missed the opportunity to back me into a corner.

Ian: If that's the case, then we'll do it this weekend. I'll help so you don't have an excuse anymore.

Sibel storms in and hits the "Be a bitch because he's being a pushy jerk" button, but I shut her down so she doesn't start an unnecessary argument.

Me: Okay...but don't be mad at me when you see how much stuff I have in my little condo.

Ian: I would be surprised if you didn't have a lot of stuff. Btw, we are taking Nana out for sushi tonight. She specifically requested you be there or she's not going.

Hmm...he got his way, so we are on to the next topic. Brat!

Me: That will be fun. I wouldn't miss it. What time?

Ian: We're picking her up at 6:30.

Me: Perfect! I'll see you then.

Ian: Why don't you leave work early so I can make you cum all over my tongue before we leave.

My God... When he talks like that, even over text, it sends a bolt of electricity straight through my body, landing joyously between my legs.

"Ummm..." Erika chimes in after waiting patiently. "I just witnessed a full range of facial expressions all in less than three minutes. You went from defensive to compassionate to pissed off to sugary sweet to completely turned on. Can I please read that full exchange so I can make sense of all that?" Her hands draw out a circle around me to reinforce her question.

Laughing out loud at her observation, I say, "I'm sorry. That man gets me so flustered I lose track of what I'm doing. Evidently, he's helping me pack the rest of my stuff this weekend, I'm officially moving into his place, we are having dinner with Nana tonight, and he's going to make me cum all over his tongue before we go."

With a straight face and deadpan tone, she says, "I'm really going to have to work hard at forgiving you for stealing my lottery ticket."

Still laughing, I dab the corners of my eyes with my napkin so my mascara doesn't smear, just as my phone pings again.

Ian: You left me hanging on that text...why?? You know what that's going to lead to.

Oh my God! I literally felt my nipples harden and heat flush between my legs.

Me: I'm at lunch with Erika, she distracted me. But I'm glad she did. Your text turned me on instantly and now my pussy is wet.

I don't think a second passes and my phone rings, spiking my heart rate even more. I'm excited and nervous at the same time and Erika is looking at me like I've got three heads. On the third ring, I answer, "Hello."

Ian's deep voice sends chills across my skin. "Are you testing me on purpose?"

The logical part of my mind is wondering how the hell that simple question spoken in that delicious, commanding voice was like adding jet fuel to my arousal. "Um...no. What do you mean?"

"I'll *show* you precisely what I mean. Be naked and standing at the foot of the bed with your back to the door at exactly 4:30. *Don't* be late." And he hangs up.

Looking down at my phone, because I can't bring myself to look at Erika right now, I let the anticipation and heat flow through me as my clit starts to gently throb, causing me to squeeze my legs together, instinctively looking for pressure. I want to text him back and tell him that I'll meet him there right now. But I know he's making me wait on purpose, and if I push it, he'll make me wait even longer.

"If I'm not mistaken, your arousal vibes just made everyone in the restaurant's phone glitch out. You do realize you're still sitting in a public place...right?" Erika says with a smirk.

Snapping out of it, I quickly look up at her, the dullness of my mind believing her sarcasm. Throwing her head back laughing, she adds, "Clearly, you don't! Either you're easy or he's really good, because you just lit up like a match—no, like a freaking blow torch—in a matter of seconds!" Still laughing, she picks up the drink menu and starts fanning me. I know that my face is red and it's not from embarrassment.

Giggling as I wipe the moisture from my hands, I respond. "Somehow, I managed to wake up the beast and for that; my day just got a lot more interesting. He wants me naked and waiting for him at precisely 4:30." I use my napkin to wipe the dampness from my neck. "Just thinking about it gives me a mini orgasm!"

"Wow. Ya know, if you were a true friend, you would at least invite me to watch."

Falling for her sarcasm, again, I look up at her only to find our teenaged waiter standing within earshot with his mouth hanging open and a look of confusion mixed with arousal on his face. Erika spots him, too, and neither of us can help it as we bust out laughing, watching the poor guy flee the scene.

Erika reaches into her purse and throws some money on the table. "Here, lunch is on me. We've gotta get out of here. I can't bear the thought of what that boy's getting ready to go do in the bathroom. You do understand we're going to be his spank bank material for the next three months, at least!"

"Oh nice, Erika! What's with you and the spank bank?" I say, grabbing my paper napkin as we go so I can fix my mascara in the car. "Thanks for that unwanted visual!"

As soon as we're out the door, she hooks her arm through mine, still laughing, and says, "Payback, sister."

TWENTY-FOUR

IAN

Nana gets annoyed if we have to wait more than ten minutes for a table, so I called in a reservation to ensure we were seated right away. It's a good thing I did because this place is packed tonight. The sushi is excellent here, and even though the decor is ultra-modern and dripping with style, the atmosphere is warm and inviting. It's a known hotspot in Miami and it's not uncommon to see celebrities and other prominent people dining here.

I have to smile as I watch Charlotte innocently talking to Nana, completely oblivious that half the patrons are staring at her, wondering if she's a celebrity. She is stunning, as always, but not showing it off like so many others do... Another thing about her I find very appealing.

Noting my attention, she pauses her conversation, offering me a natural smile. "What?" The innocence in her expression takes my breath away.

"Nothing. Just love-struck and mesmerized by your beauty."

"Hmmm...I've still got it, then? You're not tired of looking at me yet?" She laughs and playfully nudges Nana's shoulder and points at me. "What do you think, Nana? Maybe I'll have him wrapped a little longer?"

Without missing a beat, Nana pipes in with, "From the looks of your wrists, it appears you're the one that's been wrapped…to the bed, perhaps?"

Charlotte's face turns crimson as her jaw falls open, looking at me, hoping I can throw her a lifeline. She can't see the smirk on Nana's face, but I can, and I'm trying hard not to laugh.

"Nana. Was that necessary?" My tone is reprimanding.

"What? Don't act so virginal, you two. I'm observant, and I wasn't going to say anything, but then the opportunity presented itself…and I just couldn't resist." She's grinning from ear to ear and turns to Charlotte. "Don't worry about it, honey. I'm not scandalized by it and neither should you be. That's the best thing about a healthy relationship with your partner—all the fun kinky stuff you get to do!"

She's right about that. After Charlotte tested my resolve earlier and I told her to be waiting, naked, at the foot of the bed, I had a hard-on for the rest of the day that was damn near uncontrollable. I could see her in my mind, standing there with her back to me, her flawless creamy skin waiting for my touch, submitting to her need for me to take control. When I arrived home at exactly 4:30, I was not disappointed. She stayed still, knew better than to look back at me as I entered. I could sense her arousal from across the room and as I got closer, I could smell her mouthwatering scent that I had been craving all day. "Open your legs," I said, standing behind her, but not touching. She did, stepping her feet apart to give me access. I waited several seconds longer before reaching under to slide my fingers across her pussy, which was wet and slippery, as I knew it would be. I played with it, enjoying its warmth, feeling it swell, knowing I could make her cum instantly…if I allowed it. Swirling my finger around her clit, I heard her whimper. Bringing my mouth close to her ear, I said, "Don't cum," right as I pushed two fingers inside her and bit down on the meat of her shoulder where it curves to join her delicate neck. She almost lost the battle. The hours of anticipation were too much of a build-up, so I released her before she reached the point of no return.

Keeping her there, not letting her look at me, I gently placed the blindfold over her eyes then turned her around, devouring her lips and tongue in a kiss designed to make her beg. Which she did...or at least tried before I took her erect nipples between my fingers, stealing her voice as I kept her on the edge of orgasm. Once I had her tied to the bed, I teased her gently with the soft tips of her favorite flogger, then abused her breasts and nipples with perfectly executed snaps of the leather strips. Her back arched as she panted my name, each repeated syllable causing more blood to rush to my stiff cock. She begged for me to fuck her, but I did not. I was greedy and high on her lust. I engorged myself on controlling her pleasure, and when I brought out the vibrator that I chose specifically for her anal pleasure, carefully put it into place, then prepared her for double penetration with my fingers, she could no longer hold back as a powerful orgasm took hold. It was magnificent to watch... Charlotte, her gorgeous body flexed and arching, her arms spread wide as the ties on her wrists pulled tighter, her swollen mouth open and begging right below her blindfolded eyes, as her body trembled through the release.

After that glorious event, I decided to keep the vibrator in her ass while I fucked her through her second and third orgasms. The simultaneous pleasure of her tight pussy milking me and the vibration on the sensitive underside of my cock was enough to make my vision go black, my orgasm was so intense. Thinking about it now has me instantly rock hard. Thankfully, it's hidden under the table.

Charlotte is still speechless, mouth opening and closing like the proverbial fish out of water. I mouth to her, *It's okay*, and give her a reassuring nod. The look on her face says, *How did she know?* And I smile because Nana has uncanny abilities, like a master spy, taking in every subtle detail and coming up with the right conclusion. But to look at her you'd never in a million years suspect it. She knows it, too. That's why she misbehaves the way she does, because it is so entertaining...for her.

I intervene so Charlotte isn't left sitting there in shock. "To drastically change the subject," I say, looking at Nana sternly as she shrugs, then looks around the restaurant as if she's totally innocent, "Charlotte is officially moving in with me this weekend. Isn't that excellent news?"

The slight narrowing of Charlotte's eyes tells me that she is not altogether happy about me bringing it up. Likely because she knows Nana will be on my side, since on more than one occasion, she has requested that I "plant my seed" so we can get married and give her some great-grandbabies.

Always on cue, Nana raises her glass for a toast. "Great news. Here's to the next step: getting knocked up. Or you can get married first, I don't care the order, just as long I have some babies to spoil."

Charlotte is very hesitant to raise her glass and is looking at me like, *What the fuck, babe?*

Trying to appease Nana and diffuse Charlotte, I say, "You never know what fate has in store, Nana, but Charlotte and I plan on enjoying each other first before starting a family. Beyond that, I happen to be old-fashioned and intend to make Charlotte my wife *before* she becomes the mother of my children." I see Charlotte's eyes soften as her skin turns rosy, causing that familiar rush—the one that makes me want to get on my knees and beg her to spend eternity with me, to never leave my side. I have every intention of doing just that, and it will be special when it happens, but I have to wait.

She has come a long way from when we first met, when she was locked away inside the fortress her parents forced her in to. But every so often I can see remnants of her fear come to the surface. I'm afraid if I ask her to marry me now, it would be too much too fast, and I can't risk scaring her away.

"Even though the selfish old lady in me wishes she was pregnant now, I can't help but love and respect you even more for doing right by this girl." She leans over and puts her arm around Charlotte, squeezing her to her tiny frame.

Charlotte bends her head so that it rests practically on top of Nana's and closes her eyes as the warmth of Nana's love surrounds her. They have become very close over the past few months, as I knew they would. Charlotte was drawn to my grandmother's maternal nature instantly, allowing it to fill the void in her heart left behind by her own mother.

Charlotte turns and kisses her forehead. "Thank you, Nana. It will happen eventually, and you will be the best great-grandmother ever." Her smile is sincere, even though I know she is nowhere near ready to start a family.

"Thank you, dear. But don't wait too long. I'm not getting any younger. Plus, I need to catch up to Judy. She's got two great-grandchildren she's constantly going on about, and I have to say, they are pretty cute considering how unattractive the parents are." She's dead serious, shaking her head as if she can't figure out how these people actually made cute kids.

Charlotte chuckles and tries to be tactful by saying, "Well, all babies are cute, Nana."

"Ha! Oh, no, they're not! I've seen some ugly babies in my day. I had a cousin that had five of them, but lucky for them, two grew up to be okay-looking. No such luck for the other three."

This is why Jackson and I call her No Filter Nana.

Charlotte tries to hide her laugh behind her hand, unsuccessfully. Then adds, "Well, I hope Ian and I don't have ugly babies, for your sake, anyway." She pats Nana's hand in mock reassurance.

"No chance of that. McAlistairs don't have ugly babies," she succinctly replies. "The cousin I'm referring to wasn't a McAlistair, and I think her husband might have been the missing link."

Charlotte and I both bust out laughing. "You must be talking about the Petersons. They did have a little bit of a caveman thing going on," I agree.

"A little bit? I don't know what she ever saw in him. Her sister and I used to joke that he must have had a big—"

"Nana! We don't need to go there...again."

"Okay, fine. You can fill in the blanks, though. It's the only logical explanation."

Charlotte is cracking up. She thinks Nana is hilarious, but she finds the banter between the two of us exceedingly entertaining. She says Nana loves bringing out my "prudish" side, and I can't help but wonder if that was an actual conversation they had at some point.

"Yes. We can. And we will leave it at that," I end with my usual head-tip and raised eyebrow that I only use on Nana. She smiles at me with that little twinkle in her eye that spells triumph.

The rest of the evening was "delightful," as Nana said. The sushi was fantastic, and we ended up staying longer than usual, talking and laughing about random topics.

Charlotte and I have become very comfortable in our relationship, regardless of its newness. That is one of the reasons I'm anxious to have her move in with me, because the next step is me getting down on one knee. I haven't told her, but I already consider her my wife. She's mine, in the deepest way possible, and I look forward to making it official.

Once we are home, I bring it up again. "I'm looking forward to this weekend," I say, pulling her into an embrace, looking down at her as I gently move her hair behind one ear.

With a blank expression, she asks, "What's going on this weekend?"

"Charlotte." My voice is low and slightly impatient. "You know we're packing up the rest of your stuff and moving you in here...completely."

Her eyes close, and she lays her head on my chest. "I know, Ian. I was just teasing you. Although, I won't lie and tell you I'm excited about packing up what's left over there, because I'm not. When is the last time you moved?" she asks, popping her head up to look at me.

"Mmmmm…it's been a while," I say honestly.

"Yeah? And I bet when you did, someone else packed and moved everything for you."

"Yes. That may have been the case. I can arrange that for you, too. But you won't let me. I have offered, several times."

"No. I can't stand the idea of a stranger packing up my things. It doesn't feel right." She lets go and walks into the kitchen. "It's okay. We can probably get it done quickly. There really isn't that much left over there that I need. I can probably get rid of a bunch of stuff. I'm just complaining because there's a very long list of other things I'd rather do with you this weekend."

"Really? Do any of them involve you being naked and coming undone in my arms?" I walk to her, cornering her against the counter. Bending my head down to the side of her neck, I run my nose along her soft skin ending in the hairline behind her ear. *Goddamn*, she smells so fucking good.

"Yes. Most of them do, as a matter of fact," she replies as her lips connect with mine. She puts her hand on my ass and pulls me to her, pushing herself against my hardening shaft.

"You do realize that I'm about to make you have multiple orgasms right here on the kitchen counter, don't you?" I say as I unzip the back of her dress.

Leaning forward, she kisses along my neck then takes my earlobe between her teeth for a delicious bite and gentle suck that forces a growl from my chest. "I'm counting on it." Her voice is deep with desire. "I'm still wet from earlier. I need you to make me cum again."

Her body relaxes, giving itself up to me on instinct. Then, on cue, the physical evidence presents itself… her eyes turn a glossy onyx, her skin flushes that rosy pink that spikes my heartbeat, her lips soften as they part on a quick inhale. I'm completely addicted to this.

I lean down and pour all my love into a passionate kiss that leaves us breathless, then I give her what she wants—again and again and again.

TWENTY-FIVE

CHARLOTTE

The weekend is coming quickly, and I'm trying not to be anxious about it. I keep focusing on my excitement and how much happier I am now that Ian is in my life, but there is still that leftover emotion that's so negative and unbelievably powerful, though I try hard to keep it locked away.

I don't talk about it with anyone and it can be an exhausting roller coaster, but I keep telling myself that it won't be this way forever. That it's because Ian and I have only been together for a little more than five months and it's still new. That usually does the trick, and I jump easily back onto cloud nine, but this week has been a bit of a challenge. My insecurities are weighing heavily on me, and I know it's because I've committed to moving all my stuff over to Ian's. It's symbolic for me in a way that most people could never understand.

Erika swears that once I've made the move, I'll be fine. It's the leap that's freaking me out. She's probably right, but it doesn't make me hate the feeling any less.

A knock at my office door snaps me out of my worry. I expect Tracy to peek her head in to see if I'm available, but instead I'm greeted with Jackson's handsome face and smile that warms my heart. His deep voice echoes through the room. "Sorry to drop in on you like this. I was in the neighborhood."

Getting up from my desk, I walk over with open arms. "I'm so happy you did!" Giving him a hug, I finish by asking, "How have you been? I feel like I haven't seen you in so long. How's Becca? She's overdue, now, isn't she?"

"I've been great, and yes, she's about four days overdue, and she's not happy about it. I can't blame her. She looks like she's about to pop and has a hard time getting around. I check my damn phone every five minutes to make sure I didn't miss a call!" His face lights up, and I can't help but feel his excitement.

"That's so wonderful, Jackson. I can't wait to meet your baby girl." I turn toward the chairs in front of my desk. "Here, sit down."

And we both do. I am very much at ease with Jackson, I always have been, but today something is up. "Okay. So, tell me why you really stopped by, because I know this isn't as random as you're making it out to be."

Through a deep chuckle, he says, "It may not be so random, but I *was* in the neighborhood." He looks up with a smile that could disarm a highjacker. "Ian told me you're moving in this weekend."

"Yeeesss…" I say, drawn-out and questioning.

"He may have also mentioned that he felt like you had issues with it, and I wanted to come by and see if maybe you needed someone to talk to. If anyone knows how Ian's pressure can affect you, it's me." His expression is serious now, and I can tell he is genuinely concerned.

I have a slight ache in my chest thinking I've made Ian uncomfortable enough that he has to talk to Jackson about it. I've been trying to keep all of this burden to myself and not let it leech over to Ian. Looking down at my lap, fingers automatically picking at lint that doesn't exist, I say, "The only issues I have are ones with deep roots attached to old insecurities. Other than that, I'm totally fine. Thrilled, actually." I finally look up and try to smile, but the caring look of concern on Jackson's face puts a lump in my throat that I try hard to swallow down before it escapes.

"I thought that might be the case. You need to understand it's perfectly normal and perfectly understandable. I think the key is to accept the fact that you're human. Anyone in your shoes would have insecurities and doubts. You've overcome a lot, Charlotte. You're in a good place now, and even though he is controlling and intense, you're with a good man that is more in love than I ever thought possible." He laughs at that last comment, and I understand why. It's honestly a factor in the equation of my insecurities. The whole *too-good-to-be-true* factor.

"I know. I tell myself the same thing all the time, and most of the time it works just fine. But I've come to discover that my fierce independence was created as a self-defense mechanism, and moving in with Ian, regardless of how much I love him and want to be there, stirs up images of my mother and her dependence on my father...and ultimately where that led her." I'm back to fiddling with my hands on my lap so that I don't have to look at Jackson, which I know will only make me cry.

"Have you told him this?" Jackson asks—the most obvious question.

"No. I don't want him to see me as weak or as someone with issues he might find burdensome. Our relationship is amazing, and I'm so happy. I don't want to do anything to mess it up." I laugh insecurely because I know how silly it sounds.

"Charlotte. First and foremost, nothing about you would ever be burdensome to Ian. I know the man, I know his integrity, and I know how much he loves you. So, get that out of your head right now." He's giving me the stern father look, and it's anchoring me, putting me at ease.

Continuing, he says, "Have you discussed contributing to the household expenses? Setting up something you're comfortable with so that you're not completely relying on him for everything?"

"No. I don't ever bring it up because my head is stuck in the sand, hoping the issue will simply disappear." Admitting it out loud makes me see how cowardly I've been. I should have trusted Ian more, trusted myself and our relationship. "But you're right. I need to be honest with him. He deserves that. And...I think it would better if I were contributing somehow, though I know Ian won't like the idea of it, but he'll respect my feelings." A heavy weight has lifted off my shoulders, and I take a deep breath for the first time in days.

"I know it's not always easy to let down your armor when you've protected yourself with it for so long, but communication is key. I think deep inside you know that." The sound of his voice, that comforting tone, is magically releasing all my tension.

On a laugh I tell him, "I know I've said it many times, but you really could make a lot of money with that voice."

He sits back in his chair and laughs out loud.

"I'm serious! It's like what you'd think God's voice would sound like."

His eyes bulge and he leans forward again. "Well, there's a compliment if I've ever heard one. Becca would probably think it's hilarious." We laugh together then he continues. "I'm really glad I stopped by. Something told me it would be a good thing."

"I couldn't agree more." Reaching over, I place my hand over his and squeeze. "Thank you so much. I really do feel so much better. I'm looking forward to talking to Ian about it this evening."

"You're welcome," he says with a genuine smile. "Also, before I go, I wanted to thank you for the gift basket you and Erika brought to Becca's shower. It was a huge hit and she hasn't stopped talking about it."

"Awww...I'm so happy she liked it! Erika and I had fun buying everything and putting it together. We may have gone a little overboard, but once you start shopping for cute baby stuff, it's kinda hard not to buy everything," I respond, laughing a little to myself thinking about how ridiculous Erika and I must have looked while we squealed and oohed and awed at everything we came across.

Laughing, he agrees, "That's the truth. She'll be the best-dressed baby in town!" Giving me a big hug, he says his goodbyes. "Now you get back to work and I'll talk to you soon."

A few hours pass before my phone pings with a message from the dry cleaners that my clothes are ready. Good timing because I want to stop by the health food store, just around the corner from there, before heading home. Wrapping everything up, I stop by Tracy's office to drop off some schedules and detail specs for next week's banquets.

As I'm putting everything on her desk, she walks in behind me and startles me with, "Oh! There you are… Not sure you're going to be excited about this, but that Brazilian God-like creature from the Novas Alturas group is in the lobby wanting to see you." She pushes her glasses up and hugs the stack of folders she is carrying up to her chest. Good-looking men make her very nervous, but she also knows that Gabriel had a thing for me not long ago.

"It's okay, Tracy. I'm actually heading out for the rest of the day. I'll see what he needs. Hopefully they just need accommodations of some kind." I hold up my crossed fingers and wink.

"Yeah…that's not really the vibe I get from him. It's more like a lost puppy kind of thing he's got going on, and it doesn't really fit the package. Kind of freaks me out."

"Really? That's interesting. It will definitely be awkward if he's here specifically to see me. I'll take care of it, though, not to worry." I pat her shoulder in reassurance on my way out.

As I approach Gabriel in the lobby, the bright sunlight behind him has his face shadowed so I can't read his expression. But once I'm close enough, my stomach sinks from the look of longing in his eyes. *Dammit!*

"Hello, Gabriel! What brings you here this afternoon?" *Just be cordial and ignore the vibe. Ugh…*

Reaching down to take my hand...of course...he kisses my fingers while looking directly into my eyes—almost through them—and I have to force myself not to tense up. "Charlotte. You've managed to take my breath away again. Your beauty only intensifies each time it graces my vision." Most women would probably think that compliment, given in that deep, accented voice from a man as good-looking as Gabriel, would be swoon-worthy. But for me it's like an overly sweet dessert that gives me an instant headache.

Taking my hand away as quickly as possible, I respond with, "Always the charmer, you are," huffing through a fake laugh. "I'm heading out for an appointment. Is there something we can do for you?" *We, not I*...hopefully that was as obvious as it was meant to be.

"I'm sorry to catch you at a bad time. We have a group coming in from Brazil, and I was hoping your lovely resort could accommodate them." I can tell that he has more to say, but before I can cut him off and move onto the safer ground of business, he finishes with, "And...I thought we could maybe...visit, catch up...I don't know, maybe have lunch or a drink."

I know my mouth just dropped open, at least for a few seconds. I cannot believe he asked me that, knowing I am in a serious relationship with his business partner. So much for being a gentleman. *Bloody hell.*

"Gabriel, I'm going to chalk that up as a cultural faux pas and let you off the hook. But you do understand that—at least here in the States—it's considered wrong to ask someone else's girlfriend out to have lunch or drinks...right?" I'm giving him the *please-tell-me-you're-with-me* look. "And it's especially bad when it's your business partner's girlfriend."

I swear I see his eyes flash with anger, but only for a second. Nonetheless, it makes my stomach tighten with apprehension, and I'm not altogether comfortable with this situation. I can hear Sibel tapping on the window I closed on her. She'd prefer to take him by the ear and drag him out the front door, give him a swift kick in the ass and tell him to get the hell out of here. Not a terribly bad idea, except he's Ian business partner on a major project and that would make waves that could bring the whole project down.

"Please…I apologize." He puts his head down and his hands behind his back. "I didn't know you and Ian were still that serious. After all, he's a very busy man, and, well…he's rich and good-looking…and…has so many wo—"

Before he can finish, Sibel smashes through the window and snaps, "What the hell does that have to do with anything, Gabriel? And where exactly are you going with this?" My voice is loud, a few notches below yelling. "Because you need to understand something. You've crossed the line once and I let you get away with it. However, you're about to cross it again, and I have no intention of letting you get away with it a second time." My spine is straight and my hackles are up. How dare he make that kind of suggestion!

Sibel isn't finished. "This is what's going to happen." I take a step closer, finger pointed toward his chest. "*If* you truly have clients coming in from Brazil that need accommodations, you are going to contact my assistant, Tracy, and she will handle everything and ensure their stay here is beyond stellar. *Next…* you are going to turn around and leave this property, and don't you *ever* come near me again. You are clearly the *last* person that should be questioning anyone's integrity, so keep your fucking mouth shut about Ian." I'm fuming at this point, and when he tries to say something, I hold up my hand and shake my head. "Not another word, Gabriel. Get out." With a sharp 180, I turn and walk back toward my office.

Once inside, I lean against the door, my head dropping back with an echoing thud. That was the last thing I expected to happen. There hasn't been anything to make me suspect Gabriel would do something like that. I'm so shocked by it I don't know what to think. Why would Gabriel think I would be interested in his advances? Surely it's a universal understanding, you don't hit on your friend's girl. Then why the hell would he come here, now...after all these months? He's never indicated that he was interested in pursuing me since Ian and I announced we are together. What's different? Does he know something to make him think otherwise?

As my insecurity starts to rear its ugly head, I drop to the floor and sit there for a minute, adrenaline coursing through me. *Don't do this, Charlotte. You know Ian is faithful to you. He's asked you to move in with him for Christ's sake. Shake it off.*

I sit there a while longer, taking slow, deep breaths, focusing on the love that Ian and I share. How connected we are and how he fiercely protects me. Eventually, there is a steady release of tension and doubt, and I am able to relax. I get up and go over to the mirror and make sure I'm still presentable. I felt a few tears break free during my moment of weakness, but there seems to be no evidence of that. Fluffing my hair and refreshing my lipstick, I'm ready to get the hell out of here and go be with Ian.

I am grateful that I was able to sneak away without having to give Tracy the details of my awful encounter with Dickhead. Once I'm in the sanctuary of my car, I take a few more calming breaths and try to call Erika so I can vent and hopefully gain some moral support, but she doesn't answer. She's probably in a meeting, so I shoot her a text.

Me: Just had an unpleasant run-in with Gabriel. Bastard showed up at the resort basically trying to hit on me. So weird. Totally ruined my afternoon. I'll tell you the details later.

Pulling out of the parking lot, I'm halfway down the road before I remember I'm supposed to pick up my dry cleaning. I was so distracted I automatically turned right to go to Ian's condo. Now I have to do a U-turn at the next light. Knowing Gabriel made me that absentminded irritates me even more, especially since I can't stop wondering—did he seriously think I would go have a drink with him? And if so, why would he think that?

Stop it, Charlotte! I have to force myself not to overanalyze what just happened. Turning on my music, I pretend to be okay.

The traffic is kind of heavy today and it takes me a while to get to my destination, but it's a blessing because it gives me some time to chill out and get my head together. It also helps that the lady who runs the dry cleaners is one of the nicest people I've ever met, and I gobble up her good vibes. Even walking back to my car makes me feel so much better as the sun is shining bright, a slight breeze is cooling the air, and it actually smells fresh and clean outside. I think about sitting on the balcony with Ian tonight, and a smile spreads across my face.

As I turn the corner to where my car is parallel parked, I see a black Lamborghini parked across the street, several cars down. I stop, wondering if it's Ian...it has to be. There are a lot of nice cars in Miami, but probably only one that looks like that. I wonder what he's doing here. I can't really tell what all the storefronts are, but one looks like a bistro or something. Maybe he stopped there to grab a bite, although it's kind of late for that.

Just then, the door to the bistro opens. I can see that a man is holding it for someone, and I swear it looks like Ian.

What happens next causes my vision to tunnel and the blood to rush through my ears, drowning out all sound.

A very petite, very beautiful young woman walks out ahead of Ian and turns to smile up at him as they move out onto the sidewalk. Ian's back is to me as they stand in front of each other for what seems like a lifetime.

I'm completely paralyzed, my feet bolted to the concrete. *Please don't let this be my biggest nightmare come true. Please let this be something innocent that will make perfect sense.* I don't have a chance to beg the universe anymore for an outcome that won't ruin my life, because at that moment, Ian's hand comes up and his fingers run tenderly along the side of her face, exactly like he's done to me so many times before.

All the air rushes out of my lungs as my world comes crashing down. The next breath I take is filled with a blackness thick with the pain of betrayal and lies and weakness. I can't stop its inky darkness from seeping into my heart and devouring everything I thought was real.

TWENTY-SIX

IAN

Me: Hey. Is everything okay? I've been trying to call but it goes to voicemail. Getting worried.

I'm getting seriously edgy. Charlotte never lets her phone die, and she's not at work so I can't get her on a landline. I've been home for an hour, and she should have been here by now. Making matters worse, I can't track her phone because the damn thing isn't on. My gut is telling me something is up and pacing around my penthouse isn't making me feel any better, so I grab my keys and head to her place to see if maybe she's there packing and doesn't realize her phone is off. I hope.

Traffic is awful and I almost get into an accident, so by the time I get to Charlotte's…and find she is not there, my nerves are shot. *Goddammit!*

Leaving her condo, I pull out my phone and call Jackson.

"What's goin' on man?" Jackson answers after several rings.

"I'm worried about Charlotte. I can't get in touch with her, her phone is off, she's late getting home, and I don't know where the hell she is! Something's up, Jackson. She never does shit like this." Saying it out loud confirms the truth in my mind— something has happened and I'm starting to be sick with worry.

"That does sound strange. When did you talk to her last?"

"Just a quick text before lunch. Today was kind of busy, figured we'd catch up after work." A decision I'm now regretting.

"I wasn't going to say anything unless it was necessary, but I stopped by to see her after lunch today."

"Why the—" I try to interject.

"Hey! Before you start getting all crazy, I did it to help you guys out. You told me she had doubts about moving in, so I figured she needed someone to talk to...and I was right. Thing is, we had an excellent conversation and she was looking forward to talking to you about it this evening."

My anxiety is spiking as terrible thoughts start flashing through my mind. I shut it down before I lose control. "Thank you for doing that, but it's after seven and I have no fucking clue where she is!" I raise my voice and hit the steering wheel.

"All right, try to stay calm. Let's think about this... Do you know when she left work? Or have you tried to call Erika?"

"I called her office but didn't ask anyone what time she left, and no...it didn't even cross my mind to call Erika. *Dammit!* I can't fucking think clearly!" I need to pull over and concentrate. I'm not even paying attention to where the hell I'm going.

"All right. You call the resort and see what you can find out, and I'll call Erika." Without a goodbye, the line clicks and he's down to business. That's Jackson, and I'm appreciating his clear thinking right now more than ever.

Once I'm settled in a random parking lot, I call the resort and ask for Tracy, but she's gone for the day. Terrance is gone as well —apparently, the night shift crew is on and they have no idea when Charlotte left. Speaking to the manager, whom I don't recall ever meeting, I ask her if she could get in touch with Tracy and get back to me immediately. At this point, I don't care what anyone thinks, I want some fucking answers.

Less than five minutes later, my phone rings and it's Tracy. I hear trepidation in her voice, and I don't know if it's because I intimidate her or if she knows something and doesn't want to tell me. "Thank you for getting back to me so quickly. I can't get in touch with Charlotte, and I'm beyond worried. Something's not right. Do you know what time she left work?"

"Well...I...uh, yes. She left a little early today to run some errands before she went home." My stomach drops, knowing that it's been hours since she was last seen. Continuing to fumble through her words, she finishes with, "But...there was one kind of...strange thing. I don't know...I don't want to assume anything."

I'm going to reach through the fucking phone and strangle her if she doesn't spit it the fuck out! "Tracy. Tell me what's going on. Now." I almost don't recognize my own voice it's so menacing. It has the needed effect as she starts racing through her words.

"Okay. Well...before she left, Gabriel from Novas Alturas stopped by."

My heart is pounding, the blood rushing through me so fast I can hear it whirring in my ears. Fucking Gabriel? What does that bastard have to do with this? Jesus Christ...she can't be with him right now. I try to focus as Tracy continues. "He came by to ask her about accommodations for some associates from Brazil coming to town next week. But...I don't know...I...kinda thought he was acting weird. Then I saw that Charlotte was angry."

"What do you mean she was angry? What the hell did he do?" I swear to God I'm going to kill that motherfucker.

"I don't know. That's just it. I couldn't hear what they were saying. They were talking in the lobby, but too far away for me to know what it was about. But I could tell by the way she was talking to him that she was mad, and...she even pointed her finger into his chest then she turned and stormed back to her office."

What the hell is going on here? I can't imagine Gabriel would do anything to hurt Charlotte, but this is not sounding good. My hands are sweating, which has never happened in my life.

"Okay. Then what happened?"

"She was in her office for maybe thirty minutes, then left without saying goodbye. I just assumed she was too irritated to talk to anyone. Shortly after that, she sent me a text that said Novas Alturas may have people coming to town and that I was to deal with Gabriel from now on. That's all I know."

"No...that's actually a lot. Thank you very much, Tracy. I need to make some calls. Sorry to bother you." I rush through the words so I can call Jackson. But before I can dial his number, he's calling me back.

"What do you know? Because I just got a fucking earful from Tracy," I say through gritted teeth.

"The only thing I got from Erika that was good is that Charlotte is okay. She talked to her about thirty minutes ago." The tone in his voice is blasting my nerves with adrenaline.

"What the fuck is that supposed to mean, Jackson?! Where the hell is she and what the fuck is going on?" I yell, ready to destroy something if I don't get some goddamn answers.

"I don't know, Ian. Now let me fucking talk. I wanted you to know first and foremost that she's not dead!" He's yelling at me now, and Jackson doesn't yell.

"You're right. Of course, it's a relief to know she's not dead, but Tracy told me that fucking bastard Gabriel stopped by the resort right before she left and that he upset her somehow. Now you're telling me she's okay because she called Erika, but she didn't fucking call me! What the fuck did that son of a bitch say to her?" My fists are clenched, and I want Azeveda in front of me right now.

Jackson's voice is somewhat sad when he says, "I don't know what's going on, Ian. All Erika would tell me is that she is sworn to secrecy and will not break it, that Charlotte is safe, but she doesn't want anyone contacting her or trying to find her." He pauses for a few seconds, then finishes with, "Until she's had time to think."

My head falls back against the headrest as some of the fear drains from my body. She's alive and I don't suspect she's with Gabriel—both are such a huge relief I could cry.

But she doesn't want to talk to me. She doesn't want to see me. I am so confused, and the thought of her not being in my life, of walking out of it and never turning back, washes over me in a wave of pain that's almost unbearable. As I feel it coming up from my gut and into my chest, I can only get out a strained, "I'll call you back," then hang up right as the pain works its way up through my throat.

Before I can choke on whatever is lodged there, it escapes as a growling scream that feels like it's ripping a hole through me. The pressure in my head is ready to explode, and my hand may be broken from whatever I just punched. As I sit there, my heartbeat throbbing in my hand and in my head, I realize my face is wet. Reaching up, I wipe at the tears running down my cheek, then stare at the shiny wetness on my fingertips. *What the hell is happening? Why is she doing this?*

I stay where I am, sitting in my car in some random parking lot, staring at nothing for at least an hour, maybe more...I don't know...I don't even care. I can't move. It's as if I don't have the strength or even the wherewithal to do so. I'm like the dying prey of a stealth hunter, my main artery severed as I'm left to bleed out, completely drained of feeling, giving in to the numbness that nature designed to protect me.

My eyes finally close as bright headlights shine through the windshield, reminding me that I'm still alive. A car parks directly in front of me. I know exactly who it is.

I unlock the doors so Jackson can get in the passenger's seat. Finally, his headlights turn off so I can open my eyes again. Looking straight ahead, eyes half-open, head back against the seat, my voice gravelly, I ask, "Were you really that worried about me, Jackson?"

"Not so much worried, my friend. Just thought we might need to go over some things. You know...work out the problems so you don't let it stay balled up inside turning into God-knows-what inside your head." He's very calm, but I can tell he's concerned. "I tried to call, but you wouldn't answer. Naturally, I tracked your location..." He pauses when I look at him in defensive surprise, only to find him giving me a look that says *don't you dare question me*. Continuing, he says, "You've been in the same parking lot since we hung up. I didn't want the cops to get suspicious. You kind of stand out, you know what I mean?"

Damn, he knows me better than anyone and knows I'd never do anything stupid, but I can understand why he decided to come check on me. "I'm sorry. I turned off my sound. I needed to think...though I'm not entirely sure I've done any thinking at all because my brain doesn't work. What the hell is going on, Jackson? What am I supposed to think? What am I supposed to do? *Jesus Christ!* Why would she do this? All I've done is love her, and I thought it was pretty goddamned obvious that she loved me, too. But this doesn't feel like love... It's fucking killing me, man." I turn my head to look out my window so Jackson can't see my face. I feel it contorting. I heard the crack in my voice. Biting down hard, I try not to break. God, I hate this weakness. Like my insides are being ripped out and I'm powerless to stop it.

"It's all right, Ian. Don't hold back on my account. We're brothers. This shit's tearing me up, too. I can only imagine what it's doing to you." He puts his hand on my shoulder and gives it a firm squeeze as a single tear runs down my face.

Growling, I wipe the damn thing away. "I swear to God, Jackson, I have never been more scared *and* pissed off in my life. I was terrified not knowing if she was okay, not knowing where she was, who she was with, if she was hurt or scared...it makes me sick. But now...now that I know she is safe and *literally fucking* chose to leave me like this without a single word or explanation as to why...I didn't know I was capable of being this

THE ESSENCE OF FATE

angry with her. *Goddammit!* Why the hell does she think I deserve this?" I almost hit my steering wheel again, but the sharp pain that ignited through my hand when I attempted to lift it stopped me. "And I think I broke my hand."

"Yeah, it doesn't look good. We should probably have it looked at so it doesn't set wrong. I'll call Richard and see if he can meet us at his office, that way we won't have to go to the ER and wait around. But, before we do that, let me ask you something... Earlier today you said that you ran into your cousin, Phoebe, and that you ended up having coffee with her because she was so upset about having just had her dog or cat or something euthanized. Do you think Charlotte saw you with her and got the wrong idea? That's her biggest fear, ya know, that you'll end up doing to her the same thing her father did to her mother."

I turn to look at him again, speechless. That never even entered my mind. I kept thinking it had something to do with Gabriel, but no clue what—plus my mind doesn't go to the same places Charlotte's does. I would never cheat on her. I would never hurt her. Seeing Phoebe today never registered in my brain as an issue. "It's going to be pretty screwed up if that's the reason for all this. And how the hell am I supposed to know if she won't fucking talk to me?"

"Ya know, if she turned off her phone, you should be able to see her last location. Maybe that will give you a clue," he says, like it wasn't the most brilliant idea I've ever heard.

"Bloody hell, Jackson...you're right! How did I not think of that?" Pulling out my phone, I do what he suggested. After it buffers for several seconds, the screen lights up with her last location. My heart sinks into the pit of my stomach. She was on the same street as the coffee shop Phoebe and I stopped at today, and sure enough, the time coincides.

"That's it...she *was* there. That has to be what happened. You're a genius!" I'm still staring at my phone, wondering what must have been going through her head to make her react this way. Why didn't she just walk up to us and introduce herself?

"I can't believe this. I *cannot* believe this whole nightmare is because I ran into Phoebe today." Finally looking up, I turn to Jackson. "How did you figure that out, and *when* did you figure that out? I've been sitting in this fucking car for hours!" I have such a dichotomy of emotions rushing through me in opposite directions, I feel like a downed power line that landed in a puddle of water.

The relief rushing through me, knowing she's not hurt and that everything can be explained, is immeasurable. But at the same time, I can't ignore the sense of betrayal that's landed in my gut like a sucker punch.

"As usual, I laid out all the factors. From there, it really didn't take long to come up with that conclusion. What *did* take a long time was trying to get in touch with you because your damn sound was off. I really didn't want to leave if I didn't have to. My wife is going to go into labor any second...remember?" I sense a little humor in his voice.

"Dammit, Jackson. I'm sorry. This whole thing with Charlotte has made me useless and obviously very selfish. You shouldn't be here. Becca needs you at home." A wave of anger comes over me—not only at myself, but at Charlotte. I literally forgot my best friend's wife was pregnant, let alone almost a week overdue. "I'm good, man. Thank you for coming out here. You've cleared away a lot of smoke. At least now I have something to go on."

"Don't beat yourself up, Ian. I'd be no different than you if the roles were reversed. Now, let me see if I can get Richard so we can get that hand looked at."

Two and a half hours later, I'm back in my car on the way to my penthouse. My hand is broken, not a severe break—but it hurts like a bitch, nonetheless. My friend Richard wrapped it, splinted two fingers, and put it in a removable brace because I refused to have a permanent cast. I also refused to let Jackson stick around any longer. He needed to be with Becca, not me.

Walking in, I head straight to the bar and pour a heavy scotch. I opted out of the pain meds, so I down half of it then top it off again then head out to the balcony. Sitting under the starry sky with its sliver of a moon, I focus on the burn spreading around my empty stomach. I should be hungry, but I'm not. I should be tired, but I'm not. I should be a lot of things that I'm not. One in particular. I should be relieved that I know what happened today, why it happened and that there is an explanation. That this can be fixed, that Charlotte and I can go back to what we were.

But that's not how I feel...I'm not relieved at all. I'm not overjoyed. I'm not ready to wrap her in my arms and tell her it was all a big mistake... No, I'm none of that. Because I'm too disgusted. I am fucking disgusted that the woman I love beyond goddamn comprehension, beyond anything I ever thought could exist, took that love and threw it in my face like it was nothing but a bloody joke. Like it was some kind of adolescent affair where you just fuck with each other's emotions to create unnecessary drama because you're too stupid and immature to do otherwise.

She doesn't care that I actually thought, at one point, she had been abducted, and who knows what from there—potentially even dead. Those thoughts damn near killed me. Then finding out Gabriel was somehow involved tore at my soul in a totally different way, killing me another way. Charlotte never considered how scared I would be, how out of my mind I would be with worry. No, she had already made up her own mind and didn't give a fuck.

Right now, at this very moment, she is convinced that I am unfaithful to her. I understand she has issues because of her parents, and I know those issues run deep, but she seriously believes it's possible for me to even want to cheat on her. So much so, she literally left me…just up and fucking left without saying a word.

Standing up abruptly because I can't sit still, a sick feeling comes over me. The sense of betrayal lacerates through me as the sickness turns to pain. Suddenly, a violent crashing sound ricochets around the concrete walls, blasting through my ears and racing through every nerve in my body as the glass I was holding shatters into a million pieces. Standing there, teeth clenched as the heated fury swallows me whole, I grab my phone and start typing.

Me: Hello Erika. If it isn't too much trouble, would you please pass this message along to Charlotte.

The woman you saw me with today was my cousin, Phoebe. Not my mistress, not my girlfriend, not my latest hookup. My fucking cousin, whose beloved dog had just been euthanized. Your lack of faith in my integrity and feelings for you have not gone unnoticed. I'll have your things packed and moved back to your condo within 24 hours.

Send.

TWENTY-SEVEN
CHARLOTTE

I barely slept a wink. My chest is constricted, too tight to take a normal breath, and my sinuses are completely shut from crying. Lying here, looking out the window as dawn breaks through the darkness, I wonder what my next move should be.

Buying a plane ticket to Europe isn't an option...yet. I need to properly schedule time off at work first. A few days away unexpectedly is doable, but not a trip overseas. No. I'm going to stay here at my uncle's condo in Naples for another day or so, hopefully gain some strength—and courage—before heading back to Miami to set things up properly at work. After that, I will take off to France and visit Uncle James. That may be a cowardly move, but right now I don't care. A complete change of scenery is what's best for me because I certainly can't stay like this, dying from a pain that words cannot describe. Drawing my attention to it creates another lump in my throat as I roll over and curl into myself, searching for some kind of comfort.

I still can't believe all that has happened, that I was on the verge of reliving my mother's tragic life. The naive woman, head over heels in love with the gorgeous, successful businessman that clouds your vision and makes you believe in fairy tales when there could be nothing further from the truth. *My God...*

how could I let myself fall this far? Another sob breaks free as I see Ian vividly in my mind and remember the deep love that I thought we both shared, the connection, the passion, two souls reunited…

…I can't do this. My heart is pounding, too hard.

My head, the pain is making me dizzy…

…I'm going to be sick again.

Jumping out of bed, I run to the bathroom.

Twenty minutes later, I'm standing at the door, holding onto the frame for balance after another round of dry-heaving. I need to force myself to drink water…or something. What I really need is food, but I don't have the strength to prepare anything right now. I'm so weak from lack of sleep and nutrients, my head is spinning.

Suddenly, there is an image of my mother after she found out about my father's death…*and* his infidelity. My mother—that beautiful, vibrant, kind, and loving woman that would walk into a room and brighten it like a brilliant ray of sunshine breaking through the clouds, reduced to an empty shell that just existed until the last remnant of a spark was finally extinguished.

I feel my hand sliding down the doorframe as my legs give out, forcing me to sit right where I am, unable to carry the weight any longer. I despise this; I despise the weakness that has taken over every cell in my body. I don't have the strength to even sit, as my body involuntarily gives in and rolls to the floor.

After lying there for a few minutes while the blood equalizes throughout my body, Sibel finally makes an appearance as she claws her way through the crowd of zombies that reside in this dark place I've become lost in. Through the thick fog I can hear her strong—albeit confused—voice say, "Ahhhhh…why the fuck are we here?"

If I had the strength, I would laugh because this is definitely not Sibel's kind of scene. She doesn't do weakness on this end of the spectrum. She's more comfortable losing control in the form of telling someone to *piss off* while dumping a perfectly good drink over their head. Her timing is impeccable, though, because at that moment, I decide to relinquish myself over to her command—a task she is more than happy to perform as she enthusiastically walks over and gives me a proverbial kick in the ass, igniting a welcome jolt of energy.

Propping up on my elbows, I let the blood slowly flow toward my head before sitting up to take a much-needed deep breath. I do it again and again, my back against the wall for support. With a quiet thud, my head falls back as my eyes close and I patiently wait for Sibel to clean house and work her magic. I wish she had appeared sooner, like when I saw Ian caressing another woman's face. She would have gladly walked over and bashed their heads together, then walked away with a straight spine and a full sense of satisfaction. Me? No...I run and hide on the other side of the state to live in misery with the zombies and demons from my past.

After several minutes of controlled breathing and intense reprimanding from my alter-ego, I'm ready to go downstairs and find some kind of sustenance. I pray there is something palatable enough to energize me for a shower and a trip to the nearest restaurant for a more substantial meal and human interaction.

Thankfully, I don't have to go far. This area is filled with quaint little bistros and coffee shops. After ordering a man-sized meal, I sit back to enjoy my full stomach and lack of wanting to vomit. A wonderful breeze blows in off the water and I relax a bit more in the fresh air. Just then, my phone pings, startling me. I've had it off since I left Miami and must have become accustomed to the silence. Looking down, I see it's from Erika.

Erika: Hey. Assuming your phone is back on. I called the condo and got no answer. Can you talk?

Hmmm...there is a strange tone to that text, and Sibel has a vision of Erika being held at gunpoint and forced to contact me. Not wanting to continue an unnecessary back and forth, I dial her number, and, as usual, she picks up halfway through the first ring.

"Hey. How are you doing?" she asks, sounding somber and way out of her norm.

"Okay. Finally found the strength to get out of bed and find some decent food. What's going on? You sound weird."

I hear her take a deep breath. "Well, it looks like Ian did the math, with some help from Jackson, and he knows why you left." The thought of those cards being laid on the table seems surreal as I sit back in my chair. A sense of foreboding comes over me while I think of ways to defend my position.

"Yeah? Doesn't matter. It would have all come out eventually."

"Except for one problem..."

My stomach does a major flip, and there it is—the sensation of falling and there is nothing to catch me.

"...This is the text I got from Ian...*Hello Erika. If it isn't too much trouble, would you please pass this message along to Charlotte. The woman you saw me with today was my cousin, Phoebe. Not my mistress, not my girlfriend, not my latest hookup. My fucking cousin, whose beloved dog had just been euthanized. Your faith in my integrity and feelings for you have not gone unnoticed. I'll have your things packed and moved back to your condo within 24 hours.*"

There is a strange and sudden silence that encompasses everything and the odd sensation of standing outside my body witnessing this whole thing, like it isn't really happening to me. As if it's a dream. But I know the truth...It *is* happening to me. *His cousin? My God, what have I done?*

Erika breaks the heavy silence. "Are you still there?"

"Yeah. I'm trying to absorb what you said." I pause as a new kind of pain travels through me. "It feels like I've been hit in the head with a bat. I've got an instant headache and I'm nauseous again. Which isn't good because all I've done is throw-up and dry-heave since I've been here!" My voice rises and has a ring of panic to it as I finish with, "Jesus, what have I done?" I lean forward to put my head on the table in a sad attempt at steadying its spinning.

"I'm sorry, Charlotte. I wish I was there with you. I can leave now if you want me to come over." She sounds so concerned, it's making me want to cry.

Giving myself a few seconds so the dam doesn't break, I answer, "No. It's fine, Erika. I promise. I just...I don't know, I'm kind of in shock right now...I think. I know what I saw, and I know what it looked like, and I certainly know how it made me feel, especially after Gabriel insinuated that he knew something about Ian not being faithful to me. But to have Ian say it was something innocent and then break up with me...I...I honestly don't know what to think right now."

"I get it. I felt a little like that when I read the text. I mean, I know you and I know why you did what you did, and I can totally see why you would have freaked. But if what Ian says is true...I can see why he's upset as well." Pausing, she finishes with, "This is some serious talk-show shit right here!"

Leave it to Erika to try to lighten up the situation. I may have actually laughed, but I don't think it made any sound.

Sitting up straight, I put my head back and close my eyes, hoping the bright sunlight penetrating my skin will give me some kind of strength. Finally bringing my head down, I speak my thoughts. "I can't believe this is happening. I don't know what's worse, Ian cheating on me or Ian breaking up with me because I *thought* he was cheating on me. I don't know what do, and I'm sitting outside at some restaurant. I want to get back to the condo and digest all this. Can I call you later?"

"Of course, don't worry about it. But if you don't, I'll call you." She pauses, then says, "It's going to be okay, honey. It will all work out...okay?"

"I know. Thank you. I love you."

"More."

I don't remember much of the walk back to the condo, but once inside, I head straight for the couch to lie down. I am so completely exhausted, within seconds my eyes shut and don't open again until it's almost dark outside.

Disoriented from deep sleep and terrible stress dreams, I sit up to let my head clear and give myself a few minutes to ponder this afternoon's turn of events. Trying to think past the stabbing pain in my chest isn't easy. Trying to take a normal-sized breath is just as hard. I can't believe the emotional hell I've been in since that jerk, Gabriel, showed up at my office... Was that yesterday? Oh my God. It's like I've been in this black hole for an entire week. I'm so drained and miserable...and scared.

I should have confronted Ian. That would have been the normal thing to do. Even if I had flipped out on him, it could have been settled right then and there. But instead, I was *thoroughly* convinced that he was cheating on me, and the finality of it completely shattered me inside. I've known pain—terrible, excruciating emotional pain—but it was nothing like what I felt when I saw Ian with another woman. Obviously, I fooled myself into thinking I could put aside my issues and live happily ever after. I may have buried them for several months, but they were there, lurking in the corner, waiting for the opportunity to ruin my happily ever after...and they always will be.

The sound of defeat escapes as I let out a weak sigh and find the strength to stand. I wait a few seconds for the dizziness to clear, but the nausea is more persistent. Walking over to the mirror, I'm not surprised to that find my reflection is a physical reminder of the mistake I made. Yet, the longer I stare at myself, the more I start to see my father. Although I resemble both my parents, at this moment I see him—his eyes and his wide mouth, his jawline. For the first time in a long time, I have a clear vision of him and I allow myself to see him the way he was...when we loved him, when we trusted him.

A sudden burst of pain lances through my chest and breaks the lock that held my true feelings at bay for more than a decade.

"YOU FUCKING BASTARD!" I scream at the man that destroyed my storybook life...destroyed my beautiful mother.

"Why?" I continue as the sobs break free. "Why weren't we enough for you? Do you even know what you left behind? Do you know what you did to your wife...my mother? DO YOU KNOW WHAT YOU'VE DONE TO ME?"

Without thinking, my hand balls into a tight fist and shatters the mirror along with the image of the man staring back at me. My breathing is heavy as the tears wash down my face. This time, they aren't the tears of my broken heart. They aren't tears of pity for my perfect little family... No, this time they are tears of anger. Anger that is so hot and vicious, I feel it take a small piece of my sanity and lock it away in the crypt where the rest of my family's skeletons are buried.

The word *hate* flashes through my mind as I think about what I've done and why I did it. Do I hate myself? Do I hate my father?

A warm wetness lands on my foot—blood is dripping from my hand and splattering onto the white floor, its stark contrast harsh and surreal. My head falls back weakly, and I laugh, the sad sound of broken emotions. "You ruined me, Dad," I whisper. "You took my ability to trust. You took it with you, and I'll never get it back."

Several minutes later I find myself sitting on the floor, the blood thick and sticky as it dries next to me. Looking down at the cut on my hand that is finally starting to sting, I snap out of it, only to realize I decided there is a part of me that hates my father *and* myself for taking a wrecking ball to the once in a lifetime relationship I had with the man I love.

"Beyond perfect..." I moan as I slowly get up to go to the bathroom and bandage up my hand. Hopefully it doesn't need stitches, because I'm not going to the hospital. No...I'm getting the hell out of here before I go completely insane. I need to be busy, accomplishing something and not sitting here making myself sick and having outbursts with my dead father.

After a quick cleanup, I'm on the road, and fortunately it's traffic free—albeit pitch black and a little sketchy. The music keeps me company but doesn't calm my nerves as I finalize my decision. Ian is better off without me. This happened for a reason...because he deserves more than what I am capable of offering. In the back of my mind, I've always known that to be true. Yet, I fooled myself into thinking otherwise. Clearly, Ian knows it's for the best, as well. A huge lump forms in my throat as I think about the love I have for him...*if you love someone, set them free*. That never made sense to me, but it does now.

The last hour flies by, thank God, because by the time I pull into the parking garage of my condo, I'm completely wiped out again. I've barely got the strength to get to the elevator and up to my condo.

The brutal fatigue gets swallowed by a rush of adrenaline when I walk through the front door to find suitcases and several plastic totes that I assume are filled with my belongings. *Jesus Christ...how did this happen?* I suddenly feel sick and run to the bathroom.

After rinsing my mouth and splashing cold water on my face, I walk back out to the living room, determined to be strong. Standing there, looking at everything, I wonder what was going through Ian's mind when he packed up all my stuff. *Does he hate me now? Can he really turn off his feelings like that?* "It doesn't matter, Charlotte. What's done is done," I say, right as the front door opens and Ian walks in, sucking all the air from the room.

God help me...those eyes. Blazing like a mad Viking set on taking what he wants and leaving nothing but ash in his wake. "What are you doing here, Charlotte? It was my understanding you weren't coming back for *days*. Had I known you changed your mind, I would have had this task completed much sooner." His voice sounds so different, so cold and menacing. I need to say something, but what? The truth is, I want to hold him, to go back in time and make sure nothing bad ever happens between us. But I can't.

"I...um, I...just needed to get back. I...I'm sorry...I didn't know you would be here," I stutter through an explanation. He is intimidating as hell right now, emitting an energy that's about to swallow me whole. That's nothing compared to what comes next.

"Sorry? You're sorry? FUCKING SORRY?"

I jump at the awful sound and realize that I've never heard him yell in anger. I hate it. I want him to stop. Stop yelling...stop looking at me like that.

But he's not finished. He continues through gritted teeth, "Say it again, Charlotte. Tell me you're *fucking* sorry, again. Tell me that you're sorry you fucking left me without a GODDAMN WORD! That you left me worried sick not knowing where the hell you were or what the hell happened to you. DO YOU HAVE ANY IDEA WHAT WAS GOING THROUGH MY FUCKING MIND?"

The anger, the pain that I hear in his voice is too much. I can't do this. Turning toward the balcony, away from him, I hide my face and try to hold back the emotion that's ripping through my chest. *That* was a mistake.

"Don't you fucking turn your back to me!" He's suddenly behind me, grabbing my arm in a vise-grip as he turns me to face him in one swift movement. I'm forced to look at him, to smell him, to feel the heat radiating through his strong hand.

My breath hitches as the look on his face softens and his hand releases my strangled arm. "Why, Charlotte?" His voice is low now, steeped in sadness. "Why would you think the worst of me? How could you not believe in what we had?" His eyes are shining with pent up emotion and tearing my heart in two.

"I'm sorry, Ian," I whisper. Then before I lose the courage and strength to set him free, I step away and say, "It just wasn't meant to be... Please leave."

With no other sound but the familiar tap of his shoes across the tile floor, he is gone.

TWENTY-EIGHT

IAN

It's been over three weeks since I walked out of Charlotte's condo. It's been one day less than that since I broke Gabriel's perfect little Brazilian nose and sent him packing. I was pleased his father had brains enough to not use our partnership or the project that is underway against me.

Quite the opposite, actually. Lucas didn't take too kindly to his son insulting their American partners, partners that could easily walk away from the project and cost Novas Alturas a ton of money. Putting the project in jeopardy was apparently an insult to the family name, as well, so Daddy Azeveda sent his boy back to Brazil, demoted. Hopefully he's got the sorry piece of shit cleaning toilets at the Novas Alturas headquarters.

Every time I think about Gabriel and the stunt he pulled with Charlotte, I want to punch something. Jackson somehow managed to get Erika to tell him what the asshole did to upset her so badly. Sometimes I wonder if the bastard hadn't gone to her that day and planted seeds of doubt in her head, would she have reacted differently when she saw me with Phoebe. Of course, none of that matters now, it's over between us...since *it wasn't meant to be,* or should I say, since Charlotte's too blinded by her father's infidelity to live her own fucking life.

I snap the pen I was holding in half, getting ink all over my hand. "Dammit!" Grabbing a napkin, I try to clean it up and appear to only make it worse. This is my new norm, breaking shit without even thinking about what I'm doing. It's becoming a nuisance. Two nights ago, I shattered a $1,500 vase against the wall and only registered what I had done when the sound of it smashing to pieces started to echo inside my head.

Jackson thinks I need to take some time off. I disagree. What I need to do is find a ridiculously sexy woman that likes rough sex and fuck the two of us into oblivion. That would solve everything and make me feel like a million bucks, except for one major obstacle. My cock has decided it's only interested in fucking the one woman on the planet that would rather hold on to her issues than live a life people can only dream of. So, I'm left to releasing my tension via destruction of anything I can get my hands on because I'm not about to go begging for Charlotte to take me back. Why would I? So she can throw her lack of trust in my face, accuse me of cheating on her again, and turn my whole goddamn world upside down? "Fuck that!"

"Oh! Uhh...ex...cuse me...Mr. McAlistair. I...ah...I'm sorry to interrupt," my secretary fumbles, nervous after hearing my outburst.

"Yes. What is it?" I really don't want to be impatient with her, but I honestly can't help it. I've been a dick lately, and I don't have it in me to care.

"Mr. Azeveda is here. He asked if you could spare a few minutes of your time."

"Yes. Of course, send him in."

Lucas walks in, the picture of confidence and cordiality. He's been working hard on damage control ever since Gabriel left, and there is a part of me that feels badly for him. He's a brilliant man who has created an outstanding company, one he started from scratch, penniless with nothing but a vision and faith. He takes nothing for granted. I have the utmost respect for him, and we both know this project is going to be a huge success and a premier address in Miami...with or without his prick of a son.

"Lucas. It's good to see you. How was your meeting with Mitchell?" Mitchell is the real estate broker I recommended. Lucas has decided to buy a condo as his residence here in Miami instead of renting. A wise move, considering the market. It's not at the bottom, but it's definitely not at the top. Real estate is hot right now, and no matter what he buys, it will go up in value, even over the short term.

"Very well. He knows what I'm looking for and is setting up showings for the end of the week. He's sharp. I like him," he says with a smile.

"Mitchell is great. You're in good hands." Moving on to the real reason he's here, I add, "What else can I do for you?"

"I am wondering if you are available to join me for dinner this evening? Gabriel's replacement arrived yesterday, and I'd like to formally introduce you. She's been a huge asset to Novas Alturas, and I think you two will get along quite well."

Now I have to make a quick decision on going out tonight. Truth is, I'm getting quite comfortable with going home every evening and sulking with a glass of expensive scotch. But if I decline, Lucas will think I'm holding some kind of grudge against him and his company, and that is something I will not allow.

"Yes. Of course. I look forward to it. Just tell me where and when." I walk back over to my desk so he can't read my body language, which is saying...*ah, I'd rather not.*

"Wonderful! I will let you know shortly when we finalize a plan." Walking over for a brief handshake, he nods his head. "Thank you."

I didn't get much accomplished in the hours leading up to dinner. Today was a particularly bad day for whatever reason. I didn't have any specific reminders of Charlotte make an appearance, other than the thousands that already reside in my head, but she highjacked my day anyway, setting my nerves on edge.

Standing in front of the mirror while I adjust my jacket and do a final inspection of my appearance, I wonder what she's doing tonight. What is she wearing right now? Is she lounging around comfortably or is she dressed for an evening out? Is her hair up or down? She comes to life in my mind's eye as I envision her walking up behind me, that ethereal beauty stealing my breath as she wraps her arms around my waist, body pressed against my back. I'm instantly hard—rock hard—as I watch her hands drift south to tease me through my clothes. A wave of heat drifts up my spine as I feel her hand grab onto the head of my cock. It's so real, my heart is pounding. *I want you on your knees… in front of me…now*, I say inside my head with a deep command. Then, with my eyes closed, I picture her gorgeous body wrapped in a tight dress, feet strapped in sexy heels, hair loose down her back as she walks around from behind me and slowly goes down on her knees.

Fuck! My eyes squeeze tighter, holding on to my fantasy.

Looking down at her as she reaches up to undo my belt, I feel myself pulsing with need. *Take it out…wet it with your tongue.* She does what I tell her, mixing the wetness of her mouth with the pre-cum leaking from my tip. My head falls back a little as the pleasure intensifies. My hips move forward as her hands tighten around me, her warm tongue pressing against the underside of the head and then down. *"Goddammit!"* I say out loud with a growl.

A surge of anger blasts through me, intensifying the pleasure as she takes me deeper to the back of her throat. Her lipstick is smeared and her eyes are watering, but she's loving every second of it, moaning as she takes me farther and farther. My hips move faster, harder, as I match her rhythm. *Is this your way of telling me you're sorry, Charlotte?* I pump harder as a strike of pain pierces my chest. *You fucking left me…goddamn you! Why?* She tightens her grip and closes her lips around my head, sucking and kissing and licking, moaning out in pleasure and need. *Why?* I demand an answer as I grab the back of her head, wrapping her hair in my hand. She moans harder as I start to fuck her mouth in earnest, no longer able to control my need for her...my need to punish her, my need to have her...my need to love her. *You feel so fucking good, Charlotte!* I can't hold back—one last pump and I explode with the most painful orgasm of my life.

Opening my eyes on reality, I watch as my cum shoots across the vanity, into the sink and onto the mirror...my grip tight on my engorged shaft.

My eyes drift to where my hands are still milking out the last bit of pleasure. The look on my face is that of a crazed man, the berserker prepared for battle. I hate this, the look in my eyes, the pain in my chest....my fucking cock in my hand. "Motherfucker!" I lash out as I flush the evidence of my pathetic existence down the toilet. What just happened was so real in my mind—I could smell her delicious scent, feel the warmth in her touch that sends chills across my skin. Does that mean I've completely lost my mind, or do I need to find a woman that actually wants me? Give my cock a chance to feel something real and not a fantasy? I don't have time to debate that sad reality with myself, since I'm supposed to be at Fogo de Chão Steakhouse in ten minutes.

Traffic is bad and I'm more than fashionably late, putting my mood further into darkness. However, Lucas doesn't seem fazed as I apologize, acknowledging how heavy the traffic was on the way here. "Not to worry, my friend." Lucas's accented voice reassures me. "Come. Adriana is ordering us a bottle of wine."

Walking through the crowded restaurant, I see an extremely attractive dark-haired woman sitting by herself. Adriana, no doubt. The brilliant smile that lights up her face when she sees us confirms her identity. *Goddamn, she's gorgeous.* This may prove to be a much-needed distraction as my testosterone spikes in excitement.

As she gets up from the table, I can't help but notice her voluptuous form. The gods are clearly trying make up for the shitstorm they put me in for the past three and a half weeks because everything about Adriana screams fuck me and fuck me hard...after you tie me up and light up my *overly* round ass cheeks until they are flaming hot and deliciously red.

"Ian, let me introduce you to Adriana Santos, my esteemed colleague and friend. Adriana, Ian McAlistair, whom you already know I hold in very high regard."

Taking Adriana's hand, I bring it to my lips to test her scent. A slight twinge of disappointment lands in my stomach as it doesn't quite hit the mark. I'm not turned off by any means, but it isn't what my instincts are screaming for. "It is a pleasure to meet you, Miss Santos. I believe your smile lit up the entire room." My voice is deep as I play her a little, just for fun—and perhaps to support my damaged ego.

"Please, call me Adriana, and I will call you Ian."

Hmmm...the way she says my name with that accent is hot as hell. I'm beginning to hope my instincts come around because there is some serious potential in my new Brazilian partner.

"Adriana it is. Please..." I hold my hand out in invitation. "Let's sit and enjoy the wine you've chosen."

And so we do, as thirty minutes go by with easy conversation and laughter before we even order our meals. Needing to put some food in my stomach, I change the subject by asking Adriana, "Have you decided what you're having this evening?" But when I look up, expecting her to answer with a meal selection, I see the look in her eyes has made another choice altogether. How interesting. That didn't take long at all. With a half-smile and a raised brow, I acknowledge her silent request, giving renewed interest to the evening's potential.

Answering my actual question, she boldly states, "This is a Brazilian steakhouse. I'm having a flame-grilled, bone-in ribeye." Turning to me, eyes suddenly darker, she asks, "Would you like to share, Ian? It is meant to be a meal for two."

I really wish that would make my dick swell. It's supposed to, my brain knows it. I'm pretty damn sure my body knows it, but my cock is late to the show. Not wanting to focus too much attention on my deficiencies, I answer with an obvious, "Yes. That sounds perfect. You pick the sides, I'm easy."

Her smile says she is thrilled—with more than my acceptance to share our meal—and from the look on Lucas's face, everything is going precisely the way he'd planned. It dawns on me at that moment that Adriana may be a gift from Lucas, one meant to take the sting out of the burn brought on by his jack-off of a son. If so, it is certainly a generous token. Lucas believes it is entirely Gabriel's fault that Charlotte and I are no longer together and I never bothered to inform him that he's only partially correct.

My suspicions are confirmed when I ask Lucas if he's made a choice from the menu, and he responds with, "Ahh...I am sorry. You know, all the conversation, wine, and delicious bread they served has me too full to consider eating a whole meal. If you don't mind, I think I might call it a night. It's much later than I thought. I'm an old guy, you know... We go to bed early at this age." He laughs as if what he said were true, let alone funny.

Of course, I realize that I'm trapped. I can't tell him to stay, and I can't cut the evening short. We haven't even ordered. Inside my head, I tip my hat to ol' Lucas, cunning bastard that he is. His move was well played as it appears I'll be spending the rest of the evening with Adriana. I suppose it could be worse, but I'd be lying if I said I was thrilled about it.

"Of course, Lucas. I'm sorry to have waited so long to order. Are you sure you want to leave? The food is quite good here," I say, pretending not to be on to him.

"No, no. I'm fine. You get to a point in life where good company and good wine are all you need." He smiles sincerely while shaking my hand and kissing Adriana good night.

Sitting back down, I look at my "blind date" and say, "I think we scared him off."

With a sultry laugh, she agrees, "Perhaps," then flags the waiter over and places our order...for two.

A slight annoyance comes over me as I find her need to be in control very unappealing. For all of her exceptional physical characteristics, there is a very good chance we are a poor match —in between the sheets, that is. I'm starting to sense the last thing she'll want to do is relinquish control to me, but maybe the challenge of getting her to do exactly that will be the remedy I've been looking for.

The conversation continues to flow as the waiter delivers our meal. Refilling each of our glasses, I propose a toast. "To a wonderful evening and a successful project."

Adriana gives me a smirk that says she could have done better—of that I have no doubt, but something in the back of my mind is telling me not to lead her on...too much, anyway.

As she cuts into our steak, she looks up at me, desire evident in her eyes, and says, "Open up. The first bite is yours."

I want to refuse, to deny her the control she craves, but this isn't the place to put her in check. She senses my reluctance and brings the fork closer as she opens her mouth, mimicking what she expects me to do. The gesture is a complete turnoff, but I give in, opening my mouth to let her feed me.

Just as the delicious meat hits my tongue, something shifts around me, and my eyes move from Adriana's to a table across the room.

The sounds of the restaurant become muffled and my vision tunnels as Charlotte walks in and is seated in a booth that has her facing directly toward me. My hands clench as my heart rate escalates. She is so beautiful it makes my insides hurt. Yet the longer I stare, the more I notice that she looks pale, almost fragile, and my instincts are screaming at me to protect her.

I chew the bite of steak but say nothing to Adriana. My eyes cannot move; they have wanted to look at Charlotte so badly for so long, they're locked and have no intention of looking away.

Until a man walks over and sits across from her. *Is she on a fucking date?* The idea of it. That the once-in-a-hundred-fucking-lifetimes magic we had between us *wasn't meant to be.* Yet, it could with the sorry prick she's with right now? It's enough to have me up and out of this bloody obnoxious room, away from this controlling woman and back into the safety of my penthouse where I don't run the chance of seeing Charlotte *with* another man. Un-fucking-believable.

Right then, her eyes shift to mine and I can see the shock and displeasure on her face. It's like I've been stabbed in the chest with a knife, a dull knife that rips through the flesh, tearing and pulling as it makes its mark.

"The look on your face has me concerned the meat is rancid, although I find that hard to believe. I can call the waiter over to ask for something else?" Adriana is annoyed, but I don't give a shit. She's going to have to get over it.

"No. The meat isn't rancid. It's delicious." I give her a look that says *don't push me.* Continuing, I confirm, "And if it weren't to my liking, I'd call the waiter over *myself* to order something else." Does she think I'm fucking incompetent and need someone to wipe my ass for me, too? I need to move this evening along and get the hell out of here.

Taking the hint, she moves on to safer ground and spends the next twenty minutes talking about the project and some of the names they've been throwing around. I'm only half paying attention because my focus is on Charlotte and the fact that she is having dinner with another man. I'm sure Adriana knows I'm not listening, which is why she tests me with, "So which name do you like best?"

Without missing a beat, I swallow the food in my mouth and say, "None of them. This project is going to be a showcase in one the country's biggest and most well-known cities. The name is an important part of its brand. It needs to be perfect."

Her jaw drops, slightly, and I find that I like dousing her overblown ego with ice water. With a somewhat bitchy attitude, she says, "That must mean you have an idea of your own for what the name should be... Spit it out, I'm dying to hear."

Wrong again, presumptuous bitch. "Actually, I haven't really put much thought into it. It was understood from the beginning that Novas Alturas would be naming the project, so I figured whenever you all came up with something, I'd hear about it. Now...that doesn't mean I wouldn't have an opinion about it, and if I felt the name was awful and an insult to the magnificence of what we are creating, I'd definitely protest, but we haven't gotten to that point."

"Well, apparently we just did. I told you several of the names we are tossing around, and you said you don't like any of them. So I'm curious...what would you name the project?"

I glance over at Charlotte, and my timing couldn't be more perfect. At that moment, she looks right at me and the light over her table illuminates her eyes, accentuating their perfect blue-green color. It's strange, because they've always fascinated me— not only because they are so stunningly beautiful and are the window to the only soul I've cared enough to love, but they had always reminded me of something. Something specific that I just couldn't remember. I would sit and study them, sometimes draw them in hopes of figuring it out. For whatever reason, right at that moment it all fell into place...and I remembered.

The Fairy Pools on the Isle of Skye in Scotland. The mysterious, natural pools accented by majestic waterfalls that are the most incredible crystal blue or blue-green depending on the light, like Charlotte's beautiful eyes. The thought that I've solved this mystery and I can't tell her floods me with a sense of sadness.

Putting my head down for a few seconds in mock concentration, I look up at Adriana and say, "Skye...with an e."

The look on her face changes from surprise, to defeat, to exuberance all in a matter of seconds. Her mouth widens with a smile as she says, "Ian! I love it! That is absolutely perfect!" She reaches over and grabs my hand, holding it tight. "Have you really not been thinking about this? You literally just came up with that now?"

Looking down at our clasped hands, then over to Charlotte, I see her eyes are locked on our connection. Bringing my eyes back to Adriana, I respond, "No. I haven't put any thought into it." Sitting back, I release her hand and continue. "Several years ago, I traveled to Scotland to visit family and decided to visit the Isle of Skye for the first time. It's a breathtakingly pure and perfect place of beauty, and that is exactly what this project is going to be...so it seemed fitting." I don't mention it also seems fitting that it is an indirect connotation for the most beautiful woman that ever lived, but I doubt Adriana would be pleased to hear that side of the story.

"Well...it's brilliant, and I'm going to push for its approval. Don't worry, I'll give you credit," she says, as if I were worried I wouldn't get the proper accolades. What she doesn't understand is that I am not that petty. If Skye becomes the official name of the project, I would know why, and that's all that matters.

On a chuckle, I respond, "That won't be necessary. You take the credit. I'm sure it will make Lucas happy." With that, I've decided I'm done for the evening. The weight of sitting here while Charlotte is across the room in the company of another man is making my skin hurt, and the thought of Adriana dominating me in the bedroom the way I know she wants to is making my dick go into hiding.

As if he were reading my mind through telepathy, Jackson pings my phone with a text. Looking down at it, I pretend it's something important when he was only wondering how dinner went, assuming I was home by now. "I'm going to have to run, I'm sorry. Something has come up."

Adriana is no dummy and knows I'm not taking her up on her repeated invitations. I suspect she knows why, as well.

But when we finally get up to leave, this already screwed up evening gets taken to new heights as Adriana squeals in excitement. "Oh my gosh! There's Charlotte LeFay, the manager from The Clara Sea...where I'm staying! I just love her. We have to go say hello!"

You have got to be fucking kidding me. How can I get out of this? She's practically running over to Charlotte's table, and I have no choice but to join her. As I approach, about ten paces behind Adriana, my body turns into a live wire as it senses Charlotte's proximity.

Adriana has Charlotte in a bear hug by the time I approach, and it's awkward as hell. With Adriana's back to me, I'm greeted with Charlotte's face, front and center, her eyes closed. A sense of possession comes over me as I look at her. I want everyone in this room to disappear but Charlotte. I want to touch her, to run my nose along her hairline, and breathe in her intoxicating scent. I want to kiss her mouth, then bite her lip and gently run my tongue across the painful spot and hope I taste her blood. I want to punish her. Hold her. Take her tears between my lips.

I'm sure she can read my mind because she still hasn't opened her eyes to look at me, and it pisses me off. "Charlotte," I say, curt and commanding.

Her eyes pop open, making contact with mine for only a second before looking away as she pulls out of the embrace.

"You two know each other?" Adriana asks in surprise, looking back and forth between us.

Since Charlotte looks like a deer in the headlights, I answer, "Yes. We had our introductory meeting with Novas Alturas at The Clara Sea. Charlotte went out of her way to make sure we made a good impression."

Gaining a little composure, Charlotte responds with a shaky, "Thank you, Ian, but I certainly can't take credit for the impression you made. We provided a comfortable setting. You did the most important part." Her eyes are doing their best to avoid me.

Adriana enthusiastically chimes in. "I just love The Clara Sea! It's now one of my favorite resorts." She touches Charlotte's shoulder, brushing a lock of her hair over as she finishes with, "And I have stayed at a lot of resorts around the world."

She's doing her best to impress Charlotte with her compliment and being far too familiar, having only met yesterday. The thought crosses my mind that Adriana might be bisexual and is attracted to her. If so, I certainly can't blame her, but the tension this gathering is creating inside my gut is about to make me snap. So when her dinner companion stands to introduce himself, I have to hide my hands in my pockets as they curl into tight fists.

As everyone starts talking, I have no idea what they are saying. All I know is that I'm not going to be shaking that motherfucker's hand. Taking my phone out of my pocket, I put it up to my ear and say in a low voice, "If you'll excuse me," and walk out of the restaurant.

Pacing outside the front door, I wait for Adriana. When she finally arrives, she has that cat-ate-the-mouse look that says she's done the math and is deciding what to do with the information.

"Well, that was quite a fascinating little exchange," she gloats, hooking her arm through mine and steering us toward the parking lot.

"Oh?" I reply, not about to offer any information. Let's see what conclusions she's come up with.

"Had I known Charlotte LeFay was the one that got away, I would never have forced you into such a painful situation." Her sincerity catches me off guard and I stop, turning toward her.

"And you determined that, how?" I wonder if it was really that obvious and if the little douchebag Charlotte was with noticed it, too.

"Let's just say that I pick up on people's energy...very well." She looks up at me and places her hand on my arm. "Ian. Whatever happened between the two of you needs to be resolved. I have never felt such a powerful vibration between two people. And before you jump in and tell me all the reasons why that can't or won't happen, just know that I know the difference between love and hate… *That* was pure love." I swear her eyes look glassy, and this whole exchange is giving me chills.

"That's very interesting, and I will take it into consideration. However, if you are so in tune with people's vibrations, why the hell would you have ever thought I would find pleasure in being dominated by you?" Since she gave me an opening, I took it. Plus, it steers us away from my relationship with Charlotte, which is none of her business.

Throwing her head back with a deep laugh, she says, "A girl can only hope, Ian. You do happen to be one of the most attractive, desirable men I have ever had the pleasure of meeting. I tried to rein it in when I sensed you weren't having it, but you know how it goes—we are who we are…for better or worse." She looks at me for a few long seconds, her face softening, then continues. "I would be able to set…*most*…of my tendencies aside if you really needed to release some of that pent-up steam. The idea of what you are capable of is doing naughty things to my libido." Her eyes turn black and her lips part as she finishes with, "No strings attached, Ian. There's no way I could compete with whatever you've got with Charlotte. But that doesn't mean our baser needs can't be met."

There is a part of me that wishes I could follow through with her final invitation. My fantasy from earlier didn't even scratch the surface of what I need right now, and I have no doubt Adriana has some tricks up her sleeve that would leave me satisfied for the next month. But I can't, because, though I hate to admit it, the thought leaves a nauseous feeling in the pit of my stomach. "Thank you for the offer and for an enjoyable evening, but it's best that I go home alone. I'm sure you understand."

"Of course, I do. I'm an old soul—very old, I think. I don't get hurt feelings. But do me a favor. Figure out a way to make amends with her. Life is short and shouldn't be wasted on petty things like pride and misunderstandings."

"Thank you. I will think about it…I promise."

She takes both my hands in hers and pulls me to her for a

gentle kiss on my lips. Hers are soft and warm, but they feel strange to me, and her scent is too strong. The strangeness of it all distracts me, and I don't notice Charlotte walk out of the restaurant and look straight at us until Adriana's gasp catches my attention.

I turn to look in the same direction, and there she stands, eyes wide but her expression unclear in the darkness.

As her date walks up behind her and puts his hand on her shoulder, my spine tightens and I turn to Adriana, guiding her with me as I walk away, my hand resting low on her back right above the curve of her full, round ass. It's a low blow, but after tonight, I really don't give a damn.

TWENTY-NINE

CHARLOTTE

"Wow. That was intense. Are you okay?" Zane asks as we stand there watching Ian walk away with his hand resting on Adriana's ass. Zane is Erika's younger brother, which means he's like a brother to me. He talked me into going out tonight so we could cry on each other's shoulder about our breakups since Erika had a "hot date," as she called it, and neither of us had plans to do anything else other than sit around feeling sorry for ourselves. Unfortunately, I had to cut it short since the thought of food makes me want to be sick.

"Mmmm...I definitely could have done without that. Of all the places in this massive city to eat, I pick the one that puts me face to face with exactly what I *don't* want to see...Ian moving on with his life. Not even a month after we broke up." The latter I add in a low tone, as if I'm talking to myself.

"Don't do that to yourself, Charlotte. You don't know for sure that they were on a date. You said she's with the group he's partnered with on that big project. It could have been a business dinner," Zane says sweetly.

"No. Business associates don't feed each other steak and hold hands at dinner. And I don't think touching a business associate's ass is common practice, either." Finally reaching the safety and security of my car, we get inside and I finish with, "I'm not going to lie and pretend that didn't hurt like hell, Zane. Because it did. But I made this bed so I have to lie in it. That doesn't mean I'm enjoying it, though. It's like trying to get comfortable on a mattress I picked up on the side of the road with no mattress pad and dollar store sheets."

That's being generous. It's more like a bed made of glass shards. Every day I wake up and the first thought that enters my mind is that I've made a terrible mistake, and then I spend the rest of the day justifying my choice to set Ian free…for his own good. It's a vicious, repetitive cycle, and it's wearing me out.

"Oooooh…yeah, that's bad. I can deal with the dollar store sheets, but I *cannot* deal with a mattress from the side of the road. That shit just freaks me out!" The look on his face is priceless, and we bust out laughing.

Zane is about as metrosexual as it gets without being gay. He is perfectly manicured, so stylish he looks like he walked out of a magazine, is super fit but not huge, with skin that looks like a baby's. It's funny, because he's actually beautiful and gets hit on all the time by guys, but Zane is probably as crazy about women as his sister is about men, if not more so. The difference between the two of them is that Zane wants a commitment, and Erika does not. But Zane has too many choices and can't make up his mind.

"Oh my God, I know! That's why I used it in my analogy. Got the point across, didn't it?" I say, trying to go with the flow and be normal. That's another unfortunate part of my daily routine—pretending everything is normal when it very clearly is not.

I made up my mind that I'm going to visit my uncle James in France. I'm leaving in a few days and praying the distance, the change of scenery, and being with family will help get me back on track. Because right now, I'm barely functioning. It's like my body is on autopilot while the real me, my soul, has gone into hibernation. It's awful, and I simply can't do it anymore.

Then, to add insult to my self-inflicted injury, I see Ian being affectionate with Adriana Santos, of all people! The woman is so gorgeous she looks fake, and it was all I could do to act like I wasn't dying inside when they came up to our table. At first, I didn't think Ian was going to come over, but then it dawned on me that Adriana had no clue Ian and I have a history together, leaving him no choice but to pretend everything was normal. Although, when I opened my eyes and looked at him for that brief moment, I could see there was nothing normal about him. The look on his face was lethal, and the vibe he was putting off made my stomach hurt. He clearly didn't want to be there, and I was thankful when he finally walked away so I could breathe again.

Pulling up to Zane's house, I see there's another car in the driveway. "Whose car is that?"

Zane mumbles something then clarifies, "That would be Sophia…Leanne's best friend."

"Ahhh, as in Leanne that just broke up with you and that you think took a piece of your heart with her, Leanne?" I ask, somewhat shocked.

Zane's eyes look down in embarrassment. "Yeah. Sophia's been texting me, trying to be supportive. I didn't think much about it, even though she was laying it on kind of thick, but now I'm starting to think maybe she wants to fuck me." He looks up at me and waits a few seconds before his face lights up with a mischievous smile.

"You are so bad. I know exactly what you are going to do. You're going to have revenge sex with Leanne's best friend, aren't you?" I'm pretending to reprimand him.

He shrugs in exaggeration. "You never know what little trinkets the universe will send your way when you need them. Kind of seems like bad karma coming to roost for Leanne, if you ask me." His whole demeanor has changed from the broken-hearted man I just attempted to have dinner with to a predator looking forward to feasting on his next prey.

I hit him in the shoulder. "Get out of here, troublemaker! Text me later and give me the deets. I'm dying to know what happens."

Leaning in to kiss my cheek, he says, "I can do better than that…I can send pics."

"*That* won't be necessary. Just be careful, Zane. I love you." I squeeze his hand goodbye, he returns the endearment, and I'm back to my solitude.

Pre-breakup with Ian, that would have been no issue. Now… I hate being by myself. The silence makes me anxious, yet I feel so empty nothing inspires me. I don't want to listen to music, I don't want to read. I don't get up for the sunrise every morning. I don't even exercise anymore. I sincerely hope visiting Uncle James snaps me out of it, otherwise I don't know what I'm going to do.

Three days later, I'm sitting in the airport nervously waiting to board my flight. I'm trying to occupy myself with my phone in hopes that it will calm my nerves, as my leg bounces so fast it's literally a blur. I've tried to stop it, but I can't, so I give up and let it have its way. Thankfully, Erika texts me a welcome distraction.

Erika: Hey! You doing okay? Your plane is boarding soon…right?

Me: Eh and yes.

Erika: Oh no! I told you to take some of my Valium. That's a long flight for someone that doesn't like to fly.

Me: I know. I should have. I'll just have several drinks when they start serving. I wish you could have come with me. That would have really helped!

Erika: Me too. I'm sorry. The timing just wasn't right. You're going to do fine. You need this!! Who knows…maybe there is some hot French guy that is just waiting for a tasty morsel like you to come along and do all that yummy stuff that French guys do in the bedroom. Could be just what the doctor ordered

Me: Sounds more like what Erika ordered…for Erika :/

Erika: Lmao! Yeah, you're right. Shit! I'm so jealous you're going to France without me. Do you know how many fantasies I could make come true over there?

Me: Plenty, I'm sure. No doubt they include Pierre AND Francois or maybe some chick named Antoinette!

Erika: Those are some seriously generic French names.

Me: You got my point.

Erika: Yeah…a little menage could be fun. They're probably really good at it. They made it up, right?

That makes me laugh out loud. I'm so glad she texted me; it's obviously calmed my nerves because my leg has finally stopped its nervous tremor.

Me: Lol! I don't know. Maybe they just made it sound cool. Menage a trois sounds way more sexy than threesome.

Erika: Omg! I'm dying! Fucking hilarious…we are such rednecks! You are so spot on. Menage a trois sounds freaking yummy with super hotness and people that smell delicious. Threesome sounds like a creep show where everyone's got dirty feet, bad haircuts, and hygiene issues.

Me: Wow. That was a pleasant visual. Thanks.

Erika: Still laughing! This is how French people probably picture an American threesome... Let her suck my dick now Ned. Yer bein' greedy. Shut up Billy Bob and grab my balls, I'm fixin' to cum!

Me: You are twisted and are never allowed to write about redneck threesomes ever again!!
Erika: I'm going to be laughing about that for days!

I hear the announcement for first class boarding, and butterflies swarm in my tummy.

Me: Ugh...they just called for boarding. I've got to run. I'll text you when I get there. Love you!!

Erika: Okay babe. Be safe, have fun, get drunk, get laid, and tell Uncle James I said hi!:). Love you!!

A few glasses of wine chilled me out enough to induce several hours of sleep for the longest leg of my journey. The rest was spent watching movies, making the time go by quickly.

James sent his driver to pick me up at the airport, as I requested. I haven't seen my uncle in a while, and with my fragile emotions, I didn't want to risk bawling my eyes out in the middle of a public place if he picked me up.

James's home and the resort he owns are in Saint-Jean-Cap-Ferrat, which has to be one of the most beautiful places in the world. This paradise in the South of France is saturated with old money and is so exclusive, many of the world's wealthiest people pay ridiculous amounts of money to live here, vacation here, or simply hide here from the rest of society. Regardless of the area's exclusivity, my uncle's home is one of the most warm and welcoming places I've ever been. Situated on the side of a rocky hill, not quite a cliff, right above the shoreline of the Mediterranean Sea, its view expands out to the horizon, creating a backdrop of that magnificent blue that has been perfected by this small body of water.

It's a somewhat modest French Provincial home, compared to most of the houses nearby, anyway, with a massive veranda that is partly covered to shade the outdoor living and dining area. Just steps away is an infinity pool that blends into the view of the sea beyond so precisely, you can't help but pause to appreciate such a well-crafted design. The surrounding trees and vegetation offer complete privacy, while the various shades of green pop in contrast to the blues of the sea and sky.

The interior is bright and airy with big windows and doorways that make the view an integral part of the living space. His interior designer chose soft blues and greens as accents to the creamy white walls, architectural features, and furnishings, while the wood parquet floors, exposed beams, and various antique pieces anchor each room with their warm brown tones. It is truly magnificent.

As I walk out onto the veranda with my breakfast, Uncle James offers me a genuine smile and says, "Good morning, sleeping beauty. You're adjusting well. I thought you'd be asleep for at least a few more hours."

"I'm forcing myself to adjust. I want to be awake when the sun is out. It's too beautiful not to be," I say sincerely.

"Can't argue with you there. I thank God every day for my good fortune," he says, taking a sip of his coffee.

It is such a delightful morning, and we stay outside and chat a while about The Clara Sea and some of my concerns regarding updates and board members putting on the brakes. He agrees and assures me that whatever improvements need to be made will be... He'll deal with the board.

It's a relief to know he's on my side. Though my life has been consumed with all-things-Ian for the past six months, the issues at the resort have been weighing heavily in the background. Knowing that I will have a few projects to move forward with when I return gives me something to look forward to.

That afternoon, he takes me sightseeing and out to lunch at the most amazing restaurant. Not only do they serve the best food I've ever put in my mouth, it's also the most charming place, tucked into the trees that canopy the outside seating while the entire restaurant overlooks the bay. We hear birds singing as a gentle breeze drifts by, and citrusy mimosas top everything off. I am genuinely enjoying myself for the first time in a month and I don't want to leave. However, James really wants to give me a tour of the resort so I can see some of the renovations they've done and go over how they are cutting costs without altering the quality and standards that guests expect when spending that kind of money.

Entering the lobby of The Jardin d'Ferrat, I have to stop then slowly spin around, taking it all in... It's breathtaking! This showplace is the most luxurious, most exclusive property my uncle owns and has earned its reputation as one of the finest resorts in the French Riviera. As expected, I can't help but compare it to The Clara Sea, and regardless of how proud I am or how beautiful it is or how much people love it, it is insignificant compared to this.

"Uncle James, you've outdone yourself with this one," I commend, taking in the grandeur he has created.

"Thank you, dear. I thought you might like it." I can tell by the look on his face, as subtle as it is, that he is very proud—and rightfully so.

"Like? I absolutely love it...and I've only seen the lobby! I'm dying to see the rest. Let's go!" I'm so excited, I hook my arm through his and head toward the giant windows on the other side of the lobby as his laugh echoes around us.

We spend hours touring the resort. The Jardin d'Ferrat is an eye candy treat like I've never experienced. I'm so inspired I tell Uncle James that his bank account may regret showing me this magnificent place, to which he agrees. I must take a hundred pictures and write pages of notes. My brain is exploding with ideas and improvements for The Clara Sea, and it doesn't dawn on me until we get home that I spent an entire day happy, truly happy for the first time since I train-wrecked my relationship with Ian. I knew coming to France to visit my uncle, who is like a father to me, was a good decision. I feel lighter, my head seems clearer, and I'm not having that terrible anxious feeling in my chest that I hate so much.

We spend the next day out on the water, which is spoiling me in a totally different way. Everything about this place is pure opulence. The lush green of the trees and vegetation, the color and clarity of the water, the exceptional weather, the history, the architecture, the food, everything...it's truly amazing.

I think the sunshine and salt air has enabled me to sleep like a baby for the first time in weeks, too. Joining Uncle James on the veranda, a hot cup of coffee in hand, I am refreshed and ready to enjoy another sun-filled day. Selfishly, I have to say I'm happy James's girlfriend is visiting her mother in the UK for the next two weeks. I get along with her, but I don't know her that well, and I would have been less at ease if she were here. Perhaps she's a really thoughtful person and realized that, so she made plans on purpose to let us spend some much-needed time together.

"You seem like a different person from when you arrived. Apparently you needed this vacation. I'm glad you finally made it happen," James says, making me wonder how bad I really looked when I got here.

"Oh my gosh! I needed this more than you know. I am *definitely* a new person," I agree, hoping he doesn't notice my concern.

Cutting right to the chase, his deep voice echoes across the table. "Now that you've had time to release some of the tension and clear your head, why don't you tell me what happened between you and Ian," he says in a way that means he wants the truth.

A slight wave of panic sneaks in as I think about what I've done and the decisions I've made. But I answer anyway, not wanting to lie to my uncle. "Well...I made a mistake...about a month ago. A pretty big mistake. I saw Ian with another woman and assumed he was cheating on me, and I left him...without a word. When I found out the woman he was with was his cousin and everything could be explained, I knew how unfair it was to Ian. How hurtful it was. Yet, I couldn't swear that it would never happen again, that I wouldn't allow my insecurities to rule my actions, and it made me realize...basically, he is better off without me. So I never tried to make it right, never gave him a sincere apology, and I told him that it just wasn't meant to be between us."

"And how did that work out for you?" he asks in a straightforward tone.

Looking up at him, I see the concern in his eyes, and I have an overwhelming urge to cry. He probably knows this has more to do with my parents than Ian. I really don't want to go there, but I know he's not going to leave me a choice.

"Quite horrifically, truth be known," I respond on a fake laugh. "I doubt my decision every day. It has affected me emotionally, physically, intellectually...everything! I just want to go back to the day before I let my insecurities take control." I look down at my lap as the tears well up. "We were supposed to officially move in together that weekend," I say in a sad whisper.

"You already know the solution to this problem, don't you?" he asks, surprising me.

"No...I wish I did," I answer, still not looking up.

"Charlotte. Look at me," he says firmly, and I do. He's such a handsome man, like my father, but James seems wiser, more experienced. "I want to explain something to you, something important that you need to understand. My brother was a good man in many ways. He was smart and built a hugely successful business. He was so proud of you and loved you very much... and believe it or not, he loved your mother."

The tears are streaming down my face as I hear him say something that sounds foreign to my ears.

"You may not want to believe that, knowing that he was unfaithful, but the truth is that he did, perhaps too much. He thought of your mother as this perfect, fragile, rare work of art that needed to be protected and taken care of and treated with only the gentlest touch. I would occasionally tell him that she was human, an individual that had her own mind, her own needs and desires, that he should ask her what she wanted and not decide for her."

I'm glued to every word he's saying, because in the back of my mind, I remember thinking the same thing. But I was a teenager and didn't think it was my place to say anything.

James continues. "Michael's success in business was inevitable. He was always driven, took chances, and looked for any challenge that would give him an adrenaline rush. You're old enough now for me to tell you this, but men like that, especially as they get older and become mired in the headaches and monotony of their careers, they become restless and start looking for outlets to release some of the tension and light the spark that used to keep them moving full steam ahead. A lot of them can find that kind of satisfaction with their wives, but your dad didn't want to expose her to what he was craving, even though he was craving it with her. He said she was the type of woman you made love to gently, then held her after and made sure she felt special and wanted. I told him he was wrong, but he wouldn't listen, so he decided to burn off his more aggressive desires with women he didn't care about...not in the way he cared about your mother, that is."

I'm staring at my uncle, a million thoughts racing through my head, not really sure I can believe what I'm hearing. But the one thing I want to know right now escapes my lips.

"Women?" I ask.

"Yes, Charlotte. Women. Not as many as the look on your face says you're thinking. He had two affairs. The first woman allowed him to scratch the itch, per se, but she started getting attached so he broke it off. As wrong as it sounds, he wasn't looking for an emotional relationship. He had that with your mother. He was looking to spend energy he was afraid to use with Elise. The second is obviously the woman that died in the car accident. It was their second time meeting each other, and the only thing he said about her was that she was pleasant and wasn't looking for commitment." He pauses to let it sink in.

I'm a little nauseous, and my head is spinning. "What am I supposed to do with this information, James? He cheated on my mother, twice. He was looking for kinky sex, so he used other women to get his rocks off." My voice escalates before James cuts me off.

"Charlotte. That's enough. I didn't tell you this so that you could act like a sixteen-year-old. What Michael did was wrong, there is no denying that, but as screwed up as it sounds, he did it because he loved your mother. Quite frankly, to the point of obsession, and that obsession backfired in the worst way possible." His voice is sad as he finishes his statement.

"James, I'm sorry. You're right, that was selfish of me. He was more than my father. He was your brother, and I know how close the two of you were. You lost your best friend. I know that was hard." I need to stop being selfish, but at the same time, James has provided me with information that is hard to accept, let alone wrap my head around.

"Listen, I'm sorry if this seems like too much information, but it's time you knew the truth. Your dad did not cheat on your mother because he was bored or he had lost interest in her or he was just an arrogant jerk that didn't give a damn about anyone but himself. He had desires that he felt would be harmful to the woman he loved and cherished like a priceless doll. He created a fragility in his wife that was unnecessary and a sickness in his own mind that ate away at his common sense." He looks out over the water and thinks for a minute. "On the surface, what happened with your parents seems like the same thing that has destroyed marriages and lives a million times over. But it wasn't, Charlotte. I don't want you to go through your adult life thinking that your dad was a dime-a-dozen philanderer. It was more complicated than that. I knew Michael better than anyone. He loved your mother... Charlotte, he loved her so much it made him lose touch with reality."

He grabs hold of my hand. "I'm so sorry. Your parents' story ended in tragedy at a time in your life when you were most vulnerable. You've overcome so much, like a fighter, and I am so proud of you for that." He gives my hand a supportive squeeze and his voice lowers. "You and Ian are not Elise and Michael... and you never will be. You know what I'm saying is true, Charlotte. I haven't met him, yet, but from everything you've told me, it isn't hard to figure out that the two of you *were* meant to be together and are very much in love. This is your love story, honey... Why the hell would you give it away?" I can hear the disappointment in his voice—it's the same disappointment I have in myself.

"I don't know." My voice is heavy with sadness and confusion. "It was so wrong of me to do what I did to him. It hurt him badly... I know it did. My God, he moved all my stuff out of his apartment within 24 hours. He probably wouldn't take me back, anyway. That's why I keep telling myself I did the right thing...for Ian."

"Okay. Now that you're done bullshitting yourself...because you are done, understand?" His one brow is raised in authority. "Why don't we get back to the original question? What is the solution to the problem you created?"

I stare at him, somewhat taken aback by the firmness in his tone. I'm not offended, at all...but he's backing me into a corner, and I know he's not going to give me an out. I huff out a breath and stutter, "James...I—"

"Charlotte. Give me the solution to the problem," he repeats patiently.

It dawns on me at that moment that it was Uncle James's strength and faith in my own strength that got me through my father's death, my mother's addiction and inevitable passing, and all the painful discoveries in between. He always made me talk about what I was feeling, made me face my reality head-on and not make excuses. He was compassionate, but he refused to let me crumble under the weight of my emotions. I scaled hurdles that seemed impossible because James showed me that I could do it. He had faith in me then, and I can see in his eyes that he has faith in me still.

Taking in a deep lungful of the clean Mediterranean air, I answer, "I need to go to him... Tell him the truth. Tell him why I lied, that I thought he would be better off without me." Looking up at James as I wipe a tear from my cheek, I finish with, "Then let him decide what he wants."

"Yes. You took something from him that wasn't yours to take. Learn this important lesson: you can't think for other people. Look how it has worked out for you. Look how it worked out for your father." He hesitated on the last part, his voice thick with sadness.

I snap my eyes up to his, the truth of his words ringing in my ears. "My God...you're right. What was I thinking?" I rest my head in my hands and close my eyes. "I'm so selfish, he probably wants nothing to do with me now."

"I doubt it. However, if that's the case at least it will be *his* decision and not yours."

As scary as that may be, he's right. I made a mistake, and it was up to Ian to forgive me or not. I should have never tried to decide what was best for him.

Uncle James continues. "I understand that your intentions were good. You thought you were doing what was right for him, but everything that brought you to that decision was misplaced. You used a tragic story that had nothing to do with you and Ian as a couple and used *it* as the catalyst for why the two of you were better off apart. Think about it, Charlotte... How does that make any sense?"

The floodgates open as I answer, all of the emotion this conversation stirred up spilling over the surface. "I was afraid...

I've always been afraid. I let my fear of ending up like my mother take the driver's seat. It completely overwhelmed me."

Taking my hand again, James quietly reassures me with, "Now it's time to let love take the driver's seat. Fear may have overwhelmed you, and fear is very powerful..." He pauses, causing me to look up at him. "But nothing is more powerful than love."

As the sobs break free, James stands and comes over to me, holding me tightly as I let it all out...let it all go. This time for good. It hurts. The pain is intense as it leaves my heart, knowing that I am closer to reliving my father's mistakes than I ever realized, that my manipulation and lies, regardless of how good I thought it was for Ian, are ultimately no different than my father's reasoning behind his betrayal. *I did it for love...so that makes it okay.* How could I have been so selfish? The sobbing continues as I think about the pain I caused Ian. The man I love with all my heart and soul, the man that made me feel alive again, to feel whole again, to experience passion that I didn't know was possible.

Uncle James keeps holding me until I've cried the last tear. I'm exhausted from the outpouring of emotions, but at the same time, when I think about my parents, I feel so much better. As twisted as my father's justification was for what he did, knowing his intention was to protect my mother because he loved her actually makes more sense than what I've lived with for the past decade, and it soothes an ache deep in my heart.

For the first time since my mother passed away, I can picture their souls together, united in love and not lost in darkness, searching for something that will never be found. A smile spreads across my face as they come to me in a vision...the way they used to be, truly happy and deeply in love.

"Well that smile is a sight for sore eyes," I hear James say in a compassionate voice.

Sitting up straight as he moves back to his chair, I say, "I just had the most amazing image of Mom and Dad come into my mind."

"Oh?" James questions as I pause to enjoy it a little longer.

"Yes. They were together, surrounded by the pure light of love. It was the most extraordinary thing. It was so vivid, their happiness tangible." I look at him as I wipe away a tear, this time of joy. "I have never been able to do that. I've only seen them as lost souls in a dark place that's lonely and sad. I would force myself not to think about it because it was too painful. But just now...they were together, and they were happy." A huge smile spreads wide across my face as my soul wraps around the image of my parents as they were, as they were meant to be. "Thank you so much for sharing that with me."

"I'm so sorry, Charlotte. I should have told you sooner. I just, I thought you were doing so well." He's visibly upset now, and I feel badly. "I didn't know you were struggling like that. It breaks my heart to know that is how you saw your parents."

"James...please don't feel badly. I thought I was doing well, too. And maybe I was until Ian came along and started shooting cannonballs at my smooth sailing ship." I try to lighten his mood with a little sarcasm. He laughs and gestures in acknowledgment that I could be right. Continuing, I point out, "Also, I'm only twenty-eight. If you had told me all that when I was even a few years younger, I'm not so sure how I would have taken it."

"That's exactly why I didn't tell you. That, and I genuinely thought you were okay. I knew if the time came that I needed to, I would." He gives me a look that shows his love for me. "And so I did."

"Thank you. I needed to know." It's at that point I notice his phone keeps pinging with incoming text messages. I know he has a tremendous amount of responsibility, and I don't want to keep him from something important. "James, please take care of whatever that is. It could be important."

Grabbing his phone, he scrolls through the texts, smiles, and asks to be excused to make an important call. I was glad to have the time alone, looking out over the Mediterranean and beyond to the horizon, where dark blue meets the bright blue of a cloudless sky. What James told me was a lot to take in, yet I can't help but think about the way Ian expresses his passion. It's intense and sometimes even a little painful, but never in a bad way. Everything he does only accentuates the pleasure and reaches inside, attaching itself to my soul so that when I finally reach the pinnacle, it's so much more than merely a physical release. It's a magical combination of emotion, energy, sensation, and pleasure that is so powerful, so perfectly fused together it can only be described as pure ecstasy. When it's delivered by someone you love in the truest sense of the word, it's more meaningful than words could ever do justice.

I feel a sense of sadness that my parents never shared that kind of passion, that kind of trust. Perhaps it would have scared her, but I doubt it. Yet more than anything, I have a deep sense of longing for Ian. I was fooling myself before, thinking I could walk away giving him his freedom. Now that the dark veil has lifted, I can see clearly again. I know I have to make it right. I have to be honest with him and let fate do the rest.

James walks back out onto the veranda with a smile that says his conversation went very well. Sitting back across from me, he says, "I have something important I need you to do for me."

THIRTY

IAN

I ran an extra mile this morning to push myself past the exhaustion of not sleeping well again last night. It's been four days since I ran into Charlotte and that pretty boy she was with. Ever since then my sleep has been disrupted with images of her being pleasured by someone other than me...and it's eating away at my sanity. Today, however, I have meetings set up from 10:00 a.m. on, so I'll have limited time to be stuck inside my head.

At 9:15, Jackson enters my office looking a little sleepy-eyed himself. "Looks like you were up helping Becca with the baby again. I bet the last thing you want to do is sit through a two-hour meeting with the city." I laugh at the grimace that transforms his face into a clear expression of how he really feels about that.

"Man...I really don't want to deal with that circus. I'm exhausted. Forgot how much maintenance newborn babies are. She's kind of getting into a routine, but all she wants to do is eat...which means we're on a round-the-clock cycle of changing diapers. It's literally in one end and out the other with babies." Now it's his turn to laugh at the grimace on *my* face. "It's not as bad as it sounds. It's just time-consuming. Newborns only drink breastmilk. It's when they start eating baby food that things get a little gross."

"Ah...good information. I'll keep that in mind," I say, instead of what's actually going through my head.

"So what's your excuse? You look like hell." He points out the obvious then grabs us each a bottled water.

"You know exactly what my problem is, which makes that a stupid question." I may have snapped at him unnecessarily with that response. But I'm not rehashing everything with him again. As always, Jackson has been a great friend, talking me through this fucking nightmare Charlotte created, but I'm done talking. I want enough time to go by so that I start to feel like myself again and not some hopeless drug addict looking for his next fix, yet knowing it's never going to come.

"Yeah, I suppose it is a stupid question. But it's also stupid for you to assume that guy Charlotte was with is more than just a friend. You and I both know how unlikely that is." His impatient tone is pissing me off.

"That's where you're wrong, Jackson! I don't know shit! Other than the fact that the woman I loved couldn't find it in herself to trust me after I gave her a part of me that I didn't even know bloody existed! And now she knows I didn't cheat on her... She knows she was wrong, and instead of doing something—*anything*—to make it right, she walked away." My fist comes down hard on my desk, making everything on it jump. Kicking my garbage can over and putting a huge dent in it, I turn back to him and finish, still yelling even though I know he doesn't deserve it. "So...no, Jackson. I don't know how *unlikely* that is, considering I don't even know who the hell *she* is. As far as I'm concerned, she's capable of anything!"

I'm waiting for him to rip me a new one for taking it out on him like that, but instead, he says, "Love."

My back is to him, so I turn around and cross my arms over my chest, recognizing my own defensive posture. "What?"

"I said love. During your little rant, you said *the woman I loved*...as in, past tense. I was just correcting you."

He's dead fucking serious, too.

"Wow, Jackson. Don't pretend to know what's going on inside my head. Got it? Whatever my feelings are for Charlotte don't really fucking matter, because I have no intention of ever being with a woman that can't trust me. It's too important to who I am, and I'll be goddamned if I ever stay in a relationship where my woman doesn't have enough faith in me to know I won't cheat on her!" The truth in my own words lands heavily in my heart as I remember finding out why she left me. I have never had such a twisted wreck of emotions take over my mind.

"At some point you're going to have to listen to what I'm saying to you. That's not how it works! This shit doesn't just turn off and on according to who's pissed off or who's been betrayed or where the real problem lies with trust. The fact of the matter is that the two of you need to sit down and hash it out like adults! Then you can decide which way is the right way to go."

"Not happening," I respond as an image comes into my head of us hashing it out like adults, making my blood heat and my fists clench. "This conversation is over. If we don't leave now, we're going to be late and I hate being late." Back at my desk, I gather a few folders, my laptop, and my keys.

"I'll drive," Jackson says. I give him a questioning look, and he clarifies. "I'm not driving in your car with you in this mood. So you can either drive by yourself or enjoy the ride in my passenger's seat and chill the fuck out."

He's got a fair point. I really don't need to go into a meeting with the city ready to pounce on the first asshole that says something I don't want to hear.

"Fine. You drive."

Three—not two—hours later, our meeting is over, and we are on our way back to the office. I had let Jackson control most of the discussion while I sat back as the intimidating observer. Overall, everything went well, except for the new guy that apparently likes to make himself feel important by focusing on details that are irrelevant at best or blatantly nonexistent at worst. I slid a note to Jason, the head of land development, and told him to shut the little prick down or I was going to. That guy's nonsense wasted forty-five minutes of that extra hour.

Regardless, we got what we wanted and without surprise. We knew the city was going to do everything it could to pave the way for this project.

After eating a banana and half a protein bar for lunch, I was off to the next meeting with a group we are considering for the irrigation. It's a huge part of this project and has to be state-of-the-art. According to Jackson's research, these guys are one of the best in the country, and from the presentation they put on today, his research appears to be one hundred percent accurate. It is likely they will be the group we choose.

By late afternoon, I've wrapped up my last meeting with the architects and interior designers. It was a great way to end what had started out as a rather unpleasant day. The design aspect of the buildings we develop is why I love my job so much. It's a creative outlet that allows me to play with color and texture, to visualize the lines and curves, the different materials and how they all come together in a perfect balance, and to think outside the box of what is expected. My team is second to none, and our brainstorming sessions literally give me a high that no other facet of my job ever could. I do what needs to be done and I do it well, but the interior and exterior design is *why* I do it.

A tap on my door announces Jackson. He walks in and takes a seat in front of my desk. His expression says he's curious about something, and I really hope it has nothing to do with Charlotte. "So, rumor has it that Novas Alturas has officially named the project Skye...*with an e*. Rumor also has it that Adriana is insisting you get full credit for it."

Adriana is good at what she does and professional, when it comes to business, but it is becoming abundantly clear she isn't taking no for an answer.

"That's good news. That they decided on Skye, anyway. It fits quite well. As far as the rest, I really don't give a shit." I don't want to open up the conversation of Adriana again with Jackson, either. He knows she's trying to set the hook, and he's not too keen on the idea. He doesn't trust her, and frankly, neither do I.

He laughs in agreement. "Well...I'll tell you this. It's good. Damn good, man. How'd you think of that?" He leaves the question hanging while I debate on whether I should tell him the truth.

"Adriana put me on the spot last week when we were having dinner, told me to come up with something since I didn't like her ideas. Something reminded me of my trip to the Isle of Skye a few years ago, and it clicked." I don't tell him *what* reminded me. I'll keep that for myself.

He gives a slow nod that suggests he knows I left something out, but he also knows me well enough to leave it be. Changing the subject, we discuss today's meetings and any loose ends we need to tie up. All in all, today was a complete success for all things Skye.

Now, if I could get the rush I used to get after a day like today I'd be set. Instead, everything falls flat, and I hate it.

Jackson notices, saying, "You good, man? Why don't we go get a drink somewhere?"

"Thanks, but a drink is probably the last thing I need. I've been doing a bit too much of that lately, and besides, you need to be at home with your family. I promised Nana I'd stop by tonight for dinner." Which I'm only doing because I love her. What I'd rather do is go home, pour a scotch, feel sorry for myself, and go to bed. My new routine is beginning to get too comfortable.

We say goodbye as we exit the building, automatically going in for the familiar fist bump that says everything we need to say. Getting in my car, I sit there for a minute, trapped in another random daze that I constantly find myself in. Looking up, I see Jackson pull out of the parking lot in his white suburban.

I've seen his car a thousand times, drove in the damn thing today, yet at that particular moment, I see it for what it is. A family car. He bought it so he could drive his wife, his son, his newborn daughter, and any future children anywhere they want to go, and the thought of it slams into my chest like a battering ram. I continue sitting there, watching him wait at the stop sign before turning right, trying to decipher what the hell just happened. If I'm being honest with myself, I know exactly what happened; I'm just having a hard time accepting it.

For the first time in my life I have a deep longing to have a family of my own. "Excellent fucking timing, Ian," I say as the dark cloud returns. The same one that's been following me around for over a month. The same one that I hate with a passion.

Not wanting to wallow in my own pity, I start the car and head to Nana's.

As always, being in her home makes me happy. It's warm and inviting, and it's exactly what I need right now. There's a heavy weight on me that isn't getting any lighter. You'd think over time I would become resilient, yet nothing could be further from the truth. Spending time with Nana, though, gives my soul the boost it needs.

"Hello, dear." Warm hands grasp my face as she pulls me down to kiss my forehead.

"Hello, Nana. How's my favorite person?" My voice sounds flat, even to my own ears.

"I'd be doing better if my grandson was doing better." She holds up her finger and shakes her head as she turns to walk into the living room, saying in a reprimanding tone, "And don't try to feed me that line from the other day. That's another sorry attempt at bullshitting yourself, and I'm not interested in hearing it." She walks over to her chair by the window and sits down. "Why don't you try being honest with me *and* yourself for a change and maybe we can get somewhere."

She's been trying to get me to open up about Charlotte, but

all I've done is tell her everything I think I'm supposed to say, not what I really feel. "Because the truth feels like hell, Nana. That shouldn't be too hard to understand," I say, pouring a heavy scotch that I've decided I do need after all, before taking my seat across from her.

"Why don't you try it anyway, Ian. Your way clearly isn't working." She tips her head and gives an expression that says, *you know I'm right*.

"All right...the truth is..." I pause to look down at my drink and rub the back of my neck, knowing it won't relieve the pain that actually resides in my chest, but go through the motions anyway to buy some time. "I miss her. I miss her so much it's tearing me up inside." I leave it there because I need to quit talking.

"Ian. Charlotte is not dead. You can get her back and I think you know that, so what the hell are you waiting for?"

I look up at her as the thought of Charlotte no longer walking this earth knocks the wind out of me. Nana's expression now says, *I see you get my point*.

"You're right. I can't even contemplate that kind of finality. But how do I live my life with someone that doesn't trust me? Nana, I gave her everything...all of me. There was a part of me that was dead, and I didn't even know it until *she* brought it to life. That part of me is hers and no one else's. I could *never* be unfaithful to her. Ever. But *she* thinks I could." I pause to swallow down the anger that builds whenever I talk about it. "The problem is within her, and I sympathize, I really do, but how can I fix that? I can't. *She* has to fix it, and if she were willing, I could help her. But she doesn't want to." The tension is building inside as my grip tightens on the glass.

"Ian. You're complicating this, and you're wrong," she says as a ping sounds next to her. She reaches over and grabs her cell phone—that she rarely uses—smiles, and puts it back down. Did she just get a notification? Continuing, her voice is sympathetic as she says, "Charlotte loves you just as much as you love her.

Period. Yes, she screwed up by jumping the gun about Phoebe, but what the hell, Ian... Look at what she's been through! Not to mention, you said that Brazilian guy put some crazy idea in her head. What should *anyone* expect when you put all the factors of that equation together?"

"Yes, but the most important factor in that equation is that what we had was not your everyday love affair. *Goddammit!* And she knew that!" My voice rises as my anger spills over.

"True. Which is why I told you weeks ago to go sit down with her and talk. Something tells me that Charlotte loves you so much, she thinks it's a good idea to set you free...then you don't have to put up with her 'issues.'" She exaggerates her finger quotes. "People do stupid things for love, Ian. I've seen it many times. The problem I have with you right now is that you are sitting back, letting it happen. That's *not* the Ian McAlistair I know," she sternly finishes as her phone pings again. This time she actually starts typing something, and I'm stunned by her rudeness.

"Nana. What are you doing?"

"Texting someone."

"Since when do you text?"

"Just started recently. Judy taught me how." She seems so pleased with herself.

"Okay. That's wonderful, but you need to understand there is some etiquette involved here. The most important being you don't text in the middle of a verbal conversation with someone else...especially an important one!"

"Oh. I'm sorry, dear. You're right." She very politely puts her phone down and gives me a silly smile. It reminds me of a teenager showing off how skilled she is at being a smartass.

"If it's that important, please continue," I offer, emphasizing the kindness in my tone.

"No, no...it's fine. Not important." The look on her face screams mischief, and I can't help but wonder what she is up to. Before I can question any further, she boldly states, "Back to

329

where I was…enough is enough, Ian. Time to take the bull by the horns. You're miserable, I'm sure she's miserable, and none of this makes sense anymore. Not that it ever did." That last part she said under her breath, but loud enough for me to hear. "Mark my words, you make the effort, it will pay off. In spades." She reaches over and pretends to do something with her phone when I hear her mumble, "Then maybe I can get some great-grandkids before I die."

I have to smile at that, for two reasons. One, she uses those little narcissistic jabs masterfully to get what she wants, and two, because the thought of having children with Charlotte warms my heart from the inside out.

"All right, Nana. We'll see. She's in France right now, according to Jackson, who somehow knows everything, and I don't know when she returns. When she gets back to Miami, maybe I'll give her a call." The thought sends a nervous wave of excitement through my core, and I'm suddenly looking forward to something for the first time since Charlotte's false accusations ruined my life.

Nana's phone pings again and she glances over, clearly reading what's popped up on her screen. A smile spreads across her face that is so genuine I'm now curious what could have caused it.

But before I have a chance to ask, she surprises me by saying, "Good. I'm glad to hear you're thinking like the man I know you to be instead of whoever the hell you've been for the past several weeks. He was annoyingly foolish. In the meantime, I need you to do me a favor."

THIRTY-ONE

CHARLOTTE

Arriving in Scotland two days ago, I wasn't really sure what to expect. My uncle asked me to cut my visit to France short so I could fly here to check out a resort that has recently come up for sale.

When he told me it's an old castle that was converted into a hotel, I was a bit skeptical. What I pictured in my head—an old stone building, weathered with vines covering its facade and an inescapable aroma of centuries-old mildew—was a far cry from what greeted me. This place is magnificent, and my jaw literally dropped when we drove up the driveway that was designed to show off its size, architecture, and pure opulence.

The original building was built in the 16th century and has been altered and improved over the hundreds of years since. It sits high upon a clifftop on the west coast of Scotland overlooking the Firth of Clyde, a large body of water that connects to various rivers, lochs, and the Irish Sea. There are acres upon acres of the most incredible landscape, like nothing I have ever seen. So lush and green, it's breathtaking.

The interior can only be described as regal, and it's hard to fathom that it used to be someone's home. There are grand, curved staircases, intricate moldings and woodwork, massive old paintings in ornate frames, luxurious wall coverings and fabrics, and the most beautiful furnishings that are reminiscent of the history of Great Britain, yet timeless in their style and functionality. There is a spa, a restaurant that is to die for, a library, an exercise facility, an indoor pool, and gardens popping with blooms of every color outside each window you pass. This place is magical, I fell in love with it as soon as I saw it and I have already recommended that Uncle James close the deal before someone else does.

Yesterday, I went for a walk on one of the many paths that meander through the estate. The temperature was comfortably cool and the air so clean, the scent of it so refreshing, I stayed out for over two hours. The path led me along the edge of grassy knolls covered in purple flowers, through dense shaded woodlands where birdsong echoed in the trees, over rocky streams so crystal clear you could easily see every stone and pebble resting on the bottom, each one's color and texture accentuated by the sunlight shining through the water, and eventually to a small plateau overlooking the vastness of the Firth of Clyde. There was a slight breeze coming off the water, a distinct scent of brine in its freshness, and I was so energized— more spiritually than physically—I decided to meditate sitting atop a flat boulder perfectly placed near the edge of the cliff.

I often meditate to keep my mind working at its most efficient capacity and, of course, to reduce stress. Yet, since I broke things off with Ian, I have found it impossible to meditate. Each time I tried, I ended up worse off than before—my heart racing, chest tight with anxiety, and that dreadful sense of falling that terrifies me. However, here, in this place that is comforting and strangely reassuring in its familiarity, I was able to meditate so deeply, for so long, that when I opened my eyes and took in a lungful of salt air, I realized that Ian was right... This is the place from my dream. The one that came to me in a flash of white light while Ian kissed me with such all-consuming passion, demanding I tell him my true feelings. It was Scotland, and the realization didn't scare me or even confuse me; it comforted me in a way that can only be described as...home.

The whole experience rotated in my mind during the long walk back to the resort. As I put all the pieces together from the past six months...our powerful connection that refused to be denied, the electricity in our touch, a love that seemed to pick up where it left off, the vision that came to me of another place and time, Ian's history that runs deep in these lands, and the sense of nostalgia I have just being here...they finally fell into place, fitting together as they were made to, creating a picture of a true love so deep, so compelling it transcended time and brought two souls together again.

I stopped when the last piece clicked into place, sat down in the middle of the path lined with ferns and surrounded by trees, little sparkles of sunlight dancing through the leaves, and wept. I cried for the couple that found each other many generations in the past and loved one another for what I hope was a long lifetime. I cried for the love my parents shared that was cut short by misplaced intentions and an unhealthy obsession. I cried for the terrible mistake I made in accusing Ian of something he didn't and would never do, for leaving him alone, hurt, and angry. I cried for the fear that I may never be able to repair the damage I created. Yet, I refused to give up hope.

Once the heaviness of the outpouring had passed, I opened my eyes again, following the line of the path ahead of me. As the light played its fantastic game of flickering and shifting from one place to another, it caught onto a tiny winged creature in the distance and followed its random migration as it fluttered up, down, around, and over whatever caught its interest from one second to the next. A smile spread across my face as my heart expanded with joy. There she was, the portrait Ian drew of me, crystal clear in my mind, walking down a path that was identical to the one I was sitting on, smelling that delicate pink rose, its perfume both elegant and sensual, yet the meaning behind it so much more. If I had to pinpoint a moment that I fell in love with

Ian, I would have to say it was then. When he exposed a side of himself that no one else sees, a side that is vulnerable and shy, talented and raw, thoughtful and romantic. My heart was never the same after he gave me that portrait.

I stayed there, sitting on the path in the middle of a natural setting that had somehow become a part of me. I felt at home there, listening to the sounds, feeling the shift of cool air, seeing things typically overlooked by distracted eyes, and breathing in the earthy scent, a combination that was healing to my exhausted soul.

When I woke this morning to bright rays of sunlight breaking through my window, the memory of a dream stayed with me. I smile, remembering the emerald green forest, like that of a fairy tale, where I walked down a path following a little winged creature lit up by the sun's bright light, never getting close enough to determine its identity, but happy with the mystery just the same. I have decided there truly is magic surrounding this place, for here I am pretending...or maybe even believing in the fairy tales typically reserved for the innocent imaginations of children. There is a part of me that feels silly for even giving it this much thought, yet I cannot deny my excitement to go for another walk through the forest today and perhaps another chance encounter.

I am light on my feet as I head down for breakfast and two cups of their coffee that is magical in its own right. In the main corridor, just down from the restaurant, I pass the library and see a display case I hadn't noticed before. I almost keep going since I am close enough to smell the freshly brewed goodness, but something stops me and I turn back, hoping I might learn a little history or some other interesting facts about this enchanting place.

What I find is unexpected, but fascinating nonetheless. It is titled *The Poetry and Prose of Lord Alasdair Stewart*. The hairs on my neck stand as I read further. Apparently the lord of this manor, during the late 1700s, was very much in love with his wife, Lady Ella Stewart. Preserved in this case are several examples of poems he wrote for her. The paper is browned with age and the thick lined script is so perfectly written, you could mistake it for a calligraphy font printed from a modern day printer. Some of the words are hard to make out, so the historians that put together this display have them translated in Times New Roman on crisp white paper next to each one. I appreciate their effort, for now I am able to read through each without hesitation, but at the same time, I have a strange longing to go back to a time when we would sit down and hand write our thoughts and ideas…our love letters, in the practiced hand of elegant script.

I go back and forth between his original piece and the printed type, wanting to be sure I correctly read every word. He was enthralled by her beauty, captivated by her wit and clever mind. She seems to have had a love of nature and an uncommon connection with its creatures. Each poem and letter is so heartfelt, so beautifully written, it's as if I can feel his love for her.

Finally, at the end of this sentimental presentation, I get to see the woman that stole Lord Stewart's heart. There, in a copy of a painted portrait, is a blonde-haired, blue-eyed woman. She is young in this image and she is quite beautiful. A genuine smile stretches wide as a confounding sense pride comes over me. The artist has captured a mischievous glint in her eyes and for some strange reason, it pleases me immensely. I can't stop staring at her or ignore the rapid beating of my heart. Why does she seem so familiar? *Who are you?* I wonder to myself before my eyes drift to the short letter right below her portrait.

Lady Ella ~ My dearest faerie maiden,

I thank God every day that our souls found each other again.
Let us grow old joyously, knowing they will do so from now
through eternity.
   Your humble servant and loving husband,
   Alasdair Stewart ~

I feel light headed, my hands are tingling. *There's no way!* But then I step to the right to see what the last section of the display case reveals. A huge lump forms in my throat as my hand covers my mouth, muffling the gasp that tries to escape. It's him, I swear it is him. The stranger from my vision; dark hair, strikingly handsome with Ian's turquoise eyes. He's wearing the same high collared jacket with gold embellishments. Underneath the portrait his full name and title stand out boldly and reading it tightens my stomach with a mass of sensations, each one attached to a different emotion. **Alasdair Gavyn Stewart, 7th Earl of Galloway, Admiral ~ British Royal Navy**. I keep reading it, saying it over and over in my head as a familiar awareness expands outward from my core, painting my body in an unmistakable warmth that reaches to the tips of my fingers and toes.

"Alasdair." I hear myself whisper as visible chills raise on my arm.

My hands are starting to sweat as I continue to stare at him. Occasionally I glance at Lady Ella, curious to know more about her, but I want to look at him. I want to open the case and take out his image so I can hold it close, examine every detail. The vision I had, that confused...even somewhat scared me, is forefront in my mind and I have a gnawing urge to feel his warmth, smell his scent, hear him say my name.

The soft sound of a droplet landing on glass draws my attention away from his portrait. I stare at the tiny puddle for a few seconds, wondering where it came from, then notice the cool, wet trail it left on my face. My fingers come up to catch the next tear before it can fall. *My God!* I can't believe this is happening. The logical part of my brain is warring, quite forcefully, with the reality my gut is telling me to accept.

A boisterous group of guests walk by, laughing and talking loudly on their way to breakfast. I turn to watch them pass, leaning against the case that holds a mystery I'm having a hard time wrapping my head around. I feel like I'm not actually here. Like the people passing by wouldn't see me if they turned and looked this way. I feel transparent and light, floating just above solid ground. I press my back into the corner of the case, wanting to feel the sharp edge dig into my skin. I wiggle my toes in my shoes. "Everything's fine." Did I say that out loud?

I focus my vision on the massive window on the other side of the corridor overlooking the towering trees that line the main drive into the estate. I stare out over the beautiful landscape, trying hard not to picture that striking figure, impeccably dressed, atop a horse that was—no doubt, as handsome as the man himself, trotting up the drive to greet his beloved wife. A terrible sense of longing comes over me, so I turn back to the poems and images that now seem easier to handle than the picture I just had in my mind.

Twenty minutes or more must have passed before I finally decide I can't stand here any longer, staring at these people I'm desperate to know, wishing I could ask them a hundred questions and more. I pull out my phone and take pictures of Lord Stewart and Lady Ella, testing the angle to make sure there is no glare and that the clarity is perfect. I include his poems as well, otherwise it feels like I'm leaving them here and my conscience simply will not allow it.

At the restaurant entrance, I wait for the hostess, hoping it won't take too long to be seated. My legs feel strange, I'm light headed. I really want coffee and I really want to sit down. My eyes close and my lungs expand with a deep breath, hoping to calm my nerves, only to be startled by Deidra, the restaurant manager and her adorable Scottish accent.

"A good mornin' to ye, Ms. LeFay." She pauses to look at me with a creased brow. "Are ye alright? Ye look as if ye've seen a ghost."

"I think I have seen a ghost, Deidra. Two, to be exact." I feel myself try to smile and feel badly because I know it's weak. "Do you have a quiet table available?"

"Aye. Follow me, dearie. I have the perfect table by the window. Best view in the house." She guides me to a cozy little spot near the massive stone fireplace and it truly does have the best view. It's a perfectly clear morning with a sea of blue to the left, and to the right a vast expanse of every shade of green imaginable—with pops of color here and there, where several of the flower gardens come into view.

"Wow, Deidra! This is spectacular. Thank you so much." Grateful to finally be sitting down, I offer her a better smile and an apology. "I'm sorry I'm so out of it. I'm sure your amazing coffee will snap me out of it."

"That it will." She rests her hand on my shoulder and with a reassuring squeeze, she finishes, "Try to relax, dear. This is a vera' ould place and ye would'na be the first person to encounter something unexplainable. Don't be frightened, though. 'Tis always been a happy castle, none o' that crazy stuff happenin' here that keep the wee ones up at night. So, whatever spirits ye might come upon are'na here to cause ye a fright."

"Yes…uh…that's good to know and I suppose it's nothing a long walk through the forest can't cure. Thank you so much, for this amazing table and your wisdom."

"Aye, well…there are more mysteries in that forest than there are in this ould castle. Sit tight, love. I'll have Amy bring ye a coffee right away."

I'm not so sure about that, I think to myself. Bringing out my phone, I pull up the Admiral's picture. *Unbelievable!* It's definitely him. He is the man from my dream; if that's what it's called. Vision, premonition, fantasy... God, how I wish Ian were here. He wouldn't let me overthink this and we'd probably spend the next week doing research and coming up with the entire story of our past lives.

Past lives. Is that cliche or just an overused reference that everyone takes for granted? Right now it seems as real as the cup of coffee that was just placed before me.

"Thank you." I say mindlessly.

I sit in silence for the rest of my time in the restaurant, lost in thought as I look out over a view that seems to inspire contemplation. My journey from Miami to France was cathartic in a way that I never expected. What I learned from Uncle James allowed me to break free from the burdens I carried from my past. But here, in Scotland...in a refurbished castle of all places, something else entirely has happened and I realize, right here— right now in this moment—that it was meant to be. I was supposed to come here. All of the events of my life, both good and bad, have brought me to this place. The terrible choice I made to let Ian go was part of the path that would lead me here.

Even before my discovery of Ella and Alasdair, I had felt a strong connection, not only to this ancient structure, but to the trees and the flowers, the pebble lined streams, the heavy scent of brine along the shore, even my view from where I sit speaks to me in ways I could have never imagined. And the longer I'm here the deeper a sort of healing blossoms within.

I look at my phone again, less apprehensive about the butterflies in my stomach or the tightening of my chest when I see Alasdair. The more I look at him, the more I see a resemblance to Ian. Before it was just his eyes, they are truly the same, but now I see the set of his jaw, the masculine outline of his brow, and the slight depression in his cheek that becomes a beguiling dimple when he smiles. I zoom in to study it closer, smiling as I wonder if Lady Ella found his as alluring as I find Ian's. Something tells me that she did.

I click out of my pictures and turn off my phone, the black

screen becoming a mirror as my reflection stares back at me. There, I see the remnants of my fading smile and perhaps some of the mischief I recognized in Lady Ella and...it makes me happy.

I am suddenly impatient to go for a walk through my enchanted forest and make my way to the clearing to meditate again. Did Lady Ella love the forest as much as I do? From the poems Alasdair wrote, it's easy to assume she spent most of her time there. If I lived here, I know I certainly would, it seems impossible to stay away.

My pace is quick as I finally enter the woodland canopy. It's as amazing as it was yesterday—in some ways more so. I'm here several hours earlier, so there is more chill in the air, but it smells so unbelievably good the chill doesn't matter. I think it adds to the effect. There is a dewy freshness that wasn't here before, and when I finally make it to the clearing overlooking the sea, I'm so energized, I'd rather swim to the island I see in the distance than meditate. I pace around a bit, taking deep, calming breaths before finally taking my seat, comfortably facing the water, the sun at my back, gently warming away the chill.

It's surprisingly easy to come down from the high my walk here induced, but it takes me a few minutes longer to calm my mind as it cannot stop thinking about what happened this morning and the significance of its meaning. But, eventually, my breathing becomes steady, my body and mind are centered, my soul is at peace. I stay like this for quite a while, sensing the passing of time through the increasing warmth of the rising sun, too comfortable in the tranquility to let it go.

Eventually, I let my thoughts occupy my mind again. Ella and Alasdair are there and I say a sincere thank you to Fate for guiding me here...for guiding me to them. Then, I go to Ian. I see him in my mind's eye and my heart expands with the love I know we share. I ask him for forgiveness, then pray he offer it without hesitation.

Opening my eyes and shifting my position to let the blood

flow back into my legs, I stay seated while I adjust after such a long meditation. The sun is much higher now, its light glittering across the rippled surface of the water, causing me to squint at its brightness. I haven't seen it quite this beautiful before, so I grab my phone to take a picture, switching it to panoramic so I can get the full view from my special place. I am truly going to miss being here.

Standing up, I stretch my arms high over my head and take one last deep breath then walk over to the far end of the clearing where I can follow the curved progression of the coastline before it disappears behind a distant rocky cliff. Pausing to admire this extraordinary scene, I ignore the chills that cover my body, blaming it on my heightened emotions and perhaps the breeze that blew past my shaded location.

But something in the air shifted. My spine straightens out of instinct, and my skin tingles with need. *It can't be...it simply can't be him.*

But there is no denying that familiar cadence as it brings him across the rocky path. Its signature rhythm lighting a fire inside my core.

I can't move as his steps get louder and louder. I'm frozen, terrified to turn around and see that my mind has played a terrible trick on me.

"Charlotte."

I close my eyes when I hear his beautiful voice say my name. *Oh my God...this is real.*

"Charlotte. Turn around." His voice is commanding, but there is no mistaking the yearning in his tone.

I turn to face him, and my breath catches on his name as I try to breathe in and out at the same time. My eyes make contact with his, gorgeous and blazing with emotion, for only a few seconds before I drop my face into my hands as the joy of seeing him again—here, where I never expected him to be—overwhelms me. He comes to me then, whispering my name and wrapping me in his strong embrace, holding me while I let my emotions flow freely and grasp onto the reality that I am in his arms once again.

He waits patiently for me to gain control, his strength protecting me, his scent penetrating every cell in my body, causing my brain to release endorphins that Sibel is engorging herself on now that she is back where she has desperately wanted to be.

"Look at me, Charlotte," he says and releases one hand, placing it gently under my chin, bringing my tear-soaked face up to his.

"Ian..." I whisper. "I can't believe you're here... I never thought..." I can't finish as the lump refills my throat.

His thumb comes up to wipe away more tears, the look on his face shattering my fear of losing him forever. "Shhhh...it's okay. Just tell me this was the right thing to do. Tell me this is what you wanted." His grip on me tightens, his possessiveness relaxing me like the tranquilizer it's always been.

"Yes, Ian. Oh, my God, a thousand times, yes!" Reaching up, I wrap my arms around his neck, bringing my nose to my favorite spot under his ear. My lips automatically latch onto his tender skin, moving up to his jaw shadowed with the scruff of traveling across the ocean. He smells so good, I can't help biting his lip before taking his mouth in a fevered kiss that begs for forgiveness and to take us back in time, where I never let anything come between us again.

Grabbing onto my upper arms, he pulls us apart. Hard. "Charlotte." His breathing is heavy, his voice deep with pent-up arousal. "You can't do that to me here. Do you have any idea what the past six weeks have been like? Kissing me like that is torture." The look on his face is pained, the tone of his voice even worse. My heart breaks for him and the hell I put him through. I don't know that I will ever forgive myself.

Taking his hand, I turn us back toward the path that enters the woodland and pull him with me. About a hundred feet in, I veer to the left—off the main path and onto a smaller one that cuts through the dense ferns and undergrowth. "Where are you taking me, Charlotte?" I turn back to look at him, still pulling him along as I put my finger up to my smiling lips with a silent...*shhhh.*

He stops abruptly and he pulls me to him. *"Jesus Christ!"* He says against my mouth. "Do you have any idea how much I've missed your smile?" He takes my mouth fully then, eventually pausing to rest his forehead against mine. "I missed you so fucking much...everything Charlotte...everything about you."

Looking up into his eyes, I cradle his face in my hands. The joy of seeing him again, of touching him, of knowing that we have been and will be together forever; is so profound, I can feel it racing through my veins. And that's when it hits me. I let go, not taking my eyes from his and slowly begin to undress.

"Charlotte."

"It's okay, Ian. I promise." I say through the thickness in my throat.

When the last of my clothing lands beside me and the chilled air surrounds my naked body, I say, "Stay here," then turn to slowly walk away, continuing down the path.

I let myself become her, see myself as her, just as he did. I walk with the same poised grace and confidence, and with each step I let go, let myself be free...let myself be me.

A breeze blows through the forest, the smell of fresh leaves and moist soil surrounds me as it lifts my hair, swirling it around me, making my skin tingle and my lungs expand. I stop, knowing Ian is where I left him, watching me, craving me, loving me. I let the knowledge wrap itself around an unfamiliar place buried deep inside, awakening powers I didn't know I possessed. I stay with it, letting the budding flower within completely bloom, each petal gently unfolding, exposing its truest beauty. Then, as the last of the tension leaves my body, I realize I truly am everything I envied about the portrait Ian drew of me. It is part of me and always has been. The strength and confidence he admires, the natural beauty and sensuality that invigorates his desire, and the mystery and mischief that drives his curiosity and need to know more. I can fully sense the magic of what nature intended, that need for balance, the attraction of opposing forces. His masculine to my feminine, so fantastically different, yet similar in their need to be connected, to come together as one.

The wind blows from a different direction, rustling the plants surrounding me. In the movement I see a flower, easily contrasted against the blanket of green. It's small and purple, but it will do. I reach down to take its delicate stem between my fingers, breaking it free. Standing up straight, I roll it this way then that, admiring its unique beauty, so different from the one that's lived in my mind since that unforgettable day.

Shifting my body, only slightly, I bring it to my nose and am happy to find it has a subtle scent—more plant-like than perfume—and it makes me smile.

Still holding it to my nose, I turn to Ian, still several paces away, and offer him a coy grin. "Follow me...just a little farther." He does, and I guide him toward a massive oak tree in the distance. It caught my attention yesterday. It must be 500 years old at least, and I swear it was in my dream last night. Finally, we reach its canopy that expands out forever, long ancient branches stretching up and out, eventually making their way back to the ground. I pull him around to the side facing away from the main path.

"Did you recognize her?"

"Charlotte...I'll never be the same. That was a gift...One I will never be able to repay." The emotion in his voice is making want to cry again.

"Yes, you can," I assure him.

"No. You don't understand what that meant to me."

"Yes, I do."

I reach forward and start unbuttoning his shirt.

"I have so much to tell you, Ian. You were right about us... our souls reuniting. We have loved before and it was here, in this enchanted place." I stop to kiss his mouth as it turns up in a sexy smile. "But right now, I need to speak to you without words, because words will never be enough. I need to show you…"

My hands sweep across the warm skin of his shoulders, sliding the shirt down his strong arms. I can't resist leaning in to touch my lips to his chest.

"…With my body, with my heart…"

I continue removing his clothes.

"…With my soul."

Kneeling down, I remove his shoes, then his pants. I run my hands up his strong legs, gently gliding them across the base of his stunning erection.

"Char…lotte…" He grinds out my name through gritted teeth. "I can't…"

"Shhhh…it's okay. Lie down." My hands drift up his tight abdomen, gripping his sides to guide him down to the soft grass beneath us. Once he is comfortably in position, I take a moment to soak in the intoxicating image. Ian McAlistair, beautifully naked, beautifully aroused, lying on the greenest grass under a majestic oak so old, it's vibrating around us with centuries of time and knowledge trapped inside its rough exterior.

I move closer to sit by his side and run my hands across his body again, both of us trembling with anticipation. Leaning down, I kiss his lips, softly. "I'm so sorry, Ian. You didn't deserve the pain I caused. I'm so sorry." My forehead rests on his as I try to hold back the tears.

Grabbing my head in his strong hands, he pushes me up, so I can see him. "Don't. Just don't. We're here now. We both made mistakes…ones we will *never* make again. But we are here now, and that's all that matters." His eyes are glazed, his lashes damp, and I swear my heart explodes with love for him.

"Okay," I whisper and sit up, bringing my leg over to straddle his hips. I stay that way, upright on my knees, his glorious body displayed beneath me, eyes black with excessive hunger.

I place my hands on my thighs, fingers spread, and wait for his eyes to lock on them. They do, and my stomach flips with excitement. Gliding them up over my hips and across my abdomen, chills race across my skin as my fingertips barely graze my most sensitive place.

His engorged cock jumps against the tight muscles of his abdomen as a moan escapes from deep in his chest. My hands continue up past my ribcage to firmly cup my breasts and a moan of my own echoes through the silence. When I take my nipples between my fingers, my eyes close as I whisper his name. *"Ian..."* When they open, I find him up on one elbow, his humorless expression a warning of what is to come. My body instinctively translates his unspoken promise as it readies itself with a warm release at the same time his hand reaches forward to touch me where I'm screaming with excruciating need.

My hips involuntarily press down against his gentle touch, desperate for more pressure. It's not enough and he knows it. He draws out his play, teasing me so masterfully, letting the pleasure build without completion. Then he pulls away as my breath catches and brings his wet hand down to himself, coating his thick shaft, stroking it once...twice...smirking as a whimper escapes my throat.

I fall forward, my hands landing on his chest as I push him to the ground, fingernails digging into his skin. He growls out my name when I take his mouth in a kiss that is still desperate to turn back time and mend what I have broken. His arms wrap around me, so tight it's hard to breathe. I try not to fight it, I don't want him to let go, but my brain is screaming for oxygen. Finally breaking free, I fill my lungs with cool air, making my head dizzy from the sudden rush. Before I can take another breath, his hands lock onto my hips to pull me down as he drives into me, igniting an orgasm that forces me upright so I can ride him hard through its completion, crying out as he grinds himself into me harder and harder.

He's straining, trying to maintain control, but it's no use. The anger is there, the hurt. He needs this, he needs to release the pain that he thought would never end. That will likely leave a permanent scar. "Let it go... Let it go, Ian. Please... I love you. I trust you. I know you won't hurt me." That was all he needed— to know that I trust him, that I need him to be who he truly is and not hold back.

Sitting up straight, he wraps his arms around me, squeezing me hard to his body while he pulls me down to meet his thrusts. "Say it again," he says against my mouth, wet and hot.

"I love you."

"No. Say it again." Another hard thrust, then he bites my lip.

"I trust you." I can barely get the words out, though my body is screaming the truth.

"Again." He holds me tighter.

"I trust you, Ian."

Without flinching, he stands up, my arms and legs wrapped around him, and turns to press me hard against the trunk of our tree, devouring my mouth in a punishing kiss that steals my breath once again. Then slowly, one at a time, he puts his arms under my knees to hold me in place and spread me wide, allowing full access so he can take what he wants. Knowing he could push it too hard, he eases up, pulling back just enough to make the pain of the bark digging into my back a pleasant complement to the second orgasm building in my core.

"Look down." Ian growls out the command. "Watch my hard cock fuck your wet pussy." My head feels like it weighs a thousand pounds as I bring it forward and watch as his huge shaft drives in and out, my body giving and taking at the same time, the evidence of my pleasure building up around him. An indescribable sound escapes him as he pushes me harder. His entire body is flexed with exertion and passion and rage as he strains through gritted teeth, "You...are...mine, Charlotte."

I can't hold back, exploding around him as he pounds into me with bruising force, pushing my orgasm deeper as my body starts to go limp. "No!" he says with one last hard thrust and stays fully buried inside me. "Don't stop... Don't stop cumming." My head falls back against the tree as he controls my orgasm beyond what I thought was possible. His hot mouth latches onto my exposed neck as his entire body presses against mine, spreading my legs further and making full contact with my clit.

"Ian!" I cry as the pleasure becomes too much.

He thrusts hard again without pulling out, striking against my deepest wall, keeping my climax alive. Again...again...it's too much. I feel myself entering that euphoric space and I don't fight it as the darkness closes in. "Look at me!" I try to open my eyes but can't. "Look at me, Charlotte!" I hear him yell as my head pops up. What I find when my eyes finally open will be etched in my soul for eternity. Ian's face, ravaged with emotion, his eyes fierce, as if he's lived a thousand lives. But the evidence of his tears, the streaks of wetness running down his blessed face, break my heart and completely mend it all at once. I reach up to wipe them away, whispering his name.

His hard thrusts begin to slow as we stare into each other's eyes, seeing each other's souls and knowing we are home. Without a word, he gently releases each leg, my body flinching as it tries to adjust. Standing in front of him as he steadies my balance, he asks, "How is your back?"

It's then I notice the painful sting my mind had previously ignored. "It hurts," I answer truthfully.

"Turn around." His voice is a gravelly command. I do as he says and hear his breath hitch when he sees the damage. Startled by his reaction, I turn to ask, "What? Is it bad?" only to find him staring at my back with the look of a starved predator.

"Turn around," he says almost angrily, "Put your hands on the tree."

My heart starts beating faster as I do what he wishes, placing my hands on the rough surface. He doesn't come to me immediately, making me anxious about what he has planned. Then I feel his warm hands on the front of my hips. "Bring your legs back," he says in a tender voice, his foot tapping the inside of mine to make sure they are spread the way he wants them.

The next sensation makes every nerve in my body jump. "Shhhh…" he consoles as he runs his finger around and between the scratches and cuts he left behind. "I will make the pain go away." His tone is reassuring as he continues tracing a path around my back. At first, I don't like it. The nerves are raw and I want him to stop. But as he continues with his gentle touch, his voice hypnotizing as he tells me how beautiful I am, the pain starts to dissipate and I find myself getting aroused…precisely as Ian wanted me to be.

When his warm tongue glides across an open wound, he moans out in hunger. When his lips add to the warmth and pleasure-pain, I feel a throbbing in my clit that forces my back to arch and my ass to move toward him in obvious invitation.

"That's it," he says, the vibration of desire in his deep voice flushing my wet pussy with heat. His mouth is still on my back as he reaches down to tease me, making my head fall forward as I cry out and push against his hand. There is a painful tenderness everywhere, but I don't care… The pleasure is so intense. Pushing against the tree for leverage, I thrust my hips back, begging him to fuck me with his hand. Another growl echoes through the canopy as he abruptly pulls away and lights up my ass with one smack of his wet hand.

"Ian!" My voice is dry from heavy breathing.

Pulling me upright, he stands in front of me, clutching my face with his left hand and tracing my lips with the wetness on his right, his huge erection pressing hard against my stomach. Opening my mouth, I watch as he pushes his finger inside, my lips automatically closing around it. His lips part on a harsh inhale. That's when I notice the blood on his lips. Releasing his finger, I pull his face to me, taking his mouth…wanting to taste the evidence of our passion. He lets me, and the mingled taste of his mouth, my blood, and our essence drugs my brain as I unconsciously bite his lip wanting the addition of his blood to our potion.

Abruptly pulling back, he stares down at me, breath heaving from his chest. My finger comes up to touch the spot of red swelling on his bottom lip. When I bring it to my mouth, its metallic flavor spreading across my tongue, his eyes turn to onyx —a black glass that seems inhuman, possessed, a kind of wizardry that hypnotizes my mind.

Breaking the spell as his thumb sweeps hard across my lips, he declares in a voice that is not his own, an unmistakable trace of the accent of this land, "Forgive me, Charlotte. But I am not done." Chills spread across my body when he demands, "I want ye on yer hands and knees...now."

Dropping down on my knees in front of him, I look up, waiting for permission to take him in my mouth. His cock jumps as a shiny bead leaks from its tip, making my mouth water. Without warning, he reaches forward to grab the back of my head, guiding himself toward my lips. He controls my movements as he forces me to take him deep...once...twice, then holds it there before yanking it out. "No more!"

Still gripping my hair, he gently pulls my head back so our eyes can make contact. "Your beautiful mouth is too much for me...I want your ass in the air, right now." He releases me so I can take position in front of him, adrenaline mixing with excitement and arousal. I am completely exposed, exactly as he wishes. The first smack takes me by surprise. There was no soft caress prior, no warning beyond the animalistic sound that escaped his throat. The second comes immediately after, stinging more than the first. Again, no warning. The heat travels from the point of contact, around my body, then lands between my legs in a warm gush. Again, harder, and I feel myself opening to him, pushing myself toward him wanting more. Again...and this time he stops to caress the sting, absorbing some of the heat into his hand.

I'm expecting another stinging slap, but he catches me off

guard by swiping his fingers across my wet pussy, then balling his fist to roll it around my openings, switching from one to the other. The pressure he applies borders on too much and takes me right to the edge of losing control before he lights me up with another stinging smack. *My God!* Five more stings in rapid succession, then he buries his face between my legs, moaning and growling, forcing me to push myself hard against him.

Pulling away, he brings his wet face and mouth to my flaming hot skin where he cools it with his lips and tongue, soothing it with an erotic kiss that escalates the pleasure-pain to a dizzying high.

The cold air clings to the wetness he left behind as he turns to gather our clothes and lay them out in a soft bed that he directs me to lie upon. I happily abide and once I'm on my back facing him, bones the consistency of jelly, legs falling to either side, my eyes roll back in exhaustion. He reaches up to grab my face in his firm grip, then turns my head, growling out, "Look at me, Charlotte. Open your eyes and look at me."

As soon as I do, he drives himself straight to my core. I scream out as my head goes back and my spine arches to a painful degree waking up the sting his gentle touch had numbed. He drives harder and harder into me, my legs, weak from the force of his taking, barely functioning as they flail at my side. He lets go of my face and, again, reaches behind my head, wrapping my hair around his fist, pulling my face up to his. "Open your fucking eyes, Charlotte."

Mustering what little strength I have left, I do his bidding and shatter into a million pieces as his voice breaks and his thrusts become strained. "Never…again. Never…again…will you…leave me." And we both fall into a climax that surpasses anything we have experienced together before—where our souls become one, floating through space and time, creating that blinding light I have come to know as pure love.

We stay with it as long as we can, not wanting it to end.

Something this powerful doesn't happen more than once—at least not in one lifetime.

Knowing my back can't take much more, he rolls over, taking me with him so that I can comfortably fall asleep on top of him. I do, immediately. For how long, I have no idea. All I know is that when I finally wake up, Ian is on his side next to me, staring at me, playing with my hair. Leaning in to kiss my temple, he whispers, "I love you, Charlotte." Then he makes love to me so tenderly, so carefully, his heart fully exposed while he kisses away my tears.

It's true. I now know for certain that our souls have loved before, in this very place, maybe even beyond the lives of Ella and Alasdair. That it was just as deep and passionate then as it is today. And I know that when this life is over...we will find each other again.

As I lie here in Ian's arms, sated and content while he breathes gently in his sleep, I open my eyes and catch the sunlight where it follows my little winged friend, busily stopping here and there on a mission that now seems more precise than random.

As if sensing my observation, it flies over to us but pauses far enough away to keep its identity a mystery. It lingers, almost intentionally, before excitedly flying away, performing playful, whimsical aerobatics as it goes.

A soft smile lifts the corners of my mouth as I add another question to the long list I've compiled in my mind for Ella. *Did you encounter these little winged mysteries, as well?* I have no way of knowing for certain, but here, in this magical forest, I know in my heart the answer is....yes.

THIRTY-TWO

Nana: Well, that worked out well. I knew if we just guided them in the right direction they would get their heads screwed back on straight.

James: Yes, agreed. A little family intervention is sometimes necessary.

Nana: I guess I'll finally get to meet you at the wedding. I know Ian, and he won't be wasting any time making Charlotte his bride.

James: I suspect not and I look forward to it. Save a dance for me.

Nana: You can count on it :)

EPILOGUE

Ian ~ 60 years later

I've been sitting here for days, holding her beautiful hand still warm with life, knowing that it won't last much longer. She told me to be strong, for the kids...but I can't. She's everything to me, the reason I exist. How am I supposed to go on?

I break again, wracking sobs that hurt my aching chest. Holding her hand up to my mouth, I kiss her beautifully aged skin, afraid I might be hurting her I'm grasping it so hard, begging God to take me, too.

It seems like only yesterday we celebrated her eighty-eighth birthday. She was so vibrant and happy and alive... God, she was so beautiful. All the kids flew in. James, Elise, Lily, and Nicholas, their husbands and wives, all ten grandkids, and our closest friends. She wanted it to be at our estate in the Bahamas, her favorite place in the world. The place where she wants to die. If that's what she wants, that's what she will have. I've always made sure of that. Little does she know, I may never be able to set foot here again once she's gone. I don't think my heart could handle it, picturing her walking the shoreline looking for treasures or trimming the branches of her tropical fruit trees or playing with the grandkids down by the beach. It will be empty and pointless without her.

For years now she's been talking about the party she's going to throw for my 100th birthday, and I never questioned it, never doubted it would happen. I know for a fact now that I won't make it to 100, four years from now, and I honestly don't care. The kids know how much I love them. I raised them to be strong and independent, but more importantly, they know how much their mother means to me. They know I don't want to live without her.

Still holding her hand, the hospice nurse comes in to check on her, offers me a few kind words, and leaves me alone. Glancing over, I see one of our wedding pictures and my heart aches with longing to go back in time. To stand there nervously waiting for her to appear, and then she finally does, looking more beautiful than words can describe. I wonder why the universe thought I should be that fortunate.

It was a perfect wedding, intimate with family and a few close friends. It took place in Scotland, under the same ancient oak where our souls became one. That was sixty years ago; we were married three months later. God, I just want to go back. I could live my life with her over and over again…a thousand times and it would never get old.

Wiping away the tears that never seem to stop, I feel her move, coming out of her slumber. These moments have become fewer and fewer over the past 48 hours, and I cherish them more than words can express.

"Ian," she whispers, weak and gravelly.

"Yes, my love." It's hard to speak.

"Are you okay?" She asks me that every time she wakes up, and every time I give her the same answer.

"No. I'm not."

"I need you to be." She says that every time, as well.

"You know I can't." I barely finish as the sobs break free. I fall onto her shoulder, wrapping my arms around her fragile form.

"Ian." She's barely able to bring her hand up to my face. "Look at me."

I don't want to. I know what's happening, and I don't want it to. I can't accept it. I'm too selfish. She's mine. She's mine, goddammit!

"Ian...please."

"I can't do this, Charlotte. Take me with you."

"No, Ian. You have to stay...trust me." She closes her eyes and takes a few shallow breaths. "Listen to me..."

She's so weak. I can't do this. I'm not ready.

"Tell the kids...I love them...I love them so much." She pauses again, a tear falling from the corner of her eye. "Tell them...I'm sorry I couldn't wait." She's crying now, and it's tearing me apart. "I have to go now, Ian. It's time."

"No...no. Please not yet, Charlotte. I don't want to be here without you." My whole body is shaking, knowing I am powerless.

"I love you, Ian...I loved you in this lifetime...and all the others from our past...with all my heart and soul." Pausing on a few more shallow breaths, she says, barely audible, "And I will love you more...in the next...life to come...I promise."

Bringing my mouth up to hers, I tell her I love her and breathe in her last breath.

"I will find you, my love...my soul will find you...again."

ACKNOWLEDGEMENT

I would like to thank my wonderful husband for being my sounding board throughout the long writing process and my lovely daughter for her insight and advice, all of which was spot on. My son will have nothing to do with this book and is kind of mad at me for writing it...haha!

Thank you to Julie Doner (pen name Julie Evelyn Joyce), who encouraged me years ago to "just start writing!". I eventually took her advice and after writing Chapter One, I was hooked. She has taught me so much that made the writing process a deeper and more satisfying creative outlet. Julie is an amazing writer and an amazing person. You can find out more about her and her award winning books at julieevelynjoyce.com

Thank you to my editors. They did such a fantastic job and their insight, suggestions, constructive criticism, and encouragement is invaluable.
 Erica Russikoff - Beta read and proofread (ericaedits.com)
 Traci Finlay - 1st Copy edit (tracifinlay.com)
 Julie Doner - 2nd Copy edit

ACKNOWLEDGEMENT

A special thank you goes to James Fryer. He is the phenomenal artist whose drawings are featured in the story. I happened upon his work several years ago and fell in love with his series of surfer girls. Check out his beautiful and diverse artwork @james.fryer_art on Instagram and online at noahsbeach.com

Thank you to Linda Russell at Foreword PR & Marketing (forewordpr.com) for all of her great advice and patience. Launching your first book is an overwhelming task, Linda brought it all down to earth and took away a lot of the pressure. Her guidance and recommendations are honest and straightforward. I couldn't have done it without her.

Thank you Marisa Wesley at Cover me Darling (covermedarling.com) for the awesome book cover. Another woman of great patience and understanding. No matter how many times I changed something, big or small, she never made it seem like I was driving her crazy. She was truly a pleasure to work with.

A big thanks to Lori and Heidi for reading my story long before its release and giving me your honest opinions and encouragement!